In Fact

Books by THOMAS MALLON

Fiction

Arts and Sciences

Aurora 7

Henry and Clara

Dewey Defeats Truman

Two Moons

Nonfiction

Edmund Blunden

A Book of One's Own

Stolen Words

Rockets and Rodeos

In Fact

In Fact

Essays on
Writers and Writing

Thomas Mallon

PANTHEON BOOKS   NEW YORK

All rights reserved under International and Pan-American Copyright
Conventions. Published in the United States by Pantheon Books,
a division of Random House, Inc., New York, and simultaneously
in Canada by Random House of Canada Limited, Toronto.

Pantheon Books and colophon are registered trademarks of
Random House, Inc.

Grateful acknowledgment is made to the following for permission to reprint
previously published material: Copper Canyon Press: Excerpt from
"Fair/Boy Christian Takes a Break" from *The Shape of the Journey: New
and Collected Poems* by Jim Harrison. Copyright © 1998 by Jim Harrison.
Reprinted by permission of Copper Canyon Press, PO Box 271, Port
Townsend, WA 98368-0271. • Harcourt, Inc.: "My Quarrel with the
Infinite" from *Hotel Insomnia* by Charles Simic. Copyright © 1992 by
Charles Simic. Reprinted by permission of Harcourt, Inc. • Louis Simpson:
"The Hour of Feeling" from *Searching for the Ox* by Louis Simpson.
Copyright © 1976 by Louis Simpson. Reprinted by permission of
Louis Simpson.

Page 354 is an extension of this copyright page.

Library of Congress Cataloging-in-Publication Data

Mallon, Thomas, 1951–
   In fact : selected nonfiction, 1978–2000 / Thomas Mallon.
     p. cm.
  ISBN 0-375-40916-5
   1. American fiction—20th century—History and criticism.
2. English literature—History and criticism. I. Title.

PS379 .M287 2001 813'.509—dc 21   00-056503

Random House Web Address: www.randomhouse.com

Book design by Fearn Cutler de Vicq de Cumptich

Printed in the United States of America
First Edition

For Art Cooper

Contents

Contents

Up from Academe:
An Introduction

I T SAYS SOMETHING about the specialized repetitions of academic life that a journal called *Joseph Conrad Today* can be continuously published. And it says something about my days as an assistant professor that, twenty years ago, I was writing for it. Twentieth-century British literature was my field, and like most of my colleagues in pursuit of tenure at Vassar, I was accumulating "publications" in periodicals read chiefly by the other people writing in the same issue.

William W. Bonney's *Thorns and Arabesques: Contexts for Conrad's Fiction* was the Johns Hopkins University Press book I had to review for Volume VI, nos. 3–4 of *JCT*. The following sentence is typical of the book's language, an idiom spoken by the academic species one level above mine—that is, associate professors in pursuit of promotion: "In these instances, a seemingly meaningful logical surface is subverted by the ontic vacancy of raw diversity established through a plurality of multiplicative inverses, to which the very idea of orderly and sequential monogenesis is indeed alien."

Alien, indeed. "If Mr. Bonney will forgive me," I wrote after closing his quotation, "I will make my point in a mere eight syllables: no one should write like this, ever." The review's last sentences read, at this remove, like an urgent note to myself: "I fear we have entered a kind of commentators' My Lai. We have reached the point where we are destroying language in order to explain it . . . squeezing out the last humble Anglo-Saxon syllable from a critical prose that is rapidly moving beyond the Latinate and towards the Martian." I was telling myself to look for another job.

In a roundabout way that's what I began to do, by reviewing for regular newspapers and *National Review*—a magazine viewed by my colleagues as not only politically suspect but positively flashy—and by publishing a study of diaries (*A Book of One's Own,* 1984) that was a sort of belletristic curiosity. By the time I sat on the English department's hiring committee in the fall of 1987, the madly theoretical work of professors like Bonney—who scorned critical factors like biography as "extralinguistic presences"—had already given way to a preoccupation with nothing *but* the social and historical circumstances of literature. Issues of "race, class and gender"—invoked so often and with such automatic simultaneity that they seemed to be one angry word, *raceclassgender*—were fast becoming the only avenues of inquiry into literary "texts." (Talk of "books" disappeared with the ditto machine and card catalog.) And yet the language employed in these new political pursuits, evident in the dissertation chapters presented by applicants to the hiring committee, was just as pretentiously ugly as the lingo that had made the "theorists," such a short time ago, feel so smart.

By '88 I was publishing fiction along with literary journalism, and I wanted out. I gave up tenure and taught part-time for a few years, during which, I must add, I was always treated well, even fondly, like some back number spared the bindery and allowed to keep its torn cover. Just before I left Vassar for good, several months before my fortieth birthday in 1991, I gave a whole course on Mary McCarthy, the college's most famous alumna and the subject, years before, of my own undergraduate honors thesis at Brown. Mary (eventually a friend) has been without question the most enduring influence on my life as a writer. In fact, it was probably a volume of her essays, *On the Contrary* (1961), that made me want to become one at all.

Mary's glamour and reputation for sexual daring (Vassar took years to get over *The Group*) left some who read her criticism surprised by its essentially conservative nature. Her imagination was premodernist, and despite that twentieth-century academic specialty, so mine has always been. In all the years I was teaching Joyce and Woolf, my heart and mind were actually closer to Trollope and Thackeray. McCarthy's essay "The Fact in Fiction" —she was all for it—spoke forcefully to me when I read it thirty years ago, and I'm not surprised that my own fiction eventually settled into the precinct of the historical novel. Like Mary, I began publishing fiction only after I'd written a good deal of criticism and argument, and for better and worse the developmental sequence is evident: in my novels, narrative comes less easily than the construction of a character's background or commentary on his motives. Reluctant to let go of the essayist's prerogatives, I have never written a novel outside the third person. Even amongst the diarists in *A Book of One's Own*, practitioners of the ultimate first-person form, I always leaned toward the panoramic chroniclers, the ones who looked outward upon their times more than inward upon their lives. There's an element of Mary here, too: she once declared a resolute preference for sense over sensibility, and in my own essay "Enough About Me," grouped in the "Biographical" section of this book, I find myself writing this about a clutch of modern memoirs very different from McCarthy's *Memories of a Catholic Girlhood:* "I would rather end the day having had one clear thought than one strong feeling. . . ."

If I regret my long detour into college teaching—and I do; it's the vocation of first, wrong choice for most writers—I cannot say I'm sorry to have spent five years acquiring a Ph.D. My 1970s graduate education at Harvard (made sport of in my first novel, *Arts and Sciences*) was, at all events, staunchly behind the times. In Cambridge in those days, the study of literature was, more than anything else, the study of literary history. We emerged nearly immaculate of Professor Bonney's textual theory, handicapped for the job market, but in my case at least somewhat better equipped to write the sort of fiction and criticism I went on to produce during and after my long period of teaching.

More than half the pieces in this book first appeared in *Gentlemen's Quarterly,* where I got the job of literary editor in 1991, shortly after writing a piece for the magazine, included here, on John O'Hara, perhaps the most fact-heavy writer of fiction produced by America in modern times. I took to *GQ* immediately—no committees, for one thing. I bought the fiction, commissioned essays and eventually took over the books column from the redoubtable Mordecai Richler. As he was making the change, Art Cooper, *GQ*'s editor-in-chief, asked me what I thought the most important trait a book critic could have. I said skepticism; hence the column's new eponymous rubric: "Doubting Thomas." Even so, the column's dominant mode turned out to be one of qualified appreciation, as shown by the sixteen pieces in "Working Writers," almost all of them about novelists, from Ward Just to Will Self, whose works are set in a career context.

I've sorted the other two dozen or so essays into four sections. The retrospective group "Off the Shelf" begins with an early, long piece on Siegfried Sassoon (the English poets of World War I were my *particular* academic specialty) and moves on to reconsider a trio of hearty "light-heavyweights" in American fiction: O'Hara, Sinclair Lewis, and John Dos Passos. Along with some brief, more or less appalled pieces on Truman

Capote and H. L. Mencken are two short ones on McCarthy and a longer sort of literary travel essay about New Orleans in the 1960s.

I have always been drawn to literature's suburbs (those diaries) and minor keys (I used to describe my dissertation subject, Edmund Blunden, as "a major minor poet"); this book's third section, "On the Fringe," is an assortment of pieces on fan mail, plagiarism, obituary, indexes, handwriting, and book tours.

"Biographical" begins with the first sizable essay I ever published, "A Boy of No Importance," an account of my search for what happened to Edward Shelley, the office boy at Oscar Wilde's publishers and a minor (again) character in the great drama of Wilde's trials. This exercise in detection has links, I think, to the two much-later pieces that follow, in which inference goes to work on a slender trove of incidentals: "Held in Check" attempts to assess aspects of my father's character from the box of cancelled checks he left behind after his death, and "Sanctified by Blood" tries something similar with the contents of Abraham Lincoln's pockets on the night he was murdered. "Life Is Short" praises the tradition of brief biography from Plutarch to the present, while "Double Dutch" offers two cheers for perhaps the most reviled life story of our time, Edmund Morris's peculiar recreation of Ronald Reagan.

Morris's half-invented history provides passage to the book's last main section, which includes commentary on my own experience with the historical novel, and appraisals of that genre as practiced by such contemporaries as Jane Smiley and Andrea Barrett. The other "Historical Fictions" under consideration here are the Kennedy assassination as reimagined by Norman Mailer; the evolution of American political photography; the conspicuous dearth of imaginative literature prompted by the moon landing; and the tumult of the late-'60s campus revolution as I might be inclined to reconstruct it in a novel.

One might append the subtitle of that last piece, "A Minority Report," to this whole collection, whose prevailing moods and enthusiasms remain more retroverted and conservative than the academic and media cultures in which they were experienced. The actual title comes from what rereading makes me realize is my own most frequently used prepositional phrase. *In fact* is what rhetoricians call a "transitional marker"—words employed to announce a second sentence or phrase that, with a certain eagerness, elaborates upon the first. I notice that even in this short preface I could go barely more than four paragraphs without it. But as I look at them on the title page, the two words seem not so much a connective device as the single atmospheric element in which I've lived my life as a writer, even the "imaginative" part that produces novels. Those books have risen from the actual and verifiable world, its history and geography intact. The further anyone's fiction strays from those things, the less it interests me. (I cannot conceive of a phrase in which the adjective condescends to the noun more than happens in "magical realism.") Similarly, the further criticism entered its university echo chamber of jargon and abstraction, the more I clamored to flee it. The "real world"—a phrase that academics use with uncommon accuracy to indicate what's over the walls—is the one I had to get into if I was to have any chance as a writer and, I'm long since convinced, a reader.

Westport, Connecticut
August 14, 2000

Working Writers

The Fabulous Baker Boy

T HE TITLE OF Nicholson Baker's first collection of essays, *The Size of Thoughts,* reminds us that the vision he's displayed in four novels preceding it has always been defiantly molecular. Baker doesn't just count the angels on the head of a pin; he does long division with the feathers in their wing tips. The epic tininess of some of this new book's subject matter—a 150-page piece on a secondary meaning of the word *lumber* ("*old household goods, slow-selling wares, stuff, or junk*"); a "History of Punctuation" that narrows down to a treatise on the demise of the hybrid comma-dash—recalls the "plots" of his first two novels: a young man's musings during a lunch hour spent buying shoelaces and riding an escalator; a narrator's thoughts while giving his infant daughter her bottle. Mostly, this new collection reminds us that Baker has never really been a novelist at all. He has been writing essays the whole time—has been, in fact, a small master, the genre's American Fabergé.

Those first two books, *The Mezzanine* and *Room Temperature,* depend almost entirely upon association, the way one thought leads to another, a process that could keep any person with sufficient powers of observation and language wide-eyed and delighted forever. The world's lumber, after all, is inexhaustible. The difficulty comes with almost no person's having the combined gifts of sight and words that Baker does. But his readers can settle for clucking over the aptness of what's born from the author's nearly *Rain Man*–like gaze and metaphor-mad pen.

He's got a million of them: "the late-afternoon color of thermally activated elevator call buttons"; the way that, in signing a credit-card slip after a good meal, "you whip off most of your last name with the sort of accelerating wriggle that a vacuum-cleaner cord makes in retracting into its coiled place of storage"; or just the "Saarinenesque upcurve" of a contact lens. Ever since someone noticed that his love was like a rose, we have depended upon *other* things to let us truly apprehend what's in front of us, but Baker works with what he calls "vibratiuncles of comparison," tiny dog-whistle vibrations that he makes into paragraphs and even pages about the earplugs, popcorn and push-button hand dryers that stock a personal world as disproportionate as it is exact. There is something almost cyber about the way he goes fantastic-voyaging through airplane air nozzles, milk cartons and plastic coin-roll wrappers. Other writers may do the occasional riff on these things, but Baker composes one baroque concerto after another. His real ancestors are seventeenth-century writers like Robert Burton, who draped a sort of ruminative Spanish moss over their pages.

What keeps Baker's prose from being a stunt, or just a bravura sort of "technical writing" (the *Room Temperature* narrator's job), is the genuine love of the world giving rise to it. Baker may be a transistor, but he's also the kid at the other end of the radio's earphone, bopping around in wonderment and joy, feeling tenderness for even "the kind of tasteless lovable roll that was included free with your order from a nearby Chinese takeout place." He exclaims his observations in paeans and odes: "Perforation! Shout it out! The deliberate punctuated weakening of paper and cardboard so that it will tear along an intended path, leaving a row of fine-haired white pills or tuftlets on each new edge!" This particular hymn occurs in one of *The Mezzanine*'s many footnotes, a device hardly necessary, since the whole book is really a footnote.

Which brings us back to thinking about why this Lewis and Clark of gadgetry usually presents himself as a novelist. The pose won't do for two reasons, those important ones called plot and character. He has shown no real inclination to be bothered with either. Object to a novel's descriptive "clogs," and Baker will respond: "The only thing I *like* are the clogs. . . . I wanted my first novel to be a veritable infarct of narrative cloggers, the trick being to feel your way through each clog by blowing it up until its obstructiveness finally revealed not blank mass but unlooked-for seepage points of passage." Well, yes, there are these little streams of philosophy running beneath the books, some of them even deep ("reading is itself a state of artificially enhanced loneliness"), but the fiction-seeking reader must sail them alone, with no Copperfield or Clarissa, not even a Caulfield, waving from the banks. Mr. Baker may be made of flesh and love, but his narrators are androids of convenience.

That's true even in the nervy (perhaps foolhardy) novels that followed *Room Temperature*. These were *Vox,* the story of a single intercity phone-sex conversation, and *The Fermata,* Baker's much-excoriated tale of a Boston office temp with a power ("the Fold") to freeze all motion and time around him, a gift he uses mostly to take off women's clothes and have a look. The priapic nebbish heroes of these books seem like liberated versions of the shy office workers who narrated the first two novels. There was always something a little guilty in the *Mezzanine* fellow's chirpy office banter. You suspected he was a mad wanker once he got home, and when his variants showed up in *Vox* and *The Fermata,* you realized that Baker had finally allowed the young man to let loose a great titsapoppin', va-va-va-vulva, Tourette-syndrome outburst he'd kept bottled up for years.

The often funny and completely unarousing *Vox* functions via the disparities within its own highbrow dirty diction. Jim and Abby ("My clitoris is duplicitous") sound more like semioticians than phone-sex freaks, and by the end of their 165-page session, the only thing chapped is their lips. The book is nowhere near as descriptively dense as its predecessors, but this is Baker we're talking about, so the filigree remains ornate, to say the least. The angels may now be dancing on the head of a penis, but exactitude is still the order of the day. As Abby explains, finding a climactic fantasy during masturbation is a tricky business, "kind of like getting dressed for a party, and being unsure of what to wear right up to the last minute, and frantically trying on one image after another like clothes, not knowing which combination looks really *good.*"

There is plenty of sci-fi pleasure in watching Arno Strine put a periodic halt to "time's cattle-drive" in *The Fermata.* The peculiarities of the Fold—its "acoustical coziness," the problems it causes with the radio and photography—make for better reading than the book's long, and increasingly nasty, pornographic set pieces. Despite moments of happy burlesque ("Is there any other related repetitive motion that you engage in?" asks a carpal-tunnel expert of the keyboard-weary Arno), this is a novel in which one wants to skip the "good parts"—which is most of it—to get back to the Bakery basics, the superbly satisfying digressions.

One wonders if *Vox* and *The Fermata* were the author's attempt to scale one more front of his literary idol, John Updike. Between the two minutiae novels (which seem to take place in a kind of Fold of their own) and the two sex books, Baker wrote a short volume about his Updike obsession. It's a "creepy" (his own editor's word), brave book, a comic verbal stalking of the "imaginary friend" with whom Baker one day hopes to share a game of golf the way the two of them have shared formidable mothers and psoriasis. In *U and I,* Baker recognizes the thick, Updikean style of his own descriptive hothouses, and readers can relate his awe at the world's gizmos to Rabbit Angstrom's "instinctive taste for the small appliances of civilization," which once made that character think, amid the lumber of an American drugstore: "God, what a lot of ingenious crap there is in the world." But another part of Updike's achievement has been, as Baker puts it, being "the first to take the penile sensorium under the wing of elaborate metaphorical prose." There is a dizzying amount of virtuoso, lyrical sex in Updike's books, most of it still quite daring at the time the older writer was swimming into Baker's souped-up ken. It's reasonable to suppose that some of *The Fermata*'s logomaniacal fuck-frenzies originated in hero worship.

As Baker nears 40, is it fair to expect or demand a certain "growth" from this micro-megalomaniac, this maximal minimalist? His Updike book confesses plenty of literary ambition and an awareness of career trajectory that borders on the unhealthy (though not abnormal). Has he now reached the point where he will stop shoehorning his outsize gifts into such teeny-tiny books and unleash them upon some big subject and full-blown characters?

Don't bet on it. In the title essay of his collection, Baker reveals what he'll do with any "huge, interlocking thoughts" that come his way: "Once I coax from large thoughts the rich impulses of their power, I will be able to think them in solitude, evening after evening, walking in little circles on the carpet with my arms outspread." Of his Fold powers, Arno Strine admits, "I should probably make much better use of my gift than I do," but he has decided that his "foldouts should in general be short, recreational, and masturbatory, rather than deep and pained." Imagine what Julien Sorel, or Raskolnikov, might have done with this power! Arno won't even use it for practical jokes, let alone bank robbery. He leaves behind cash for the small items he takes from stores with frozen clerks. "The last thing in the world I want is to be seen as a threat," he explains, and so it is with his creator. "We don't want the sum of pain or dissatisfaction to be increased by a writer's printed passage through the world," declares the author of *U and I*. His mother told him that his reluctance to use painful family memories in his books "was admirable and kind of me but bad for my writing, because it severely limited my range." It's this emotional resistance, besides his philosophical bent, that's keeping his books small.

Perhaps that's all right. Depth of talent is a rarer thing than range, after all, and some of his recent work, like a piece on the abandonment of old library card catalogs, has a surprising measure of passion. Still, Baker's first novel suggests there might be one big subject to which his bug-eyed magnifications are supremely well suited. While riding the escalator, *The Mezzanine*'s narrator plays "a superstitious game" whose object is "to ride all the way to the top before anyone else stepped onto the escalator behind me or above me," because "if someone got on either escalator before I finished my ride, he or she would short out the circuit, electrocuting me." This is mentioned just minutes before he cleans his eyeglasses "with the fifth paper towel." There is a great American novel waiting to be written about the little looming agonies of OCD (obsessive-compulsive disorder), a condition whose hilarious-seeming symptoms are suffered heroically—and suspensefully—by thousands of *real people*. Baker's imagination was born to write it.

I urge him toward it with fellow feeling. *Mon semblable! Mon frère!* How can I not essay a short B-and-I close about the three times our type-ridden paths have crossed? There's that reference to me, in the Updike book, as a quick interruption to your life and work—"My wife gave me Thomas Mallon's brand-new *Stolen Words* for Christmas (yes, it is already December 28, 1989, and I have only gotten this far in this essay!)"—and there was the time I asked if you would write for *GQ* about your *Vox* book tour. You politely declined, saying you were still in the middle of the experience I was asking you to describe; if I'd read more of your work than I had (I didn't own up to this), I'd have known that in the wordage I had to offer, you probably couldn't have finished describing how you put on the TV-interviewer's clip-on mike. And finally, there was the quite unexpected time when the link between us was made by none other than Updike himself, who was reviewing a book of mine and noted that I too was something of a "precisionist"—was, in fact, stylistically "like Nicholson Baker, if not with the same antic effect." How flattering (Baker was, from what I'd then seen, awfully good), but how crushing (was I, by comparison, some literal-minded sobersides?).

Could I, if I wanted, take my own detailed sightings up to the 300x power of yours? No, I couldn't, for the big, simple reasons you put down with a shudder while considering Updike: *"He writes better than I do and he is smarter than I am."* The italics were yours, and this time, with your six books and whatever reservations in front of me, they're mine.

Speed the Plot

October 1994*

O LD JOKE: Panhandler accosts businessman for spare change. "A loan," he says. Businessman refuses but imparts some literary financial advice: " 'Neither a borrower nor a lender be.' William Shakespeare." Panhandler replies: " 'Fuck you.' David Mamet."

Since the 1970s, in plays from *American Buffalo* to *Oleanna*, Mamet has made himself famous with dialogue that is faster, filthier and more fractured than any other important dramatist's. His characters shout at and over one another, like shortwave radios barking cross talk. Take the following typical exchange between two of the middle-aged real-estate agents in *Glengarry Glen Ross:*

> AARONOW: *Well.* Well . . .
> MOSS: *Hey. (Pause.)*
> AARONOW: So all this, um, you didn't, actually, you didn't actually go talk to Graff.
> MOSS: Not actually, no. *(Pause.)*
> AARONOW: You didn't?
> MOSS: No. Not actually.
> AARONOW: Did you?
> MOSS: What did I say?
> AARONOW: What did you say?
> MOSS: Yes. *(Pause.)* I said, "Not actually." The fuck *you* care, George? We're just *talking* . . .
> AARONOW: We are?
> MOSS: Yes. *(Pause.)*

*Review of *The Village,* by David Mamet (Little, Brown).

The above is so unreadable that, seeing it on paper, one can forget how effectively it works onstage. Mamet's dramas *play* well enough to survive such things as the casting of Madonna (in the 1988 Broadway production of *Speed-the-Plow*), but one cannot read them. They offer not the slightest linguistic pleasure on the page; the static that crackles on the stage is ugly and arrhythmic in a book. And this is not a small thing, because genuinely great and even just good playwrights, from Shakespeare through Tennessee Williams, can be read with as much pleasure as they can be viewed—perhaps even more: Early nineteenth-century critics like Hazlitt preferred their Bard in a book instead of on the boards, because his characters were more likely to be understood through careful savoring of the playwright's language than through passive witness to an actor's histrionics.

In his essay "A Playwright in Hollywood," Mamet confessed: "It is much easier to write great dialogue (which is a talent and not really very much of an exertion) than to write great plots. So we playwrights do the next best thing to writing great plots: we write *bad* plots. And then we fill up the empty spaces with verbiage." The prospect of a novel by Mamet was intriguing. What would he do with the fullness of the form, in which dialogue is only one component among many? The answer turns out to be precious little. *The Village* is set in rural New England, but far from "lay[ing] bare the dark heart of small-town America," as his publisher rather desperately promises, the book performs a triple bypass, neglecting the novel's traditional realms of characterization, chronicle and social texture in favor of nervous interior monologues that seal up the village's population, one by one, like pears in a row of Mason jars.

Chief among the characters is Henry, whose mind has begun to wander, either from—it's never clear—the natural forgetfulness of age or something more clinically sinister, like aluminum cookware. In any case, he spends most of the book sinking into contemplative deliriums: " 'Was I asleep?' Henry thought. 'Or was I hypnotized? Did I lapse into some Hindu State of Consciousness? Or did I drift away? What was I thinking of?' " Much of the time a reader has very little notion of, let alone interest in, what that could be, but Mamet treats him to long, dull replications of Henry's consciousness as the character makes tea, prepares a campsite or—most numbingly—decides not to employ the same parking style as his neighbor:

Each time he returned to his own home, after having seen the Trooper's car, he debated parking his truck in the driveway nose-out in emulation of the Trooper. He was restrained by the fear that neighbors would feel he was posing, and, so, he always parked in the same manner—straight-in, between the house and the small barn. "Well," he thought, ending his debate with himself as it always ended, "at least I am capable of decent self-restraint, and lay no claim to attitudes and accomplishments I have not worked to possess."

The Trooper is another self-torturer, someone we eventually learn is named Billy and is feeling guilty over an extramarital affair. There's also a sexy, surly girl named Maris who gets everyone worked up when she walks through town; a hardware-store owner named Dick who is facing foreclosure; and an old farmer and World War II veteran, Lynn, who, while out walking his dog one day, spots Maris making love to a man by a dried-up stream. If all this sounds disjointed, it is; if all this is intended to make some point about the isolation of individuals in such a village—or just in such a sad world as ours—it doesn't.

Instead of a bad plot, there is no plot. Some slam-bang developments take place toward the end (one character's children are involved in a terrible accident, and it seems as if the befuddled Henry may have done something terrible without being quite aware of it), but these are *occurrences,* not at all the same thing as a plot. The bulk of the book moves in a sludge of consciousness. There is a terrible tentativeness to everything everyone does, whether it's driving into town, repairing a clock or catching a fish. It's as if they all somehow can't manage, as if they and the world are ready to shatter like glass. "He moved back to the toaster, and took the toast and buttered it with a large, black-bladed knife. He took a heavy white plate from a rack at eye level, and used the knife to slide the toast onto it": Not since the old *nouveau roman* has one heard such ticktocking monotony. Dick, the hardware-store owner in trouble with the bank, spends an entire paragraph in internal debate over the rightness or wrongness of storing an electric fan in a plastic bag.

For a brief while, the reader experiences a grotesque fascination with the pointless elaboration. It's like watching one of those single-camera public-access cable shows, which lull you into a sort of drooling attentiveness until the phone rings or the cat makes a noise and you surface toward actual consciousness with a vague sense of disgust over the way you've permitted your heart and brain to slow to such a dangerous level. In the case of Mamet's novel, your head jerks toward wakefulness with the question: Why didn't he endow the characters with something like life histories and personalities, textured pasts and quirks, instead of presenting all these long, dull replications of the immediate moment? And do all the accompanying philosophical musings rise much above Robert Fulghum? " 'Just like the plane,' he thought. 'It's here, and then it's gone, and whatever you're looking at, is—while it's there—then it passes on.' " As any number of Mamet's dramatis personae might once have said: no shit.

The narration reads like stage direction ("Dickie's hand came back and took the pipe. He filled it from a tin at his right hand. Next to the tin sat the pad with the mortgage figure. He filled and tamped the pipe while looking at the pad"), and the internal monologues sound like spotlighted soliloquies (" 'I don't want sympathy, understanding, or a special break from anyone that lives' "). Halfway through the book, some of the characters finally start talking like the playwright's old creations (" 'Hell of a fucken fucked-up world,' the third man said. 'I b'lieve I'll have a drink. *Bill?* ' "), but profane speech can't save the novel from its sacramental pretensions. The bits of dialogue that Mamet does present convince one he could have done a fine job spitting out a play's worth of the gravelly pellets of New England speech, with even some wit thrown in (" 'He looks like he was born with his face washed,' Dick thought"); but everything lively is hunted down and choked before it can realize itself.

Not content with creating the most subtle fiction of his age, Henry James broke his back and heart trying to write a hit play. For his pains he received thunderous catcalls. Deep down, he must have known better, and so must Mamet as he moves in the opposite direction. "Let's be serious," he once wrote at the beginning of an essay against amplification in the theater. "If you are an actor and you can't make yourself heard in a thousand-seat house, you're doing something wrong—you should get off the stage. . . ." And if Mamet can't handle the social scope and carpentry of a novel, he should get back *on* it and return to the business of machine-gunning audiences with the dialogue he sprays faster than anyone else. Buying his glacial first novel is like paying money to see Carl Lewis walk.

Writing Like the Dickens

Pᴇʀᴄʏ Bᴜᴄᴋʟᴇ. Mercy Larkin. Mr. Figgs.

Exactly right!

The publisher of Peter Carey's new novel, *Jack Maggs*, promises a "Dickensian" book, and the author has come up with a dramatis personae worthy of the adjective. What better moniker for a pretentious housekeeper than "Mrs. Halfstairs," caught as she is between the up and the down? Welcome, lady, to the grand company of compounds—Murdstone, Honeythunder, Tulkinghorn—conjured by the master to whom your creator now pays tribute.

If moviegoers who have just seen *Oscar and Lucinda* go back to the decade-old Carey novel on which it's based, they will be able to find there, too, considerable literary homage being paid. Carey's story of the Reverend Oscar Hopkins owes much of its feel to the novels of Thomas Hardy (especially *Jude the Obscure*) and some of its character conflict to *Father and Son* (1907), Edmund Gosse's memoir of his upbringing by a Darwin-defying churchman.

This time it's Dickens, and the gifted Carey has gone whole hog—or, shall we say, plum pudding? *Jack Maggs* is full of cruelty, goodness, merriment and terror, mysterious inheritances, plot-driving coincidences and sharp-eyed generalizations about segments of the endlessly proliferating human species: "She did not lift her head, but she had that capacity, commonly found in the short and shy, for peering up whilst seeming to look down." The census of any Dickens novel was always so large that the characters had to be outfitted with not only their preposterously appropriate names but also, if the reader was to keep them all straight (particularly the reader who said good-bye to the characters for a month at a time during a novel's initial, serial publication), voices uniquely their own. We appreciate

13

some novelists as masters of regional dialect—Hardy, in fact, is one of them—but Dickens is remembered for his idiolects, one-of-a-kind combinations of syntax and diction by which his minor people imprint themselves upon the ear. In *Jack Maggs,* the tragic footman Edward Constable is sprung to life, in part, by the choppy way he gives instructions to a new servant. " 'Sideboard,' whispered Constable. 'Put tureen.' "

One measure of Carey's success is the impossibility of a reviewer's doing what he would ordinarily do at about this point—namely, summarize the plot. *Jack Maggs* is too Dickensianly jammed with incident and accident and sheer population for anybody to recap. And yet it is very easy for a Dickens lover to explain it: *Jack Maggs* is an inverted chunk of *Great Expectations* that's been fleshed out with *Oliver Twist,* jazzed up by *Edwin Drood* and put inside a biography of Dickens himself.

This is not as silly as it sounds. Well, it is silly, but it's also entertaining and not beyond sorting out. The novel begins with its title character taking the Dover coach to London in 1837. Jack Maggs's principal baggage is, in the Dickens manner, his shadowy origins and unclear purpose. We soon see him exhibit not only a painful facial tic, but also scars on his back and violent mood swings—the last done to great menacing effect: "He stepped out into the road, and raised his stick as if he intended to chase the offender and punish him, but a moment later he was a perfect gent, presenting himself at the doorstep of 27 Great Queen Street with his distress reduced to a small flickering on his left cheek." Before long we know that he has come to London "to meet with Henry Phipps," a wealthy young man who has the house next door to the one where Jack joins Edward Constable as a footman. The callow but dissipated Phipps, his mouth "being one moment utterly persuasive of its charm, and the next distinguished by its churlishness," is frightened of Maggs and resists his approaches.

The pennies begin to drop, and then cascade, well before the reader learns why Maggs has made Phipps the heir to his secret wealth. Years ago, having been sentenced to transportation as a thief, the manacled Jack grew hungry during the coach ride to the boat that would take him to exile in Australia. While stopped at a blacksmith's forge, Maggs spotted 4-year-old Henry Phipps holding a pig's trotter: "First he ran away. But then, two shakes later, his little head appeared up amongst the baggage on the coach and he held out the very thing I might have stolen from him. When he saw my chains would not allow me to eat it without assistance, he did the holding for me, so I could gnaw each morsel off that bone." Yes, that's right: Phipps is Pip, and Maggs is Magwitch, and we're back in the churchyard in *Great Expectations*. Except that Magwitch is now the main character.

And except that Maggs is also Oliver Twist. At one point in Carey's novel, Jack begins writing down his true history (in invisible ink) for Henry Phipps. This story-within-a-story tells of his being forced into thievery as a child, by a Fagin named Silas Smith. Plunged down the chimneys of prosperous houses, young Jack was made to pass the silverware to a confederate at the kitchen door.

Henry Phipps is the only creature Maggs wants to confide in. But Carey's other main character, Tobias Oates, is determined to extract Maggs's secrets by means of mesmerism, or what used to be called "animal magnetism," before the term became a synonym for sex appeal. Oates hypnotizes the scary new footman, promising to cure his tic and to extract whatever "phantom" is tormenting him from within. But, in the language of his first profession, Maggs feels "burgled" by the treatments. As well he might: Oates really wants Maggs's story for a book.

And that's because Tobias Oates is really Charles Dickens. A young writer ambitious to surpass Thackeray in reputation, Oates is the author of a highly successful comic novel, *Captain Crumley*—i.e., *The Pickwick Papers*. Up from poverty; a crusader in the press against injustice; better at dealing with humanity in the abstract than in its individual forms; a devotee of amateur theatricals; and peculiarly close to his sister-in-law. It's all there. All right, Dickens probably never slept with Mary Hogarth, as Oates does with Lizzie, but he was wildly devoted to her, and shattered by her death in 1837—the year in which *Jack Maggs* takes place, and one year before Dickens attended Professor John Elliotson's animal-magnetic demonstrations.

In a book on the subject, *Dickens and Mesmerism,* Fred Kaplan points out the phenomenon's effect on any number of Dickens novels (including *Oliver Twist* and *Great Expectations*) and the high probability that it holds the key to the unfinished *Mystery of Edwin Drood.* In that last book, Dickens's narrator declares the "criminal intellect" to be "a horrible wonder apart" from the average man's mind; in *Jack Maggs,* Tobias Oates recognizes the "Criminal Mind" as just such a discrete physical phenomenon.

Carey is so good at reproducing the yellow fogs and gothic dangers of 1830s London that he can't help occasionally overdoing it, letting the time reach "six of the clock" and having Maggs curse not a policeman but "a bobby, an esclop, a frigging peeler." Not everything seems audibly authentic ("Bullshit"? A "rat's fart"?), but the book has the right spirit of excess, exactly what's needed to replicate the least minimalist novelist of all time. Observe Jack Maggs writing in his invisible ink through the eyes of the little housemaid, Mercy Larkin:

> She watched how those immense thighs jammed beneath the dainty little desk and, when his feeling ran away with him, how they lifted the desk clear off the floor so that the cedar top tilted like the deck of a ship at sea. Throughout all this turbulence he would keep on writing, back to front like a Chinaman, until Mercy thought she saw a kind of glow, from behind his neck and shoulders, like the light from a furnace door. As he wrote, his thick lips moved, and his eyes screwed almost shut.

Now set this passage before a Dickens fanatic and watch him spend a fair bit of time trying to identify it before you tell him it's not Dickens at all.

In the course of antiquing his own imagination and style, Carey resists any counter-urge to modernize Dickens—except when it comes to sexual candor. We learn that the laconic Constable has not long ago been seduced and abandoned by the grown-up lad Maggs considers his son. He "heard his soft promises; he had heard himself called Angel; he had taken his manhood deep inside of him. . . . For two weeks in 1836, Edward Constable had been drunk with Henry Phipps, dreamed of Henry Phipps, had been reamed, rogered, ploughed by Henry Phipps so he could barely walk straight to the table." A passage like this makes one realize why there was never any need for or possibility of graphic sex in Dickens. With such a frenzy of other activity taking place every cornucopian minute, making the characters have sex, too, would have been like asking a gymnast to comb his hair during a triple somersault: superfluous. The failure of Carey's sex passages becomes only one more index of how well he has succeeded overall; his book is too much like one of Dickens's to accommodate them. In fact, he is not just writing like Dickens. As they say in movie posters, he *is* Charles Dickens. We are told, after all, that Tobias Oates will one day succeed in writing a novel called *Jack Maggs*.

Finally, though: why? What is the point of Carey's hypnotizing himself into the literary shape of the long-dead master? Is it a failure of the imagination, equivalent to the complaint made halfway through the novel by Mrs. Tobias Oates? " 'You never needed magnets before. You used an ink and pen. You made it up, Toby. Lord, look at the people you made. Mrs. Morefallen. Did you need magnets to dream her up?' "

Given the imagination that Carey has long displayed with such boldness in his books, one doubts that he suddenly "needs" the literary past to sustain his present. It's more that he cannot resist it. He may be Australian and living these days in the United States, but his approach is decidedly that of the modern English novelist, who tends to see history as *literary* history. If Britain is, as we're so often told these days, no more than a theme park on the world stage, its literature is the big ride, the giant Old Curiosity Shop. British novelists—among them Peter Ackroyd and A. S. Byatt and, if one goes back to *Orlando,* Virginia Woolf—will take a turn at writing in the manner of Trollope or Austen or even Thomas Malory, because this great Everest of writing is there, ready to be gamboled over, with the gamboling a sufficient end in itself.

America's novelists are more likely to search the past for history per se. Whether it's William Styron or Gore Vidal or Russell Banks (his enormous new book, *Cloudsplitter,* is told from the point of view of John Brown's son), the American historical novelist usually has allegory in mind; he wants to see our present woes in terms of earlier experience. The great national love of utility is at work—how can we use the past to improve the present? —whereas the English, shrunk back to their island shores, are content with the aesthetic approach. One doesn't find American novelists trying to "do" Hawthorne or Melville so much as grapple with the same guilty themes and white whales. We have heard much of late about the emotional Americanization of England, supposedly visible in the free-rein grieving for Princess Diana. But the two nations' literary sensibilities remain far apart.

There will be those who see *Jack Maggs,* with its focus on the Magwitch figure instead of Pip, as a victim-based update of *Great Expectations:* very '90s. Well, as Mr. Grimwig would say, "I'll eat my head" if that's the case. Carey knows that the greatest reforming novelist of all time hardly needs sensitivity training from the likes of us. Like the Fat Boy in *Pickwick,* Carey just "wants to make your flesh creep," and he's done a rattling good job. If there's any irony to his undertaking, it lies in the way the book makes us realize the greater vitality of Dickens's relationship to the past than that of any modern novelist, curating English or crusading American. In Dickens, the past is neither literary nor historical. It is the dark well of personal mystery, the place where the key to everything will be discovered: the foundling's parents, the long-lost lover, the stolen fortune. What turns up, in the last hundred pages, will redeem the several hundred that went before. "Recalled to Life" is the title of the first part of *A Tale of Two Cities*. But it's what all Dickens's heroes are waiting to be, as soon as he starts mesmerizing.

Dead Ringer

August 1994

H ALF A LONG lifetime ago, in an autobiography written as he
entered his forties, Sir Stephen Spender expressed displeasure with "something about the literary life which, although it offers the writer freedom and
honor enjoyed by very few, at the same time brings him a cup of bitterness
with every meal. There is too much betrayal, there is a general atmosphere
of intellectual disgrace. . . ." The past year has involved the poet in what
is likely to be the last dustup of a career stretching back to the 1920s, and
provided American novelist David Leavitt with the first real setback to a
critical reputation that took off with the publication of his first volume of
stories (*Family Dancing*, 1984) at the age of 23. Like most literary quarrels,
Spender and Leavitt's has been protracted beyond all usefulness, though its
last acts have yet to be played out on both sides of the ocean.

The trouble began last fall, with the publication of Leavitt's novel *While
England Sleeps,* the story of two Englishmen caught up in the Spanish Civil
War, that magnet for young left-wing writers of the 1930s who were eager to
oppose fascism abroad and advance their notions of social justice back in
England. In Leavitt's book, Brian Botsford, a recent Cambridge graduate,
"a social, rather than an ideological, Communist," attends an Aid to Spain
meeting one night in 1936 only to find himself falling less in love with the
cause of antifascism than with Edward Phelan, a ticket taker on the London
Underground. Ignoring his aunt's efforts to fix him up with a suitable girl,
Brian arranges for Edward to share his room—only later to fall prey to his
latent conventionality and try making a go of it with Philippa, the suitable
girl. On the weekend Brian attempts to get her to accept his marriage pro-
posal, Edward, feeling abandoned, enlists with the international brigade in
Spain. Unable to bear it once he gets there, he deserts, is captured by his

own side and imprisoned. Now realizing the depths of his love, Brian travels to the Spanish frontier to find Edward and bring him home.

Like most novels, Leavitt's was based on a true story. The book's ensuing problems didn't lie in that story's truth; they lay in its recognizability. E. M. Forster, whose spirit figures largely in the novel, once said of fiction writing that "[w]hen all goes well, the original material soon disappears. . . . " *While England Sleeps* went badly. The source of its plot was clearly Spender's 1951 memoir, *World Within World,* and in a review in the *Washington Post*'s "Book World," Bernard Knox (a survivor of the international brigade) laid out the parallels others were also beginning to realize: Brian Botsford's liaison with Edward Phelan was created out of Spender's youthful relationship with "Jimmy Younger," and many details of Brian's attempt to rescue Edward were obviously drawn from Spender's own mission to Spain in 1937.

David Streitfeld's column in the same issue of "Book World" challenged Leavitt on the matter and reported his admission of having withheld an acknowledgment of Spender's book on advice from his publisher's legal counsel—presumably since such an admission would have given a legal wedge to Spender, if he were displeased enough to take action. "Are you supposed to ignore the advice of lawyers?" Leavitt had argued to Streitfeld.

That anyone could ask such a question in connection with a matter of common courtesy speaks more about our age than most novels are able to. There is no telling how Spender might have behaved had Leavitt approached him early on; perhaps he would have been charmed into accepting a contemporary rendition of his story. In the event, alerted to the existence of *While England Sleeps,* he brought the inevitable lawsuit. After some months, a settlement was reached, stipulating that the American edition of Leavitt's novel could still be sold but not reprinted (a revised paperback edition will supersede it early next year) and that the British hardback suffer a much unkinder fate. Instead of being allowed to limp toward the remainder table in the usual way of literary fiction, it has been pulped.

———

When writing *World Within World* at midcentury (it went back into print in 1994), Spender had to torture the reality of his life with the pseudonymous Jimmy Younger into an evasive jargon that must have rendered it unrecognizable even to himself:

We had come against the difficulty which confronts two men who endeavor to set up house together. Because they are of the same sex, they arrive at a point where they know everything about each other and it therefore seems impossible for the relationship to develop beyond this. Further development being impossible, all they can do is to keep their friendship static and not revert to a state of ignorance or indifference. This meant in our case that loyalty demanded, since the relationship itself could not develop, that neither of us should develop his own individuality in a way that excluded the other. . . . The things I am now writing of are difficult to explain.

By contrast, once Leavitt turned Spender into Botsford and Jimmy into Edward, he was free to go to town, '90s-style:

Then I touched my slick palm to his penis, and he opened his mouth as if to scream, but held his breath. Three steady strokes and he came, the semen spurting out in thick streaks, some of it landing in his hair and his mouth. His abdomen rocked like a stormy ocean as the orgasm subsided. He heaved. I was afraid he might choke.

One gets the feeling Leavitt thought he was doing Spender a favor, unshackling him from the old conventions with these Stakhanovite climaxes: "He knelt in front of me to get a better look, and I came ferociously, all over his face." But there's a boilerplate ecstasy to the sex scenes ("I knew there was no limit, no distance we could not go with each other"), and the only thing they excited in Spender was contempt: "I don't see why [Leavitt] should unload all his sexual fantasies onto me in my youth." In fact, Leavitt's departures from *World Within World* distressed Spender more than the similarities.

Still, he complained of "a total lack of invention in the novel," and a reader of *While England Sleeps* will quickly realize that the borrowings from *World Within World* are the least of its literary debts. The whole production is a sort of syllabus, the Bloomsbury unit preceding classes on the Auden Generation, the Victorian references and bits of Dickensian coincidence retrieved from last year's prerequisite courses. The Edward character is little different from Forster's Leonard Bast or Virginia Woolf's Septimus Smith, though he underlines his role in worse dialogue than one will find in *Howards End* or *Mrs. Dalloway:* "I believe in improving myself, even though I'm not highly educated." He stumbles through a book that makes the same dichotomy between British uptightness and southern European naturalness that Forster did in *A Room with a View* and *Where Angels Fear to Tread.* "Mediterraneans would have gone mad," says Botsford about some awful London weather. As a worker, of course, Edward is, from Botsford's refined viewpoint, the closest thing to an uninhibited Italian that Britain can produce: "[H]is breath went in and out, sweet as a baby's. How content—how *easy*—he seemed to be with himself. He did not question, as I did. I suppose it was a matter of class." The other characters are also from stock. John Northrop, a Communist organizer, is even described as "a proper Shropshire lad, right out of Housman," and Edward's lively, much-married mother ("There was something so *fresh* about Lil!") could be dolling up for a date with Alfred Doolittle.

In *World Within World,* Spender owned up to a sexually charged worker-worship of Jimmy Younger ("Nothing moved me more than to hear him tell stories of the Cardiff streets of Tiger Bay, of his uncle who was in the Salvation Army"), the sort of thing Leavitt's Botsford displays again and again: "That he was of the working class, I had to admit, thrilled me inordinately." The Phelan house emits a proletarian ambrosia ("What smells! Cabbage and beef, child's vomit") that perfumes Botsford's overscrubbed class burden. The thought of violating British propriety acts as an aphrodisiac: "How thrilling and dirty it was to strip off at five in the afternoon, to stand naked and hard in the immodest light, while upstairs our lady neighbors spread their toast with Marmite and spoke of the Royal Family!"

Leavitt is at least as good a novelist as Spender was a poet, and *While England Sleeps,* within the bounds of formula, is frequently affecting. From time to time it contains the taut language ("A wounded blue dark was descending") and sharp observations ("lust . . . the *doppelganger* of dread") with which Leavitt has filled many of his short stories. But the derivativeness is pervasive and fatal. The railway station as modern life's "cathedral" is warmed-over Hardy, and Botsford's reply to the card-carrying-Communist question ("I never carry cards. One is so likely to lose them") is Hollywood's idea of Oscar Wilde. Even the soiled bedspread ("mineral oil and snot and piss and spunk") seems an homage to the early, grody Martin Amis.

For the past decade, in four books before this one, Leavitt has been so identified with family themes (divorce, parental illness, the coming out of gay children) that it is hard not to see this latest work as an attempt to broaden his subject matter, to give it a historical heft, the literary equivalent of his real-life foray into Act Up, which he described several years ago. Running into an acquaintance at one of the group's meetings, Leavitt noted how "seeing me, [the man] seemed, at the same moment, surprised, skeptical—annoyed that I hadn't come sooner, and very pleased that I'd finally gotten there. It was as if I were a late arrival at an inevitable realization everyone else had already come to." But this new venture into history—albeit, finally, a defense of the personal's claim over the political—seems thin. There is an unearned feeling to the narration, whose history is often cardboard—"the European nations had signed a nonintervention treaty in regard to Spain, which the Germans and Russians appeared to be blatantly defying. Curse Eden! Curse England for her cowardice!"—or just off the mark. Nonstop listening to the wireless, wondering if war had come, was really a fact of life in 1938, not 1936, a year when Wallis Simpson (absent from this book) would have figured rather dominantly on the Christmastime airwaves.

In fact, the best moments of *While England Sleeps* are small nonhistorical ones that take place away from the Spanish battlefields or even the pounding walls of Brian and Edward's bed-sitter. A map of the Underground, the source of Edward's livelihood and a matter of fascination for Brian, gives rise to this fine passage: "[I]t magnifies the clogged network of veins that underlies the City, it smooths out every unsightly curve and angle. The result is an illusion of order and coherence, discrete and colorful lines seamlessly linking one destination to another. Yet riding on the underground, one *believes* that map. . . . Aboveground the world continues in its orderly ways; belowground everything connects." (More Forster: the famous epigraph—"Only connect"—from *Howards End.*)

The Spender lawsuit, Leavitt admits, transformed him "from an Anglophile into an Anglophobe." In a counterattack in *The New York Times Magazine* ("Did I Plagiarize His Life?"), he said he "became increasingly aware of the extent to which a strain of brutality, even barbarism, underlay the factitious veneer of English 'gentility,' particularly where homosexuality was concerned." This is actually a rather smelly red herring: if anyone suffered at the hands of English homophobia it was Spender, who, amidst the different literary standards (and criminal codes) of 1951, became a self-made pod person, cobbling reticence and refraction into what he called an autobiography. It's one thing for Leavitt to appropriate the older man's story; it's another for this young, liberated writer to make off with Spender's victimization.

Like Botsford, who becomes "ill disposed toward the country of [his] birth" before spending "the nefarious decade of the fifties" in America as a victim of McCarthy, Leavitt has recently had trouble deciding which world, the New or the Old, has let him down more. During the Bush years he raised the possibility of "a mass exodus of artists out of America to Europe, where state support of the arts is already much stronger." Now it's England—whose BBC a few years ago filmed Leavitt's novel *The Lost Language of Cranes* after American producers showed little interest—that "may well be on its way to becoming a nation in which writers are simply afraid to write."

While England Sleeps makes much of Forster's questionable (but never questioned) idea that "if I had to choose between betraying my country and betraying my friend, I hope I should have the guts to betray my country." Botsford has no time for Northrop's screeching Communist zeal ("Don't you see? He doesn't matter! None of *us* matters!"), and yet it's all right for Leavitt, in his *Times* piece, to brush aside Spender's personal sensitivities in the name of that great cause, Art: "Yes, these 17 parallels existed; but they constituted only the smallest percentage of both works. They had been picked with legal tweezers out of a narrative that was as intricately woven as a Persian carpet." Leavitt has no trouble hoping others will honor *his* feelings, of course: "Please don't put me on the spot," he told the *Washington Post*'s Streitfeld after volunteering more about the book's composition than he should have; he'd "spoken too freely, trusted too much."

Leavitt concluded his *Times* piece by saying, in effect, Take my life, please: "I am 32 and I have never written an autobiography; but if I ever do, and if something in its pages grabs some young novelist's attention, I hope he'll feel free to take whatever he wants from the story. Indeed, I can't think what greater homage could be paid a writer than to see his own life serve as the occasion for fiction." He listed a number of other writers who, he claimed, had done as he had with Spender. He's only acted as "Susan Sontag did in 'The Volcano Lover' (about Lady Emma Hamilton); as Pat Barker did in 'Regeneration' (about Siegfried Sassoon); as Mary Renault did in 'The Persian Boy' (about Alexander the Great)." The obvious distinction—that Lady Hamilton, Sassoon and Alexander were all gone before they were novelized—seems to elude him, unless, at 32, he can't help but think anyone 84 might as well be dead.

Spender's duty, it seems, was to hurry up and make himself available. Leavitt's apologia shares with *While England Sleeps* a kind of petulant narcissism, an inability to see events in anyone's terms but the protagonist's. When Edward is dying of typhoid, Botsford's moral quandaries seem more important than the boy's physical agonies ("Edward, listen to me. There's something I must tell you. . . ."). The body of the novel concludes with the line "It was April 1938, and I was twenty-four years old," as if that is the most important thing to be said of April 1938; just as a hundred pages before, the reader was informed, "It was the winter of 1937, and I was twenty-three years old." The *Times* article opens with Leavitt pouting: "Six months ago a famous writer accused me of stealing his life. As a result, I lost six months of mine."

This sense of entitlement has even before now marked Leavitt's career: "I had my N.E.A. grant in 1985, in another time," he wrote in a 1990 piece attacking the new post-Mapplethorpe puritanism of the National Endowment for the Arts. "Perhaps those of us who depended on the National Endowment, regularly or sporadically, got too comfortable, too complacent, cozying up as we did to a Government that handed out the money and never asked questions." One question that he might have asked is why *any* writer—let alone a 24-year-old whose first book was nominated for a PEN/Faulkner Award—should require or be given federal funds to produce a novel.

Early on in *While England Sleeps,* Botsford loses an expensive umbrella he borrowed from his rich aesthete friend Rupert Halliwell. The umbrella is a nice thematic and period touch (Neville Chamberlain), and Botsford will later have reason to regret his carelessness, but for the moment he can only excuse himself by saying, "Certainly had I been aware that it was not just an ordinary umbrella, I never would have taken it. . . . Was I a fool not to have appreciated its value? No, just irrevocably middle class—it had never occurred to me that there could be such a thing in the world as a hundred-pound brolly!" Leavitt's own incapacity for realizing the value of an old man's memories may not be one of breeding, but it is certainly one of manners. And good manners are at the core of this little controversy.

Plagiarism is a matter of word-for-word replication and has no more relevance here than homophobia. (The lawsuit was foolish and the settlement needlessly harsh.) Feelings, however, are quite to the point. Aside from the poet's, Leavitt expresses little concern for those of Mrs. Spender. After hearing about "an eminent English novelist who declared her support of Spender not on moral or literary grounds but because she felt sorry for his wife," Leavitt can only ask: "Was the right to write freely to fall so easily before the sentimental goal of status-quo maintenance?" Brian Botsford, supposedly writing many years after the death of Edward Phelan, declares: "I believe what courage I have shown is in the telling"—a line that Leavitt uses in the novel's dedication. It would have been more courageous for him, instead of fanning his smoke screens, to do what he has Botsford doing, making a "frank admission of moral failure." For that, however small, is the sort of failure we're talking about.

Read It and Beep

*June 1995**

OF ALL FORMS of artificial intelligence, none exceeds that possessed by a graduate student on the day he sits his qualifying exams. I was never more knowledgeable, or less thoughtful, than that May morning, more than twenty years ago, when I took the test for my master's degree (a speed bump en route to the Ph.D.) after a year spent stuffing myself like a Christmas goose (Dickens) from the groaning board of books on the prescribed reading list. Augustans, medievalists, Renaissance men—Ascham, Massinger, Spenser, Jonson—the force-feeding went on, month after month, until I was able to respond to such pressing questions as "Suggest an adequate definition of the literary genre 'Breton Lai,' and support your definition with specific references to appropriate examples."

Today's list would be more multicultural and ax-ground, but the fattening rite goes on. It lies at the heart of Richard Powers's extraordinary new novel, *Galatea 2.2*, in which a researcher in neural simulation bets that a computer can not only absorb such a reading list but also learn to explicate it with the same facility as a living student. The tormented, sarcastic 60-year-old Philip Lentz, described as the electronic equivalent of Geppetto, wants ultimately to know "Is the brain an organ or isn't it?" and he warns a skeptical colleague not to "throw this 'irreducible emergent profusion' malarkey at me. Next thing you know, you're going to be postulating the existence of a soul."

For a "test domain," Lentz will use the reading list for a Master's Comprehensive Exam taken years before by the book's narrator, a 35-year-old novelist who has returned to his alma mater as the "token humanist" at its Center for the Study of Advanced Sciences. Readjusting from seven years

---

*Review of *Galatea 2.2*, by Richard Powers (Farrar, Straus & Giroux).

abroad and the failure of his marriage, the confused, still-young writer gets drawn into collaborating with the older, abusive scientist: "I followed along, moving my lips like a child, while Lentz declared in print that we had shot the first rapids of inanimate thought."

The narrator carries the author's own name, Richard Powers, making *Galatea* part of a growing literary genre one might call virtual realism—not exactly autobiography but a coyly forthright version of the usual novel refracted from an author's real life. (Consider Peter Høeg's recent *Border-liners,* narrated by Peter Høeg.) Powers the character describes some of Powers the writer's earlier novels, such as *Three Farmers on Their Way to a Dance* and *The Gold Bug Variations,* even citing the same *Time* magazine review that's quoted in the publicity package accompanying this new book. In the absence of facts, a reader will assume—rightly or not—that the story interwoven with the fictional experiment is largely the author's own: marriage to a former student who moves the two of them back to her parents' native Holland, where the more successful Powers is with his writing, the more she declines into self-dislike: "Her devotion to my project, fierce and unquestioning, was bitterness by another name."

Lentz and "Powers" program eight different "Implementations," Imps A through H, each one "nested" in the others that succeed it, like a series of Russian dolls or the successive periods of literary history. The Imps ascend in cognitive power: A can be read to; B can manage syntax and the beginnings of content; Imp F makes inferences and even metaphors; and G can dream a sort of cyber-dream, though it still can't handle irony.

But then along comes Imp H, which begins not only to make critical judgments but also to express something like human desire. Asked to explain Frederick Douglass's sentence "Once you learn to read you will be forever free," H responds, "It means I want to be free." Powers, thrilled and fearful, grants the mechanical heart's desire, sitting up nights in the lab inputting book after book with his own voice, reading aloud to the machine as he and his wife once read to each other. Inevitably, Imp H is named and sexualized—though the "Helen" she becomes, however dangerous the name's implications, is less the incendiary prize of Troy (whose story is part of her reading) than Helen Keller, never mentioned in the book but, as someone given a second life by language, inevitably rising to the reader's mind.

Lentz revels in Helen's *dissimilarities* to people. They will help him win the bet. After all, she doesn't have to be given sensations or physicality, and as he tells Powers, "We can beat the hell out of a developing infant, in any case. First off, our baby never needs a nap." But Powers is not so sure, and it is his doubts and anxieties that create the novel's drama. He argues with the older man: "Knowledge is physical, isn't it? It's not what your mother reads you. It's the weight of her arm around you. . . . Reading knowledge is the smell of the bookbinding paste. The crinkle of thick stock as the pages turn." Much is at stake in Lentz's experiment, as well as in the novel. What is cognition? And how is "comprehension bred, or aesthetic taste, or temperament?" Is memory, as Lentz insists, just a mental parasite that "opportunistically used perception's circuitry for its playback theatre"?

Powers cunningly introduces minor characters on the extremes of human intellectual performance—a child prodigy, a boy with Down's syndrome, a stroke victim (Lentz's own wife)—who function as controls, against which the reader can consider more typical capacities for thinking. The narration is speckled with witty lines ("as literal as a lawyer giving the keynote at a libel convention") and dozens of lightly concealed quotations ranging from Shakespeare to Pope to Yeats, though Powers's own descriptive prose is occasionally so overrich that a reader wants to rip out some of the book's wiring, just as Lentz has to do with Imps A and B.

Galatea 2.2 is entertainment of a very high order, and likely to be remembered as one of the best books of the year, because its erudition is nourished by genuine feeling. "Helen" is a noble savage undergoing the kind of civilization visited upon Dr. Frankenstein's creature (he had a reading list, too) as well as Tarzan and even the frantic, preliterate Helen Keller. This new Helen's accumulating fund of knowledge is so full of gaps and incongruities that the list of what Powers must impart to her reads like one of the Homeric catalogues she's getting in her epic poetry:

> We taught her never to draw to an inside straight and never to send a boy to do a man's job. We laid out the Queen's Necklace affair and the Cuban trade embargo. The rape of continent-sized forests and the South Sea bubble of cold fusion. Bar codes and baldness. Lint, lintels, lentils, Lent. The hope, blame, perversion, and crippled persistence of liberal humanism.

The perils of unexpected learning have been around since the creation of Caliban, whose eventual profit from being taught language, one will remember, was knowing how to curse. Powers can protect Helen from the barbarity passing for today's literary criticism, but he cannot forever shield her from the blood-soaked nightly narrative we call the news—not if she's going to grasp one of the chief rules of literary interpretation: "how little literature [has], in fact, to do with the real." Helen's deferred encounter with life itself is the novel's most poignant moment.

It would be easy to put Powers into the sort of category those master's tests are built around. Let's call it "Fiction Writers Grappling with the Cognitive Consequences of Advancing Technology: Wells, Snow, Pynchon, Lightman . . ." But to do that is to put academic shackles on his novel just when it's aborning in bookstores. Let Powers be read before he's studied. Besides, if his blocked but eventually inspired narrator reminds a reader of anyone, it's not some fixture of the syllabus but clever old Scheherazade, who extended her life, and enlivened ours, by staying up nights to tell a thousand and one stories.

Joan Didion: Trail's End

August 1984

As AN EPIGRAPH for her first novel, *Run River,* Joan Didion, sixth-generation Californian, chose an observation from *Peck's 1837 New Guide to the West:* "The real Eldorado is still further on." That line says a lot about pioneering, an endeavor and state of mind that for a long time preoccupied Didion, who once registered suspicion of any code of conduct other than "wagon-train morality": "If we have been taught to keep our promises—if, in the simplest terms, our upbringing is good enough—we stay with the body, or have bad dreams." Conservatives may have been annoyed by her recent book on El Salvador, but irrespective of administration policy toward Central America, they would be hard put to read her twenty years' worth of books and not conclude that she is among the most fundamentally conservative writers in America.

Cant is cant, on whatever political wing it flies, and Didion's ear has in the past performed synesthetic miracles that let the reader hear the stench. In *Democracy,* her latest novel, she can still rise to the occasional smell. A put-upon ambassador is playing host to Harry Victor, a liberal Democratic congressman, during riots in Jakarta in 1969: "the ambassador was interviewed and expressed his conviction that the bombing of the embassy commissary was an isolated incident and did not reflect the mood of the country. Harry was interviewed and expressed his conviction that this isolated incident reflected only the normal turbulence of a nascent democracy."

It is a pleasure to find her still able to do this in *Democracy*. It is, however, less agreeable to realize that, having borrowed her title from Henry Adams, she has lifted almost everything else from her own earlier novels.

This book is principally about Inez Victor, Harry's wife, who has never gotten over Jack Lovett, an adventurer who spent much of the two decades

31

before the fall of Saigon dealing in arms, currency, technology, and maybe drugs. "It was kind of the place to be" for Jack, who years before played regaling Othello to Inez's all-ears Desdemona, and whose right if shady stuff never lost its appeal during her long marriage to Harry, who can't even win something as worthless as the 1972 Democratic nomination. It's no wonder that Inez (not to mention Didion) prefers Jack to Harry, who has all the depth of a press release. He's even stuck her with a kid named Adlai. You know she's finally going to bolt. She doesn't do it until one of her kids has run away from a methadone program to Saigon (in the spring of 1975) and her father has killed her sister, but she gets around to it, and when she does, Jack is there to go with her.

Pardon me, miss, but haven't we met before?

Three times, in fact. Inez Victor has in the past gone by the names of Lily Knight McClellan, Maria Wyeth, and Charlotte Douglas. They were the heroines of Didion's first three novels, and they're still the heroine of this one. All four women have the same frayed psychic wiring. Inez's "capacity for passive detachment" proves to be "the essential mechanism for living a life in which the major cost was memory." A native of Hawaii, she once "believed that grace would descend on those she loved and peace upon her household on the day she remembered the names of all ten Star Ferry boats that crossed between Hong Kong and Kowloon." What she remembers from the aforementioned Indonesian grenade-throwing is "the green lawn around the ambassador's bungalow at Puncak, the gardenia hedges." When she finally washes up in Kuala Lumpur tending to refugees (remember Charlotte Douglas inoculating the population of Boca Grande?) and is pressed by Harry's adviser for a reason why, she writes back: "*Colors, moisture, heat, enough blue in the air. Four fucking reasons.*" Like Maria Wyeth in *Play It As It Lays,* she learns to ask why not instead of why. Like all the rest of the heroines she can be tough, both practically and morally, during certain emergencies, but she spends most of her life drifting in the wake of second-rate men and almost remembering something ineffable that somehow got lost.

Democracy is, by the author's admission, a failure. It got written when Didion detoured from the novel she originally intended to write about Inez's family in Hawaii. "Of the daughters I was at first more interested in Janet, who was the younger, than in Inez." No, this is not something Didion said in an interview. It's on page 25 of *Democracy,* which, in addition to its other problems, is a novel about novel-writing. "You see the shards of the novel I am no longer writing," the author tells us. "I lost patience with it. I lost nerve." This is fair enough, but why an author who has in the past written brilliantly about cutting one's losses and burying one's dead chooses to advertise her failure in this awful old-hat *nouveau* way is mysterious and sad. Didion even decorates the failure with her own supposed presence in her characters' lives: "The first time I ever saw Jack Lovett was in a *Vogue* photographer's studio on West 40th Street, where he had come to see Inez. Under different auspices and to different ends Inez Victor and I were both working for *Vogue* that year, 1960. . . ." Didion *was* in fact working for *Vogue* then, but if she thinks it's somehow imaginatively interesting to claim that the demonstrably unreal Inez was as well, she's wrong. There's a sort of desperation to the device, and as this unholy marriage of author's biography and characters' non-lives proceeds, the reader winces and, finally, wearies. Two thirds of the way through the book, Didion writes:

> I plan to address Jessie [Inez's daughter] presently, but I wanted to issue this warning first: like Jack Lovett and (as it turned out) Inez Victor, I no longer have time for the playing out.
> Call that a travel advisory.
> A narrative alert.

I'm not surprised that the blurb to *Democracy* gives no hint of its format. What surprises me is that Didion expects us to care about a story she apparently ceased to.

I have not been so disappointed by a novel in years—partly because as *Democracy* clanks along Didion keeps giving brief reminders of her great gifts. Her dialogue is wonderful. After listening to Inez's sister Janet make conspicuously consuming chat about childhood servants on a *CBS Reports* during the '72 campaign, Harry's adviser says: "Ask Mort how he thinks the governess from Neuilly tests out. . . . Possibly Janet could make mademoiselle available to do some coffees in West Virginia." A firm believer in the you-are-what-you-own theory of characterization, Didion stocks the Victors' Central Park West apartment with the ideological and careerist clutter of a lifetime:

... the Canton jars packed with marking pencils, the stacks of *Le Monde* and *Foreign Affairs* and *The Harvard Business Review,* the legal pads, the several telephones, the framed snapshots of Harry Victor eating barbecue with Eleanor Roosevelt and of Harry Victor crossing a police line with Coretta King and of Harry Victor playing on the beach at Amagansett with Jessie and with Adlai and with Frances Landau's Russian wolfhound.

But some of the techniques that have served her so well in the past are worked too hard in the attempt to light these by-now-too-familiar faces: the litanies ("By which I mean to suggest" opening three paragraphs in a row); the caressing of scientific diction as an antidote to the abstract ("Technical death would not occur until they had not one but three flat electroencephalograms, consecutive, spaced eight hours apart"); the sentence fragments that used to be so arresting but now often seem just a nervous refusal to finish a sentence:

> See it this way.
> See the sun rise that Wednesday morning in 1975 the way Jack Lovett saw it.
> From the operations room at the Honolulu airport.
> The warm rain down on the runways.
> The smell of jet fuel.

One can sit down with the same syntax too many times, just as one can bump into the same heroine once too often. More than anything else *Democracy* suggests that it is time for Joan Didion to break camp, to realize that this particular vein is exhausted, to summon the courage to pack up her enormous talents and once more, for the sake of imagination, head west.*

---

*She didn't. Her 1996 novel, *The Last Thing He Wanted,* contained, to a startling degree, all the same elements and character types.

And Quiet Flows the Potomac

June 1997

T HE POTOMAC HAS NOT exactly flowed with fiction like the Thames or the Seine. Washington novels, such as they are, tend to be found on racks at National Airport, the raised gold letters of their titles promising a bomb on Air Force One or a terrorist kidnapping of the First Lady. There's a reason for all the goofiness. A serious novelist must take his characters seriously, regard them as three-dimensional creatures with inner lives and authentic moral crises; and that's just what, out of a certain democratic pride, Americans refuse to do with their politicians. Somehow, treating them as pasteboard figures to be knocked around on the Sunday "discussion" programs proves that one knows better and refuses to accord them a deference dangerous to liberty. As a result, the Sportswriter and the Moviegoer grab more of the American literary novelist's attention than the average senator ever will.

The fictional dearth isn't helped by all the mandatory memoirs that politicians turn out. These first-person tales of coming to the capital, of being made a better man by victory and defeat and a forced return home, have a standard narrative arc, as well as an agreed-upon measure of falsification, and their steady consumption may wipe out the market for serious political fiction. But along comes, this month, a serious novel about politics by the attractively serious Ward Just, who years ago left a career in journalism (*Newsweek* and the *Washington Post*) to write novels in which he could more fully imagine the kind of people and events he had merely reported on. His great theme has been compromise, that necessary, honorable and not-so-honorable public art. The reluctantly antiwar LaRuth, title figure of "The Congressman Who Loved Flaubert," a story Just wrote a quarter century ago, "has no secret answers. Nor any illusions. The House of Representatives is no simple place, neither innocent nor straightforward. Ap-

35

pearances there are as appearances elsewhere: deceptive. One is entitled to remain fastidious as to detail, realistic in approach."

In his fiction, Just claims the same entitlements, avoiding both the flashy and the affectless, putting up solid, old-fashioned constructions that are inevitably compromised by the awkwardness peculiar to any political fiction, in which great events must be discussed with a casualness that always seems too studied; invented presidents must oust real ones from the years that they served; and the novelist shuffling résumés into a plot may appear to be picking a staff instead of a dramatis personae. Like a dedicated legislator who will never reach the presidency, Just will probably never snag any of the big literary prizes. What he will leave, like that legislator, is a record, a body of work whose accomplishments are obscured by the manner—"fastidious as to detail, realistic in approach"—in which it was compiled.

Echo House is his new three-generation chronicle of the Behl family, occupants of a Washington mansion where Lincoln once conferred with General McClellan and to whose billiard room Grover Cleveland went to unwind. Shortly after World War I, when the book opens, the socially dull, civically dutiful Senator Adolph Behl and his wife, Constance—now at "base camp of the summit of her ambition"—are awaiting the telephone call that will make him his party's vice-presidential candidate. When it doesn't come, Behl makes the deliberately fatal mistake of showing his emotions and burning his bridges—a scene and a lesson his son, Axel, will never forget.

This scion becomes the novel's chief character, a pillar of the establishment during the country's long zenith: a hero twisted with war wounds, an insider's insider with touches of James Jesus Angleton, Joe Alsop, Clark Clifford and any number of others who have run the country, sometimes with portfolio, more often without. Axel Behl becomes trapped in a bad marriage and haunted by the moment of his crippling: the sight, just as he was wounded, of a beautifully mysterious French Resistance fighter has resulted in a lifelong conflation of eros and duty that will be his curse and his luck. "Hard to explain about the government," he'll tell his son, Alec. "It's a religion, I suppose, and you either believe in it or you don't. The people who don't believe in it think it's an opiate. Too bad for them."

Alec himself gets religion at an early age ("Growing up in Washington, you weren't Irish or Italian or German or Jewish; you were a Fed"), his confirmation coming when, as a college student, he joins his father and Adlai Stevenson on election night 1952 at the governor's mansion in Springfield, Illinois. "They want a hero instead of a wiseacre," he hears a young woman saying into the telephone. Just lets her go on, in a nice example of dialogue that gets away with a lot of expository and thematic heavy lifting: "I don't know what Adlai thought he was running for, maybe president of the Triangle Club. Everyone told him that Americans like their politics sober and every time he cracked a joke he lost ten thousand votes, and he knew it, too, but couldn't help himself." The speaker is a statistician, a sort of Ur-Dick Morris, and she will become the perfect first wife for Alec, soon to be a lawyer because "to be a lawyer now was like being a religious in the Middle Ages; it opened any door."

Echo House takes Alec and his father through Camelot and Watergate and on beyond Reagan, a long era during which a new arbiter of power, television, renders politicians familiar and thereby contemptible, at least to those "beyond the Beltway." Just lays on a lulu of a climax that may be slightly more appropriate to those novels with the raised gold letters, but even it contains a lovely, knowing touch.

The book is full of intelligent conversation. Its spoken abstractions matter in themselves, not merely as indices of character. At one point or another, every figure in the book is a voice for the author, a flagpole up which to run an idea. We get Axel's wife, Sylvia, with her "hydraulic theory" of capital gossip ("the first draft of scandal [is] tasted on the higher slopes of northwest Washington") and Willy Borowy, with his notion that Nixon was "Washington's Jew" ("If only they get rid of Nixon, Washington will be sound once again") and Wilson Slyde, who reads the Bible in American-historical terms ("Job and Ecclesiastes were the Lincoln and Roosevelt administrations"). The idea that politics is art—sometimes in the form of a novel, sometimes verse—is a recurring theme, and there are passages in *Echo House,* lyrical set pieces about the Senate chamber or the figurative bridges that Axel builds (and, unlike his father, never burns), where Just decides to outdo himself—and does. But he quickly gets back to his knitting, because he's more comfortable being the faithful civil servant of action, character and interpretation than some literary candidate begging for cheers.

———

The day after Senator Behl loses that vice-presidential nomination, he gives Axel a present: a signed first edition of Henry Adams's novel *Democracy*. "Some day it'll be yours," Axel later tells his own son. Adams and his book are a motif in *Echo House*, one that fairly insists a reader go back to that 1880 novel right after finishing Just's.

Because Adams published it anonymously—an action he sustained with greater success and class than Joe Klein managed—*Democracy* was sometimes mentioned during the recent *Primary Colors* contretemps. But Adams's story of how Washington works is more comparable to Just's book than to Klein's tale of one outsider's scramble to the top. Mrs. Lightfoot Lee, the young widow who is Adams's peculiarly idealistic heroine, arrives in the capital not to conquer it in the manner of, say, Pamela Harriman, or even to find out how the political game is played. She seeks to know whether democracy is worth the bother it causes.

> With a sigh of despair Madeleine went on: "Who, then, is right? How *can* we all be right? Half of our wise men declare that the world is going straight to perdition; the other half that it is fast becoming perfect. Both cannot be right. There is only one thing in life," she went on, laughing, "that I must and will have before I die. I must know whether America is right or wrong."

The human laboratory in which her researches are conducted is Indiana's Senator Silas P. Ratcliffe, a much-compromising and much-compromised figure whose career includes vote fraud and bribery—and for all that, an undeniable record of achievement. Whether Madeleine Lee will resist or accept his advances provides *Democracy* with its chief suspense, and the novel's cast—a reformist congressman, an ideological editor, some courtly European diplomats—gives a latter-day reader many pleasures. A number of first-rate scenes unfold, such as Madeleine's horrified viewing of a White House receiving line ("I wish the house would take fire. I want an earthquake. I wish someone would pinch the president, or pull his wife's hair"). A reader also takes in the consoling it-was-ever-thus continuities: The novel's womanizer is a senator named Clinton; Ratcliffe's campaign-financing defense has a familiar sound ("We strained every nerve. Money was freely spent"); and once again Washington is mad about a Madeleine.

But there's another kind of pleasure to be had discovering that Adams's novel is not as good as one remembers it from impressionable youth. One can now observe a surprising broadness here and there ("Democracy, rightly understood, is the government of the people, by the people, for the benefit of Senators") and an overreaching specificity to its lowdown: "For simple, childlike vanity and self-consciousness nothing equals an Italian Secretary of Legation at twenty-five." The author strains himself in dandy-ish attempts to sound like some proto-Wilde of paradox.

Ward Just, a century and more later, hold his own quite nicely. His observation of Axel's aging generation at a party—their ringed, arthritic fingers clutching mixed drinks—is distinguished not only by its accuracy but by an unsentimental sympathy, an appreciative dimension that Adams, disgusted by the venal rough-and-tumble, refuses himself. The answer that Adams makes Mrs. Lee give to her own question ("She had got to the bottom of this business of democratic government, and found out that it was nothing more than government of any other kind") is one Just declines to accept. The real insider's lesson he has to impart is that outsiders have become too cheaply cynical, which is to say naive. Axel Behl's civil religion may have too much zeal and a share of self-interest, but it came along during a century when Americans could hardly fail to make distinctions between their kind of government and the other, usually murderous, variety. *Democracy* was written by a man who couldn't get over how government had passed out of his own family's hands. *Echo House* stays vitally interested in what one fictional family does to keep earning its place.

The Best Man

November 1995

N INETEEN FORTY-EIGHT was supposed to be the year that
Gore Vidal, like Thomas E. Dewey, finished himself off. The 22-year-old
writer, whose first book, *Williwaw,* had put his handsome face (along with
Truman Capote's babyish pout) into a *Life* magazine feature on important
young writers, elected to publish *The City and the Pillar,* a novel about
homosexuality that, in '40s parlance, was "too frank" for anyone's good. Ignored or abominated, most famously by *The New York Times,* Vidal realized
he had solved his dilemma about whether to pursue a career in literature or
"the family business" of politics: *The City and the Pillar* ruled out both.

Entering his "literary blackout," the grandson of Senator Thomas Pryor
Gore spent a decade regrouping. Under the pseudonym Edgar Box, he
wrote several mystery novels (praised by the *Times*) and, using his own by-
line, about two dozen television plays, whose success only further confined
him to the margins of literary reputation: "There might have been a certain
sad prestige had I failed in television, but to have been successful was a sign
of fundamental flaw." Still, he was on his way to financial independence and
the chance to sit in his library writing, at first for mere intellectual profit, essays. Over the next forty years, Vidal would rescue both of his thwarted
early ambitions, earning a permanent place in American literature as the
best essayist of his age, the only one among the contenders whose subject
was always, in the fullest sense, politics.

Palimpsest is a memoir of his first forty years, and he admits to giving
away its "Rosebud" in the early pages: James Trimble III, the "J.T." of *The
City and the Pillar*'s dedication, a blond boy killed on Iwo Jima before his
twentieth birthday. Jimmie was, Vidal believed from the moment they met
at school, the twin he had longed for. Even the more sophisticated book
buyers of 1948 (the year of Dr. Kinsey, too) might have been able to deal

40

with the adolescent love affair between bookish Gore and baseball-loving Jimmie, "belly to belly" on the bathroom floor, as the sort of "phase" that "normal" boys pass through and "outgrow." Vidal, however, outgrew neither the phase nor the boy. What made *The City and the Pillar* unthinkable was its projection of a later, disastrous encounter between Jim Willard (Gore) and Bob Ford (Jimmie).

Jimmie Trimble was the only real passion of Vidal's life. Together they "reconstitut[ed] the original male that Zeus had split in two." The author is still, a half century later, wondering whether Jimmie would "have continued to recall what was for me a completing of the self but might have been for him nothing at all." To get the answer, he seeks out the 90-year-old mother and now late-middle-aged girlfriend who survived Jimmie and discovers— among other surprises—that he is composing "for the first and last time, not the ghost story that I feared but a love story. . . ."

As the rigorously rational Vidal made his way through the world, thinking of Jimmie or calling his name could make the wind rise and the white-caps swell; with anyone else, sex and love were strictly unblendable, a matter of simple reality and considerable relief. Vidal contented himself with "a thousand brief anonymous adhesions, as Walt Whitman would put it," holding to a set of rules that forbade going to bed with anyone drunk or older or a friend. He broke them for a brief encounter with Jack Kerouac, which is described, atypically, at some length. In this one of life's departments, pattern reveals much and details just about nothing, so Vidal's excellent standard for recollection is candor (the only wile, as Whitman's competition put it) without particulars. In late-1940s New York:

> I did enjoy my daily meetings with strangers, usually encountered in the streets. We would then go to one of the Dreiserian hotels around Times Square. Most were poor youths my own age, and often capable of an odd lovingness, odd considering the fact that I did so little to give any of them physical pleasure. But then, even at twenty, I often paid for sex on the ground that it was only fair. Once Truman [Capote] said to me, "I hear you're just the lay lousé."
>
> "At last, Truman, you've got it right."

Vidal's sexual history has shown some flexibility as to gender, and to the annoyance of almost every side in the sexual-politics war, he maintains that there are only homosexual acts, not homosexual people. For the past forty-five years he has lived, in chaste amity, with Howard Austen, realizing that, while the absence of "tempestuous love affairs" has left him without some of the key stuff of memoir, it's also saved him a lot of time.

Time, for instance, to complete his plan for financial independence by 1960 and to make a long-shot run for Congress. He was urged on by his Hudson Valley neighbor Eleanor Roosevelt, at whose funeral two years later, her pallbearing sons passed in front of him: "The smell of alcohol was overwhelming." Soon after that, Vidal decamped to Rome and began writing the historical novels that would usefully stimulate American readers—who prefer feelings to ideas in their fiction—and irritate the professors of history's "agreed-upon facts."

The books have infuriated Vidal-haters by selling well, but as their creator long ago learned about the movies, commercial productions "are often rather better than those of solemn *auteurs*." Back in 1992, while I was struggling with the structure of my own novel about two of the bit players at Ford's Theatre, I asked the author of *Lincoln* for some advice. "I'd start with the bang-bang," he said with weary generosity, adding, "It's the hack's solution"—a respectful nod to what works.

Lincoln is an exceptionally artful novel. Most of the "hacks of academe" (a favorite Vidal phrase, this time pejorative) don't even guess what its shifting points of view are up to. *Palimpsest* is similarly sly. It takes its name from reusable parchment, the right material for "*re*-vision—literally, a second seeing, an afterthought." Readers don't look at Vidal's past so much as watch him watching it. The verb tense shifts in and out of the present, and as often as we're in 1948, we're with the beta-blocked and soon-to-be-70 author in 1994, at his Olivetti typewriter on the Italian coast or on new journeys to the places where he grew up.

From Senator Gore, his blind, populist grandfather, the young Vidal received "the ability to detect the false notes in those arias that our shepherds lull their sheep with," as well as "the curious flaring Gore nostrils that most of us have inherited, including our young cousin who currently lives in vice-presidential obscurity, a sort of family ghost flickering dimly on prime-time television." With each rubbing of the palimpsest, the author's mother (Senator Gore's daughter, Nina) grows only more hideous, the object—except perhaps for Truman Capote—of Vidal's most unyielding disgust. He records her rages, her drinking, her lying, her inability to bear the spotlight's being on anyone but herself. When Vidal's father, Gene, Franklin Roosevelt's air-commerce director, appeared on the cover of *Time,* Nina flung the magazine in his face; forty years later, after Gore occupied the same iconic slot, she wrote a long denunciation of him to the editors.

It was through Nina that Vidal became connected to the Kennedys, whom he would eventually name "The Holy Family" but now settles for calling a "pretty deplorable" (no comma) bunch. Nina Vidal and Janet Bouvier successively married Hugh Dudley Auchincloss, Jr., thus making the eventual Jackie Kennedy into Gore's stepsister-once-removed. Young Jackie moved into Vidal's bedroom at Merrywood, "Hughdie's" Virginia home, where she and the future president at least once in a while slept on the same twin beds Gore and Jimmie had. Jackie was dying as Vidal wrote *Palimpsest,* and his view of her remains harshly, if hilariously, mixed. Her "boyish beauty and life-enhancing malice were a great joy" to him, even if she was "selfish and self-aggrandizing beyond the usual." She comes to mind when he recollects his World War II military training in Colorado Springs: "Once, after I was blown by an old man of, perhaps, thirty—my absolute cut-off age—he offered me ten dollars, which I took. As a result I, alone in the family, did not condemn Jackie's marriage to Onassis, since I, too, had once been a small player in the commodities' exchange market."

Vidal's own sex life was actually more similar to JFK's. The two of them got on well; as the memoirist points out, the only thing he wanted from Kennedy was his job. As for Bobby, his and Gore's mutual loathing climaxed at a famously unpleasant White House party. The attorney general's ardent homophobia proceeded, Vidal feels sure, from anxieties on the sexual front: "Anyone who has eleven children must be trying to prove —disprove?—something other than the ability to surpass his father as incontinent breeder." Rudolf Nureyev, believe it or not, weighs in for the prosecution here.

Even before he walked through Camelot, Vidal's life had a kind of Gumpian ubiquity and, as he tells it, influence. He watched FDR's second inaugural with his father; saw Neville Chamberlain, on his way to declare war, during a school trip to Europe; worked down the hall from Fellini while doctoring *Ben-Hur* for William Wyler; helped make JFK president (by urging Richard Rovere not to write about his Addison's disease); got Jackie to wear sunglasses; and gave us Ronald Reagan, too, by opposing his being cast in Vidal's play *The Best Man:* "Melvyn Douglas played the part;

won prizes; and his career was hugely revived, while the rejected Reagan, at a loose end, became governor of California."

The gossip value of *Palimpsest* is enormous (Joe Alsop and Tennessee Williams's boyfriend? Jackie and William Holden?), and with every clod of dirt that's flung a score is settled. For someone with a "lifelong reluctance to read anything about myself," Vidal has certainly managed to keep up. *Palimpsest* is compulsively retaliatory, a sort of human nuclear strike against Arthur Schlesinger, Henry Kissinger, Anaïs Nin, Lee Radziwill ("Only recently have I learned that [her Secret Service code name] . . . was 'Rancid-ass' ") or, again and again, in cold blood, Capote. During a moment of speculative charity, he pronounces it "a mystery that [Truman] never used his truly uncanny inventiveness in his attempts at fiction."

In my early years of doing what Vidal always calls "book chat," I frequently wrote for his archenemy William F. Buckley, Jr.'s, *National Review.* Buckley, who will no doubt be the Capote of *Palimpsest II,* would often enclose short, handwritten notes with one's freelance paycheck, something as simple as "Nice going" to sweeten the $125 being tendered. In August of 1982, after I'd gone on about Vidal's brilliance, the check arrived with an unsigned, typewritten note that read, "Mr. Buckley is out of the country at the present time." A good thing for me that he was, I suppose. It was pretty big of them even to run the piece; Buckley must have understood (perhaps in a weak moment shared?) my difficulty: What are politics compared with writing as good as Vidal's?

All the familiar complaints against the "National Security State" are here in *Palimpsest,* all the forecasts of repression and apocalypse. To have read them so delightedly and for so long is to have believed none of them, but listening even now to the Gibbon of Ravello ("As Christianity began to obscure our bright world . . .") makes me muse on his indispensability, and pity a liberal world that will one day try to make do with Barbara Ehrenreich and Frank Rich. There has not been anyone as good as Vidal, nor anyone who came to his beliefs in quite the same way. It was, he says, his own hard-earned dollars that turned him left: "If the government was going to take so much of our money, then let the government give us health care, education, and all those other things first-world countries provide their taxpayers."

That sexual courage should have kept him from a career in the Senate (or, God forbid, beyond) is a deplorable mercy, but by now the literary blessing has long exceeded the political one. He remains vastly under-honored ("My receiving a literary prize [is] an event as uncommon in my native land as Halley's comet"), but the long view will kick in before all that melting polar ice he so looks forward to, and it will note that of all the '40s wunderkinder he was the most lengthily gifted. Capote drank away a second shelf of books he could have written; Mailer pulled himself together to compose another half dozen that will only diminish his reputation.

Early on in *Palimpsest,* Vidal makes a conventional distinction between mood-driven memoir and systematic autobiography, but this new book far transcends the former category, into which he puts it. His view of himself is too coherent, too much from without as well as within. He has lived a life that *adds up,* even after a reckoning that still has decades to go. If, in the unchronological manner of memoir, he has seen himself unsteadily, he has nonetheless seen himself whole—which is to say half, the prodigious half that survived Jimmie.

True Crit

I T'S BEEN SAID THAT, like most big movie stars, John Wayne always just played himself. No similar secret explains the success of Garry Wills, who has taken his subjects from all over the political and literary map. Maybe best known for *Lincoln at Gettysburg* (a Pulitzer winner) and *Nixon Agonistes,* he has also produced books about the Catholic church, *Macbeth* and Jack Ruby. All through recent decades, when the unspecialized "public intellectual" was supposed to have disappeared, Wills wrote seriously about pretty much whatever was on his mind. So his decision to explore *John Wayne's America* comes as no particular surprise.

Just what the book aims to accomplish is somewhat less clear. Its subtitle, *The Politics of Celebrity,* sounds like the afterthought of a catalog writer and offers no real clue to what follows. A famously lapsed conservative, Wills certainly welcomes the chance to decry Wayne's eventual status as right-wing icon; he claims to be tracing "the history of 'John Wayne' as an idea" and admits to concentrating only on the actor's work with "directors who helped create or advance [Wayne's] ideological image." But like some rogue steer in *Red River,* Wills keeps meandering off the trail, writing paragraphs and pages on topics, from Howard Hughes to the OSS, that lie a bit beyond the borders of his chosen Dukedom.

This is "not the biography of a man," Wills insists, but it has plenty of biography's elements, and as the author goes about piercing Wayne's "aura of slumberous power," he revises the man's résumé with a literalist's relish. No, in contrast to what the actor claimed, Wayne could not have seen the silent-screen star Helen Holmes performing her stunts for a series of Westerns called *The Hazards of Helen,* because "the nine-year-old Wayne arrived in Glendale a year after she had completed the serial." And no, it was Wayne's slowness, not any injury, that forced him off the USC football squad. Compared with other stories being told these days by former USC football greats, Wayne's doesn't seem so bad; and despite what he says, Wills isn't correcting "myths" so much as amending factoids, little flakes of rust on the collective brainpan.

The energy for the effort comes from an underlying political animus as well as the author's natural pedantry: on virtually any subject, Wills has shown himself a born corrector. This is an admirable enough critical occupation in some of the realms he's previously visited, but how far does this approach take a reader looking for the meanings of Hollywood? To hear that Gary Cooper was *really* Frank James Cooper tells one nothing about Gary Cooper, let alone what he meant to all those wonderful people out there in the dark.

After a couple of years moving props on the Fox lot, the young actor Marion Morrison (who, like Ronald Reagan, had come to California from Iowa) more or less "wast[ed] his twenties in trivial productions" churned out on Hollywood's Poverty Row. At Monogram the legendary stuntman Yak Canutt became a useful mentor to the renamed John Wayne, but the actor's big break didn't come until he was past 30 and John Ford offered him the part of the Ringo Kid in *Stagecoach* (1939). In a sentence that allows the author to knock both director and actor, Wills debunks Ford's colorful tale of their first meeting as "a little movie Ford later ran in his mind, not a real encounter with a property-moving nobody on the Fox set."

Ford's penchant for making up stories about himself is more than enough to activate the correctional officer in Wills. No matter how much artistry he credits Ford with, the author absolutely loathes the director, a sentimental martinet who could be found "salivating heavily" when he drank, or confining insufficiently servile actors to his personal "dog house" for years at a time. (Ford is introduced in a chapter Wills simply calls "Sadist.") And for all their collaboration (thirteen films, eventually), it wasn't Ford who made Wayne a huge star. That would happen only after another ten years, when Howard Hawks took an actor turning 40 and aged him even further to play the heroic but distinctly unpleasant Tom Dunson in *Red River* (1948).

Wills offers some provocative close readings of the major Wayne movies, but at moments in these exegeses he seems to be bucking for tenure in the film-studies department—listing, for example, the eight major elements of a westward "migration movie" or making the lit-crit observation that some

47

"bullets are frustrated expressions of love." During his lengthy treatment of *Stagecoach,* he feels compelled to point out that Dry Forks is "a name suggesting barrenness," while missing, I think, a few crucial hints that the Ringo Kid is less naive about Claire Trevor's wicked recent past than the author says he is.

It is the postwar Wayne, the developing symbol of right-wing superpatriotism, that disturbs Wills most. "Moving under a variety of masks, Sergeant Stryker," the roaring Wayne character in *Sands of Iwo Jima,* "is still with us to this day—out on the hustings with Pat Buchanan, presiding over the House of Representatives, and lurking in thousands of men's own adolescent pasts." (Maybe even Bill Clinton's?) The three Seventh Cavalry movies that Ford and Wayne made out of James Warren Bellah's magazine stories were, Wills argues plausibly, as much about the fear of Communism as about Indian raids. Yet Wills's take on the whole business is marred by the usual anti-anti-Communism of the American intellectual, be it public or academic: "The Cold War would take many more casualties than artistic integrity, but in this case it also victimized art." The art in question here is *Fort Apache.* Those other casualties presumably include many millions in the gulag, but as always, these souls don't get the space required to make amends to the Hollywood Ten.

However clumsy Wayne's propagandizing may have been—in the again-metaphorical *Alamo* (Wayne directed, but Ford showed up and kept butting in) or the laughable *Green Berets,* in which the sun sets east of Vietnam—Wills's deflation of it suffers from his own willingness to say almost anything about the Cold War except the rather large facts that (1) we were on the right side of it and (2) we won. He is so intent on skewering Wayne for the actor's hypocritical avoidance of service in World War II that he will even use Ronald Reagan's military experience as a moral counterweight: "Reagan did not serve abroad because he was practically blind without his contact lenses—but his military film work for the Signal Corps kept him from commercial movie-making and definitely hurt his career." Back in 1987, when Reagan was doing so much to make possible large fact number two (see above), Wills sounded rather more sarcastic about that actor's World War II years. In *Reagan's America: Innocents at Home,* the author wrote: "Reagan obviously believes he was 'off to war.' He was in a never-never-land of publicity absences and fan-magazine presence."

Similarly, in the *Alamo* chapter of this new book, Wills suddenly notes what a nice guy Wayne was offscreen, an observation so out of keeping with everything preceding it that a reader remains puzzled until the end of the paragraph, whose purpose, it becomes clear, is to show, by contrast, what a son of a bitch Ford was. When necessary, a target can always be made into a foil.

Despite the praise he grants Wayne for *The Quiet Man* and *The Searchers,* and even with a Duke-knowledge whose exhaustiveness seems to bespeak a fan's devotion as much as a scholar's doggedness, Wills almost never drops the sneer. "There is no humor or forgiveness in the tale," he writes of the Maurice Walsh short story that, once leavened with those qualities, became the "material" for *The Quiet Man.* But Wills has kept his own production pretty much free of any such gentling. The spirit that animated *Lincoln at Gettysburg*—a broad, if unhagiographical, admiration—led to deeper insights, and to better word of mouth than this book is going to have.

John Wayne's America desperately needs a more personal approach, Wills's consideration of just why Wayne remains so deep under his own skin. In one or two places, the first-person pronoun makes a momentary emergence, but the author squelches it like one more incorrect "fact." What might be a self-indulgence in other critical enterprises is, where the movies are concerned, a sine qua non. Without the author's willingness to speak about his own feelings when the lights go down, the mystery of Wayne's durability (one 1995 poll had him as the most popular American film star, and this summer the writer Dan Barden will publish *John Wayne: A Novel*) remains mysterious to the end. "Down the street of the twentieth-century imagination," Wills writes, with some felicity, "that figure is still walking toward us—graceful, menacing, inescapable." But *why*? The author may be good at framing the problem, even by analogy—"Judith Anderson was a far greater actress than Marilyn Monroe; but she took up less psychic space in the movie audience's dreamworld"—yet he seeks too many of his answers in the realm of the political.

His concluding chapter, "American Adam," is more about the West than about Wayne, and his thesis that Wayne succeeded as an "unwitting heir to [a] long tradition of anti-intellectualism" makes a cultural matter of what the movies have always actually been about: sex and self-projection. Wills is right about Wayne's having had fewer female fans than most comparable male stars. But one of them, Joan Didion, explained her attraction to the actor in an essay written more than thirty years ago, "John Wayne: A Love Song." In 1943, as an 8-year-old, she had heard him "tell the girl in a picture called *War of the Wildcats* that he would build her a house, 'at the bend in the river where the cottonwoods grow.' " And that, Didion wrote, "is still the line I wait to hear."

But that doesn't account for the 8-year-old American boys, the ones who grew up into the anxious, self-doubting American men who still vote for John Wayne in those movie-star polls. It was another line that they heard, one Wills examines more for its acoustics than its psychological force. It was a line that American boys would ever after keep waiting to hear being said about *them* by a real-life man who looked and talked and, above all, walked like John Wayne. Just those two words he said about the kid he decided had enough potential to be worth hiring in *Red River:* "He'll do."

The Bronx, with Thonx

S OMEWHERE ALONG THE WAY, moving out of which house or dorm room or apartment I'll never know, I lost (threw away?) my Ralph Branca autograph. He'd signed it for me at a Little League banquet—one of those Swiss-steak father-and-son affairs—in, I would guess, 1962. As he stepped up to the microphone to make his after-dinner speech, my teammates and I exchanged glances behind our fathers' backs: Who is this guy?

We had all been born in '51, the year of his split-second, defining misadventure—the single pitch that rendered him the schmuck of all time and gave him this second career, off the mound and behind the dais, listening to the nostalgic laughter of our newly middle-aged dads. Driving home, however, some of them would swear that, on a long-ago afternoon when they were awaiting our births or changing our diapers, Branca had broken their goddamned hearts.

Most of us heard the story of October 3, 1951—the Giants' ninth-inning playoff comeback against the Dodgers—for the first time that night, and it made no impression at all. We were Yankee fans, accustomed only to victory—in baseball, over polio and eventually, we were certain, against the Russians. We did not know, as Don DeLillo's epic new novel tries to demonstrate, that Bobby Thomson's home run off Branca was an occurrence deeper than politics and war.

In *Underworld,* Thomson's homer is the linchpin and the propellant for a thousand actions by dozens of characters. It is a myth, a mystery, a masterstroke by the Prime Mover; an event whose significance lies not in itself but in its power to make apparent the infinite connectedness of everything happening on the lighted ball field that is Earth. DeLillo's long opening account of what transpired at the Polo Grounds is panoramic, spooky and essentially comic. He puts J. Edgar Hoover, Frank Sinatra and Jackie Glea-

51

son in the stands, all of them palpable and emblematic, part of a crowd whose members, after Thomson's redemptive, last-minute swing, will have "their hands in their hair, holding in their brains." Much to the distress of the fastidious Sinatra, Gleason, at the crucial moment, has just thrown up, not from excitement but from overeating. A Homeric shower of paper is pouring from the stands—"faded dollar bills, snapshots torn to pieces, ruffled paper swaddles for cupcakes," as well as a torn *Life* magazine reproduction of Brueghel's *The Triumph of Death*. It lands on Hoover, the painting's grisly profusion exciting the coiled heat in "a man whose own sequestered heart holds every festering secret in the Western world" and who has just been given word of a successful Soviet atomic test.

In the last line of this prologue—"It is all falling indelibly into the past"—the adverb glides by almost without notice, though it is the most important word in the sentence. Similarly, the pleasures of DeLillo's half-historical fantasy go down so easily that a reader may fail to realize the story is not being written, as it is always told, from a Dodger-tragic point of view. Like the dog that doesn't bark, this is significant. Freestanding, the prologue is a tour de force; as the springboard for the huge, perhaps great, novel that follows, it is a signal that tragedy is too small an outlook, and that the author intends a much bigger, more generous explanation for the world and time he is about to re-create.

On one level, DeLillo's book belongs to a literary genre we 10-year-olds at the Little League banquet had already left behind: the "adventures of a penny" exercise from fourth-grade composition. In *Underworld* the penny is the home-run ball, its adventure the trip it takes from Branca's hand to Thomson's bat to a stanchion in the old Polo Grounds' left-field seats, where it picks up "a small green bruise" before disappearing into a chain of eager human hands. The first of those belong to a Harlem kid playing hooky, Cotter Martin, whose father will sell the ball to a white ad executive, who will pass it on to his son, a B-52 crewman in the Vietnam War.

Years after all this, Marvin Lundy, a baseball memorabiliast who resembles "some retired standup comic who will not live a minute longer than his last monopolized conversation," conducts an obsessive search for the ball across America, "through cities with no downtowns," toward dozens of leads, a hundred blind alleys and such characters as the "gospel singer named Prestigious Booker who kept a baseball in an urn that held her lover's ashes" and the "woman on Long Island, what's-her-name, whose husband was at the game—she served instant coffee in cups from a doll museum." Lundy's search will demonstrate to him the "shock, the power of an ordinary life . . . a thing you could not invent with banks of computers in a dust-free room."

It will also, eventually, put the ball (whose provenance is never totally established) into the hands of Nick Shay, DeLillo's chief character, a man whose age (57) and origins (the Bronx) are close to the author's own. The only major figure given a first-person voice, Nick extends the neutral narrative intelligence presiding over the rest of the novel's vast, connected landscape. We first see him in the early 1990s, living in the Southwest and working for a firm that "entomb[s] contaminated waste with a sense of reverence and dread." DeLillo beautifully renders "the marriage sensurround" created by Nick and his wife, Marian, all the loving cross talk and evasions. But mystery and edginess surround Nick, too. When asked about his past, he sometimes replies, "I live a quiet life in an unassuming house in a suburb of Phoenix. Pause. Like someone in the Witness Protection Program." He's not in the program, actually, but Shay isn't his original name, either. When Nick was still a child, his father, a well-liked Bronx bookie, disappeared, the victim of a small-time execution, his son likes to think: "I believe they were waiting for my father when he went out to buy a pack of cigarettes and they took him and put him in a car and drove him somewhere near the bay." (The true story will prove less dramatic, more shameful and, finally, more interesting.)

Nick walks with another shadow: the memory of having shot a man when he was only 17, around the time of his brief affair with Klara Sax, a frustrated painter married to the Bronx science teacher who coached Nick's brother in chess. Forty years later, she reenters Nick's life, after he reads a magazine article about how Klara, now a well-known artist past 70, is spray painting an assemblage of 230 deactivated B-52s in the western desert. She is a woman "drunk on color," at her peak of sexual and artistic vitality. Her story and Nick's emerge slowly, as *Underworld* moves back and forth through the past several decades, sometimes arbitrarily (though this is how memory works) but never confusingly (a testament to DeLillo's construction skills). We learn that certain characters are dead before we have our first extended meetings with them. The novel resembles Marvin Lundy's quest narrative, a "whole wandering epic, skimmed here, protracted there," always aware of "the past that never stops happening."

Underworld continually circles back to the source of its characters and visions, the Bronx, whose "old demotic song" still infuses the author's. There we find the childhood Nick; Klara's ex-husband and his forgetful sister, Laura; as well as the aging Sister Edgar, who once ruled her parochial-school class with an iron ruler and now stays on, bewildered and determined, in a burnt-out, AIDS-thinned neighborhood, where victims of gunfire turn into spray-painted angels on a graffiti artist's wall and a racing, feral girl dubbed Esmeralda, "the fleet leaf-fall of something godly blowing through the world," lives in a vacant lot.

The choice of "Underworld" for a title seems deliberately, and deceptively, cheesy. It makes the book sound like a Mafia thriller involving, well, the waste-disposal industry, whereas DeLillo's novel is really about the hidden, linked life of everything we only think we have abandoned. The waste Nick Shay works with is "the secret history, the underhistory" of the world. The book suggests that people are beginning to perceive this in a dimly literal, environmentally conscious way: They "look at their garbage differently now, seeing every bottle and crushed carton in a planetary context." With *Underworld* DeLillo means to tell them they don't know the half of it. Cotter Martin's Harlem classmate, who eats pages from his history book? The joyful shower of paper at the Polo Grounds? All of it is going into the same cosmic landfill toward an as yet uncertain recycling and rebirth.

In its big, eight-cylinder American way, *Underworld* is as intricately cat's-cradled a novel as *Pale Fire* or *Ulysses*. A reader cannot begin to appreciate it without stopping to chart some of its dozens of connections. Whom does Sister Edgar, in her prime, most resemble? Why, J. Edgar Hoover. Both are fiercely anti-Communist, germophobic and fascinated by the private lives of Hollywood stars; she has her stash of movie magazines, and he has his FBI dossiers. In the 1970s, Ismael Muñoz is "Moonman 157," a subway graffiti artist whom Klara's art dealer is trying to sign up; in the '90s, he'll be the man painting angels on the wall in Sister Edgar's neighborhood—an act similar to what the long-gone Klara Sax now performs on her B-52s in the desert. In the early '60s, Charles Wainwright, the adman owner of the Thomson ball, imagines pitching the Minute Maid account: "You show the froth on a perky housewife's upper lip, like the hint of a blowjob before breakfast . . . you can suggest, you can make inferences, you can promise the consumer the experience of citrusy bits of real pulp—a glass of juice, a goblet brimming with particulate matter, like wondrous orange smog." Thirty years later, after feral Esmeralda has been thrown off a Bronx rooftop, her image will appear when the lights of a passing train strike a billboard advertising orange juice. An alert reader will also note, though hundreds of pages separate the two pieces of information, that Nick pays $34,500 for the same baseball Wainwright purchased from Cotter Martin's father for $34.50. When Nick's mother finally moves out west to join him and his wife, one long-ago ticket holder at the Polo Grounds, Jackie Gleason, comes too, via *Honeymooners* reruns. "We felt better with Jackie in the room, transparent in his pain, alive and dead in Arizona."

Many of the connections are terrifying, such as the work of the "Texas Highway Killer," captured on an amateur videotape that most of the characters watch. All the dark preoccupations of DeLillo's previous novels—the Zapruder film (*Libra*), crowds (*Mao II*) and poisonous chemicals (*White Noise*)—are also on display. And yet, even though Marvin Lundy's obsessive, often forensic search for the home-run baseball is said to be "an eerie replay of the investigations into the political murders of the 1960s," and even though DeLillo brilliantly resurrects the vision of persecution in Lenny Bruce's nightclub act, *Underworld* amazes a reader—and stakes whatever claims it has to being a great novel—with the lack of paranoia in its spider-web design.

When Nick considers history, he pronounces it "not a matter of missing minutes on the tape," concluding, "I did not stand helpless before it. I hewed to the texture of collected knowledge, took faith from the solid and availing stuff of our experience . . . a single narrative sweep, not ten thousand wisps of disinformation." About technology, that witch's milk of paranoia, he declares, "Bemoan [it] all you want. It expands your self-esteem and connects you in your well-pressed suit to the things that slip through the world otherwise unperceived." The grailish baseball, its 216 stitches enumerated, its "drag coefficients" and "trailing vortices" described in Pynchonian physics, is still not the paranoia-catalog item that Pynchon made Lot 49. Even Hoover is given his human, three-dimensional due. Instead of the by now tiresome drag queen, he's an "old stopcocked soul" deriving power and poignancy from his "self-repression."

These connections are more profound than those of conspiracy. Marvin Lundy believes the "wellsprings" beneath the world are "deeper and less detectable, deeper and shallower both, look at billboards and matchbooks, trademarks on products, birthmarks on bodies, look at the behavior of your pets." The links may be sinister, inhuman, but DeLillo would not wish them away, and he will not ascribe them to some secret world government.

The first cause of all these connections? There is the "clammy . . . hand of coincidence" to consider, and there is God. *Underworld* is finally, if tentatively, a religious book, awed and frightened by its own visions. Esmeralda's billboard apparition will wind up on a Web site devoted to such phenomena that Nick Shay's son likes to visit. The Web, of course, invites its own paranoia ("All human knowledge gathered and linked, hyperlinked, this site leading to that, this fact referenced to that, a keystroke, a mouse-click, a password—world without end, amen"), and DeLillo asks the most frightening questions anyone has yet asked about the planet's new wiring: "Is cyberspace a thing within the world or is it the other way around? Which contains the other, and how can you tell for sure?" Still, fear does not send him running for the off switch. Some incoming virus might, for all we know, bring revelation.

And revelation is still required by a world that can't make up its mind about luck and misfortune. To Nick, the home-run baseball is "not about Thomson hitting the homer. It's about Branca making the pitch. It's all about losing." But to Cotter Martin, falling asleep in his room with the ball on October 3, 1951, the game's mystery is nearly the opposite: "The game was lost and then they won. The game could not be won but then they won it and it's won forever. This is the thing they can never take away." (He doesn't know that his father is about to steal the ball and sell it.) To Marvin Lundy, the "ball brought no luck, good or bad. It was an object passing through. But it inspired people to tell him things. . . . Their stories would be exalted, absorbed by something larger, the long arching journey of the baseball itself and his own cockeyed march through the decades." The ball is his reason to live.

———

Underworld's flaws are conspicuous enough. Its refrains are overplayed; its nostalgia is every so often an egg-creamy end in itself; the speech of both Nick and Lundy is asked to haul a lyric and a thematic weight it cannot plausibly bear. The novel is too long by at least a couple of hundred pages. But none of this changes the fact that DeLillo has written the first defining novel of what we are still calling the post–Cold War period. If his definition consists less of attributes than absences, he faces the latter head-on. Explaining her B-52 project, Klara tells Nick, "Power meant something thirty, forty years ago. It was stable, it was focused, it was a tangible thing. It was greatness, danger, terror, all those things. And it held us together, the Soviets and us. Maybe it held the world together. You could measure things. You could measure hope and you could measure destruction. Not that I want to bring it back. It's gone, good riddance. But the fact is." Lundy, who sees Latvia and the collapse of the USSR in Gorbachev's birthmark, warns that "other forces will come rushing in, demanding and challenging. The cold war is your friend. You need it to stay on top." Maybe we are, and maybe we aren't, at what Francis Fukuyama calls the end of history. Either way, as that old Cold Warrior Sister Edgar knows, "All terror is local now."

Toward the end of *Underworld*, Nick is in Russia meeting the marketers of a nuclear solution to toxic debris: "They will pick up waste anywhere in the world, ship it to Kazakhstan, put it in the ground and vaporize it. We will get a broker's fee." Perhaps this is what that Soviet atomic test of October 1951 created: both a problem and a solution. Not necessarily a bad thing, "but the fact is." The fact is *what*, exactly? More than anything else, it's that we pine for faith. "Don't underestimate our capacity for complex longings," says Jesse Detwiler, a waste-industry visionary with whom Nick is acquainted. "Nostalgia for the banned materials of civilization, for the brute force of old industries and old conflicts." Communist ideologues used to prophesy "the garbage heap of human history" for their enemies. Now Communism itself—what I most loathed, most feared and was most right about in life—is part of the heap, decomposing with my Ralph Branca autograph. It was the black half of the Manichaean world I lived in for forty years, and not the least effect of DeLillo's vast, disturbing novel is having to face how much I miss it.

Book of Revelation

June 1998

I
T'S REGGAE NIGHT at the Bixx Bar in Jerusalem, and as the narrator of Robert Stone's cacophonous new novel reports, "The place was full; there were Viking quasi-maidens, Ethiopians with Malcolm X hats, Romanian pickpockets and American Juniors Abroad in kibbutznik hats. Each boogied according to his covenant." You want multiculturalism? Stone's Israel makes the most polyglot American borough look like a Rotary breakfast in Cedar Rapids. It's the mix that interests him—not only the casserole of cultures simmering on the disco floor but also the crazy soup inside each cranium. A decade ago, the author surveyed an audience he was addressing and hypothesized, "If we took the fantasies, the perversities, the madnesses, the weirdness, the strangeness, the odd directions, our own crippled making-it-through-life psyches . . . if we took our mentalities, or even mine, and projected it on a wall, we'd drive each other mad."

That's the chance you have to take reading *Damascus Gate,* in which Stone looks at Israel's stunning, violent juxtapositions of historical circumstance—resort hotels near refugee camps, both of them a day trip away from the Holocaust memorial, Yad Vashem—and tries to decide whether they have meaning or are instead a kind of Babel. History might, after all, be "moronically pure, consisting entirely of singularities. Things had no moral." Maybe there is no casserole, only ingredients; and maybe history is only its parts, not even their sum. But Stone is determined to look at, and play with, everything at once.

Since his first novel, *A Hall of Mirrors,* set in the still-segregated American South of the early '60s, and on through *Dog Soldiers* (Vietnam) and *A Flag for Sunrise* (Central America), Stone has been drawn, by his own admission, to political explosions; his new book takes him toward apocalypse. In the Middle East of 1992, it is "a banner year for martyrs," a time of *in-*

58

tifada and fundamentalist preoccupation with an Armageddon that's supposed to start in Israel. The fiction Stone builds on this time and place is a dizzying combo: an action thriller–cum–novel of ideas. Its mechanisms are as old as Chaucer (throw some pilgrims together) and as modern as Le Carré (make the reader figure out who's really working for whom). *Damascus Gate* is best practiced daily, like religion: Put it down for too long and you'll lose both the story line and the strange brew of its mood, a kind of giddy melancholia suspended in fear. It is not an easy book to enter, especially given the number of plot wires Stone has to run. But by about page 50, he has most of them crossed and ready to spark.

The author's alter ego is Christopher Lucas. (Exegetes: Get your pencils out and start with that name.) A freelance journalist and the author of a book on the Grenada invasion, Lucas is the product of an extramarital liaison between a Jewish Austrian father who became a Columbia professor and a Catholic mother, a sometime singer who drank too much. The character's childhood obliquely suggests Stone's own. He too was raised in New York City by a troubled mother, and he had the same sort of painful Catholic-school experience he now gives Lucas, whose early years—a mixed religious background with no real belief—leave him with "the idea of a great absconded Creator [that] must reflect, had to reflect, some actual state of things." He does not know whether to consider himself a Jew or how serious his spiritual longings are. He has, in fact, come to Jerusalem to "cure" himself of an underdeveloped, "silly regard for religion" but soon realizes he's in the only place where he would "trade his sanity for faith."

Seedily tending toward drink and impotence, prone to despair, desiring to confess, conscious of faith itself as a kind of temptation, the middle-aged Lucas so resembles one of Graham Greene's netherworldly heroes that Stone's usually springy writing about him sometimes gets flattened by the load of affinities: "The river running beside them still seemed at the point of manifesting a great holiness. Something Lucas felt himself unworthy to see. Something dreadful that he required. He was having trouble letting go of it all. He so wanted to believe." But the mad jumble of circumstance keeps the character alive and awake.

Two big stories present themselves as possibilities for Lucas's freelancing efforts: a gang of Israelis who beat stone-throwing Palestinians near settlements in occupied Gaza ("The beatings were egregious and outside the rules as generally understood by both sides") and, more tantalizingly for a lapsing agnostic, the mental condition known as Jerusalem Syndrome, a Messiah complex wedded to geographic opportunity. Dr. Pinchas Obermann, the German-accented psychiatrist who deals with this hot millennial topic, explains a hypothetical case: "A young man of scant prospects receives a supernatural communication. . . . He must go to Jerusalem at the Almighty's command. Once here, his mission is disclosed. Often he is the Second Coming of Jesus Christ." And sometimes he decides he's supposed to blow things up.

These two stories will eventually become one, owing to Stone's skill at plotting and the way Jerusalem has replaced Berlin as an ideal venue for the highbrow spy novel: "It was hard to tell who anyone was and what they wanted because the emergency basis on which the state proceeded created constant improvisations and impersonations." Strapped with political, spiritual and pathological agendas, the characters Stone fires through his double-barreled narrative depend on such improvisations, too.

One of Obermann's patients is Ralph Melker, a.k.a. Raziel or Razz, son of an American congressman, clarinet player, intermittently recovering drug addict, former Jew for Jesus. "*Always smiling,* Lucas wrote in his notebook . . . *Patronizing arrogant but probably sincerely nuts.*" Raziel is assembling a new cult around one Adam De Kuff, an older, whacked-out seeker he meets in Obermann's waiting room. In Raziel's hands, De Kuff becomes a holy Manchurian candidate, a Second Coming coming attraction who makes a splash when preaching, "his face glowing with mad enthusiasm," at the Pool of Bethesda.

Also high on the fever chart of local fanaticism is the House of the Galilean, a group of Christian evangelicals who, in preparation for the Messiah, want to rebuild the Temple of Jerusalem on the Temple Mount—a project that would, however they finesse it in discussion, require the destruction of the mosques there. The House provides Stone with some of his most amusingly villainous characters. Janusz Zimmer, another of the book's ideological vagrants—a Polish Communist who has moved from the party's defunct altar to extreme Zionism's—is the evil hand who brings together the violence in Gaza and the plans for violence on the Temple Mount. Whose hand guides Zimmer's is the novel's seventh seal of plotted revelation.

But nothing—neither the plot nor the novel's emotional life—would be possible without Sonia, the most gorgeously parti-color figure in Stone's testament. A Jewish, biracial Red-diaper baby who spent years in Cuba, Sonia has lately been following a Sufi master and singing jazz at Mister Stanley's, a Tel Aviv nightclub. She also does occasional human rights work with her friend Nuala Rice, an Irish radical at the International Children's Foundation who runs guns and drugs in and out of Gaza. Sonia happens to be the ex-girlfriend of Raziel, and, still living "in hope," the new disciple of De Kuff.

She is also the new love of Christopher Lucas, with whom she debates faith and doubt. She doesn't think he can be happy without belief; he is determined to overcome her credulity:

> "You're too hip and beautiful and smart to believe this garbage. It's dangerous. And because misery loves company, and if I can't have all these pretty dreams and illusions, I'm going to take them from you."
>
> "But, Chris," she said, laughing, "they're my joy. They make me happy."
>
> "Well, I don't want you happy. You're too good a singer. I want you like me."

But he also wants to be like her. He used to rid his life of such pushovers for enthusiasm and madness, but now (with an echo of Kierkegaard) Sonia is "the leap he could not make"—and, as such, unbearably attractive. With her in his life, Lucas feels "a slackening of the critical faculties," a desire for the two of them "to be subsumed in ongoing mystery." He even experiences a "flutter of mindless hope" when he traipses along with Sonia's new cult. "Did it not matter that Raziel was the flake of flakes, De Kuff a dying reed, Sonia so good and smart she turned foolish?"

That is her glory, and her problem, as a character. Together she and Lucas make the novel's beautiful music, but Sonia is sometimes more poignant than fully believable. The wonder that leaves her so open to possibility and forgiving of disappointment is also the exasperating naïveté that helps ignite the book's climax. Her valediction—"When I'm not here trying to be the best Jew I can be, I'm going to be in Liberia. Rwanda. Tanzania. In Sudan. Cambodia. I don't know, man, Chechnya. Every township and barrio and shit town"—sounds like a goofball parody of *The Grapes of Wrath*. Sonia and Lucas never make complete sense, individually or together, but if the reader can suspend disbelief—which is to say, take his own leap of faith—these two characters may wind up being his favorite literary couple in some time.

It's amazing what Stone gets away with, until you examine the steady display of improbable skill. The novel's style is as dichotomous as Lucas's psyche. Consider this one sentence, about his and Sonia's lovemaking: "And she sang and screamed and afterward Lucas cried the tears of a happiness he could not measure or analyze or otherwise molest with self-examination." Up until the last verb phrase, it's pure best-seller-ese; from there to the end it's the customized craft of real writing. This stylistic mix of the earthly and the divine is perfectly in keeping with the novel's crazy toss of characters and concerns. When he's in the mood, Stone oils his lyrical pipes for passages like the book's beautiful close:

> It meant, he thought, that a thing is never truly perceived, appreciated or defined except in longing. A land in exile, a God in His absconding, a love in its loss. And that everyone loses everything in the end. But that certain things of their nature cannot be taken away while life lasts. Some things can never be lost utterly that were loved in a certain way.

This almost sounds like an homage to the last lines of *The Great Gatsby*, the novel Stone has said made him want to be a novelist; if he gets away with this, too, it's because, quite simply, he's good enough.

Writing about William Burroughs, Stone once located the "moral element" of that writer's violent, dope-drenched work in its humor: "Laughter represents a rebellion against chaos, a rejection of evil, and an affirmation of balance and soundness." *Damascus Gate* is full of terrorism, revenge killings, madness and memories of genocide; it is also, in places, a scream. The humor runs from quiet stand-up to Chaplinesque pratfall to gonzo riffing. Of the Christian fundamentalists' rapture, that apocalyptic occasion when true believers will be plucked heavenward, even if they happen to be on the freeway, Lucas figures: "Since born-again Christians tended to be concentrated in states with high speed limits, things would get ugly." In the middle of a beautifully written riot, Lucas's Muslim guide convinces the mob that a famous writer has been spotted in the neighborhood: " 'Death to Salman Rushdie!' He could speak without fear of contradiction."

The worse things get in this novel, the more comical it somehow becomes. "You think this is funny?" the reader may want to ask, perhaps as he did when reading Allan Gurganus's recent *Plays Well with Others*, an AIDS novel from which, in places, you could die laughing. Of *course* it's funny, and He, who has the most perverse sense of humor of all, and who has far more explaining to do than we, knows it. "You know what I think," Lucas says, warming to regional custom at one stressful point. "God's going to get his fucking hand cut off someday." The character who, on hearing this line, covers her ears in horror, is the biggest, most destructive nitwit in the novel. Genuine lovers of the word, and the Word, will know enough to smile, to take it as one more piece of God's plenty, and to be grateful for this big, good book.

The Norman Context

Howard Norman's four works of fiction amount to only about a thousand pages and seem somehow less like an oeuvre than an eccentric stash, similar to the cryptic paintings and antique radios and wooden bird decoys that line the pages of the books themselves. And yet, for all their humble clutter, they prove exquisite, like pieces of folk art whose simplicity postpones a sly impact.

A naturalist and a translator of Native American tales, Norman came late to his career as a novelist. When he published *The Northern Lights,* in 1987, he was approaching 40, and even that book—the story of young Noah Krainik in rural 1950s Manitoba—hesitated, like a boy's changing voice, unsure whether it wanted to be a collection of set pieces (the mad quilting woman, the beautiful, nude-bathing Norwegian wife) or a full-throated novel, which it becomes only toward the end, when Noah, having survived the loss of his boyhood friend Pelly Bay, moves to Toronto to help his abandoned mother rejuvenate the movie theater where she worked as a young woman.

If you read *The Northern Lights* after you've read Norman's other books—and thereby made acquaintance with his patterns and preoccupations—you won't be surprised to find that the theater is more important than the movies it shows; or that a Cree Indian family is living in the projectionist's booth; or that the accident that kills young Pelly is beautifully macabre (his unicycle falls through the ice). Norman's heroes, who always tell their own first-person stories, are boys and young men, orphaned or otherwise sundered from their parents. Despite what Pelly's uncle Sam says about how "people should not become their losses," the protagonists are a combination of what they've lost and what they can't have, the latter sure to be an enchanting and impossible young woman.

In Noah's case, that's his cousin Charlotte (herself an orphan), "a very opinionated girl," whose birthmark betokens "a rare, stubborn character." And Charlotte is nothing compared with Imogen Linny, the object of desire in Norman's new novel, *The Museum Guard,* set in Halifax in the late 1930s. This time the hero, DeFoe Russet, has lost his parents in a zeppelin accident. From the age of 9, he's been raised in the Lord Nelson Hotel by his randy uncle Edward, who resembles the life-loving panders of Renaissance comedy, trying, sometimes cruelly, to inject a bit of friskiness into his solemn nephew. DeFoe guards a gallery in the Glace Museum not far from the one Edward looks after. Imogen (another orphan) works at an even quieter job, caretaking the Jewish cemetery in Halifax. Her romance with DeFoe is marked by protracted periods of "celibacy and quarrels," her moodiness and passive aggression leaving the poor young man quite beside himself, especially when he's beside her: "Often I found I had to circle around her with words. . . . Even lying next to her in bed, pitch-black room, or a strip of light from her kitchen floor lamp showing under the closed door, she did not always seem directly approachable."

Imogen's headaches and scoldings and mixed sexual signals prefigure the difficulty she will present after developing an obsessive identification with the subject of a painting, *Jewess on a Street in Amsterdam,* on loan to the Glace from Nazi-threatened Holland. "Here's what I think," she tells the sweet, literal DeFoe. "I think she's living a true life and I am not." So Imogen decides to live the Jewess's life, to continue the existence of the artist's wife who modeled for the painting and was killed by the Germans after Kristallnacht. Imogen's madness begins with her determination to commune—all alone, overnight—with the canvas. DeFoe, in one of the wild gestures that eventually burst forth from Norman's polite heroes, steals it for her.

Norman always tells you the worst in the first paragraph or even sentence. "The painting I stole for Imogen Linny, *Jewess on a Street in Amsterdam,* arrived to the Glace Museum, here in Halifax, on September 5, 1938": So begins *The Museum Guard.* And so began *The Northern Lights:* "My father brought home a radio. 'It's got a sender and a receiver,' he said. 'Now you can talk to people other than yourselves.' He fit the earphones over my head. And the first news I heard was that my friend Pelly Bay had drowned." The author doesn't just tip his hand; he spreads it faceup on the table and then takes you back to events occurring well before whatever explosion he's already detonated. The effect is peculiarly artful, the disclosures creating the very suspense they ought to be destroying. One wonders, uneasily, during the muffled comedy that usually follows the opening revelations, how the books will break out of their Cornell-boxed charms and get to their announced tragedies. *The Museum Guard,* peopled as it is with lecherous Uncle Edward and the forbearing curator, Mr. Connaught, and the pretentious tour guide, Miss Delbo, reads almost like a Friday-night Britcom—daffy staff in provincial museum—until Uncle Edward gets shot and Imogen takes her delusion to Amsterdam and DeFoe waits for news of her from prison.

By the end, the novel is about art's transformational power and how—as in Norman's books—that power often depends on what's at the margins. In the shop window in the *Jewess* painting, which DeFoe ponders every day from his guard's vantage, are "all sorts of toothbrushes. The toothbrushes made one laugh. They quickly put me in a good mood. But then I looked close up at the Jewess' face; I was sunk from that mood in a second."

In *The Bird Artist* (1994), the novel for which he is best known, Norman made the hero a painter. Fabian Vas, who turns 20 in 1911, lives in Witless Bay, Newfoundland, and is learning to draw and paint birds via a correspondence course. His mother has an affair with the local lighthouse keeper when his father is off hunting; and Fabian, dreading the marriage his parents have arranged for him, is of course smitten with someone difficult—a willful, funny, alcoholic redhead named Margaret Handle:

"You are a blunt woman, Margaret."

"Fabian, dear, I'm only exactly as blunt as life is, forgive the preachy sentence. You're going to marry a stranger. Your mother is adultering nightly. Your father's got one hell of a homecoming in store. How much more bluntness do you want?"

We know that Fabian's impending nuptials will be the least of his woes, since the book's first paragraph has already had him announcing the real catastrophe. "I am a bird artist, and have more or less made a living at it. Yet I murdered the lighthouse keeper, Botho August, and that is an equal part of how I think of myself." So we wait, thoroughly attentive, for Fabian's id to break through his fastidiousness. (During nervous spells, he drinks coffee; DeFoe Russet irons shirts.)

The Bird Artist's bleak Newfoundland landscape will turn gaudy with blood and recrimination, and at the end, the book's melodrama will be replicated in a supposedly penitential mural that Fabian paints for the local church:

> Botho stands in the topmost window of the lighthouse, black wings spreading from his back, three splotches of blood on his nightshirt. He is the presiding angel of Witless Bay. . . . On the rotted dock at the southernmost point of the harbor, Margaret is a grown woman riding her bicycle.

———————

Most novelists—more troubled than they like to admit by the enduring equation of the picture and the thousand words—seek to achieve a painterly vividness in their work. But Norman seems unsatisfied until, in the course of each book, his heroes can transform their spoken narratives into actual pictures. Once in prison, DeFoe Russet has "a view of Halifax Harbour and can see the topmost masts of the historical schooners. Hour after hour, that is my framed view." Near the end of *The Northern Lights,* when Noah arrives in Toronto, he sleeps in a room with two portraits of himself that were done by the now dead Pelly back in Manitoba.

Any good novel will take you out of your own world; ones that actually put you into another one—instead of leaving you in the mere suspended state of "reading"—are rare. Norman's are among them. Fictional kingdoms like his are so strongly imagined as to be a bit oppressive, and their writers labor under something of a compulsion to re-create them from book to book. What makes these novelists unique is also what circumscribes them; their greatest strength is necessarily their worst weakness. An extreme example of such repetition can be found in the work of the English novelist Anita Brookner, whose lonely London flat dwellers need to get out more but simply can't and finally shouldn't: too much activity would kill their odd reality.

Norman's novels are all variations on a dream. His tricky northern landscapes, both homey and stark, have a demon's face glowering up through the ice. *The Museum Guard* may play itself out a bit slowly toward the end, but the author's work is generally as lean as a sled's runner. In an age of biblio size-worship—a comically obvious affliction among ambitious male novelists—Norman writes to exactly the right modest length, just as Alice Munro, who also works the Canadian past and may be the greatest contemporary writer of fiction in English, has found a natural habitat not in the novel but in the long short story. As DeFoe tells his uncle Edward at one point in *The Museum Guard,* "What I'm saying is some things are my big subjects. . . . They might be smaller, but they fit my life. So leave me alone about it."

What for another writer would be motifs are, in Norman, almost the melody. Those radios, for instance: They're not the symbol of long-distance projection and communion; they're the fact. In *The Northern Lights* (a book Norman says he began as a radio play), a shortwave set may bring the news of Pelly's death, but it was another radio, shared by Pelly and Noah, that once took the boys far from Quill, Manitoba:

> It was a brown Grundig-Majestic, about two feet high. . . . At nine o'clock, *Great Books* connected us to the libraries of the world. This program began with the reader, Fabian Bennet, announcing in a British accent, "Here, once again," then a background voice hushing him. Bennet would say, "So sorry," and lower his voice.

At one point in his story, when Noah has an attack of misanthropy, he doesn't drink coffee or iron shirts; he dismantles and reassembles a shortwave set. He has to shake the feeling that Pelly "drowned inside the radio," just as, in a heartbreaking story of Norman's called "Jenny Aloo," an Eskimo woman feels certain her son has disappeared into a jukebox. In *The Museum Guard,* the Fabian Bennet figure is Ovid Lamartine, whose dire broadcasts from Europe in the fall of 1938 help lure both Imogen and Uncle Edward toward calamity. Nothing in fiction succeeds like obsession; Norman's is the airwaves ridden by birds and sound alike.

He may set his books in 1911 and 1938 and 1959, but one can't really call him a historical novelist. The novels aren't heavily textured with period detail, and the author's dialogue, fine at fostering the illusions it's designed to, is more charming than credible. The past per se doesn't matter so much as do its remoteness and the demands its primitiveness makes on the imaginations of those inhabiting it: the slowness of letters; the wait to be endured after ordering a catalog item; the need to make up faces for the voices coming out of those radios. By setting *The Northern Lights* in 1959, Norman chose the last possible moment when a rural boy might become a teenager without having dialed a telephone or seen a movie. In making DeFoe a museum guard and Imogen a cemetery caretaker, Norman is making them walk in his own backward footsteps.

A story of Norman's called "Old Swimmers" concerns an aging character named Helen, the survivor of a long-ago ferry disaster. (In Norman's books, ferries are meant to sink, as planes must crash and zeppelins explode.) Helen explains to a nephew her reasons for marrying so late in life: " 'Because . . . Thomas, my fiancé, chooses to remember the same things I do.' " Even more tellingly, Norman has the narrator in "Jenny Aloo" declare, "My father told me once that the importance of any event was measured by your memory's loyalty to it. When he said that he was facing away from me at his work table, painting on a wing stripe."

A painter—of wooden birds or Dutch streetscapes or church murals—always has the chance to paint over a bit of his paintings. It's one more possibility in visual art that the writer, after publication, may envy. A reader must ask whether Norman, burdened with the irrevocability of both past and print, didn't conceive his new book with the sudden, possessed boldness of his heroes. Return to the author's 1989 short-story collection, *Kiss in the Hotel Joseph Conrad* (it contains "Jenny Aloo" and "Old Swimmers"), and you will find that the title piece begins in 1943 with a character named Imogene Linny. Could she, with her additional *e*, be the same Imogen Linny of the 1998 *Museum Guard*, who disappears into Holland—hopelessly, it seems—in 1938? Is her later/earlier life an extension/precursor of her earlier/later one? Which is the bird, and which is the decoy? Norman knows, and word artist that he is, he's not telling.

Tom Wolfe Bonfires Atlanta!

No, *A Man in Full* is not as good as *The Bonfire of the Vanities,* so why don't we get that out of the way right here at the start, and even offer a couple of excuses. For one thing, few American novels of the last twenty years have been as good as Tom Wolfe's first work of fiction (published in 1987, when he was 56), and for another, the '90s haven't been anything so wonderful—*O tempora! O mores!*—as the '80s. Back then we had a real presid—

No, let me restrain myself. Let me start over. Let me make the simple bipartisan literary point that when it comes to subject matter, the '90s have not been quite so outsize as the '80s, which is only to say that no current novel can be expected to get so gaudy a purchase on this period as *Bonfire* did on its own. And which is not to say that Wolfe doesn't try (sometimes too hard) to do things here that he did in the earlier book. Clearly, two of his essential subjects, money and sex, remain as connected as ever: "The lawns rose up from the street like big green breasts, and at the top of each breast was a house big enough to be called a mansion."

That grass tells you we have moved away from the co-op canyons of Manhattan. *A Man in Full* takes place mostly in Atlanta, and since Atlanta is no more New York than the '90s are the '80s, one never completely loses the feeling that one's watching a road-company version of *Bonfire.* The cities do have similarities—Wolfe notes, through his protagonists, that in Atlanta honor consists of "the things you possess"—but a certain paleness results from the change of venue. Atlanta, for example, may have its white-establishment Piedmont Driving Club, but there isn't the sort of old money, one of the hidden combustibles in *Bonfire,* that you find in New York. Wolfe displays his fine eye (and, as always, even better ear) for the folkways of his new locale, but he can't keep things from feeling a bit . . . suburban: "There was something so damned gloomy about dinner at these fancy restaurants in the mall. It was so damned dark, since all the shops were closed."

The problem, of course, is that Atlanta is mostly suburbs, or a collection of "edge cities," as the early-'90s vogue term had it. As Wolfe explains, "From now on, the growth of American cities was going to take place not in the heart of the metropolis, not in the old Downtown or Midtown, but out on the edges, in vast commercial clusters served by highways." The first of these, Buckhead, is home to many of *A Man in Full*'s players, and it becomes an ongoing reminder that no peach ever gets as red as an apple.

Even so, this new book's protagonist, Charlie Croker, is bigger, brawnier and altogether more satisfying than Sherman McCoy, the hero-by-accident of *Bonfire*. Charlie really is a Master of the Universe, a self-made, sixtyish football legend (Georgia Tech's defense- and offense-playing "Sixty-Minute Man"), now a big developer whose dream has been to build Atlanta's newest edge city and have the gall to name it Croker. On winter weekends, he upholds a nouveau riche idea of plantation culture down at "Turpmtine," a huge old farm whose workers always mispronounced the stuff they drew from its pine trees. Charlie goes there to hunt quail, entertain businessmen and feel himself the benign overseer of his own set of black retainers. The rest of the time he's living with Serena, his much younger second (of course) wife in a Buckhead mansion decorated by Ronald Vine, one of those interior designers and architects at whom Wolfe has been laughing, in godalmighty disbelief, for decades. (Vine, in fact, makes an appearance in *Bonfire*.) Poor Charlie, whose prostate may be giving out with his knee, has to relieve himself in the middle of the night amidst the "wall sconces, downlighters, beveled mirrors, and glistening marble" of Vine's masterpiece bathroom.

Charlie's real problems, however, are neither medical nor aesthetic. They're financial. His plan to build Croker has depended, like plans for many edge cities, on the success of an initial office tower-cum-galleria—in Charlie's case, the forty-eight-story Croker Concourse, which now sits "60 percent empty and hemorrhaging money." The "workout artistes" at PlannersBanc have already called him in to discuss the optimistic loans they made him a few years before. They're ready to seize his Gulfstream jet and

Turpmtine; now that he's devolved into a "shithead" (semiofficial parlance for debtor), he'd better know they at last mean business. The "workout" is conducted by Harry Zale and seen from the perspective of Raymond Peepgass, a senior loan officer at the bank:

> "I wanna know if *you* know," said Harry. "Think of this as an AA meeting, Mr. Croker. Now that the spree is over, we wanna see some real self-awareness here. You're right, we called this meeting, but I want you to tell me *why*. What's it all about? What's the problem here?"
>
> Peepgass watched Croker's face. Oh, he loved this part, too, the moment when the shitheads finally realized that *things have changed,* that their status has taken a header (into the excrement).

Charlie needs tenants and cash to deflect not only the creditors but also his own imaginings of what people may have started saying behind his back. In fact, his financial crisis is a semispiritual one; he's losing what Wolfe calls "man's sixth sense, his sense of well-being," and his good ol' boy's touch seems to be failing. He invites Herb Richman, owner of the fitness-club chain DefinitionAmerica, down to Turpmtine for some business courtship and winds up, at a crucial moment, calling him Hebe instead of Herb.

When it comes to plotting, Wolfe likes to stage leisurely train wrecks, letting two or three big, chugging engines come together for a satisfying smashup. *A Man in Full*'s second plot is racial, involving a huge, sullen Georgia Tech running back, Fareek "the Cannon" Fanon, an African-American who wears "a gold chain so chunky you could have used it to pull an Isuzu pickup out of a red clay ditch." Fareek may or may not have raped the daughter of Inman Armholster, a pillar of the white establishment. The situation presents problems not only for Tech's coach, Buck McNutter, but for Mayor Wesley Dobbs Jordan, a Morehouse man who had always been a leader "because he was . . . *going to be a leader.*" This moderate practitioner of the Atlanta Way—remember "The City Too Busy to Hate"?—is no Reverend Reginald Bacon, the fabulously Sharptonesque black "leader" in *Bonfire,* but in the two-book, two-city competition, one must call Atlanta's literary loss its civic gain.

The black corporate lawyer called in by Coach McNutter is an old college buddy of the mayor's: Roger White II, or, by his own and others' reckoning, Roger Too White, successful and assimilated to the point of self-hatred, a man whose ambivalences Wolfe puts on perhaps too-obvious display when he has him drive to Coach McNutter's Buckhead house during Freaknic, the annual black-undergraduate blowout. Appalled to see these middle-class college students shaking their booties and booming their car radios and mooning some horrified whites on the terrace of the Piedmont Driving Club, Roger also has "another feeling entirely . . . sweeping through his loins. Deep inside he was . . . *exhilarated.* The freedom of these young brothers and sisters, the abandon, the Dionysian fearlessness on the very threshold of the Piedmont Driving Club—"

Any mishandling of the charges against Fareek will threaten not only Mayor Jordan's reelection campaign against a much less white-accommodating black opponent but also the peace of the city. And whom should Jordan and White and McNutter begin seeing as the key to, the way out of, the potential savior in this whole situation? Charlie Croker. If Charlie, an old friend of the may-or-may-not-be victim's father, will get up at a press conference and warn people against prejudging Fareek—after all, big sports stars have always been, even in Charlie's gridiron-glory days, vulnerable to wild calumnies and manipulations—then Charlie will have not only done a good turn for up-from-the-ghetto Fareek, and not only saved the delicate fabric of Atlanta, but also, just incidentally, bought himself the time he needs to get over his financial woes. The mayor will see to it that Planners-Banc, which has no more interest in racial apocalypse than he does, gets off Charlie's back.

While this situation does provide Wolfe's main character with a dandy moral dilemma—fiscal salvation in exchange for saying a few good words about this decidedly scary running back ("Now they be messing with my endorsements!")—it may be wishful plotting on the author's part to imagine this case's having "the potential to do more damage to this city than anything since the murder of Martin Luther King or the Rodney King riots." Still and all, the mixture of legal manipulation, miscegenation and media does combine to make *A Man in Full,* among other things, the last O.J. book.

Wolfe doesn't manage the black-on-black dialogues at City Hall with anything like the verve and authenticity of his all-white workout sessions, but in a lot of places he plays the literary race card with superior skill, enough to make him one of the few important white novelists putting racial reality at the center of entertaining, out-of-line books, instead of just letting it loom like some guilt-producing abstraction. We get Freaknic scenes in which the "*jeunesse dorée* of Black America" gives its chalky fellow citizens "a snootful of the future"; conversations that are "a delicate business in upper-stratum white Atlanta, particularly if the subject moved onto the terrain of racial . . . tendencies"; and black characters who are neither cardboard paragons nor villains. Wolfe loves creating rap lyrics—

HOW'M I SPOSE A LOVE HER
CATCH HER MACKIN' WITH THE BROTHERS?
RAM YO' *BOO*TY! RAM YO' *BOO*TY!—

whose Day-Glo diction and punctuation aren't far from the stuff he's been doing since *The Kandy-Kolored Tangerine-Flake Streamline Baby* (1965).

One cannot read *A Man in Full* or *Bonfire* without taking into account Wolfe's prior quarter century as an essayist. Mostly for better, occasionally for worse, his earlier methods remain a large part of what he's now doing in fiction. A reader gets reportage on American business-meeting posture ("They perched on an arm or a back or on the edge of a cushion or the marble ledge with their thighs ajar in an athletic sprawl, as if they were bulging with so much testosterone they couldn't have closed their legs if they tried"); a mini-essay on those edge cities, tweezered through Charlie's brain; Mayor Jordan's too-long disquisition on politics; and, in the novel's least successful stretch, a guided auto tour of rich and poor Atlanta that the mayor conducts for Roger White, a lifelong resident of the city. (The inescapable impression is that Wolfe himself has seen most of the city's poor precincts only from the backseat of a limo.) Nonetheless, unlike the average American literary novel—that ever more pious confection of authorial self-love and sensibility—*A Man in Full* is *about* something, and something big at that.

Wolfe has always been lovingly alert to American ugliness, especially assaults upon the national language. He delights in the current risible rash of fused corporate nomenclature ("NationsBank, SunTrust . . . Cryo-Life . . .

XcelleNet") and the "technogeekspeak" of Charlie's financial officer, Wismer Stroock, who wears titanium-frame glasses that make his eyes "look like a pair of bar-code scanners," and is forever speaking "this word *paradigm.*" Lower down the social scale, Wolfe explains the "beavering" of prisoners' girlfriends, who show up for their across-the-glass visits "wearing mini-skirts and no underpants" in order to mime "the motions of sexual ecstasy." He even creates some country-metal lyrics ("Brain Dead" by Pus Casserole) to go along with the rap ones. Wolfe has the most sensitive ear since Sinclair Lewis, a writer he admires, with the difference that while Lewis was repelled by what he heard, Wolfe is enchanted. *Bonfire* put a half dozen or so noun phrases into general circulation, among them "social X rays" and "Masters of the Universe" (placed, most recently and ridiculously, on the lips of James Cameron's *Titanic* passengers). Expect to be hearing talk of "saddlebags" (giant sweat stains under the armpits) and the "Pizza Grenade" neckties ("the sort of tie that looked as if a pepperoni-and-olive pizza had just exploded on your shirtfront") throughout 1999.

––––––––––

Eleven years is a long time to go between novels, even big ones; 1993 or 1994 might have been a better publication date for *A Man in Full.* Charlie's problems seem to have been conceived by his author during the first, recessionary '90s rather than the booming '90s that soon followed. *Bonfire,* published weeks after the '87 crash, had better, if accidental, timing. The defining novel of the '80s seemed to be an instant elegy for them.

Wolfe also can't help repeating himself on a number of subjects, so here and there this latest book has a certain greatest-hits feeling. The "pictures so baffling they were bound to be worth a fortune" hark back to *The Painted Word* (1975); the complaint that architects are really just "neurotic and 'artistic' hired help," to *From Bauhaus to Our House* (1981). Hobbyhorses are meant to be ridden, of course, but some of the repetitions are specific enough that they'll grate on fans who cherished their original appearance. Carpets in corporate Atlanta are made of the same "Streptolon" we heard about in *Bonfire;* the "red dog" of Raymond Peepgass needs to be taken "out for a romp" just as Sherman McCoy's "rogue hormones" needed to be aired in exactly the same prepositional phrase. At a charity event, Charlie's first wife, Martha, eager to be back among males, discovers that she's invisible to the two she sits between:

When Sonny Beamer, who was on her other side, turned their way to listen in, Oskar von Eyrik began to look right past *her* and direct the entire story into *the man's* face.

In a vignette published twenty years ago, Wolfe's "Invisible Wife" observed that

> when the man sitting on the other side of her turned their way to listen in, the Investment Counselor looked right past her and directed the entire story into *the man's* face.

A Man in Full also contains some internal repetitions and overelaborations (do we really need to have the slang term "Oreo" defined?), and sometimes, in the big, bouncy mattress of Wolfe's prose, a little too much batting surrounds the springs: Atlanta's towers look "like a miniature Oz." Too many nod-and-a-wink underlinings of southern speech—" 'I'm gon be tied up here for a spell.' *Spale*"—create a small strain, just an annoying little ding, but one that's still audible as this great big Buick of a book gobbles up the road.

––––––––––

And yet it's not just out for the drive. Wolfe is determined to get someplace, to his book's big theme, the way Lewis always had one in each of his novels. As the title suggests, Wolfe's theme is Manhood, what it is and what it's worth. From the moment we meet Charlie Croker, we're told that, at least in his own mind, during weekends at Turpmtine, he's not "merely a real estate developer, he [is] . . . a man." Even the near bionic Wismer Stroock, Charlie's financial wiz, pointlessly trying to live forever on long runs and bottled water, is in "unconscious awe" of something in Charlie, "and that thing was manhood. It was as simple as that." Charlie's own worries about his private-schooled son Wally—"a boy embarrassed by his advantages, desperate to hide them, eager to dress in backward baseball caps and homey pants and other Ghetto rags, terrified of being envied, a boy facing the world without any visible signs of the joy of living and without . . . balls"—are presented as a kind of comic inner cry, a complaint strangled by '90s-P.C. propriety, but Wolfe takes all this seriously, as he does the often perfectly silly Charlie himself. There's never, in fact, been a conflict between the silly and the serious in Tom Wolfe's view of the American male. The astronauts' hotdogging exploits may have amused the author of *The Right Stuff;* they also awed him.

This sort of dual vision is something like the opposite of ambivalence. It's the ability to *like* both views of a thing, to guffaw and pay homage all at once. It's been the secret to some of Wolfe's best writing, including some of what's here. When Charlie insists on showing Herb—not *Hebe!*—Richman and some other weekend guests the couplings of a prize stud in the Turpmtine stables, the bravura scene that results is equal parts amusement and wonder: "The three stable hands leaned in at a fierce angle, shoving the mare's flank and skittering across the dirt, three frantic little tugboats attending a stupendous, thundering act of coitus beneath the very belly, beside the very rutting rod, of the stallion." Exit laughing, but reverently.

What Charlie requires—as his holdings, self-worth and right knee begin seriously to crumble, and as the distasteful press conference looms—is a clear-eyed messenger of truth. One will finally arrive in the person of Conrad Hensley, the novel's other main protagonist, whose fortunes we follow, in more or less alternating scenes, from the book's beginning. Conrad is a nice fellow in his early twenties, the son of some particularly distasteful hippies, a working-class guy who married and fathered two children quite early for our day and age. He's trying, out near Oakland, to earn enough money to put his family into a decent condo, showing up nights as one of the "fat gray ice weevils" lifting eighty-pound blocks of meat in the "Suicidal Freezer Unit" within the warehouse of Croker Global Foods—an incidental part of Charlie's empire through which pink slips are about to flutter. Wolfe does great work taking us along on one shift of this job that's given Conrad forearms all out of proportion to the rest of his body. But the young man's story really gets rolling, all downhill, once the layoffs hit, and a comedy of nightmarish mishaps over a towed car—rendered superbly, like an anxiety dream—lands Conrad in the Santa Rita prison.

Santa Rita is even worse than the South Bronx lockup into which Sherman McCoy got thrown. The Okie, black, Latino and "Nordic Bund" prisoners make its inmate "pod" a soul-killing, mind-destroying Dolby-sounding boiler, day and night:

> Masturbation was so prevalent at Santa Rita after lights-out, you
> could actually hear the joints and flat springs of the metal bunks

groaning and squeaking. Conrad could hear them now. He could hear undisguised groans *Unnnh . . . Awnnnnnnnnnnhhhhhhhhh . . .* He could hear exclamations of satisfaction. . . . *God-damn! . . . Good jookin'! . . .* And now, amid the whiffs of body funk, urine, bowel movements, and Bugler smoke, there arose, as it did every night, the sickly sweet smell of semen. Geysers of it! Gallons of it! Jook! Jook! Jook! Jook!

Conrad, through his already good character and the accidental discovery of a volume of Stoic philosophy, survives. He rejects the pod's punk-raping notions of manhood in favor of Epictetus's: " 'What are you, slave,' Epictetus had demanded, 'but a soul carrying a corpse and a quart of blood?' What was this body of his, which he was so worried about, but a corpse and a quart of blood? The living part of him was his soul, and his soul was nothing other than the spark of Zeus." Conrad, who can say and mean lines like "This is—not right!" may seem a sentimentalized Everyhero, and he is, but he's also a touching, noble creation, a descendant of Tom Joad in *The Grapes of Wrath,* a volume for which the politically conservative Wolfe still manages to profess the highest admiration.

Getting Conrad's plot to train-wreck with Charlie's requires an earthquake (literally) and some intercontinental coincidence. Readers will have to measure for themselves the plausibility and the punch of the philosophical conversations these two get into, during which the younger man sounds like an amalgam of Gus Grissom and Gordo Cooper in *The Right Stuff* ("Well—I'm not the final word on this, Mr. Croker, but he's saying, it seems to me . . ."). There will be those readers who could more easily imagine Charlie trying to parlay all this Stoical business into a buck (maybe by writing a management-style book? *Turn Your Zeus Loose?*) than using it to the serious, life-changing purpose he does. They will have to decide, too, whether a press conference is enough of a climax for a book this big; whether Wolfe loses track of too many plotlines (that election campaign); and whether, on the last page, Roger Too White has lost his soul or made himself newly useful in the Realpolitik way of Mayor Jordan.

However they decide, readers should avoid the temptation to make the near-perfect *Bonfire* the enemy of the merely terrific. A third of the way through *A Man in Full,* Harry Zale, the workout artiste, reminds his colleagues of how years ago General Curtis LeMay appeared before a Senate committee asking for ten thousand nuclear warheads for the Air Force, and one of the senators, Everett Dirksen, says, "I thought you told us that with six thousand warheads you could reduce the entire Soviet Union to cinders. Why should we give you ten thousand?" And LeMay says, "Senator, I wanna see the cinders *dance.*"

This new bonfire of Wolfe's may not blaze quite so high as the last one, but the cinders are definitely dancing—in a fine, lurid light.

Snow Falling on Readers

May 1999

Historians of publishing are likely to remember David Guterson's fantastically best-selling novel *Snow Falling on Cedars* as the first Oprah book. They will be wrong—it never received Winfrey's imprimatur—but the mistake will be understandable. With its clear-cut moral issues and underlined emotions, *Cedars* could be the keynote volume for a series whose books have often been more heartfelt than well written. Oprah's picks tend to get an astonishing second wind after they've been dying, or at least sleeping, on the shelf. In Guterson's case, it was a PEN/Faulkner Award that finally got the ball rolling into a word-of-mouth avalanche.

Three and a half years after the *Cedars* paperback appeared, it is at last time for the release of Guterson's next novel, *East of the Mountains,* whose first printing of 500,000 copies will arrive in stores on a precise "laydown" date (April 20), like a rock album. The marketing budget is a half million dollars. Guterson has said that sustaining the *Cedars* phenomenon, through readings and interviews and the tending of subrights, became "a full-time job." So in order to understand the business of David Guterson—the values and outlook of this literary phenomenon—one would do well to postpone looking at the newest book until one has traveled through the three Guterson volumes that preceded it.

Let us start by trying to divine the appeal of the by now ubiquitous *Cedars.* Its setting is exotic, its cast of characters at least initially intriguing. In 1954, on San Piedro (in real life, Bainbridge) Island, a Japanese American named Kabuo Miyamoto stands accused of murdering his fellow fisherman Carl Heine. The prosecutor has circumstantial evidence and a possible motive: A decade earlier, when Kabuo's family was sent to a wartime internment camp, Carl's mother used some sharp practice to wrest the Miyamotos' seven-acre strawberry farm from them.

But the real reasons for suspecting Kabuo, here on this rain-soaked island whose "verdant beauty . . . inclined its residents toward the poetical," are racial. He might have served with the American army in Europe, but his skill at *kendo,* a form of Japanese stick fighting, and his general, yes, inscrutability are enough to convince courtroom observers of his guilt: "The man before them was noble in appearance, and the shadows played across the planes of his face in a way that made their angles harden; his aspect connoted dignity. And there was nothing akin to softness in him anywhere, no part of him that was vulnerable. He was, they decided, not like them at all." Which is to say—and the author has no problem with your thinking this— that Kabuo is better than most of them. Indeed, his "detached and aloof manner" really proceeds from the guilt he still feels over having had to kill a German soldier during the war: "What could he say to people on San Piedro to explain the coldness he projected? The world was unreal, a nuisance that prevented him from focusing on the memory of that boy."

In contrast to Kabuo, we get Ishmael Chambers, the local newspaperman, who years ago had a puppy-love romance with Kabuo's wife, Hatsue. (Throughout early adolescence, the two of them cuddled in a hollow cedar tree.) The once idealistic Ishmael, alas, now exhibits moral degradation: In the years since his arm was blown apart during fighting in the Pacific, he has, from time to time, actually felt provoked to utter the word *Japs.* And, wouldn't you know it, he now secretly holds information that can prove Kabuo's innocence.

For all those—apparently no more than a handful of Americans—who have not yet read this novel, *Snow Falling on Cedars* might best be described as a p.c. police procedural that has been padded out 150 pages past its necessary length. The courtroom scenes run on like transcript, and the supporting characters—including an upright, aging, half-blind defense attorney (Max von Sydow in the movie coming this fall)—are as boilerplated as their activities. The coroner feels "the need not merely to know but to envision clearly whatever had happened. . . . [It was] all recorded, or not recorded, in the slab of flesh that lay on Horace Whaley's examination table. It was his duty to find out the truth."

None of the book is half so well written as an episode of *The Practice,* and one does not have to be a devotee of mystery novels to spot the red her-rings swimming with the salmon around San Piedro. Guterson works with an iron-heavy hand throughout, speechifying all the crucial dialogue, such as this explanation from Hatsue's mother (a strawberry farmer, mind you): "The whites, you see, are tempted by their egos and have no means to re-sist. We Japanese, on the other hand, *know* our egos are nothing." Ishmael's mother reminds her son that "facts are so cold, so horribly cold—can we depend on facts by themselves?" She, by the way, supposedly a great reader of the classics, seems never to have informed him that he has a namesake in a novel called *Moby-Dick.* He doesn't open that book until he's a college student home from the war: "The narrator, he found upon reading the first sentence, bore his own name—Ishmael, Ishmael was all right, but Ahab he could not respect and this ultimately undermined the book for him." It would not surprise me to find that Guterson feels the same about Ahab—so dark, so obsessive, so *negative*—since he seems more interested in taming his own characters' passions than in letting them rip. He would like them to quiet down and behave, to earn good-conduct medals instead of the vivid-ness that arises from compulsion. In *Cedars,* Ishmael will redeem himself by doing what is right, which is to say sensible.

I must confess that the real mystery to me is not what happened to Carl Heine aboard his fishing boat but just what on earth the PEN/Faulkner ju-rors were thinking—and beyond that, what all the local book-group readers who have made this No. 1 can be seeing. A majority of these group readers —a discerning constituency who do much to keep literary fiction alive in America—are women, and it's the female characters in Guterson's books who are flimsy to the point of mere functionality, projections of male desire and indecision. Even Hatsue, the most fully drawn woman in *Cedars,* is little more than a quiverful of cultural vectors who emerges from her youth-ful worldly desires "as if from a dream"—i.e., with arbitrary suddenness— "discovering the truth of her private nature: it was in her to have the composure and tranquility of an island strawberry farmer." Well, if the au-thor says so.

———

Guterson's first book, a 1989 short-story collection called *The Country Ahead of Us, the Country Behind,* provides considerable evidence of the au-thor's overall sensibility and methods. These stories are mostly attitudes—

teenage anomie, loathing of the suburbs, ambivalence about hunting—in search of plots. "Day of the Moonwalk," a late-'60s tale of two brothers, trips over itself in a race toward higher meaning: "Now, if a move to a new place is an opportunity for change in whom we have thus far played at being. . . ." Guterson strains to load every rift with ore and inflicts a lot of pain on the fillings of any reader attempting to chew through it: "It was the day of the moonwalk, a thing that seemed to us more distant than the moon; while planets disintegrate and stars are born, we migrate, love, make plans, pare our fingernails, hate one another ceaselessly." This is a sigh masquerading as reflection; there is, in the end, no reason at all for the story's principal event—the narrator's brother blows out his knee playing basketball—to take place on the day Armstrong and Aldrin landed.

The stories display an aspiration to purity, sometimes an adolescent revulsion from sex that their grown-up first-person narrators haven't quite overcome. The adult teller of "Aliens" recalls his high school admiration for a self-possessed boy named Dan Wyman and explains how, years later, when he was 24, he spotted Dan playing pool with some other guys in a Seattle bar: "It was not so much something in their appearance, or even in their manner, that suggested what I came to conclude from the scene: that Wyman was gay, a homosexual. It was rather their intimacy that suggested it, the way in which their pool game shut them off from the world and made them a society unto themselves." (The fact that Dan "gently place[s] his palm on his friend's buttock" is also something of a tip-off.) The revelation sends the narrator scurrying home to his high school yearbook and the story's last lines:

> *Daniel Richard Wyman* it said beneath his picture, a handsome boy in a white tuxedo suit, white teeth, combed hair. *Woodworking, Hunting. Automobiles.*

It's as if we're in 1952 and Dan Wyman has suffered some terrible, resonating fate. But the story isn't really homophobic so much as agoraphobic, in the way it gapes at the fleshly everyday. What the narrator finally can't stand is the way Dan has been revealed to be sexual, period, a creature with grubby appetites like everybody else. In this collection, as in *Cedars*, Guterson seems to wish that people could be more like landscape, that they could just sit there with a lot of chiseled dignity.

He appears to regard the world as a kind of contagion. His second book, published in 1992, between the story collection and *Cedars,* is a little non-fiction manifesto called *Family Matters: Why Homeschooling Makes Sense.* As polemics go, it's rather odd, full of concessions and sweet reasonableness toward the opposing position, but also prone to vociferous lurches: "The doctrine of school's necessity, which we early imbibe in the very belly of the beast, is inevitably supplemented once we're disgorged." The book is short on practicalities, and Guterson's wife—who shoulders, one suspects, the greater portion of hearthside pedagogy—remains a curiously absent figure, as underdeveloped as his run of female characters. One might set this volume aside, see it as a curious literary detour, if it didn't feel so connected to the worldview in Guterson's whole oeuvre, the desire to be sealed off from the impure, materialist, overpopulated world. The author does "not claim any sort of moral superiority for homeschooling parents," but self-regard is everywhere evident, from his declaration that homeschooling must be practiced with "sensitivity to the nation's social needs" to the high seriousness with which the vehicular progress of the author's son is described: "Taylor, for example, our oldest boy, articulated for some time prior to an initial practice session an interest in riding a bicycle."

I have been against homeschooling ever since that family-taught girl won the national spelling bee a few years back. This child who became such a point of pride to homeschooling parents couldn't stop shouting and jumping around and crowing about her moment of onstage accomplishment. I didn't care if she could spell *arrhythmia* backwards; this unsocialized kid needed Miss Crabtree to put her in the corner. Still, at least she was in the game. *Family Matters* exhibits a pervasive dislike for the competitive rough-and-tumble of the larger world outside the house. "I think of [a student named] Caroline," writes Guterson, "a brilliant watercolorist, and her anguish about the C she received, after much effort, for her essay on Rudyard Kipling." *I'm* thinking that the proper course for Caroline right now is to put down the paintbrush and try harder, until she can write a grammatical sentence, because if she's getting a C in today's public schools, you can bet that her Kipling exegesis suffers from more than a lack of critical penetration. Guterson neglects the extent to which many children find school a relief from what they experience at home; they're really better off in a room with thirty others like themselves, instead of on the back porch, or snuggled away in the hollow of a cedar tree.

Without a shred of evidence beyond the author's own wishfulness, *Family Matters* flies off on a *Greening of America*-style retro high: "A home-schooling society might also nurture the kind of independent-minded, critical electorate our republic now desperately needs; it might infuse our tired democracy with a new, grass-roots energy." Guterson insists he does not romanticize the primitive, but such sentiment is all over his broadside: "Hunter-gatherer and agrarian cultures were arranged so that one's satisfaction was derived not from personal or material success but from relationships between family members and between members of the tribe." There's an exceptional humorlessness to all the author's books, as if laughter were one more gross self-indulgence to be risen above.

––––––––––

The success of *Cedars* has now dragged Guterson into the faddish pop culture he deplored in *Family Matters*. (" 'Twin Peaks' one year," he wrote, " 'The Simpsons' the next, the death of 'Dallas' as a historical event, Disneyland, Madonna talking about group sex, Hulk Hogan, and Pee-wee Herman.") Guterson did overcome his squeamishness long enough to pose for *People* magazine's "50 Most Beautiful People in the World" issue, and that photograph is now being sent out in the publicity package for *East of the Mountains,* which turns out to be just the sort of novel you would wind up writing if people had spent the last four years talking about your sensitivity, family-mannishness and broad shoulders. It is a book held hostage to its own high-mindedness.

Ben Givens, a widowed 73-year-old heart surgeon, is dying of colon cancer. To avoid burdening his grown daughter and grandson with this news, and to spare himself the disease's gruesome crescendo, Ben decides to kill himself with his father's old shotgun. He will arrange the suicide to look like an accident that has occurred in the course of a hunting trip he's taken with his dogs, the sort of expedition he's been making for years into central Washington's sage-smelling landscape. But a freakish car accident disrupts Ben's plans. Banged up but otherwise all right, he is diverted onto an odyssey of self-discovery, during which, over the course of a few days—on foot, in truck cabs and aboard buses—he will save one of his dogs from a pack of hounds, get help for a tubercular apple picker and, with the assistance of a dwarf, deliver a migrant worker's baby.

"It's good you're here," she said to Ben.

"How long has she been in labor?"

"A long time. Too long," said the dwarf.

Ben's selfless adventures would wear out a 25-year-old triathlete, but for this terminal septuagenarian they provide fresh awareness and renewal. Suffice it to say there is never any doubt Ben will get a little of his life-affirming groove back.

For stretches, *East of the Mountains* unreels like a geriatric *Easy Rider,* during which the protagonist bumps into a lot of youthful wisdom and alternative viewpoint. Kevin and Christine, two golden ski bums, give Ben pumpkin seeds and Himalayan incense. These two don't "need a piece of paper" to cement their union. "We're soulmates," Christine says. "We're forever." Ben confides the secret of his cancer to a drifter, who gives him some marijuana and assures him, "We're all dying. You're just closer to it." A girl on the same bus with the sick apple picker explains her studies at WSU: "It's like there's this spiritual dimension people just don't see. Because they're so occupied with the material world. And in anthroposophy you try to reach it." You would think Ben's bump on the head in the car accident had pushed him back in time thirty years.

This new book, one quickly comes to understand, is less a novel than an anti-yuppie tract, a scolding of all those SUV-driving materialists too wrapped up in their jobs to homeschool their kids or give Ben a lift: "Who would stop for an old man with two dogs and a black eye? The drivers speeding past were from another universe—the universe he'd inhabited as a Seattle physician—and hurtled past his extended thumb without concern or apology."

A work of fiction is in serious trouble when its flashbacks are more interesting than its main action. Ben's earlier life comes to us in two chunks, one that deals with his apple-farming parents and the other his army experience in the mountain divisions during World War II. The military training and battle scenes are done, as in *Cedars,* with surprising power. These new ones include a deft bit in which young Ben, not unlike the guilt-ridden but fine-soldiering Kabuo Miyamoto, gets to have it both ways morally: His hesitation about shooting a German causes one of his comrades to be badly wounded, but that gives Ben the chance to save his buddy with an on-the-spot blood donation. However vividly these early-life episodes are rendered, they remain awfully remote from the older Ben Givens. We are shown next to nothing of his life between 1945 and 1997; perhaps we're meant to think it's been wasted tending to all those urban consumers' clogged heart valves.

A peculiar mismatch of sensibility and style governs the narrative, as if the author were trying to wrap Hemingway's butch code in Fitzgerald's gorgeous prose. Some of that sage gets pretty purple: "On the night he had appointed his last among the living, Dr. Ben Givens did not dream, for his sleep was restless and visited by phantoms who guarded the portal to the world of dreams by speaking relentlessly of this world." That the most admirable characters should be so deliberately laconic while the narrator is so verbose becomes one more mystery of disjunction. All sorts of mannered and even ungrammatical moments arise—"He hit Stackhouse in the chest with no small violence"; "The rest of the world obliterated"—and the decades-old sex that Ben recollects seems to have had periphrasis, rather than orgasm, as its goal: "She unbuttoned his pants and clutched him so that he flooded thickly against her arm and fingers. The next day Nora left to pick fruit in Okanogan County." Why Guterson can describe the effects of colon cancer in plain, powerful English but feel compelled to render a hand job as if it were a meteorological phenomenon is one more thing beyond me. The author compiles so many wearying catalogs of landscape features and camping equipment—all twenty-two items in Ben's rucksack—that a reader wishes he would send out for more verbs.

It's all right that Ben Givens never clearly arrives at "some view of death that made leaving the world endurable," but the author might face more squarely the way his character's good deeds do not conquer his cancer so much as merely take his and the reader's minds off it. Nonetheless, what's most objectionable about *East of the Mountains*—and the rest of Guterson's work—is its lofty distaste for so many of the world's human messes. One begins, after a while, to notice how in Guterson's books the physically favored tend to behave better than the fat. One also begins to recoil from descriptions of Seattle as standing "incidental to the force of the rain" and "an addendum to the water, the sky and the listless rain," as if people—at least middle-class ones—were nothing but clutter. (The ill-favored migrant pickers on Ben's bus, with their Cheetos and Cokes and Almond Joy bars, get a pass because of their victim status.)

In *Cedars,* Arthur Chambers's widow tells her son Ishmael that his father "loved humankind dearly and with all his heart, but he disliked most human beings." The judgment is never really substantiated in our glimpses of the elder Chambers, but the line will stick with a reader who has to drive east of the mountains, and all through the rest of these books, on the fumes of their author's fine feelings.

Is God Read?

February 1999

NOVEL READERS CAN find Him on the Web—though the "most relevant matches" of God + Fiction come from sci-fi conference sites. He can be found at Barnes & Noble along a whole stretch of shelving labeled "Religious Fiction"—but what's there is only pastel-covered inspiration, novelized tracts designed to lighten one's load in this vale of tears. If readers of serious novels head into the literary-fiction precinct where they usually shop, still seeking Him, like the women at the tomb, they too will be told, "He is not here."

God has not so much risen off the pages of imaginative literature as disappeared, and so the publication of an anthology called *God: Stories,* edited by C. Michael Curtis, the fiction editor of *The Atlantic Monthly,* immediately intrigues. The volume is endorsed by Jack Miles, author of the Pulitzer Prize–winning *God: A Biography,* whose boffo title seems to have called forth the one for this volume containing twenty-five "stories about spiritual experiences of several sorts." Curtis's collection might also seem to promise fictional treatments of God Himself—whose character potential should be, even now, incomparably juicy—and yet for all the faith-hungry humans and moments of apparent grace in this nicely done gathering, there is precious little imagining of the deity, in His anthropomorphic or more ineffable guises. Just as we no longer take the Bible literally, we no longer take Him literarily. This new anthology gives us a chance to consider the reasons He's missing.

Let's start with the rule-proving exception. The white-maned, roaring God of the Sistine ceiling makes only one appearance in Curtis's collection, in a story by the late John Hersey, "God's Typhoon." Its readers are clearly cued to see this archaic archetype, projected by a stern Christian missionary onto the mind of a child, as something destructive.

Dr. Wyman preached a God I couldn't quite see in my mind, and certainly couldn't love. I dimly pictured some kind of Grandfather, who dealt out to bad people their awful "just deserts," which I thought must be poisoned food at the end of delicious meals. . . . This Grandfather apparently spent most of His time on the lookout for ways of punishing everybody's "trespasses" and "sins of pride."

This is the image of God that modern people are supposed to get over, or grow out of, lest they be burdened with neuroses and guilt in adulthood. But before the Enlightenment (that self-congratulatory term for one more shabby human century!), this baleful, billowing patriarch of the clouds was the real, unquestioned Thing. You can find the grandfather of Hersey's Grandfather-God enthroned in Book III of *Paradise Lost.* No king ever seemed so implacably self-centered as Milton's top deity, who thus assesses the fall of man:

> whose fault?
> Whose but his own? ingrate, he had of mee
> All he could have; I made him just and right,
> Sufficient to have stood, though free to fall.

A couple of dozen lines before drafting Christ to go down and raise man back up, God makes it clear where the ultimate credit for any redemption will lie:

> once more he shall stand
> On even ground against his mortal foe,
> By me upheld, that he may know how frail
> His fall'n condition is, and to me owe
> All his deliv'rance, and to none but me.

Me, Me, Me—a pretty unappetizing picture overall. And yet I can recall Professor Herschel Baker lecturing in his infallible way and faint Texas accent one morning twenty-five years ago at Harvard: "Some readers have found God the Father in Book III to be arrogant, haughty, complacent." Long pause, as we waited for the point that always came, like water out of a cactus. "Well, why shouldn't He be?"

Perhaps the only thing more presumptuous than criticizing God's appearance on the page is attempting to create Him there in the first place. He creates us, after all, and John 1:1 makes clear that the Word, written or otherwise, is nothing but His exact synonym. Voltaire may have declared that if God didn't exist, it would be necessary to invent Him, but who wants to go first? Any believing artist is held back by fear of committing the same idolatry for which a wife, in Curtis's Flannery O'Connor selection, scalds her husband after he's tattooed himself with the image of the Lord. Before beating him almost senseless with a broom, Sarah Ruth reminds Parker that God "don't *look*. . . . He's a spirit. No man shall see his face."

Which leads to the second great problem—not a moral one, like presumption, but the purely aesthetic difficulty of being able to imagine something almost any way one wants. The bad writer thinks that's freedom; the good one knows it's a surefire ticket to failure. Consider dreams in fiction: Am I the only reader who skips right over these phony little constructions in which the writer has infinite license to allegorize and underline the much more difficult wakeful action, which is held in check by standards of plausibility? God offers too *many* possibilities to the good writer, who can give Him three heads or make Him into a twinkling photon. Have it Yahweh.

What modern American writers have tended to do, when still inclined to the task, is cut God down to size, to make Him, one way or another, fit for democracy—someone like us, only nicer. Norman Mailer's Christ, in *The Gospel According to the Son,* comes off as dignified, self-doubting and precise. "Exaggeration is the language of the Devil," He assures the reader. In fact, He's smaller and less boastful than many of Mailer's fictional heroes and self-incarnations, with aspects of the Christ in Martin Scorsese's *Last Temptation,* who was all too human for the Catholic League.

Hollywood used to view the Bible as source material for big, bare-chested epics that remind one of the old line about "what God would do if He had the money." The God of film was eventually replaced not by a new secularism but by George Lucas. Who needs Revelation when you've got Industrial Light and Magic? Out on the coast, Old Testament figures and God live on as Jewish comedians—Mel Brooks or George Burns. (There's a print version in Joseph Heller's *God Knows,* where He's glimpsed as an angry Sunshine Boy taking a lot of guff from David.) Robin Williams is obviously working up to the role—an apotheosis of the empathetic doctors and saintly street people he's played of late. Guardian angels from Henry

Travers to Della Reese are even safer screen bets. Toned-down gods or souped-up mortals, call them what you want, they're guaranteed crowd pleasers, soothing persuaders instead of avenging scolds, ready to lead their beleaguered human charges toward the big guy with the "Hi, My Name Is Jehovah" name tag.

———

Our great national subject is the country's uneasy variety, and in much modern American fiction, religion is only a form of race or ethnicity, one more social fault line and cause for misunderstanding. In a few gifted hands, these dramas of affiliation transcend themselves and are born again as crises of belief. Philip Roth's "Defender of the Faith" is one such rarity in Curtis's anthology. It's the story of a war-toughened Jewish army sergeant trying to resist the endless wheedlings of Private Sheldon Grossbart, who wants Sergeant Marx to identify with the Jewish GIs and act, in everything from dietary questions to the granting of weekend passes, as "one of them." Grossbart is an outrageously persistent fake, but he will not be denied. Marx has a desperate inkling that the private may be something more; he asks, in fearful exasperation, "What are you, Grossbart? Honest to God, what are you?" Grossbart is, in fact, what the poet Francis Thompson called the Hound of Heaven, that relentless beast whose job it is to pursue the doubter home to belief. Marx banishes Grossbart—perhaps even to his death in the Pacific theater—but his ultimate effect on the sergeant remains unclear. What exactly is the "fate" he says he's accepted? The God-free life of a solid modern citizen? Or hungry exile in a secular wilderness?

Still, all this only makes Grossbart God's instrument. Direct depictions of God are even harder to come by. The anthology contains one remarkable story by Andre Dubus, in which a father's protection of his daughter, after she's committed a hit-and-run killing, becomes a secret—and the subject of direct dialogue—between himself and God. As the two of them speak, father to father, the protagonist admits he would not suffer the same risks and guilt for one of his boys:

Why? Do you love them less?
I tell Him no, it is not that I love them less, but that I could bear the pain of watching and knowing my sons' pain, could bear it with

pride as they took the whip and nails. But You never had a daughter, and if You had, You could not have borne her passion.

So, He says, you love her more than you love Me.

I love her more than I love truth.

Then you love in weakness, He says.

As you love me, I say, and I go with an apple or carrot out to the barn.

It is a brilliant, nervy conclusion, a last line that blows the roof off the story and makes it something much bigger, a story about God's nature, which the writer, however tentatively, imagines as less than perfectly strong.

I tried this once myself, and ran away from what I started after a single paragraph, the last one in a novel called *Aurora 7*. The book is set entirely on the day of Scott Carpenter's nearly disastrous 1962 spaceflight and is mostly about an 11-year-old boy named Gregory Noonan who is obsessed with the astronaut. My original plan was to have Gregger be run over and killed by a New York City taxicab in a sort of cosmic exchange: God lets the much-prayed-for astronaut get safely home, but only at this price. In the end, I couldn't go through with it. For one thing, since Gregory was essentially me a quarter century before, I would be killing myself—creepy—and for another, I realized I didn't believe God worked this way. The God I feared existed was marked by the "caprice" Jack Miles talks about. If anything, this figure who came and went in the book's last sentences was like the rest of us—existentially confused. He might have all the power, but He didn't have all the answers.

He hadn't intended to reunite the boy and his father. He had intended for some weeks to send this one of His field's lilies, this one of His sparrows, whom His eye is always on, to his death, under the wheels of Checker cab number 7D22, just as He had planned to let Carpenter skip off the earth's atmosphere and keep orbiting until he suffocated. But His moods change. Five days from now the papers will report that twelve-year-old Kenneth Shickley, Jr., while chasing a squirrel near Shamokin, Pennsylvania, has fallen down a 550-foot mineshaft to his death. "Mercy" is not a word expounded upon by the Baltimore Catechism, and as such is not an idea that Gregory

Noonan ever pondered before falling asleep and into his dreams tonight. But he did say his prayers before going to bed, and he did make the customary petition that God's will be done on earth as it is in heaven.

This bit of hesitant blasphemy (I didn't even give God a speaking part) has haunted me, like the dream of an ocean I approached and then fled. But the tide had raced away from me, too. Having grown up with the illustrated versions of that Baltimore Catechism—in which God's white beard flowed and the denizens of hell were a lurid pink—I was hustled through the let's-please-everybody changes of Vatican II and into the college chapel, where God was now on lithium, no longer promising the fires of hell, just sweetly recommending the grape boycott. The Old Man was as dead as Patton.

––––––––––

If the God of modern fiction had an honorific, it would be His Immanence. Unwilling to show Him directly, the writers in Curtis's collection will occasionally tell you He's all around and inside everything. In Alice Munro's "Pictures of the Ice," the retired minister "rarely mentions God. Nevertheless, you feel the mention of God hovering on the edge of [what he says], and it makes you so uneasy . . . that you wish he'd say it and get it over with." It's the same with the writers of those stories in which God makes Himself known through little grace notes and mysterious ways, arriving in characters' lives like an anonymous bank deposit or a basket left on the porch. Modern readers won't accept God's personal appearance, but they'll allow Him to phone in His work—so long as in the course of these manifestations He does not lord it over the modern world. Flannery O'Connor and Mary McCarthy—a fervent and a lapsed Catholic, respectively—disagreed about Graham Greene's 1950s play *The Potting Shed,* in which a miracle (the resurrection of a suicide) occurs. But they both understood Greene's basic M.O., in book after book. "What he does, I think," wrote O'Connor, "is try to make religion respectable to the modern unbeliever by making it seedy." McCarthy, with more exasperation, observed that God "permeates [Greene's] novels and plays, with His unfailing presence, and in turn He soaks up the smells of His surroundings—bad cooking and mildew and dirty sheets and stale alcohol. You would not think that this was well calculated to make religion attractive to the general public. But the public is titillated by this deity, created in its own bored image."

The power of prayer has its own narrative potential. Allowing a character to prompt God's manifestations makes the petitioner into a sort of sympathetic antagonist, somebody who wants something, may get it or not, misuse or deserve it, be grateful or otherwise. In William Hoffman's "The Question of Rain," a minister is inveigled into devoting an entire service to praying for the end to a drought. When the downpour comes, he experiences more apprehension than relief, worrying what compensatory (or capricious) calamity may now visit him. Curtis's anthology is full of these clergymen whose crises make them into spiritual lab rats and scapegoats for the religious-minded writer. Most amusingly included is the Reverend Swain Hammond, in Peggy Payne's story "The Pure in Heart," a comically poignant illustration of Thomas Szasz's famous observation that "if you talk to God, you are praying; if God talks to you, you have schizophrenia." The Reverend Hammond's deity isn't much more vocal or visible than the Immanent Beings in so many of the other stories, but the minister has heard some unmistakable monosyllables and fragments—none of it joyful to his ear, either—and he feels an obligation to report the experience to his congregation. The church operations committee is soon recommending, by a five-to-four vote, that he seek "professional help."

Big Brother, the Wizard of Oz and the White Whale may be bona fide political and psychological preoccupations, but they are also God substitutes, displacements of a Father whose possible existence slowly became too embarrassing and retro to handle in literature. With the eighteenth century, Reason became God, and happiness replaced salvation as the end of life. But the human need to be terrified of something omnipotent, to supplicate and to taunt, remained. And so an array of spooky God replicas, some as inanimate as Dr. T. J. Eckleburg's billboard eyes in *Gatsby*, have ever since been around to pick up the slack of terror and devotion.

God's most frequent modern literary stand-in is, of course, the Devil, an unfailing showstopper from *Faust* to *Damn Yankees;* he is at least somewhat powerful and otherworldly, and he makes writers and audiences much less uncomfortable than his celestial counterpart. There's never any sense of presumptuousness about writing lines for him, and the words that come out of his mouth, along with the toads, are usually more memorable than

God's. Even in *Paradise Lost,* he puts on such a rhetorical performance—
" 'Better to reign in hell than serve in heav'n' "—that Blake later pronounced Milton "of the Devil's party without knowing it."

Still, today even fewer people believe in the Devil than in God, and the
resulting man-centeredness of fiction makes it a kind of pre-Copernican
universe in which there's nothing more central than us. This is the real presumptuousness the writer of fiction commits, and the likelihood of his over-
coming it is pretty slim, considering the other, occupational hazard holding
him back from the contemplation of God—namely, a sense that the deity is
creative competition. Look at these sentences in the John Updike story
picked by Curtis, "Made in Heaven."

> With their own young the Schaeffers were lucky—the boys were a
> little too old to fall into the heart of the drug craze, and the girls were
> safely married before just living together became fashionable. One
> boy didn't finish college and became a carpenter in Vermont; the
> other did finish, at Amherst, but then moved to the West Coast to
> live. The two girls, however, stayed in the area and provided new
> grandchildren at regular intervals.

How can we expect the writer of even such a religion-minded story as this
to lose the sense that *he* is the one flinging a whole little world into being, even faster than God tossed off His production over the six days of
Genesis?

Among all the important American novelists of his time, Updike has
been the most attentive to God, in part through the sporadic heavenly musings of Rabbit Angstrom, who once told his minister, "Somewhere behind
all this . . . there's something that wants me to find it." It's what many novelists, typing away in God's vineyard, feel, too. But how to tear one's attention from the other servants and the grapes? If the world is too interesting a
distraction, Who's to blame?

A Measure of Self Esteem

Parlor-game question: who's the most misnamed novelist of our time?

Answer: Will Self, since his books show neither a belief in the first nor a permanent sense of the second.

In Self's first novel, *My Idea of Fun,* the life of its young protagonist, Ian Wharton, is run by an all-powerful character called the Fat Controller; and "Between the Conceits," a story in Self's collection *Grey Area,* posits that eight quite ordinary-seeming Londoners psychically direct the existence of every other person in the city. As one of them explains:

> I make more calculations in an hour than Kasparov does in a year. I stretch, then relax—and 35,665 white-collar workers leave their houses a teensy bit early for work. This means that 6,014 of them will feel dyspeptic during the journey because they've missed their second piece of toast, or bowl of Fruit 'n' Fibre. From which it follows that 2,982 of them will be testy throughout the morning; and therefore 312 of them will say the wrong thing, leading to dismissal; hence one of these 312 will lose the balance of his reason and commit an apparently random and motiveless murder on the way home.

As a London teenager, the now 38-year-old Self was labeled a borderline schizophrenic by psychiatrists. It would be tough for the novelist to talk his way out of such a diagnosis on the basis of the half dozen or so aggressively imagined works of fiction he's produced in the past decade—not with all the distant, fateful string-pulling and sudden mad morphing that go on in every one of them. In *Cock & Bull,* an early pair of novellas, a man acquires a vagina and a woman grows a penis. (Once the latter, Carol, gets her membership in the male sex, she rapes and murders her husband. The clockwork-orangey aspects of Self's world also wouldn't score points with any white-coated examiners.) His most recent novel, *Great Apes,* has the painter Simon Dykes discovering one morning that his girlfriend, Sarah, is now a chimpanzee; in fact, chimps and humans have changed places running the world. Simon doesn't seem to realize that he's now an ape, too, but Sarah can feel "his fingers move with something like import, and she could mark out a few signs, shaped with spiky terror. 'Beast,' Simon signed, 'fucking beast.' Then he sprayed her."

Self is perhaps most often compared to Kafka, though he has plenty of domestic ancestors, too: Aldous Huxley, Anthony Burgess, J. G. Ballard, Martin Amis—all those inventive, dystopian British writers who came of age during different stretches of the century, but none at a time when it was possible to imagine an English future as anything but grubbier and more oppressive than the present. Back beyond these, Self has a number of forefathers from the nineteenth century, the one in which Britain ruled the world and still had a lot of time for nursery nonsense. Lewis Carroll and Edward Lear both prance behind some of the grossness and dislocation in Will Self's imaginings. He's gone through a looking glass, too: a computer screen with some coke lines on it.

Self's latest book, *Tough, Tough Toys for Tough, Tough Boys,* takes its goofy title from an old ad slogan for Tonka trucks. The eight stories it contains are ugly, inventive and amusing in a manner that by now seems trademark. "Flytopia" concerns the division-of-labor pact made between a work-at-home indexer and the insects in his cottage: "Teams of earwigs were at work in the bathroom, and in the kitchen all signs of his breakfast, right down to the ring of coffee powder he had left by the jar, were eradicated by the industrious ants." In "A Story for Europe," the British parents of little Humphrey Green learn that their baby is speaking not gibberish but business German: " 'Some people might say it was a great asset,' says Dr. Grauerholtz, 'especially in today's European situation, yes?' "

Self sometimes doesn't know what to do with his own creative gusher. His work is more vivid than shapely. It lacks the crazily thorough micromanagement that, here in America, Nicholson Baker gives his equally peculiar, and brilliantly childish, books. In Self's "Caring, Sharing," the futuristic story of how humans, sick of sex and emotional complications, let themselves be nuzzled and nannied by big, apelike androids called "emotos," the author brings the nicely conceived business to a close with a lazy, predictable twist (the emotos turn out to be quite sophisticated once their human masters go to bed for the night). "The Rock of Crack As Big As the Ritz," about a giant mine of dope under an ordinary London house, just stops, as if the author preferred going on to another bravura setup instead of fulfilling this one.

Johnny Carson used to say, "You buy the premise, you buy the bit." The guarantee doesn't apply to Self's high-concept comic creations, since the premise sometimes ceases to govern the story halfway through. He's not content, for instance, to let "The Nonce Prize" remain a black-comedic nightmare about a man framed for the murder of a child; he steers it into a satire on the nature of aspiring writers—rather as *Cock* takes time out from its genital surprises to make astute, if somewhat extended, fun of twelve-step counseling.

One is tempted to decide that Self's problem with follow-through is a deliberate aesthetic obstinacy, that he's making one more point, through form, about the instability of human nature and earthly circumstance. But it's really more a matter of being too fertile for his own good. "I have often thought," says Dr. Zack Busner in *Grey Area,* "that a suitable epitaph for me—given the gad-fly nature of my enthusiasms—would be 'He had no interests but interest.' " The line works for Self too. God knows, he has no need of Inclusion, a mood-altering drug invented by Busner, which permits the taker to become absorbed in anything, even televised curling competitions and dramatizations of Sir John Betjeman's poetry. (It helps to have spent a bit of time in Britain to get not only some of Self's slang but also the spot-on funny nature of little cultural references like these.)

Zack Busner is Self's Dr. Frankenstein, a recurring manipulator and enemy and alter ego. A few years after writing "Inclusion®," Self reintroduced him in *Great Apes,* where he became the chief chimp shrink: "Dr. Zack Busner, clinical psychologist, medical doctor, radical psychoanalyst, anti-psychiatrist, maverick anxiolytic drug researcher and former television personality, stood upright in front of the bathroom mirror teasing some crumbs from the thick fur under the line of his jaw." Readers of Self's 1991 collection, *The Quantity Theory of Insanity,* will recall the "anti-psychiatrist" phase of Busner's career from the title story. There he was directing the Concept House, "an autonomous community of therapists and patients, except that instead of these roles being concretely divided among the residents all were free to take on either mantle at any time."

Recurring characters are, of course, a writer's prerogative; readers have met them from Falstaff to Rabbit Angstrom, and part of the pleasure in a second or third encounter comes from figuring out whether to put the latest piece of life story before or after the stretches of it that one has read previously. Self sometimes works this way—*Tough, Tough Toys* has two stories apiece about a philandering doctor and the crack-dealing O'Toole brothers—but some of his encores are freakishly nonlinear.

Consider the following: Simon Dykes, the painter in *Great Apes* who continues to believe he's human, has come up against Dr. Zack Busner in an earlier book—as a test subject for Inclusion. In fact, one Dr. Anthony Bohm suspects a connection between Dykes's *Great Apes* "breakdown" and the drug trial run by "that pushy, exhibitionistic chimp, Busner." But more weirdly, the reader has also seen Dr. Bohm and Dykes together in a previous volume—specifically, a nasty little environmentalist nightmare called "Chest," where the inhabitants of a fogbound English town are forever hacking up great gobs of phlegm. There one Anthony-Anthony Bohm is the local GP and Simon-Arthur Dykes his patient—two incarnations that seem more like recombinants than extensions of the Bohm and Dykes in *Great Apes*. The characters are the same but not the same. They're literary mutants, like women with penises.

The doppelgänger—the idea of a double, or "secret sharer," as Conrad put it—has always been a surefire source of reader intrigue. But in Self the off-center recurrences have a nauseous, cloned feel; one wants to flee the replicants. *Grey Area* has stories in which every restaurant waiter is writing a novel and every couple is quarreling. Most oddly, people with the name Dave proliferate all over Self's work: In *Cock* we're told that one friend of Carol's husband must be called Dave 1 "because Dave 2," an alcoholism counselor, "comes later"; in "Chest" the newsagent is "Dave-Dave Hutchinson"; and then, climactically, in the new *Tough, Tough Toys* story "Dave Too," we get "a world with so many Daves, Daves running, Daves walking, and Daves standing." The reader gets a horrible sense of interchangeability, a feeling that there's always someone about to replace him in a push-pull world, where everybody unknowingly connects to somebody else. In "Between the Conceits," all that one of those eight people controlling London has to do is groan, "turning on his day bed—and forty-seven of his people lose control of their vehicles and drive into the vehicles of forty-seven of [the narrator's] people." For little Humphrey to advance in his business German, somewhere in Frankfurt an economist must have a stroke and begin speaking baby talk.

It's all related to the "Quantity Theory of Insanity" developed by an early Self narrator. Like Newton's third law of motion, the QT posits that "there is only a fixed proportion of sanity available in any given society at any given time" and that "any attempts to palliate manifestations of insanity in one sector of society can only result in their upsurge in some other area of society." In other words, each person's soundness of mind depends on someone else's being nuts. We're not people so much as components, lock-stepping Daves, the crash-test dummies used in the illustrations for *Grey Area*.

Sustained reading of Self's books will leave you feeling lulled or edgy, depending on your temperament and, to some extent, brain chemistry. Self's own has been altered by drugs, prescription and otherwise, for many years. (In 1997, while working as a reporter for the London *Observer*, he was famously caught using heroin on Prime Minister John Major's campaign plane.) Self's fiction—its subject matter, themes and metaphors—is filled with dope, whose addictive repetitions dovetail with the replicating Daveness of the author's world. As Tembe O'Toole realizes about crack, "The whole hit of rock is to want *more rock*. The buzz of rock is itself the wanting of *more rock*."

A junkie-disgust runs through the figurative language of the whole Self shelf, including this new volume: "Turner, Bill thought, would have painted this greying haze, had he been alive to suck the butt-end of the twentieth century." Paranoid motifs are discernible even in the writer's nondrug preoccupations. Like Carol, who's just developing the fixation in *Cock*, Self has "an unreasonable interest in everything to do with the road." Britain's numbered motorways, forever being driven by his characters, thread the country and the stories like a computer's hardwiring or the body's own accessible veins.

The author's most frequent tone is a deadpan, aerial detachment: "She wore a blue, nylon coverall, elaborately yet randomly brocaded with the abandoned hairs of a sector of the population." This is what can unsettle you on one page, anesthetize you on another. Self seems to seek, overall, what in "Dave Too" he calls an "objective creepiness." He can describe the sending of a fax and the rape of a child with the same virtuoso affectlessness.

"Satirist" is the label most frequently stuck on him. Goodness knows it's an elastic enough term, having been made to fit everyone from the forgiving Horace to the world-hating Swift to the amused Tom Wolfe, who reserves his greatest affection for his biggest targets. When trained on the way-we-live-now specifics that are always the social satirist's fodder, Self's wit and powers of observation operate at a terrifically high level: One "awful, venal, unprincipled and deeply alluring woman" has "a horrible, expensive, phone-your-divorce-lawyer kind of laugh." But the author has trouble sustaining his gaze. It's not just that he's interested in something he thinks more fundamentally and frighteningly rotten. It's also that the atoms in front of his eyes keep shifting and reproducing and mutating; before he's finished looking at any one element, he's already spotted its isotope. A year and a half ago, when *Great Apes* came out in the States, he scolded an interviewer from *Publishers Weekly:*

> "I'm telling you the absolute fucking gospel truth. You can't sit down as a satirist and think, 'oh, these people are behaving dreadfully badly. I must write this satire about apes to show humans that they've all got to be much nicer to each other. I'm very upset about it and I'm going to lock myself up in this room . . .' It doesn't work like that. You just get very bored, and start writing books."

As far back as *Cock & Bull*, he picked an epigraph from Byron that emphasized the medium instead of any message—"as I said, / I won't philosophize and will be read"—and his latest book carries one from Wilde, with the emphasis again more on his needs than the reader's: "Life is a dream that keeps me from sleeping."

The fiction he's writing is full of brilliance; but as the oeuvre grows, volume by volume and a bit relentlessly, it's showing signs of repetition, a certain Daveness. One can't get rid of the feeling that Self's whole prolific, off-kilter enterprise is moving too fast, that it may soon short out, stop and be forgotten. But as the doctor tells the parents of little German-speaking Humphrey, "If there is a real problem here . . . I suspect it may be to do with a gift rather than a deficiency."

Off the Shelf

The Great War and
Sassoon's Memory

1983

THE STAGE NERVES that Siegfried Sassoon may have experienced before addressing the Poetry Club at the Harvard Union in the spring of 1920 were surely mitigated by the assurances of Miss Amy Lowell, who had recently written to tell him that he "was the one man whom the Harvard undergraduates wanted to hear." Such guarantees were more necessary than might be supposed; Sassoon had discovered upon arriving in New York in January that, a year after the Armistice, more than enough British authors were touring America to fulfill the already slackening desire to hear from and about the soldier-poets. In fact, the war was receding enough from people's minds that Sassoon had to rely on himself, rather than the Pond Lyceum Bureau, to scare up most of his engagements. But at Harvard Sassoon did find a receptive audience for the last of his pleas against militarism, and he finished the tour feeling that his "diminutive attempt to make known to Americans an interpretation of the war as seen by the fighting men" had been "not altogether ineffective."

In some respects the Harvard appearance marked the end of a three-year phase in Sassoon's life that began in 1917 with the appearance of *The Old Huntsman* and his public statement against the war; climaxed with the publication of *Counter-Attack* on June 27, 1918; and had its denouement in his post-Armistice lecturing. In less than four years he had gone from being a sometime versifier to an international literary celebrity, the man who more than any other had brought about the post-Somme poetic rebellion in diction, subject matter, and outlook. These were the most public years of his life, and nothing in his later works would so impress itself on readers' minds and literary history as the angry ironies of "Base Details," "The General," "To Any Dead Officer," and "Suicide in the Trenches."

He would continue publishing poetry into the 1960s, including some beautiful and neglected religious verse, but after *Counter-Attack* he is best known as a memoirist who twice wrote three volumes about his early years. The "fictional" memoirs, with the non-poet George Sherston as Sassoon's reductive stand-in (*Memoirs of a Fox-Hunting Man*, 1928; *Memoirs of an Infantry Officer*, 1930; *Sherston's Progress*, 1936) were followed by the "real" autobiographies (*The Old Century and Seven More Years*, 1938; *The Weald of Youth*, 1942; and *Siegfried's Journey*, 1945). The Sherston books run from George's childhood until 1918; the second trilogy takes Sassoon two years beyond the Armistice. Lines marking the refraction of actual experience are not clearly drawn in either set. In the Sherston books, for example, the actual Dr. W. H. R. Rivers (who treated Sassoon in Craiglockhart War Hospital, site of his famous conversations with Wilfred Owen) makes more than one appearance, like a "real" character in a historical novel. Conversely, in the autobiographies, Sassoon admits occasionally to bending material toward a particular logical or aesthetic effect, and he will sometimes refer readers to the Sherston memoirs, where the fictional treatment of actual experience is close enough to the way events really happened to make further discussion redundant.

Readers who make a gingerly commute between both sets of books will eventually understand the salient features of the author's mind and memory, and come to realize how the Great War, which transformed his poetry and destroyed much of his world, left Siegfried Sassoon essentially, and bewilderingly, unchanged.

"Pre-lapsarian" is one of those overused academic adjectives, but is it ever less avoidable than in discussions of the doomed patterns of English country life in the last years before 1914? That those patterns would be extinguished by conflicts originating on the remote continent of Europe was unthinkable to most of the young men who had grown up slowly and securely in English villages. Sassoon's Sherston says that before the war "Europe was nothing but a name to me. I couldn't even bring myself to read about it in the daily paper." The only notable conflicts in Sherston's prewar world are manufactured and ceremonial ones—hunts and horse races.

Sassoon's own childhood was spent amidst the considerable comforts assured by an unusual pedigree. Siegfried grew up in a large Kentish house, educated mostly by tutors, played with by older brothers, cast in his mother's *tableaux vivants,* and exposed to such venerable villagers as Miss Horrocks, whom King George IV had once kissed. An impractical boy, regarded as delicate, he was quite unsingle-minded about anything. He would later recall himself at age eleven: "My undistracted imagination had been decently nourished on poetry, fairy-tales, and fanciful illustrations, and my ideas of how people behaved in real life were mainly derived from *Punch, The Boy's Own Paper,* and F. Anstey's *Voces Populi.*" Sherston is depicted enjoying the same sort of undemanding security as he approaches adolescence. "In this brightly visualized world of simplicities and misapprehensions and mispronounced names everything was accepted without question. . . . The quince tree which grew beside the little pond was the only quince tree in the world."

Fox hunting and poetry became the chief imaginative excitements of Sassoon's youth. Economics gently curbed his pursuit of the first; poetry, practiced intermittently, touched in him "a blurred and uncontrolled chord of ecstasy" and became associated with "an undefined heart-ache." This uncertainty of response (as well as spotty, haphazard reading) gave his own first efforts at composition "a fine frenzy of aureate unreality" that, by his own admission, he could still lapse into many years later, even after he had achieved the disciplined fury of his antiwar productions. He collected books as much for the feels and smells of their bindings as any revelations within. The experience of Cambridge remains almost completely unchronicled in the Sherston memoirs and only hastily recounted in the autobiography. Sassoon says that he left the university convinced of his desire to be a poet, but the enervating split between his comfortable "reynardism" and casual versifying would be part of his life for several more years, until the Great War arrived.

In each set of memoirs, the announcement that the subject has reached his majority provides the reader with one of the few starts he receives from the tranquilly beautiful narratives. Sherston and Sassoon both seem, at twenty-one, not just far away from adulthood, but also uninterested in it. Sherston recalls: "The word maturity had no meaning for me. I did not anticipate that I should become *different;* I should only become *older.* I cannot pretend that I aspired to growing wiser. I merely *lived,* and in that condition I drifted from day to day." Already more predisposed to remember than anticipate, Sassoon and Sherston impress themselves on the reader as static and ambered; the effect is beautiful in the way that innocence can be, but troubling, too, like a plane unable to gain altitude.

In all six volumes, which take the persona and the person past the age of thirty, sexual exploration is almost eerily absent—even by period standards of reticence. Protected from the emotional ravages of love, Sherston and Sassoon seem deoxygenated, like toys under glass. Women who appear are generally aunts. Men may be models of grace and bearing—like the fox-hunter Stephen Colwood, or Denis Milden, Master of the hunt—but their erotic attractions are carefully blunted. The figure who is Milden in the memoirs and Norman Loder in the autobiographies provides one of the key differences between the two sets of books. The real Loder is considerably endowed with virtues, but of a rather unglamorous kind: "He was kind, decent, and thorough, never aiming at anything beyond plain common-sense and practical ability." Milden, however, even while behaving with similar straightforwardness, has a more romantic allure. Sherston meets him when they are both boys: "Already I was weaving Master Milden into my day dreams, and soon he had become my inseparable companion in all my imagined adventures. . . . It was the first time that I had experienced a feeling of wistfulness for someone I wanted to be with." Years later an invitation from the hunt-master is still cause for rapture in Sherston, and the dependable simplicities of Milden's routine are observed with something like awe: "Meditated on the difference between Denis hunting the hounds (unapproachable and with 'a face like a boot') and Denis indoors—homely and kind and easy to get on with; would he really want me to come and stay with him again, I wondered." These are the familiar thrills and worries of schoolboy crushes; but Sherston is twenty-five.*

London failed to galvanize his character any more than romance had. As an uncertain young poet in the city just before the war, Sassoon was aided

---

*Sassoon's *Diaries 1920–1922,* published more than a decade after his death, show his involvement in two homosexual affairs during this period. He writes on August 13, 1922: "I must remember all the years of sexual frustration and failure, and be thankful. I must not ask too much of P. who has limitations which at present are charming to me." But "this cursed complication of sex"—made worse, one feels, by what he admits was his "prolonged youthfulness"—remains a frequently unhappy and confused theme. Annotating these diaries in 1939, Sassoon wrote: "Homosexuality has become a bore; the intelligentsia have captured it."

and encouraged by such professional encouragers as Edmund Gosse and Edward Marsh. But his vocation was hardly overpowering, and he continued to move confusedly between the field and the desk, his métier no more defined than his personality: "I may have wondered why it was so impossible to amalgamate my contrasted worlds of Literature and Sport. Why must I always be adapting my manners—and even my style of speaking—to different sets of people?" This adaptability, a kind of active passivity, is something Sassoon repeatedly ascribes to Sherston and admits in himself. In his diary from 1922, Sassoon refers to his own "mental coma," and of the diary itself he writes: "From this jungle of misinterpretations of my ever-changing and never-steadfast selves, some future fool may, perhaps, derive instruction and amusement."

In the summer of 1914, having moved to Gray's Inn at the suggestion of Edward Marsh, Sassoon felt "on the verge of some experience which might liberate [him] from [his] blind alley of excessive sport and self-imposed artistic solitude." The war would turn him into a poet with a mission. But despite Sherston's claim that the war "re-made" him, the evidence suggests that Sassoon himself emerged from it the same protean and tentative creature who had embarked for the Front. His splendid military performance and brave subsequent protest didn't synthesize him into a solid character any more than fox hunting and poetry had. If anything, Sassoon had his constitutional capacity to shift and adapt made even more habitual. Wilfred Owen may have approached him as novice to mentor while they were both in Craiglockhart War Hospital, but in *Siegfried's Journey* Sassoon admits: "When contrasting the two of us, I find that—highly strung and emotional though he was—his whole personality was far more compact and coherent than mine." The war transformed Owen with almost molecular thoroughness; it left Sassoon's most inner dimensions unpenetrated.*

*Paul Fussell, in *The Great War and Modern Memory* (Oxford: Oxford University Press, 1975), offers a view of both Sassoon and the construction of the Sherston memoirs that is very different from the one put forth in this essay. He sees a great change between "prewar and postwar Sassoon," whereas I would emphasize similarity; the Sherston trilogy, which I find loose and episodic, appears to him "elaborately structured." Readers of this essay may want to contrast its argument to that found on pp. 90–105 of Fussell's book. In addition, an extended and workmanlike discussion of both the Sherston memoirs and the autobiographies can be found in Michael Thorpe's *Siegfried Sassoon: A Critical Study* (Leiden: Universitaire Pers Leiden, 1966).

Both Sherston and Sassoon volunteer for the army with the sort of dutiful inertia that led many of the educated soldier-poets to the Front. Irony and bitterness set in a good deal later. Sherston listens uneasily to the same "Spirit of the Bayonet" lecture that Sassoon did. Echoing Prince Hal's remark about Hotspur and the Scots, he reflects: "Man, it seemed, had been created to jab the life out of Germans. To hear the Major talk, one might have thought that he did it himself every day before breakfast." But a raid can still be as important to the ego as a point-to-point race, and after protesting the war, being hospitalized (instead of court-martialed) and then pronounced fit to return to the Front, Sherston can still have war dreams in which he is "vaguely gratified at 'adding to [his] war experience.' " (Indeed, there is good reason to believe that Sassoon himself conceived the famous lines of "The Kiss"—inspired by the bayonet lecture—in a pre-Somme spirit of romance, and only later invited them to be read as satire.) Even after Sherston has learned to be bitter towards the "happy warrior attitudes" imagined back home and recommended by superiors, he can still—a year after the Somme—assume a heroic stance as a kind of prophylactic against danger and death: "I had always found it difficult to believe that these young men had really felt happy with death staring them in the face, and I resented any sentimentalizing of infantry attacks. But here I was, working myself up into a similar mental condition, as though going over the top were a species of religious experience. Was it some suicidal self-deceiving escape from the limitless malevolence of the Front Line?"

It was, in fact, self-preserving. To act from a sense of purpose, with whatever suspension of disbelief that may require, is to reduce the possibilities of panic and despair that would follow a sense of absurdity. So, even after he knows better, Sherston plays "at being a hero in shining armour." It was the same with Sassoon himself. After rereading his actual war diary from the end of 1916, he notes in *Siegfried's Journey:* "Some of its entries suggest that I was keeping my courage up by resorting to elevated feelings. My mental behaviour was still unconnected with any self-knowledge, and it was only when I was writing verse that I tried to concentrate and express my somewhat loose ideas."

While Sherston is convalescing from a "blighty," he makes a comic list of the chameleonlike poses he adopts. Each depends on his visitor: to a hunting friend he is "deprecatory about sufferings endured at the front"; to the sister of a fellow officer he is "jocular, talkative, debonair, and diffidently heroic." When alone except for other patients, he is "mainly disposed toward self-pitying estrangement from everyone except the troops in the Front Line." The reflexes here are more psychological than social, part of an instinct, in the absence of fixed character, to improvise selves as needed.

Siegfried's Journey gives reasons to believe that Sassoon, during his 1917 protest of the war, was not quite so dependent on Bertrand Russell and H. W. Massingham as he made Sherston be on their fictive refractions, "Tyrrell" and "Markington." Even so, Sassoon's whole antiwar gesture contained plenty of personal ambivalence. Just as so many English poets of the 1930s would have secret difficulty casting their lot with a politics designed to sweep away the privileged milieux in which they had learned so many humane values, so Sherston, at home on leave, wonders whether his indictment is too inclusive:

> Walking round the garden after tea—Aunt Evelyn drawing [Captain Huxtable's] attention to her delphiniums and he waggishly affirming their inferiority to his own—I wondered whether I had exaggerated the "callous complacency" of those at home. What could elderly people do except try and make the best of their inability to sit in a trench and be bombarded? How could they be blamed for refusing to recognize any ignoble elements in the War except those which they attributed to our enemies?

He concedes that his protest "was an emotional idea based on [his] war experience and stimulated by the acquisition of points of view which [he] accepted uncritically"; and that in this period he was as interested in becoming a good golfer as an intellectual.

The real Sassoon, in *Siegfried's Journey,* confesses that his protest "developed into a fomentation of confused and inflamed ideas" and that his "disillusionment was combined with determination to employ [his] discontents as a medium for literary expression." The suggestion by the portrait painter Glyn Philpot that the protest is a Byronic gesture helps "to sustain [his] belief that [he is] about to do something spectacular and heroic." He soon realizes that "army life had persistently interfered with my ruminative and quiet-loving mentality. I may even have been aware that most of my satiric verses were to some extent prompted by internal exasperation."

Like much else about Sassoon, the protest was more or less impromptu. As it crumbled and its consequences became felt, he had few certainties of intellect and character to fall back upon. He went back to the Front still as inchoate as he was gallant.

The anger Sassoon felt toward the war had an almost boyish sense of right and wrong as its propellant. He endowed his fictional isotope with the same. Shortly after Dick Tiltwood, another ideal friend—"a young Gala-had"—is killed at the Front, Sherston says: "I was angry with the War"—an emotionally genuine declaration, not the literary understatement employed for effect by Great War poets and memoirists. After observing an unforgiv-ably severe doctor during his convalescence, Sherston says: "I hope that someone gave him a black eye"; in real life Sassoon had an altercation with a photographer disrupting the dignity of the grave site of T. E. Lawrence— whose *Seven Pillars of Wisdom* exhibits, like Sassoon's books, heroic be-havior proceeding from a curiously ad hoc and incipient personality.

Very late in the war, Sherston is at Company HQ in a chateau behind the lines at Habarcq. In his diary he locates himself in "this quiet room where I spend my evenings ruminating and trying to tell myself the truth—this room where I become my real self, and feel omnipotent while reading Tol-stoy and Walt Whitman." But how can one's real self reside in the fantasies insurgent from reading? Here again Sherston seems younger than his age. It is a year since his protest, and his diary records his confusion: " 'I want to go up to the Line and really do something!' I had boasted thus in a moment of vin rouge elation, catching my mood from those lads who look to me as their leader. How should they know the shallowness of my words?" He is still taking his character from momentary circumstance.

The memoirs end with Sherston once again in hospital, almost thirty-two and despairingly baffled about whatever meaning the war may have had for him. Rivers, the mind's physician, appears as a deus ex machina. His smile is a "benediction," and Sherston understands that this is what he has "been waiting for": "He did not tell me that I had done my best to justify his belief in me. He merely made me feel that he took all that for granted, and now we must go on to something better still. And this was the begin-ning of the new life toward which he had shown me the way." In this bibli-cal language, Sherston delivers his will into Rivers's hands.

———————

The autobiographies give evidence that their author reacted to the first year of peacetime with many of the same traits, and much the same uncertainty, that he displayed in London before the war. Sassoon turned fitfully to reviewing and to Labour Party politics as he made the acquaintance of many of the day's important writers. *Siegfried's Journey* shows him encountering Hardy, Masefield, Bridges, T. E. Lawrence, Galsworthy, Firbank, Blunt and Belloc. In most cases he is accompanied or propelled by someone like Osbert Sitwell or the indefatigable Ottoline Morrell, his literary celebrity now managed by others the way, several years before, his obscurity had been by Marsh. He exhibits the compelling blankness with which Virginia Woolf endowed Jacob Flanders, destined to move from party to party and house to house and be appreciated for his freshness and potential—but to remain somehow ungraspable, leaving more of an afterglow than an impression. Aware of his still diaphanous personality, Sassoon recalls:

> I am sure that if, for example, my Gosse, Galsworthy, Marsh, and Arnold Bennett selves could have been interchanged, some perplexity would have been present in their acutely observant minds. I resembled the character in a Pirandello play who was told, "Your reality is a mere transitory and fleeting illusion, taking this form today and that tomorrow, according to the conditions, according to your will, your sentiments, which in turn are controlled by an intellect that shows them to you today in one manner and tomorrow . . . who knows how?

Sassoon's diaries from the early 1920s show a persisting split between the worlds of the Morrells' Garsington and "Loder-land," with sometimes literature and sometimes sport gaining sway over his ambitions and routine. But his literary moment was receding, even as he attempted to find his place in it. With wartime subject matter gone, Sassoon's bold diction and "knockout" last-line ironies had fewer poems to go into. He was left with his prewar pastoralism and regular Edwardian metrics, having traveled a very fast sound wave from being *le dernier cri* to a respected echo. As the above list of arranged literary pilgrimages shows, he was really more attuned to the writers of an earlier generation, soon to be the literary past, than to those who would would create the great modernist poetry and fiction of the '20s.

His premature eclipse complemented his constitutional attraction to the past. In *The Weald of Youth* Sassoon imagines that "the present is only waiting to become the past and be laid up in lavender for commemorative renewal." During his childhood, even his grandmother Thornycroft's senility had appealed to his imagination as a kind of magic carpet flying backwards in time. Sherston makes fun of himself as a "professional ruminator" inclined "to loiter . . . as long as possible" among details of the past. Sassoon may refer in *Siegfried's Journey* to his "comparisons between the crude experience and its perspectived proportions as they emerge in matured remembering," but even in the autobiographies the past seems more often conjured than interpreted. This would be so in a man who can recall experiencing "the first instance . . . of a detached sense of proportion about [his] doings in relation to life as a whole" at the age of twenty-seven. He makes frequent use of the present tense ("I see him, chalking the dates of famous battles on the blackboard"), calling the dead and the past to life in the same sort of séance manner he used in a number of poems about the dead, enacting Sherston's frequent assertion that the past is apprehended more vividly than it was when it was merely the present.

Sassoon's sense that "when you get close up to life, little things are just as important as big ones" displays perhaps the single affinity between his mind and the modernist sensibility that produced *Ulysses* and *Mrs. Dalloway*—one that sought, with the logic of paradox, to achieve universality by exploring the particular with more particularity than ever before. But a gentle un-Joycean fastidiousness prevents Sassoon from depicting any earthy or unpleasant minutiae. Indeed, even in the autobiographies the author confesses to enough distortions to make shaky any claim that those books focus more sharply on reality than did the Sherston memoirs: "I prefer to remember my own gladness and good luck, and to forget, whenever I can, those moods and minor events which made me low-spirited and unresponsive. Be at your best, vision enchanting, I cry."

One need not recall one's school days with Dotheboys horror or even the detachment of Orwell's "Such, Such Were the Joys," yet all but the most naive reader will be left more quizzical than charmed by the way Sassoon romances schooltime unpleasantness into the picturesque. It's the same with parent-child relations. Conflicts between Sassoon and his mother are only hastily alluded to in the autobiographies; in the Sherston memoirs the deserted and, one suspects, complicated Mrs. Sassoon is woollied and neutered into "Aunt Evelyn." In both sets of war recollections the sharp sarcasm of a Graves is avoided in favor of an understatement like Edmund

Blunden's, as well as humorous, self-protecting periphrasis: "This was a mistake which ought to have put an end to my terrestrial adventures, for no sooner had I popped my silly head out of the sap than I felt a stupendous blow in the back between my shoulders."

Sassoon admits that the "unrevealed processes of memory are mysterious," and he refrains from probing them too strenuously. Throughout the first two volumes of the autobiography he draws attention to the unsystematic nature of his mind, the traits that leave it more liable to intense apparitions than chains of thought. He says that information best reaches him slowly and visually, that "abstract ideas are uncongenial," and that the study of history made sense to him only in terms of drama or chronology. The progression of titles in the autobiographies (*The Old Century, The Weald of Youth, Siegfried's Journey*) seems to suggest a steady movement toward personal definition: the name of a time, then the name of a phase, finally the name of the person. But this is misleading, because Sassoon's character hardens very little; his retrospection relies throughout on the movement of time, rather than particular traits or any ruling passion, for its narrative trellis.

The episodic recollections of all six volumes are often extremely beautiful. To read of the lonely young Londoner's accidental encounter, at the Regent's Park zoo, with his old, defensive friend Wirgie, or of Sherston sitting in a dugout, "tired and wakeful and soaked and muddy from [his] patrol, while one candle made unsteady brown shadows in the gloom" is to experience moments of great and quiet power. In each set of recollections the opacity of the central figure's character is as appealing as it is frustrating. The presentation, like the personality, tantalizes; both excite, entice, and somehow defeat the reader. T. S. Eliot's remark that Henry James "had a mind so fine that no idea could violate it"—offered as a kind of awed compliment—could be applied, in something of the same spirit, to all Sassoon's books of memory.

On his American tour, Sassoon stood and talked with Carl Sandburg on the roof of a large building in Chicago during a sunset. Years later in *Siegfried's Journey* he took exception to Sandburg's definition of poetry as "a series of explanations of life, fading off into horizons too swift for explanations," raising the following Frost-like objections: " 'Explanations of life' should be evolved and stated once and for all, not incontinently ejaculated in blissful immunity from the restrictions of versecraft." Sassoon's own metrics may have been anachronistically regular, but his prose recollections exhibit just the formlessness he criticizes above. That they do will impress the reader of all six volumes less as an aesthetic decision than as a psychological inevitability.

———

The *Imperator* (a ship confiscated from the Germans by the Allied governments) brought Sassoon home from New York to Southampton in the summer of 1920. He was the same man who, six years before in London, could be irresolutely "reduced to boarding an omnibus just to see what sort of places it went to." It is unsettling and wondrous that gunfire, celebrity, and the simple accrual of years made so little difference to the unformed spirit of the thirty-four-year-old man set before the reader's eyes for one last look. The man in his late fifties who puts him there says that he may, even in these "real" memoirs, be rendering him "stupider than he actually was" in an attempt "at unity of effect," an admission that indicates his own belief in a substantial difference between the pliant youth and the matured autobiographer. In fact, there wasn't much of one.

Sassoon says that the self who stood in a sunny Trafalgar Square one day after his arrival from America "realized that he had come to the end of the journey on which he had set out when he enlisted in the army six years before. And, though he wasn't clearly conscious of it, time has since proved that there was nothing for him to do but begin all over again." But if he did begin again, it was mostly to explore his "impercipient past." Certainly nothing to equal the literary impact of *Counter-Attack* was ever again to come from his pen. He went home from that Saturday afternoon in London more to recall life than to live it; his uncertain efforts toward existence were mostly over, and a sort of afterlife had begun. After his peculiar relationship with the aesthete Stephen Tennant, and unhappy marriage to Hester Gatty, Siegfried Sassoon would end up as the hermit of Heytesbury.

In the final pages of *Siegfried's Journey,* he speculates:

Once in his lifetime, perhaps, a man may be the instrument through which something constructive emerges, whether it be genius giving birth to an original idea or the anonymous mortal who makes the most of an opportunity which will never recur. It is for the anonymous ones that I have my special feeling. I like to think of them remembering the one time when they were involved in something unusual or important—when, probably without knowing it at the time, they, as it were, wrote their single masterpiece, never to perform anything comparable again. Then they were fully alive, living above themselves, and discovering powers they hadn't been aware of. For a moment they stood in the transfiguring light of dramatic experience. And nothing ever happened to them afterwards. They were submerged by human uneventfulness. It is only since I got into my late fifties that I have realized these great tracts of insignificance in people's lives. My younger self scornfully rejected the phrase "getting through life" as reprehensible. That I now accept it with an equanimity which amounts almost to affection is my way of indicating the contrast between our states of mind. The idea of oblivion attracts me; I want, after life's fitful fever, to sleep well.

The older autobiographer is just giving final intellectual acceptance to what, for all its fitful rebellions and genuine heroism, was the essentially passive temper and practice of his youth. The later perspective isn't so long as the older Sassoon thinks; nor is the sensibility so different. The narrative lacunae, present-tense reveries, and watercolored judgments found in the autobiographies all spring from the mental and emotional habits of his younger days. The dreaming and tentative boy-poet was not meant to become a thinker at thirty-four or even fifty-nine. To say that this is a limitation in his character is to say very little, because it is also the key to that character's unusual beauty. There was something permanently inviolate and unreachable about it, even in the most exciting and dangerous circumstances.

It took a higher power to break the spell. God came to him late, but succeeded in transporting him fully and finally. Religion brought his last volumes of verse new life, and he awaited the next world with far more sustained ambition and interest than he ever really displayed toward this one. But that is another, and better, story.

Babbitt Redux

CALVIN COOLIDGE PRESIDED over the American Twenties like a Latin teacher manning the punch bowl: He didn't like the dancing, and he didn't get the music, but the kids were basically all right, so he pursed his lips and let them party. He was, according to William Allen White, a Puritan in Babylon.

Actually, there were two Puritans there. The second was Sinclair Lewis, an altogether more sophisticated scold, a small-town boy turned cosmopolite, who between 1920 and 1929 scorched the national landscape and pride with five programmatic novels: *Main Street, Babbitt, Arrowsmith, Elmer Gantry* and *Dodsworth*. Lewis chose Big Themes (Conformity, Religious Hucksterism, Knowledge Versus Commerce) the way James Michener picks out geographic entities, and throughout all five books he sprinkled, like itching powder, a host of American irritants that included boosterism, Prohibition, the endless *talk* of Prohibition ("the one required topic"), public speaking, press agentry, statistics, standardization, pep, baseball and the Republican Party.

"Their life," he writes of some minor married characters, "was dominated by suburban bacchanalia of alcohol, nicotine, gasoline, and kisses." These are the kind of things that a half-century or so later would make John Updike's Harry Angstrom feel that "all in all this is the happiest fucking country the world has ever seen," but Lewis approaches them with all the affection of Savonarola. He was a one-man cultural elite who, by the end of the decade, had produced his five-part symphony of sourness, a body of work that would take a permanent, deserved place in American literature, but not before its author's reputation, along with the stock market, plunged off the ledge.

It has taken ten years for the Library of America to get around to including Lewis in its handsome series of national classics; even Jack London and Frank Norris made it in before he did. But this fall, with the single-volume reissue of *Main Street* and *Babbitt,* Sinclair Lewis will once again be taking American readers to the woodshed.

Main Street was published in 1920, the year "a Mr. W. G. Harding, of Marion, Ohio, was appointed President of the United States." This story of Gopher Prairie (more or less Lewis's native Sauk Centre, Minnesota) announces itself with typical sarcastic overkill: "Main Street is the climax of civilization. That this Ford car might stand in front of the Bon Ton Store, Hannibal invaded Rome and Erasmus wrote in Oxford cloisters."

Fortunately, Lewis believed in building his books around a single character, and *Main Street* is brought under control by its heroine, Carol Milford, an idealistic young woman who has studied library science in Chicago and worked in St. Paul. When she marries Dr. Will Kennicott, she must resign herself to a life in Gopher Prairie, which she greets much as the young Hillary Rodham must have greeted Fayetteville, Arkansas:

> Main Street with its two-story brick shops, its story-and-a-half wooden residences, its muddy expanse from concrete walk to walk, its huddle of Fords and lumber-wagons, was too small to absorb her. ... They were so small and weak, the little brown houses. They were shelters for sparrows, not homes for warm laughing people.

Carol throws herself into a series of "reforms" for Gopher Prairie, everything from beautification projects to serious social work, though she knows from the start that her dreams are "hopeless." For 486 pages, she stumbles between resignation and renewed faith, puzzling the town and trying the patience of her good-natured husband. (Lewis's marriages can be wonderfully convincing. The spouses, usually incapable of serious communication, are frequently on to each other.) By the end of the book, Carol's only accomplishment is the honorableness of her defeat:

> I do not admit that Main Street is as beautiful as it should be! I do not admit that Gopher Prairie is greater or more generous than Europe! I do not admit that dishwashing is enough to satisfy all women! I may not have fought the good fight, but I have kept the faith.

To what sensible purpose, a reader is never sure.

What Carol shares with most of Lewis's principal characters is a desire for admiration, a slightly guilty sense of superiority, and that peculiarly American conundrum known as the pursuit of happiness: "She tried to be content, which was a contradiction in terms." Happiness is what most of Lewis's people seek, in fitful, self-deluding ways. Only Elmer Gantry, his most gorgeous creation, that self-adoring glutton for power and adulation, has anything like relentlessness; otherwise, Lewis gave to American literature a gallery of ditherers. Dr. Martin Arrowsmith, attempting devotion to pure science against the blandishments of money and fame, is really an eternal protégé, chasing one false mentor after another. Babbitt, the great American blowhard, "stopped smoking at least once a month. He went through with it like the solid citizen he was: admitted the evils of tobacco, courageously made resolves, laid out plans to check the vice, tapered off his allowance of cigars, and expounded the pleasures of virtuousness to everyone he met. He did everything, in fact, except stop smoking." When a business and marital crisis takes sympathetic Sam Dodsworth, the automobile magnate, to Europe, this man, "apparently as dependable as an old Newfoundland," realizes he isn't very sure of anything; but once he knows what he wants, he seems afraid to take it home.

If tragic drama required its heroes to persist in self-delusion, the novel, since its beginnings in the eighteenth century, has always demanded of its protagonists a growth in knowledge. The lack of much emotional development in Lewis's characters may make for a certain psychological realism, but it also results in narrative tedium. These very long books consist largely of characters who are constantly lapsing back into being themselves, opening and shutting like morning glories. It is odd that novels with such attitude, such thematic edge, should be so shapeless, so spasmodic and repetitious. If Carol is to suffer petty annoyances from Main Street's shopkeepers, she must suffer them three times in two pages or else, Lewis seems to fear, his point will not be taken. Even *Dodsworth,* which has richer writing and more emotional shading than the other four novels, is really a 350-page short story. The truth is that Lewis's narrative economy was every bit as lazily unsupervised as the larger one in the hands of Coolidge and Andrew Mellon.

Still, even if his books are distinguished chiefly by the *saturation* effect that Henry James noted in the novels of Arnold Bennett and H. G. Wells, there are plenty of skillful tricks that a reader will find swimming inside them. Lewis is to slang what Mark Twain is to dialect. He has a grotesque facility for reproducing it, a talent like playing the saw or cracking knuckles. The listener concedes the skill being displayed while begging the performer to stop. Whether it's Elmer Gantry's sermons (he has one called "Whoa Up, Youth!") or the patter of Babbitt's little manicurist ("[B]elieve me, I know how to hop those birds! I just give um the north and south and ask um, 'Say, who do you think you're talking to?' and they fade away like love's young nightmare"), Lewis has some of the sharpest nails on the American blackboard. The British edition of *Babbitt* even required a glossary.

Lewis is not memorably metaphorical, but he bats out good lines steadily enough to keep his place in the literary lineup and avoid being traded by posterity to Sociology or Historical Curiosity. A colleague of Arrowsmith's has "put on weight and infallibility," and the late-night conversationalists at a Gopher Prairie party "[sit] up with gaiety as with a corpse."

As befitting a doctor's son, his great scenes tend to be medical: Martin Arrowsmith racing to another town in the middle of the night to get antitoxin for a child with diphtheria; Carol Kennicott assisting her husband at a kitchen-table amputation ("It was not the blood but the grating of the surgical saw on the living bone that broke her").

The medical episodes complement Lewis's essentially clinical interest in the human species, which is further evident in his naturalistic descriptions: Some rural deacons in *Elmer Gantry* are shown "wiping their mouths with the hairy backs of their paws," and Babbitt often seems to be a creature who has just exchanged flippers for opposable thumbs. In the bathtub, he is

> a plump, smooth, pink, baldish, podgy goodman, robbed of the importance of spectacles, squatting in breast-high water, scraping his lather-smeared cheeks with a safety-razor like a tiny lawn-mower, and with melancholy dignity clawing through the water to recover a slippery and active piece of soap.

Nature prompts the grumpy novelist into passages more obligatory than observant; we know that spring has arrived in *Arrowsmith* because "the first insects . . . were humming." Lewis is brilliantly alert to his human creatures' habitats, but when it comes to their interiors, he doesn't so much describe as vandalize them. Here is part of the inventory for Mrs. Cass's parlor:

One small square table contained a card-receiver of painted china with a rim of wrought and gilded lead, a Family Bible, Grant's Memoirs, the latest novel by Mrs. Gene Stratton Porter, a wooden model of a Swiss chalet which was also a bank for dimes, a polished abalone shell holding one black-headed pin and one empty spool, a velvet pin-cushion in a gilded metal slipper with "Souvenir of Troy, N.Y." stamped on the toe, and an unexplained red glass dish which had warts.

Every object in Fran Dodsworth's bedroom is a dozen steps beyond Mrs. Cass in price and taste, but each one is just as remorselessly typifying. One can no more deny the brilliance of these catalogues than one can feel entirely comfortable—even in the case of the monstrous Fran—with their heartlessness.

There are places in fictional America that one shouldn't even want to visit—Faulkner's Yoknapatawpha County, Kennedy's Albany, O'Hara's Gibbsville—but where one might actually consider living, so rich with unmanageable life did their creators make them. But Lewis's locales—the village of Gopher Prairie, the state of Winnemac, the city of Zenith (really Minneapolis, home to the Babbitts and the Dodsworths and, for a time, the Arrowsmiths)—are all aggressively uninhabitable, made by an author bent on being a sort of anti-chamber of commerce. (You can add Rotarians to that list of American irritants.)

He found nearly as much material in his handmade universe as the aforementioned writers found in theirs, but across Lewis's landscape the temperature almost never gets above freezing. As a satirist, he is more a chilly Juvenal than a forgiving Horace. In our own day, his opposite would be Tom Wolfe, whose affection for all he attacks is so obvious as to sometimes risk undermining his enterprise. But in the course of Lewis's long novels, what's profitably withering can sometimes turn unimaginatively cruel: What on earth is so bad about the poor rubes of Gopher Prairie having a few laughs over the Mack Sennett kind of comedy playing at the Rosebud Movie Palace? Yes, Lewis gives Will Kennicott a sensible rejoinder to Carol's disapproval, but read Chapter 16 and decide whose view the novelist really shares.

There are gentle moments in the books, though they tend to be carried in and deposited like a hot towel by some minor character who disappears before you can thank him. Perhaps the nicest person in all Lewis's work is Arrowsmith's first wife, Leora, whom the novelist characterizes, with a certain astonishment, as having "an immense power of accepting people as they were."

The decision to combine *Babbitt* with *Main Street* reaffirms one's good opinion of the Library of America's editorial judgments. Not only do these two books hold up better than the others; rereading them reveals that they weren't quite what we thought. If *Main Street* now seems as much about feminism as small towns, *Babbitt* turns out to be a victim of its own fame: So much has its hero's surname come to stand for the middle-American philistine that we have forgotten all the hints of something more in this character, forgotten how the book depicts the first midlife crisis in modern American literature. *Dodsworth,* which came along seven years later, is about one, too, but Sam Dodsworth's is provoked from without—by the takeover of his company and his wife's outrageous behavior. Babbitt's bubbles up almost entirely from within, from the wellsprings of a thwarted romantic self.

He has a dream life (this is probably what makes him such prey to the subliminal nature of advertising), and its chief denizen is a "fairy child . . . so white, so eager! She cried that he was gay and valiant, that she would wait for him, that they would sail. . . ." She regularly visits his sleep, the emotional world apart from his realty business, his loud friends, his quarrelsome children, his dull wife. There are moments when Babbitt, so frightened of loneliness, seems almost like a Cheever hero, experiencing a rush of well-being or dread, a sense of something more, in suburban twilight. His fantasies are stunted by his circumstances (he pictures heaven as being "rather like an excellent hotel with a private garden"), but he has a susceptibility to beauty—including such beauty as the city of Zenith has to offer: "the storming lights of down-town; parked cars with ruby tail-lights; white arched entrances to movie theaters, like frosty mouths of winter caves; electric signs. . . . He loved his city with passionate wonder." We've always known that Sinclair Lewis ridiculed and tormented George Babbitt; what we've forgotten is that he sometimes envied him.

Babbitt's crisis renders him temporarily "converted to dissipation" and dangerous thinking. After carousing with questionable women and expressing too much sympathy for some strikers, he needs to be paid a visit by the vigilantes of the Good Citizens' League. Being a Lewis hero, he eventually falls back into being himself, even to the extent of joining the detestable League. ("But, dear," his wife had warned, "if you don't join, people might criticize you.") Still, Babbitt's rebellion has left him with a smidgen more generosity than he had before, enough at least to approve of his son's decision to elope:

> "Now, for heaven's sake, don't repeat this to your mother, or she'd remove what little hair I've got left, but practically, I've never done a single thing I've wanted to in my whole life! I don't know's I've accomplished anything except just get along."

One finishes the novel thinking that Lewis has understood this one of his ditherers better than the others, perhaps because the author had traces of the sloganeering businessman within himself. In a letter written to Alfred Harcourt on July 12, 1921, Sinclair Lewis sounds a good deal like George Follansbee Babbitt:

> He's started—*Babbitt*—and I think he's going to be a corker. I've been working on him for a week now. . . . I think that Babbitt is the best name for him—and the best title for the book as well. One remembers name-titles really better than apparently more striking titles, and it so causes the public to remember the name of the central character that he is more likely to be discussed.

Serious discussion of Babbitt subsided long ago, but we've been mentioning him for seventy years. He is the fictive abbreviation for a whole historical moment and, just as surely as Uriah Heep and Iago, an entire personality type. By these things alone, he is Lewis's guarantor of immortality.

In his speech accepting the Nobel Prize in 1930, Lewis took the trouble to mention novelists he thought more deserving than he, among them Theodore Dreiser and Willa Cather. In dedicating his books, he also tended to honor his fellow writers. *Babbitt* was for Edith Wharton and *Elmer Gantry* for H. L. Mencken, whom Babbitt himself regarded as the author of "highly improper essays, making fun of the church and all the decencies." Mencken returned the compliment, correctly prophesying that Babbitt "should become as real as Jack Dempsey or Charlie Schwab." So much reality did Lewis's books have throughout the Twenties that each new one was almost compelled to refer to the ones before. "Lord, how that book of Lewis', 'Main Street,' did bore me," says the otherwise sensitive Philip McGarry in *Elmer Gantry;* and when Sam Dodsworth is feeling self-doubt, he reminds himself that, aside from not being an Elk, a deacon or a Rotarian, "He was not a Babbitt. . . ."

If forced to find Lewis's contemporary equivalent, one might settle on Gore Vidal, another (more gifted) misanthrope who ended up in Italy. It was inevitable that Lewis himself would go quickly out of fashion. How could anyone in 1932, reading *Main Street* to pass the time in a bread line, sympathize with Carol Kennicott's perception of Gopher Prairie's bigger houses as "soundly uninteresting symbols of prosperity"? Lewis may have been right in everything he said about the Twenties, but who wouldn't prefer them to the decade that came after? Even Lewis must have been left nostalgic: The novels he managed to publish in the Thirties include such completely forgotten ones as *Work of Art* and *The Prodigal Parents.*

Nevertheless, even if American life is lacking in second acts, no one can dispute the ability of the country's decades to revive themselves, like summer-stock productions. There were plenty of Levittown wives who could have responded to *Main Street* in 1955, and some of the fund-raising rhetoric in *Elmer Gantry* ("In making my own appeal for contributions, I use 'love offering' ") seems like a sound track by Tammy Faye Bakker. We are told by Lewis that, in the false economy of the Twenties, Babbitt "made nothing in particular," like a lot of other men, then and sixty years later, who "were urging on nerve-yelping bodies and parched brains . . . hustling to catch trains, to hustle through the vacations which the hustling doctors had ordered." What goes around comes around, again and again. In Sauk Centre, Minnesota, Main Street is still Main Street, but the street on which he was born is now Sinclair Lewis Avenue, an occasional tourist destination whose rechristening proves that the business of America is, still, business.

U.S.A. Today:
Dos Passos Reconsidered

November 1996

"Dos' *1919* is knocking people cold," Dawn Powell admitted to her diary, with a touch of envy, in March of 1932. The reception of the second novel in his *U.S.A.* trilogy made it clear that John Dos Passos (1896–1970) was "no longer a promising writer but as arrived as he can ever be—like Lewis or Dreiser. . . ." By now he's barely on the syllabus, let alone in anyone's actual fund of reading, but with the issuance of *U.S.A.* in a single massive volume, the Library of America treats Dos Passos to the literary equivalent of video release, letting him join those other two long-since-departed arrivals in a Pléiade that now runs to nearly a hundred titles.

Never much skilled at the creation of characters (try to name one), Dos Passos preferred to concentrate on the churning panorama of America between McKinley and Hoover. But a return to *U.S.A.* reminds one that the main portions of all three novels (*The 42nd Parallel, 1919, The Big Money*) are headed with the names of a dozen recurring figures whose individual fortunes carry the narrative and paint the big picture, and one can only begin making sense of this triple-decker with a partial survey of its principal players.

Fainy "Mac" McCreary and Joe Williams are the working-class heroes, the first an itinerant printer, book salesman, "pearldiver" (dish washer), Wobbly sympathizer and, finally, bystander to Zapata's rebellion in Mexico. "I wanta study an' work for things," Mac tells his freight-hopping friend Ike Hall: "you know what I mean, not to get to be a goddam slavedriver but for socialism and the revolution an' like that. . . ." The less enlightened Joe, a big galoot of a merchant mariner, exists mostly to be knocked around by the capitalist system. Prey to shipwreck, false arrest, unemployment and VD, he is a sort of walking folk song, a brawler whose literary cousins fill the novels of London and Farrell.

126

In the years leading up to *U.S.A.,* Dos Passos's left-wing credentials were well in order (on the board of *New Masses;* author of a famous pamphlet in defense of Sacco and Vanzetti), but the America he chronicled was never the one despised by latter-day radicals. It was rough but redeemable (by socialism), and it left even a critical observer more awestruck than sour. (Just contrast Dos Passos's nation of immigrants with the one grotesquely imagined in E. Annie Proulx's new novel, *Accordion Crimes,* where America is less a WPA mural than a Hieronymous Bosch painting.) In *U.S.A.* even a put-upon radical like Ben Compton probably means it when he says, "It's a great life if you don't weaken."

Dos Passos's "depiction of women," as the academic matriarchy likes to phrase it, is distinctly on the harsh side: there are far more money-mad graspers than idealists here. Eleanor Stoddard is a Chicago stockyard worker's daughter who will lie to herself and anyone else as she claws upward through art classes, a lace shop and a job at Marshall Field's. With Eveline Hutchins, a wellborn dilettante from North Shore Drive, she opens a decorating business and then designs theatrical costumes, an enterprise that soon takes them to New York. It's hard to read about these two without thinking how much more Scott Fitzgerald could have done with them, but Dos Passos does manage something essential by making Eleanor the mistress of J. Ward Moorehouse, his on-the-make public-relations pioneer.

Moorehouse is the novel's perpetual-motion machine, manufacturing nothing out of nothing. Believing his own bromides about p.r.'s contributions to "industrial peace," he shows up at the Mexican revolution; committee meetings in Washington; the Paris Peace Conference; or just his office at the Graybar Building in New York, where he looks at the ceiling, "his big jowly face as expressionless as a cow's," thinking how much more attractive patent medicines would be if they were renamed something else. His faithful secretary is Janey Williams—Joe's sister—who in 1915 tells the boss about the torpedoing of her brother's ship and hears him respond with some words "about being patriotic and saving civilization and the historic beauties of Rheims cathedral."

The closest Dos Passos comes to an autobiographical analogue is the character Dick Savage, who after Harvard joins the ambulance corps in Europe. For the vaguely left-leaning Dick and some of his friends, the Great War seems like a drunken lark, their months at the Peace Conference a junior year abroad. "It's a magnificent tragic show," he says; "the Paris fog smells of strawberries . . . the gods don't love us but we'll die young just the same. . . . Who said I was sober?" He'll never be fully sober again, certainly not when he's in New York working for Moorehouse and indulging the self-pity that starts coming out of him at the end of *1919*, just before they bury the Unknown Soldier: "I wish I was hard enough so that I didn't give a damn about anything." Given the number of pages spent on them, Moorehouse and Savage don't come terribly alive, but with the two of them Dos Passos had made an early sighting of an American subspecies for whom adolescence would be a constant instead of a phase. They are the Ur-Boomers, coasting across the landscape.

In *The Big Money*—even with Wall Street and Prohibition and conspicuous consumption to cover—the author manages to slow down and tell the tale of Charley Anderson at a little more leisurely pace than usual. First seen at the end of *The 42nd Parallel,* Charley, a hard-drinking, whoring Swede out of Fargo, returns after four hundred pages—having become an air ace in the war—to begin making money in aviation and the stock market. Vainly pursuing the glamorous Doris Humphries, who would prefer an exiled Russian prince, he winds up unhappily married to someone else and on his way toward ruin and delusion in the arms of Margo Dowling, a minor vaudevillian and eventual Hollywood star, a tough little con artist who prefigures some of the dames in Raymond Chandler and John O'Hara: "They made Savannah late that night and felt so good they got so tight there the manager threatened to run them out of the big old hotel. That was when Margo threw an ashtray through the transom."

And then, after twelve hundred pages, all of them, and a bunch of others besides, are just gone.

It's hard to say why one set of literary characters proves more evanescent than another, but Dos Passos's were partly suffocated by their packaging. Sixty years after its completion, *U.S.A.* is remembered chiefly for its incidentals, the various "devices" that garnish the main text like elaborate epigraphs. The trilogy's sixty-eight "Newsreels," each a page or two long, combine headlines (both serious and tabloid) with snatches of popular song:

**GERMANS BEATEN AT RIGA   GRATEFUL PARISIANS
CHEER MARSHALS OF FRANCE**

U.S.A. TODAY: DOS PASSOS RECONSIDERED

Oh a German officer crossed the Rhine
He liked the women and loved the wine
Hankypanky parleyvoo

———

PITEOUS PLAINT OF WIFE TELLS OF RIVAL'S WILES

The effect must once have been fresh, even dazzling, but at this remove it seems more lazy than enlivening, as if with these quoted scraps Dos Passos had given over the literary creation of time and place to the efficiency experts he elsewhere decries. (The whole text is dappled with silly fusions—"downattheheels," "powerfullybuilt"—that seem to reflect some long-ago belief in linguistic progress, like Shavian spelling or Esperanto.)

The "Camera Eyes" are the worst, swatches of avant-garde kitsch (what's more quaint than "modernism"?), in which the author, through a lot of unpunctuated Joycean singsong, remembers the way he saw things himself. Here is Dos Passos recalling the Russo-Japanese war from his own eight-years-old point of view: "and we played the battle of Port Arthur in the bathtub and the water leaked down through the drawingroom ceiling and it was altogether too bad. . . ." These brief, interminable bits read like Steinbeck attempting Faulkner, to no clear purpose besides a sense of obligation to prevailing trends. Their subjectivity ("Camera Eye" is a complete misnomer) only contradicts Dos Passos's basic aim of conveying the roll and sweep of whole decades and continents. His art really pointed *backwards,* to the nineteenth-century novel; its up-to-date look was mostly a jazzy camouflage. Today's readers will be tempted to skip most of the little inter-sections, the way they do the cetological chapters in *Moby-Dick.*

The exception among the "devices" is the thumbnail biographies, both scathing and reverent, of actual figures. These are still well worth reading—though better as a separate collection than interruptions to the narrative. This celebrity *Spoon River* features, among many others, Eugene V. Debs, Isadora Duncan, Joe Hill, Edison, Veblen, and "Meester Veelson," that hero of the Europeans, "talking to save his faith in words, talking to save his faith in the League of Nations, talking to save his faith in himself, in his father's God."

Dos Passos declared that "mostly *U.S.A.* is the speech of the people," and its thousand-plus pages do clang with the sound of them, out on the street and in one another's faces, their group names—Bohunks and Polaks and Shanty Irish—less offensive than the nascent market-tested language of Moorehouse and the p.r. men. In subject matter and descriptions, these three novels still display a grit that hasn't fully lost its effect; they brim over with prostitution, adultery, abortion, armpits. Dos Passos can't show a burlesque girl's gams without zeroing in on their vaccination mark.

Alas, the entire production moves with the curious stasis of a marathon dance. A certain shapelessness may be part of the point (these books can no more truly begin or end than a newspaper, or history itself), but the protagonists' rushed, episodic adventures weary a reader. Even when they're thinking, Dos Passos's people never seem to stop walking, and their sheer number forces the author to stop and restart his book, over and over, just to keep us current with all of them. World War I seems to break out a half dozen times, sacrificing, to say the least, a measure of narrative impact. A handful of fine scenes and phrases ("the dark theater full of girls and jazz") can't make up for the effortful bulk of the whole, or for its occasional just plain clumsiness: no one can run down stairs "three at a time."

U.S.A. concludes with a kind of *New Masses* cartoon: above a lonely hitchhiker some coast-to-coast air passengers "sit pretty," except for one who symbolically "sickens and vomits into the carton container the steak and mushrooms he ate in New York." In fact, as he wrote these lines in 1936, Dos Passos had already begun his long journey toward conservatism. The radical had been feeling prematurely anti-Communist even before the Moscow Trials, and Soviet behavior in the Spanish Civil War only further dampened his leftist ardor. By the 1960s he would be pro-Goldwater and writing for *National Review,* a career turn presented as a form of senility by most literary historians of our time. "Henry Ford as an old man / is a passionate antiquarian," the author himself had written in one of the thumbnail biographies; the irony of his own retreat from millenarianism, however principled, could not have been lost on him.

His reputation will have to content itself with the sort of *pro bono* resurrection offered by the Library of America, whose volumes, complete with page-marking ribbon and rustling paper, have the feel of a missal. The series' relative lack of footnotes does suggest a sensible hope that the books will be read instead of studied, but one suspects Dos Passos's will simply be shelved: authentic literary revivals (the sort that dark horse Dawn Powell is now enjoying) happen less by deliberateness than little accidents of the Zeitgeist. Nonetheless, it's right to give these three volumes two cheers, if only for the way they remind us of a time when private literary enterprises could be as grandly programmatic as the biggest public-works projects, of an era when the Great American Novel seemed not only achievable but important.

Scrappy Days:
The Life of H. L. Mencken

*January 1993 ⃰

HE WAS A literary machine, self-designed and chiefly for killing. Shortly after the century turned, H. L. Mencken says he was "full of lust to function, and before I was twenty-five it was already plain that my functioning would take the form of a sharp and more or less truculent dissent from the *mores* of my country." His literary autobiography, published now for the first time, amounts to about 40 percent of an enormous manuscript Mencken dictated between 1942 and 1948, when he suffered a stroke. It covers the years before 1924 and *The American Mercury,* the period when he was editing *The Smart Set* with George Jean Nathan and having a personal success with *A Book of Prefaces* and *The American Language.* It is the memorable record of a killer's progress, a body count conducted with Whistlerian relish ("In March 1909, I made another violent enemy"), even as it insists its author "was far more eager to discover and proclaim merit."

Every susceptibility of the booboisie and intelligentsia is once more on display here. As Mencken shoots them down again, like carnival ducks, the reader watches nostalgically. He refights Mencken's wars against "comstockery" and the "Anglomaniacs," laps up his contempt for anyone caught mucking about in "the swamps of the uplift," and appreciates his still-amusing contempt for the literary seacoast of Bohemia:

> *Ulysses* seemed to be deliberately mystifying and mainly puerile, and I have never been able to get over a suspicion that Joyce concocted it as a kind of vengeful hoax. Writing excellent stuff in conventional patterns, he got very little attention and was so hard up that he had to

⃰Review of *My Life as Author and Editor,* edited and with an introduction by Jonathan Yardley (Knopf).

go on teaching languages to keep alive, but from the moment he took to the literary bizarreries of Greenwich Village and began to push them further than Greenwich Village (or even the Left Bank) had ever dared, he was a made man.

There are the incidental bashings, too ("New Orleans and Providence, both intellectual slums"), compulsive animadversions from a man who says, correctly, that "moral indignation . . . was foreign to [his] nature."

My Life as Author and Editor stands, for better and worse, as a matchless guide to American literary life in the years just before and after World War I. Mencken's superb retrospection introduces readers to such forgotten writers and literary personalities as the short-story writer Lilith Benda and the poet (later publisher) John Farrar:

> He was slim and graceful and had the peaches-and-cream complexion of a young girl not yet condemned to night work. As a result, he became at once the darling of all the fat women who like to rub noses with authors, and in a little while he was touring the country haranguing the women's clubs and driving the old girls crazy. Of that dismal trade there was never any more successful practitioner, at least in my time.

Benda's and Farrar's names are comparatively enduring; Mencken lists fourteen others that he can find "over and over again in the disintegrating files of the *Smart Set*" without being able to remember a thing about any of them.

This says a mouthful about obscurity, and certainly nothing against Mencken's powers of recall, which are so formidably specific that they produce not only a peerless record of his trade and era, but also—even after Jonathan Yardley's yeoman slashing of the manuscript—some awfully dull reading. Much less about advertising lineage, sales figures, and the number of incoming manuscripts would still have gone a long way. Even the more interesting tales of business rivalry and shifting ownership sometimes make a reader feel as if he's been locked in a library seventy years from now and condemned to read page 3 of every issue of *The New York Observer:* When Hastings Harcourt "was introduced into the business and began to take a more and more active hand in it, the father's partner, Brace (Howe had meanwhile retired), and the principal employees were full of disquiet." But the book never takes long in coming back to life with blunt truths, small cruelties and amusing lines: "Claire [Burke] added the detail that [Willard H. Wright's] addiction had made him impotent, and thereby caused a rift in the lute of their domestic felicity."

The portraits Mencken offers of still-read writers are the portions of text exhibiting true shapeliness and polish, because with these he's willing to get ahead of himself, to jump into the future to finish them off. He shows the naive, awkward Theodore Dreiser lurching from one publisher and woman to another, hurt that Mencken's admiration for his work does not extend to personal approval: "he was . . . upset by my skeptical attitude toward his removal to Greenwich Village and his arty life there with [the actress] Kirah Markham. While he lived uptown with [his wife] Sarah he led a thoroughly bourgeois life." Dreiser must have realized at some point that Mencken's championship of his books was as much a matter of personal ambition as disinterested homage. Around 1909, Mencken says, he needed "an author who was completely American in his themes and his point of view, who dealt with people and situations of wide and durable interest, who had something to say about his characters that was not too obvious, who was nevertheless simple enough to be understood by the vulgar, and who knew how to concoct and tell an engrossing story." *Jennie Gerhardt* came along two years later.

Mencken takes up F. Scott Fitzgerald at the outset of his alcoholic ruin ("so shy a young fellow by nature, that he not only mistered Nathan and me, but also sirred us"), and makes every stop along Sinclair Lewis's downhill slide, saving his best shots for Lewis's second wife, Dorothy Thompson:

> the true daughter of her Methodist pa—a tin pot messiah with an inflamed egoism that was wholly unameliorated by humor. Her eight years abroad as the correspondent for a third-rate newspaper had filled her with the conviction that she knew all that was worth knowing about the political, social and economic problems of the world, and her views, stated freely, had all the confidence of divine revelation.

A letter Mencken wrote to Ezra Pound in November 1936—"You made your great mistake when you abandoned the poetry business, and set up shop as a wizard in general practice"—makes one realize that Mencken traveled something of the same route himself (he was writing triolets in 1900) with greater cunning and steadier success. Each one's anti-Semitism, however, came from a different mental precinct. Pound's was a predictable ingredient in the simmering crackpot of his "system." Mencken's, as this book amply shows, was something else—an almost physical compulsion, a Tourette-like discharge of poison he seemed doomed to vent at regular intervals while the proud machine of his judgments kept chugging on and laying down the law. This was no incidental flaw, no posthumous discovery limited to his private diaries (he was called on the matter as early as 1930), and not something that can be explained away by making allowance for the era and circumstances in which he lived. "Jew-like"; "a Jewish law firm called Fishbein, Goldfarb, Spritzwasser and Fishbein, or something of the sort"; "prehensile kikes"—and so on and on. These are less the genteel barbarities of another age than the eternal chant of the crazy who's just boarded the subway car.

One would be hard put to find any book more indicative of this particular hatred's being, literally, a mental illness, one that in Mencken's case led to breathtaking abandonments of logic. In a single paragraph of his admiring treatment of his publisher, Alfred A. Knopf, Mencken says, first: "I had little if any prejudice against Jews myself." Six lines later we are told that Knopf "showed a certain amount of the obnoxious tactlessness of his race." Twenty pages later, in a discussion of the actor-producer Edgar Selwyn, cause precedes effect: "there was but little suggestion of the Jewish in his appearance and manner, and I got on with him very well." Finally, three pages before the book breaks off, this risible imparting of information: "Isaac Goldberg, like DeCasseres, was a Jew. . . ."

Mr. Yardley, who seems to have thought about this issue honestly and long, reaches the following conclusion: "if by the standards of our day Mencken was anti-Semitic, by those of his own he was not. Inasmuch as he lived in his time and not in ours, it is by this we should judge and, I believe, acquit him." But Mr. Yardley acknowledges the existence of "legitimate objections" to this view, and one must raise strong ones here. Mencken's anti-Semitism, by any definition, and in any time or place, was *spectacular*—gaudy, energetic, and marked by, to use a Mencken term, "salacity." His editor's excuses are overly sophisticated, and they're offered with a certain embarrassment: "there is the old some-of-his-best-friends argument, which in Mencken's case carries considerable force." To Yardley's credit, he has presented this uncivilized material in a civilized way, taking care "not to excise any material that might be unfavorable to Mencken in that regard," and finally to let the reader make up his own mind.

Like many witty people, Mencken lacked humor. Even worse, he was low on normal measures of self-awareness. On this point Mr. Yardley is acute and unsparing: "Mencken's impregnable self-confidence is, to my taste, the least appealing of his traits, suggesting as it does an incapacity for self-doubt or real self-scrutiny." Eventually more conscious of being a symbol than a man, he came to view himself as a petrified phenomenon passing into posterity on a schedule of his own choosing. (The boxes containing the memoir were opened in Baltimore's Enoch Pratt Free Library on January 29, 1991, exactly thirty-five years after the author's death.)

His soundest bit of self-appraisal came in a review of his activities around the time he was thirty-six: "No reasonably attentive reader of my monthly discourses, by the beginning of 1917, could be in any doubt about my fundamental ideas, which were, in the main, scientific rather than moral or aesthetic: I was in favor of the true long before I was in favor of either the good or the beautiful." He reviewed according to standards instead of theories, even if in summarizing his principal one, he chose the other word:

> My central theory was that an author was entitled to choose his own manner, his own weapons. If, having made his choice, he produced a work of genuine vitality, giving a plausible picture of human life as he had seen it, and devoid of fustian and brummagem, then I was for him; but if there was any sign of falseness or affectation in him, then I was against him.

On balance, if we look at his work by his own lights, we should probably be for Mencken—but also not unrelieved to board the train out of Baltimore and get the hell away.

Appointment with O'Hara

December 1990

ALMOST EVERY HOUSE on Parnassus is a triplex. Wordsworth, Coleridge and Blake live behind Keats, Shelley and Byron, who face onto Tennyson, Browning and Arnold. Of such triads do we assemble literary history. Think of the American Renaissance novel and you'll find Hawthorne, Poe and Melville bunched together as its worshiped trinity. Then fast-forward a hundred years and find the Big Three of the American Century: Hemingway, Fitzgerald and Faulkner.

No matter how hard John O'Hara tried out for the trio, he was never allowed to be more than a backup player. Good, even damned good, but not good enough. In talent, they would all concede, he abounded. But too little art and too little doom clung to him. His sentences were tough and efficient, not gorgeously gilded like Fitzgerald's, not dangerous cobras like Faulkner's, not self-parodic spitballs like Papa's. Though he wrote better about the subject than any of the above, he didn't go in for suicide, either the fast- or the slow-motion kind. Drinking oneself to death was common enough among American writers. O'Hara did something rarer: He *quit* drinking, at 48, and his already high productivity shot up even higher. In literary memory he remains a kind of butch, American version of Somerset Maugham—awfully smart, extraordinarily prolific and dependably observant, but belonging to his period, surely, not to the ages.

On Thanksgiving Day John O'Hara would say grace and calculate the percentages. It was the day on which he liked to publish his books:

> Thanksgiving Day is a holiday. You don't go to work. You get up maybe a little later than usual, and have time to read all of your paper —including the book reviews. Then a couple of days after, come the Sunday papers—a chance to read other reviews on one big weekend.

137

Then Monday—who knows?—you can stop off at a store on the way downtown and get the book.

In fact, when it came to O'Hara's sales, it was always the Christmas season: By 1965 there were 20 million copies of his books on the world's night tables. A quarter century later, most of the hardbacks have gone the way of garage sales and almost all of the paperbacks have crumbled.

But try to understand the literary present without him. If you do, you'll fail to figure out a big part of what's going on with some of its conspicuous figures, from John Gregory Dunne (another loud deracinated Irishman and obvious O'Hara pretender) to John Updike, over whom O'Hara's ghost could fight a paternity suit with John Cheever's, to whom custody is usually awarded.

In the years since his death in 1970, O'Hara has pretty much defied resuscitation. Some of the novels and Frank MacShane's 1984 selection of O'Hara's short stories remain on bookstore shelves. But no one seems to be reading him. The recent dustup between Tom Wolfe (who calls for renewed production of the kind of sociological fiction O'Hara wrote) and defenders of the minimalists (who can reproduce brand names but seem willfully ignorant of any social pattern larger than that of a dysfunctional family) sets one to wondering: Why isn't O'Hara seen as a kind of bridge between the two camps? One would think his gift for working in short forms might make him attractive to the postmodern crowd that has found small so beautiful and the story a more natural form of expression than the novel.

All in all, it's a rather insulting excuse for going back to a writer—asking him to help make sense of what came after him. (Especially in the case of this writer, whose epitaph reads in part, "Better than anyone else he told the truth about his time.") But if, twenty years after his death, it's the only street some readers will walk toward O'Hara, they ought to go down it. Because when they get to him, they won't believe their ears.

He was so aware of his gift for speech that he coined "O'Hara's Law, that an author who does not write good dialog is not a first-rate author." In *BUtterfield 8,* Gloria Wandrous has the perfect pitch of a girl trying to stand on her dignity and come off as just a little more educated than she is: "I don't know. What do you want that you've been calling me all over, as you put it, although I don't know where you'd be apt to call me except home." Twenty years after *Appointment in Samarra* (1934), Julian English shows up in a section of *Ten North Frederick* set in 1930, and his voice has such a Lazarene fidelity to what you remember of him—what made him so real in the first place—that you jump a little, as if at that moment the novel's noise-reduction button had been switched on: " 'No,' " he tells Edith Chapin after she admits she won't even try to appreciate her son's talent for jazz piano. " 'You have a Steinway, it isn't even in tune.' "

O'Hara could write a drunk the way only a few actors can play one—convincingly. Consider the tipsy actress in *We're Friends Again* (1960), deciding whether or not to call it a night:

> "Oh, yes. The big *question. Is.* Do we go to Harlem and I can't go on tomorrow night and I give my understudy a break. *Or. Or.* Do I go home to my trundle bed—and you stay out of it, Jim. You're a rat. I mean stay out of my trundle. Nevermore, quoth the raven. Well, what did my understudy ever do for me? So I guess we better go home. Right?"

Beyond dialogue, there was trialogue; O'Hara was a master at the game of keeping three characters talking on the same page. He'd move the shells faster and faster and never let the reader lose track of the pea. But let the reviewers he despised grudgingly acknowledge his gift for speech and he'd throw the bouquet back in their faces for not being big enough: "Many of my critics seem to feel that they have to say, or strongly imply, that my gift for dialog is all I have. . . . I do not believe that a writer who neglects or has not learned to write good dialog can be depended upon for accuracy in his understanding of character. . . ." He understood his characters, all right, perhaps best when he shut them up and put them in their place. Edith Chapin "dressed like a Member, belonging exactly to her class, with a Yale husband in the background, tennis and swimming for exercise, Protestantism for her religion, extravagance nowhere in her character, and discontent never far from her contemplation."

Knowingness—being wised up to the way America operated—was what people read him for. His books form a single great chronicle, the same characters and family histories turning up in them until Gibbsville became more thickly textured, and finally more real, than what it started out as—O'Hara's hometown of Pottsville, Pennsylvania. At home or in the city, he liked to do figure eights of economic and sociological exactitude:

He stopped at a place in Lexington Avenue, bought a bottle of the six-dollar gin, had a drink on Matt, the proprietor, and took a taxi, one of those small, low Philadelphia-made un-American-looking Yellows of that period.

No one could pile up the social, and social-climbing, details the way he could; no one could more reliably tell you which boys would join what fraternity and which girls would go "all the way," a subject O'Hara sang about more often than Sinatra.

Sometimes the knowingness was showoffish and baroque, but more often than not it was a cultural passkey. He forgot nothing. Frank Zachary, the editor of *Town & Country* who in the early 1930s was O'Hara's copyboy at the Pittsburgh *Bulletin-Index,* remembers running into him years later at Brooks Brothers—a store mentioned so frequently in O'Hara's books that he should have been on commission. They got to talking about someone they'd once worked with, and O'Hara "started describing him in detail after detail, down to his diamond stickpin . . . an incredible performance."

Frances Kiernan, a writer and former *New Yorker* editor, says she used to read O'Hara thirty years ago, when she was a teenager, in order "to find out how the world worked." But people don't do that anymore, she says; the information is too dated to be useful, not outdated enough to be exotic. "A writer belongs to his time," O'Hara had his fictional alter ego, Jim Malloy, say in 1960, "and mine is past." It'll be a few more decades, says Kiernan, before O'Hara comes back, the way Edith Wharton (a writer he admired) eventually did. I taught his stories a year or so ago in a writing class at Vassar. The students let themselves be led toward Gibbsville as if it were a huge antique model railroad O'Hara had created. They were duly impressed, though the nature and the scale of the enterprise seemed eccentric, almost frightening, and they were glad to say a quick, polite good-bye to the old man who had made it.

A doctor's son who could have gone to Yale, O'Hara decided not to, choosing instead a lifetime of besotted preoccupation with Ivy League trappings, first from a newspaperman's desk and finally from a house he built himself near Princeton. Maybe keeping an informed distance was good for his art; maybe it let him preserve something on the order of what Malcolm Cowley described as Fitzgerald's "double vision" of his subjects. O'Hara saw himself as an inevitability:

My father was a successful small-town doctor who also made a little money, and I was born and brought up a Catholic. My antecedents, even those who came here in the eighteenth century, were practically all Irish except for a few drops of English and German that it is too late for me to do anything about. All my life I have been rebellious. My father and mother were well-educated people, and I am not. Put those items through an International Business Machine and out comes a card marked Writer.

He was sure his Irishness gave him perspective on the hypocritical country-clubbers who were so often his characters. Actually, he was one of those dangerous, diluted Irishmen who are at their worst when proclaiming their Irishness as their essence. Jim Malloy, for example, gives a barstool speech about a fifth of the way through *BUtterfield 8:*

> "First of all, I am a Mick. I wear Brooks clothes and I don't eat salad with a spoon and I probably could play five-goal polo in two years, but I am a Mick. Still a Mick. . . . We're Micks, we're non-assimilable, we Micks. We've been here, at least some of my family, since before the Revolution—and we produce the perfect gangster type."

This rings so loudly false that you wish the fully assimilated O'Hara had reworked Robert Frost's advice to John F. Kennedy—to be "more Irish than Harvard"—into a plaque for his desk top: "BE LESS IRISH AND MORE YALE."

As an artist (a word he properly insisted on for himself), he wanted to be prized not just for knowingness but for knowledge, which is something else, something a few long stops up from knowingness on the novelist's highway, something en route to wisdom. "Social history," O'Hara once said, "has absolutely no standing in the world of art as I see it." If this knowledge isn't put to the service of character creation, the writer "is converting himself into historian or journalist" and missing the core of the novelist's matter, which is the working of individual human hearts.

During his productive peak, O'Hara read little fiction and seven newspapers a day. For better, and for worse, his early training in deadlines made him a one-draft writer. Frank Zachary recalls his coming into the offices of the *Bulletin-Index* and inserting a blank page into his manual Underwood.

Two and a half hours later he'd have a story ready to be mailed to the *The New Yorker*.

O'Hara found his happiest medium in the novella, the form he is still least known for, even though he wrote several excellent ones, including *The Farmers Hotel* (1951), in which he throws a party for his snowbound characters and then, just when the reader is feeling well fed, makes sure two members of the cast are brutally killed. The three short novels making up the *Sermons and Soda-Water* trilogy (1960) show an astonishing ability to make decades pass steadily and convincingly in a hundred or so pages. But by the time he wrote them, he had too much invested in hating critics to accept their praise; he was still smarting from their response to the 897-page *From the Terrace* (1958). He explained the different receptions this way: "A critic who writes, say, three 500-word reviews a week, is irritated by a *From the Terrace* because after spending all that time—all *what* time?—reading my long novel, he has only the material for a single review. It's as simple and disgusting as that." In fact, his shorter works (*Ten North Frederick* is the exception) are usually better, and they make a better transition to the screen, too. *From the Terrace* was pointlessly CinemaScoped into proportions as needlessly large as the book; just recently public television turned his sixty-page Hollywood story, "Natica Jackson" (1966), into a snug hour.

If you read any O'Hara when you were a kid, you remember him not as a sociologist or a cynic or a seer but as a writer whose books were appreciably dirty and still somehow available from the town library. You go back to him thinking that after the past twenty-five years he'll seem laughably tame, and you're surprised to find that he isn't. Your eyes don't exactly pop, but you're pleased to wonder what Bennett Cerf made of page 125 of *Ten North Frederick* (1955), where some Philadelphia prostitutes are said to accept "any perversion that did not involve the drawing of their blood or the burning of their flesh," or the coarse, risible lyricism on the next page: "And thus the chambermaid became the last woman to receive the seed that reposed in the body of Ben Chapin."

Lesbianism appalled and appealed to him in such an unrealistic, compulsive way that if he had lived into the age of video, one would have a pretty good idea of what his rental record at the local Blockbuster might look like. They're *everywhere* in his books, going at it in every locale, from Edith Chapin's boarding school to Ada Ewing's farmhouse bathtub. Jim Malloy and Isabel "go steady" in an on-and-off affair that runs from *BUtter-*

field 8 (1938) to a story thirty years later called "A Few Trips and Some Po-etry," in which O'Hara, while still open-mouthed, brings himself to see Isabel's conversion to homosexuality as something more than a porno-graphic disaster: "This was what the Lesbians themselves called a marriage, and it was love." Well, he'll be damned.

The authorial freedoms of the Sixties and Seventies, when they arrived, did him more harm than good, affording him the chance to breathe hard over subjects about which he'd usually been more than frank enough in the first place. *The Ewings* (1972), his last and arguably worst novel, leaves a reader just plain embarrassed. The widow Ada, before getting Priscilla into the tub, has an adventure with Palm Beach gigolo Will Levering that leaves her certain of one thing: "As she walked to the train that day there was life in her derriere that had not been there for three years."

O'Hara's outsize faults are more interesting than the tame virtues of so many contemporary writers of fiction; the faults themselves make him worth reading again. But don't look for an O'Hara revival to come from the crazily politicized academy. He's too white, too belligerently male and too class-conscious. Class consciousness may be an obsession among literary academics, but only because of a professed disgust with class barriers. O'Hara wouldn't have dreamed of tearing them down. They were the steel beams of his world, and he wouldn't have known what to do without them. He has had a large biography (*The O'Hara Concern*, 1975) written by Matthew J. Bruccoli, who is indeed a professor but, more important, a kind of publishing industry unto himself, respectful of prodigiousness in a way that most professors fear. Still, Gibbsville remains a ghost town to profes-sors and students, even though O'Hara wrote one of his finest sentences ever, a Tolstoyan one, when he summed up his life's creation:

> Gibbsville was like any other American town in that the first impres-sion and the last impression it created was that the traveler would have been safer at home—except that in the traveler's home town conditions were identical with the conditions of Gibbsville.

For all his disdain of book reviewers, those arbiters of the short term, he was surprisingly confident about the long run: "I am immodest enough to believe that the opinion of posterity is the least of my worries, and should be the least for anyone who writes about contemporary life. I say that because I have written so accurately and so honestly that my overall contribution will have to be considered by future students of my time."

If there can be "round" characters, ones capable, in E. M. Forster's terms, of "surprising in a convincing way," then O'Hara should figure in our minds as a round author, one who, despite his wishes, is usually more knowing than wise and yet sometimes—surprisingly, convincingly—turns out to be the latter. "It is always a pleasure," he writes in *We're Friends Again*, "to discover that someone you like and have underestimated on the side of simplicity turns out to be intricate and therefore worthy of your original interest. (Intricacy in someone you never liked is, of course, just another reason for disliking him.)" He might have been speaking here to the posterity he craved. He wasn't, though; he was just telling readers something large that they knew but didn't realize. At moments like this he flirts with a sort of incidental greatness, giving the reader more than enough reason to give thanks for O'Hara and more than enough reason to make friends with him again.

The Big Uneasy

October 1998

I T WAS A BOOK only a mother could love—not even a book, not yet and probably never; just a manuscript, "a badly smeared, scarcely readable carbon," recalled the famous writer to whom it was brought in 1976 by the mother of its author, a hugely unhappy man who had killed himself seven years before. Five years after the mother's importuning, *A Confederacy of Dunces* won John Kennedy Toole the Pulitzer Prize. The story is now a legend of maternal devotion, and much of the novel involves a mother-son relationship, albeit not one to warm the heart; something more on the order of what one remembers between Victor Buono and his squawking mum in *What Ever Happened to Baby Jane?*

As *Confederacy* opens, its huge hero, Ignatius J. Reilly, clad in a green hunting cap, a plaid flannel shirt and suede desert boots, waits for his mother by the clock outside the D. H. Holmes department store on Canal Street in New Orleans: "Shifting from one hip to the other in his lumbering, elephantine fashion, Ignatius sent waves of flesh rippling beneath the tweed and flannel, waves that broke upon buttons and seams." Told to move along by a policeman, he replies with his first epic rant against the modern world, a sort of anti-ode to his hometown:

> "This city is famous for its gamblers, prostitutes, exhibitionists, anti-Christs, alcoholics, sodomites, drug addicts, fetishists, onanists, pornographers, frauds, jades, litterbugs, and lesbians, all of whom are only too well protected by graft. If you have a moment, I shall endeavor to discuss the crime problem with you, but don't make the mistake of bothering me."

New Orleans has taken his point. Instead of driving Ignatius from the spot, it has fixed him to it forever, as a bronze statue. The Holmes department store may now be the Chateau Sonesta, but Ignatius Reilly is still standing outside, dressed in all his too-warm absurdity. He is, in the sculptor's rendition, not nearly fat enough, but if you stand behind the statue and off to one side and look into its left metal eye, you may gasp at its poignancy. It's Ignatius to the life; if, of course, he'd ever been alive.

It's safe to say most tourists and natives don't know who it is they're passing on the Canal Street sidewalk. New Orleans's literary history is more familiarly commemorated by the Hilton's "Streetcar Desires" café or the young man in a black robe on Royal Street hustling Anne Rice readers with vampire lore. But it is John Kennedy Toole's book that represents the comic high point of a great, edgy period in the city's literature, the 1960s, a decade, at least locally, more seedy than swinging. It gave rise to a quartet of manic, paranoid volumes—*Confederacy,* Robert Stone's *A Hall of Mirrors,* Walker Percy's *The Moviegoer* and James Kirkwood's *American Grotesque*— whose terrain is still there for the bookish pilgrim willing to walk not only the French Quarter and Canal Street but also a few neighborhoods off the tourist maps.

With a small degree of perversity to match what's found in the books, I decided to travel down to the city during a hot summer week to tramp their locales and see if the fumes of their ethos didn't rise a bit more strongly when they were considered in the place that produced them. I carried the books with me, but mentally I was bringing Newcastle to the coals.

New Orleans is a creepy place, a town where the *bons temps* don't *rouler* so much as ooze past your feet, and the volumes I had along were the sort of baggage to let one go with the oily flow. I had come to groove on the twitchy and the dark, not the music and the food. I asked for a quiet room at my hotel on Gravier Street and got a tiny one at the back whose windows took in no sunlight and whose only sound was a sinister clicking that came out of the phone even when it was hung up. I was off to just the right start.

––––––––––

Even if he could step out of his sculpted eternity, Ignatius Reilly would be loath to act as a guide. Like a Tennessee Williams heroine, he suffers from a medical hysteria ("Oh, my valve! It's closing!") that leaves him disinclined to venture forth from the house he shares with Mother on Constantinople Street. At home he is free to hurl insults at *American Bandstand* ("Do I believe the total perversion that I am witnessing? . . . The children on that program should all be gassed") and write his running indictment of the world on a series of Big Chief tablets. A failed medievalist, he still corresponds with his onetime graduate-school friend Myrna Minkoff, who is now back in New York. There are more problems than distance in the relationship: She is a lefty who once traveled "the rural South to teach Negroes folk songs she had learned at the Library of Congress"; Ignatius is a royalist.

Going out always involves calamity, like the minor but plot-starting auto accident the Reillys suffer at the corner of Bourbon and St. Ann, today a venue for gay bars and gift shops festooned with rainbow flags that would call forth God knows what denunciations from the sex-terrified Ignatius. (For an erotic outlet, he makes due with a rubber glove, an object presented with heroic discretion.) Driven into the labor force, he blusters and shirks, a sort of voluble Bartleby, as a clerk at the Levy Pants factory, before leading the firm's black workers in a strike he dubs the "Crusade for Moorish Dignity" and whose goal he of course despises: "I do not wish to witness the awful spectacle of the Negroes moving upward into the middle class. I consider this movement a great insult to their integrity as a people."

A second, enforced round of employment puts Ignatius, in a pirate's outfit, behind a Paradise Vendor hot-dog cart. He eats most of the contents, since "tourists were not apparently coming to colorful and picturesque old N.O. to gorge themselves upon Paradise products." The real-life tourist can still spot "Lucky Dogs" wagons—a "New Orleans Tradition Since 1948"—being pushed around the city; in fact, a few days after arriving, I notice that one of them sometimes parks itself at the corner of Bourbon and St. Ann, as if waiting to be hit by Mrs. Reilly's car.

Ignatius is a viceroy of verbiage, and the plumminess of his tirades carries over into the simplest sentence of Toole's narration ("There was a localized explosion on top of the stove"). The novel sings with dead-on voices, from the jivey questions of the Night of Joy's porter ("How come a white cat like you, talkin so good, sellin weenies?") to the kindly whine of Darlene, a hapless stripper ("Harlett O'Hara, the Virgin-ny Belle") who works in the same Bourbon Street joint.

But the reader never laughs for very long. Listening to Ignatius while considering his doomed creator is like watching the fat comic you know is only one movie away from early death. Ignatius is helpless against the *rota Fortunae* of the medieval world he once studied: " 'Oh, Fortuna, blind, heedless goddess, I am strapped to your wheel. . . . Do not crush me beneath your spokes. Raise me on high, divinity.' " He expects debasement but has megalomaniacal longings; he knows that the world can turn any which way and that each spin has no more meaning than the one before. He is a paranoid, but manic enough for moments of ecstasy, and as such the Everyman of his literary place and time.

The cracked protagonists of 1960s New Orleans tend to come and go by bus. Ignatius leaves the city only once, on a fruitless academic job hunt to Baton Rouge, and he continually recalls the vomitous journey home—during which a Greyhound Scenicruiser acted like the whale to his own cetaceous Jonah—as the central nightmare of his life.

At the opening of Robert Stone's first novel, *A Hall of Mirrors* (1967), the bus on which the no-first-name Rheinhardt drifts toward the city affords, by contrast, an "anonymous protection." Only thirty but already a killing-himself alcoholic, Rheinhardt slips into a bad hotel before his inevitable bender and eviction by the proprietor's Deadbeat Tattoo ("three dull slaps against your door with the open palm, so spaced as to form a modest crescendo") force him to move on to the Living Grace Mission.

His New Orleans life really commences when he stumbles into the right-wing enterprises of M. T. Bingamon: a chemical company whose workforce of cons, drunks and mental patients is being "rehabilitated" into a private militia; and WUSA, Bingamon's radio outlet, where Rheinhardt, a failed musician with some on-air experience, starts doing a jazz-tempo newscast of inflammatory political items. Success begins awakening his "sublime needs" from their boozy suspension.

On the same day Rheinhardt arrives, Geraldine, a hooker who's lost a child and been scarred by her pimp, rides into town on a fruit truck. She's fighting off panic, trying not to feel anything, and soon trying to cling to Rheinhardt, the two of them "fearing each other's desperation." Geraldine's instincts, better than his, tell her that "something fucking awful is happening all the time."

Is it ever. Despite skids of hipster humor that would become a staple of the author, *A Hall of Mirrors* (filmed, and forgotten, as *WUSA,* with Paul Newman and Joanne Woodward) is mostly one bleak binge of dread. Rheinhardt and Geraldine settle into an apartment at 920 St. Philip, behind the closed shutters that make houses in the Quarter look like books hiding stories from a neighborhood whose slightly sickening smell—"of green things, of black soil and blossoms mixed with river and damp old stone, grinding coffee and something that might be saffron"—never leaves a visitor's nostrils.

But the Quarter is not this novel's epicenter. The radio station, at the corner of Canal and Burgundy (a few blocks up from the Holmes department store), brings you closer to it, as does the nexus of Canal and Rampart, which is even now in a district of check-cashing outlets and pawnshops, where Rheinhardt, gazing at a window display of weaponry, finds "poetry . . . in the razors." Stone goes on about them for a few terrific paragraphs that finally take him over the top:

> Somewhere, [Rheinhardt] thought, shivering—somewhere, in the heart of a stone mountain sits a scarred and demonic old man with a striped shirt and one suspender, and with teeth clenched and spittle on his chin he takes that razor and cuts a dirty piece of string. And he kills me. The American Fate, the angel of American Death, His Razor.

When Stone is good ("Rheinhardt went through the rear door and into a faceful of sunlight"), he's very good, and when he's bad, he's as purple as a bruise.

Still, the novel keeps you going, keeps you looking for its diseased locus, which for a time seems to lie inside City Hall, an aqua-glassy, red-lettered part of the Civic Center put up in the late '50s, a sort of urban-renewed Brasília standing under what Stone calls "the joyous, brutal blue sky of the Caribbean," which caps New Orleans when humidity doesn't block sight of it. In *A Hall of Mirrors,* City Hall is the Muzak'd, air-conditioned nightmare to which nervous Morgan Rainey (Anthony Perkins in the movie) reports to work on a survey of the city's welfare recipients, a job obviously derived from one Stone had as a census taker. The horrors he witnesses door-to-door—and then the revelation that he's really aiding a politician's scheme to trim the relief rolls and please white voters—shred his already frayed spirit. Wobbling between self-hatred and the messianic ("Even though my weak life is lost I set myself against them and I shall not be moved"), scared of his shadow and cheered on by voices, Rainey starts his own spin on the *rota*

Fortunae. Rheinhardt, just as severely split, a juicer with those "sublime needs," hates Rainey from the moment of their acquaintance.

Their stories converge at the novel's actual ground zero, the "Sport Palace" (not the current Superdome, which looks like wet clay spinning on a potter's wheel), where Bingamon has arranged for a giant rally and a phony race riot. With "peculiar vermin gamboling at the field's edge, darting among the rest of the spectators, light reflected on their teeth," Rheinhardt splashes the already berserk crowd with some rhetorical gasoline about his modern version of Columbia herself: a racially terrified, Communist-threatened "fat old lady on her way to see the world's fair." She's riding a Greyhound, probably a Scenicruiser, to get there.

———

It's on April 16, 1963, that Morgan Rainey writes in his diary, "Today—Back of Town—I came away feeling broken." One day later, a real-life 23-year-old native of New Orleans told his Russian-born wife that he was heading home from Dallas to the city of his birth. Lee Harvey Oswald, self-described as "the son of a Insuraen Salesman whose early death left a far mean streak of indepence brought on by negleck," had tried unsuccessfully, a week before, to kill the right-wing extremist General Edwin Walker in Dallas. Insofar as he was capable of linear thought, Oswald had probably decided it was time to get out of town.

The city to which he returned—by bus, the same way he would leave five months later—has far more claim to him, and a far stronger hold on the minds of JFK conspiracy theorists, than Dallas. In the mid-1950s, Oswald lived with his dropsical, angry mother, Marguerite, in an apartment above a pool hall in Exchange Alley, a dank little pipe of a block that still connects Canal Street to the Quarter. During this teenage period, he is said to have first fantasized about acquiring a gun, an automatic pistol he planned to steal from the window of a shop on Rampart Street, perhaps the same one displaying the "great American razor" that Rheinhardt covets.

By the summer of '63, Oswald had legally acquired, through the U.S. mail, both a pistol and a rifle, the gun he would play with on the porch of his apartment at 4907 Magazine Street, a frame house still quite as it was, in a neighborhood a couple of miles from his coffee-company job and the Canal Street corner on which he would be arrested for distributing Fair Play for Cuba Committee leaflets. (It's not far from where Patrolman Mancuso tries running in Ignatius Reilly.) This was a season, as even the whacked-out Geraldine notices, with "stories about Castro on the front page," but it would take the post facto imagination of the real-life district attorney Jim Garrison—the ultimate paranoid auteur of this period—to make Oswald the trompe l'oeil element of an assassination designed in the French Quarter by a band of anti-Castro homosexuals.

On a hot June afternoon, I walk up Dauphine Street, all the way to the 1300 block and past the stretch where, long before gentrification, Ignatius Reilly's mother grew up poor. I'm only one street up from Bourbon, but it's so quiet I can hear the rustle of plastic garbage bags; except for the architecture and a midget, dressed all in black, riding past on a bicycle, I might forget I am even in the Quarter. At the corner of Barracks stands Kaboom, an excellent, sweltering used-book store, where on a back shelf James Kirkwood's *American Grotesque,* an unlikely nonfiction account of the Garrison freak show, awaits a buyer. The autographed volume contains a yellowed clipping from the defunct *New Orleans States-Item* dated June 5, 1967: RUBY, SHAW LINKED—DA.

In Garrison's mind, everything was linked. As a resident of the city tells Kirkwood, "Holy Smoley, the only group not charged is the Girl Scouts— and they'd better stop pushing cookies!" The elegant man put on trial for Kennedy's murder was Clay Shaw, retired director of the city's International Trade Mart, a discreetly homosexual pillar of the city's establishment who had a great deal to do, over many years, with reversing the Quarter's slide into slumminess. This Francophile preservationist probably had less desire to replace Jacqueline Kennedy with Lady Bird Johnson than anyone imaginable, but in Garrison's mind, Clay Shaw, alias Clay Bertrand, was the queen bee of a murderous operation that included Oswald and freelance cancer researcher David Ferrie, an eyebrowless ex–airline pilot cashiered for his fondness for young boys.

Half a block from Kaboom, on the same side of the street, I'm tempted to knock on the red door of 1313 Dauphine and wait to see if anyone looks through the peephole that Shaw put in after Perry Russo, Garrison's crackpot informant, showed up, pretending to be a Mutual of Omaha salesman, and fingered Shaw as the man he once heard discuss killing Kennedy with Oswald and Ferrie—each by then as dead as the other.

Kirkwood arrived in New Orleans with his mind, like most better-functioning ones, already made up against Garrison. "How can I be objec-

tive?" asked the future coauthor of the book for *A Chorus Line,* hardly anyone's idea of a trial reporter. Kirkwood's just-post-Stonewall introduction
to *American Grotesque* serves oblique notice that his book has been conceived in a spirit of gay solidarity with Clay Shaw, whose homosexuality
was central to his villainy for Garrison. (The D.A., later years would show,
had a wee bit of personal conflict in this area.)

The idea of gay conspiracy is older than Salem. In fact, when Ignatius
Reilly converses with the flamboyant Dorian Greene from behind his hot-
dog cart, he supplies the Dark Ages context for Garrison's fantasy:

> "In a few years, you and your friends will probably take over the
> country."
> "Oh, we're planning to," the young man said with a bright smile.
> "We have connections in the highest places. You'd be surprised."
> "No, I wouldn't. Hroswitha could have predicted this long ago."
> "Who in the world is that?"
> "A sibyl of a medieval nun. She has guided my life."

Ignatius attends a party in Dorian's apartment near the corner of St.
Peter and Royal, where the frantic guests wear a lot of jewelry and leather:
"A cowboy with a little riding crop flicked the crop at one of his fans, producing a response of exaggerated screaming and pleased giggling." Clay
Shaw's own whip, confiscated by Garrison's searchers, along with a black
hood and chains, occasioned much pretrial comment. It was part of his
Mardi Gras costume, Shaw's supporters explained; people had seen him in
it repeatedly. One would not be surprised to know that he'd also carried it
over the years to more than a few parties like Dorian's, or that he'd made
some halfhearted use of it in the privacy of his restored home, but for the
duration of the trial it was necessary for him to appear only as a credit to his
orientation. In *American Grotesque,* Shaw emerges as the manly hero, fighting off Garrison's assault with quiet wit and stoicism. Years after the trial,
the D.A. would get the film director he thought he deserved in Oliver
Stone, who coaxed a hilarious portrayal of Shaw, as bad as it was untruth-
ful, out of Tommy Lee Jones.

In Kirkwood's invaluable 650 pages, witnesses zanily proliferate, accuse
and self-destruct. Charles Spiesel, a tax accountant, says that Ferrie once invited him and three others from LaFitte's Blacksmith Shop, the oldest bar

in the Quarter, to an apartment near Dauphine and Esplanade, where Clay Shaw joined a discussion about providing a getaway for whoever would kill the president. Spiesel loses a bit of credibility when, under questioning by Shaw's attorney, he says he's been hypnotized by fifty or more different persons conspiring against *him*. Some of Garrison's Dealey Plaza testimony comes from a man who, Kirkwood notes, "had not seen the President's head blown off, Governor Connally shot, or Jackie Kennedy crawling back onto the trunk of the car, but [who] had traced the path of a bullet as it furrowed through the grass."

Everyone else in the courtroom does get to see the salient occurrences of November 22, 1963, since Garrison repeatedly shows the Zapruder film, which in those days had yet to be seen by any member of the general public. The "anxious, ill-tempered and, if not blood-thirsty, most definitely morbid craning mob of voyeurs" in the courtroom is denied its viewing pleasure only on Mardi Gras, when court is in recess and Kirkwood awakens at 6 A.M. to the sight and sound of "three young men dressed as nuns, striding along with arms locked, singing 'Roll Me Over in the Clover.'" Shaw spends the day behind his locked red door on Dauphine Street, his whip still unreturned by the district attorney's office.

What Oswald really did in the spring and summer of 1963, rather than exchange dark whispers up in the Quarter with Ferrie and Shaw, was to go, quite often, to the Napoleon branch of the New Orleans Public Library, today the Children's Resource Center. The first of thirty-four books he checked out was *Portrait of a Revolutionary: Mao Tse-Tung*. My trip to the main library, right near the Brasílian City Hall, reveals that the system still holds one copy of that title, at the new Martin Luther King branch on Caffin Avenue, a long cab ride over the bridge crossing the Industrial Canal, from which I can't help looking for a glimpse of what might have been Levy Pants.

The Mao book is on the shelf, with one stamp identifying the date it was acquired (NOV 28 1962), and another, the branch of the library that first owned it: NA901894—sure enough, Napoleon. I can imagine Ignatius Reilly logging it in during the two weeks he held a job in the central cataloging department of the N.O.P.L. ("On some days I could only paste in three or four slips and at the same time feel satisfied with the quality of my work"). One suspects that, during his brief tenure, the same part of Ignatius prone to shrieking at the TV screen made him deface at least a few books with his opinionated marginalia; alas, I discover that *Portrait of a Revolutionary* bears not one jotting by Lee Harvey Oswald, who we know had his polite and meticulous aspects. Maybe one or two of the dog-ears are his doing, and maybe one of the buffs who still talk nightly about Garrison on the alt.conspiracy.jfk Web site will one day find a significant pattern to all of them.

Meanwhile, a plaque commemorating Clay Shaw's efforts to restore the French Quarter can now be found on Governor Nicholls Street, a few blocks away from both Shaw's home and the Kaboom bookstore, where Kirkwood's signed volume still looks for a buyer. Shaw and Garrison are both dead now, and so is Kirkwood. The apartment he rented for the duration of Shaw's trial is on the corner of St. Philip and Royal, one block from LaFitte's and two from where Rheinhardt went to live on the day Mr. Bingamon, explaining his political worldview, assured him that "there is a pattern" and that other people, the enemy, "keep that pattern obscured."

———

Binx Bolling, the hero of Walker Percy's *The Moviegoer* (1961), enjoys riding a local bus that still runs from suburban Gentilly down Elysian Fields and into the Quarter, a neighborhood whose "old world atmosphere" he dislikes as much as the "genteel charm of the Garden District." Binx prefers living among Gentilly's "old-style California bungalows" and "new-style Daytona cottages" in an apartment that is deliberately impersonal. A still-young Korean War veteran, Binx runs the neighborhood branch of a brokerage firm, delights in making money, dates his secretaries and has no real friends or deep involvements. He appears to float upon modern life with an equanimity to rival Ignatius Reilly's screaming malcontentment: "It is a pleasure to carry out the duties of a citizen and to receive in return a receipt or a neat styrene card with one's name on it certifying, so to speak, one's right to exist."

Above all he goes to the movies, whose formulas furnish his frame of reference and contribute to a calm acceptance of his real life. They even allow him to entertain pleasant alternatives to actual disappointments. When Binx sits next to an attractive girl on the bus, he muses:

What a tragedy it is that I do not know her, will probably never see her again. What good times we could have! This very afternoon we could go spinning along the Gulf Coast. What consideration and tenderness I could show her! If it were a movie, I would have only to wait. The bus would get lost or the city would be bombed and she and I would tend the wounded.

In *Confederacy*, when Ignatius goes to the movies, he behaves no differently than when he's watching *American Bandstand* at home on Constantinople Street. "Filth!" he screams at one on-screen all-American heroine. "How dare she pretend to be a virgin. Look at her degenerate face. Rape her!" Binx would just ask her out.

And yet, for all that, there is another layer to Binx, a spiritual precinct that is "never a moment without wonder." In the middle of his suburban, cinematic round, he can be as crazily elevated as Ignatius or Rheinhardt or Jim Garrison or Morgan Rainey. From time to time, Binx goes on a "search" for ultimate meaning, a search that "anyone would undertake if he were not sunk in the everydayness of his own life." The anodyne happy-ending movies he cherishes are really lures into the condition defined by the novel's epigraph from Kierkegaard: "The specific character of despair is precisely this: it is unaware of being despair."

Early in the novel, after riding the bus into the Quarter, Binx spots William Holden, in New Orleans to make a movie, coming out of Pirate's Alley. Along with some tourists, Binx follows him for a while, until Holden turns down Toulouse Street, "shedding light as he goes." When I re-create Binx's movements from the time he gets off at Esplanade and walks down Royal, observing the carriageways and courtyards and the "ironwork on the balconies [that] sags like rotten lace," I realize just what the sudden sight of Holden prevents Binx from seeing: Saint Louis Cathedral, the next thing that would have appeared on his left. Once more it's the movies that defeat his aspirant spirit, distract him from a search that eventually led Walker Percy into the Catholic Church.

For the rest of *The Moviegoer*, the feckless hero must fight off "malaise," the comfortable torpor that leaves modern man unable to sin very big because "nowadays one is hardly up to it." Sex is a sort of "sickness . . . longed after as a fruit not really forbidden but mock-forbidden and therefore secretly prized, prized first and last and always by the cult of the naughty nice." The novel's serious sexual interest—not Binx's latest naughty-nice secretary—is Kate, a 25-year-old manic-depressive stepcousin, who has had a breakdown and even skirted "political conspiracy here and now in New Orleans with the local dirty necks of the bookshops and a certain oracular type of social worker"—perhaps Morgan Rainey himself. Asked by his aunt to keep Kate on an even keel, Binx instead takes her, without telling anyone and after what looks like a suicide attempt, on a convention trip to Chicago. When Aunt Emily tracks them down, they return to New Orleans—on a Scenicruiser—arriving, like Rheinhardt, the day after Mardi Gras.

Instead of the hangover Binx might have had, a giant case of malaise begins to settle in, and on his thirtieth birthday he serves up a rant that could, but for its dead seriousness, be bellowed by Ignatius Reilly.

Living in fact in the very century of merde, the great shithouse of scientific humanism where needs are satisfied, everyone becomes an anyone, a warm and creative person, and prospers like a dung beetle, and one hundred percent of people are humanists and ninety-eight percent believe in God, and men are dead, dead, dead; and the malaise has settled like a fall-out and what people really fear is not that the bomb will fall but that the bomb will not fall—

When you reread a passage like this, it makes more than enough sense that the famous writer to whom Thelma Toole brought her son's manuscript—the man who rescued *A Confederacy of Dunces* from oblivion—was Walker Percy. In fact, if you take Binx's bus ride down Elysian Fields, you'll pass number 1016, the tiny hotbox of a house that Mrs. Toole lived in after her son's suicide.

On his trip to Chicago, Binx talks about the "genie-soul" of places, the presence that "wherever you go, you must meet and master first thing or be met and mastered." The secret for traveling down to New Orleans and back thirty years into its literature is to meet the genie-soul and *be* mastered, for these four books from that period—each with its "search" or "pattern" or *rota Fortunae* or conspiracy-so-immense—posit a world in which someone or something, God or an underground network, is fully in control of you. The only available response is surrender, in its paranoid or ecstatic forms.

In the heat, the improbably regular grid of streets in the Quarter begins to feel like a chip someone's planted in your brain; the clouds always ready to burst over City Hall and Magazine Street start looking pregnant with revelation as well as relief. New Orleans remains the least American of all the country's cities not just from the blood mix of its many conquerors but because, more than any other place, it sets no premium on, or even possibility of, free will. Years before he became a best-seller, the vampire was abroad in its books.

Too Good to Be Tru

*December 1997**

HALF HIS WRITING LIFE was aftermath. The baby-faced literary sensation of 1948 took eighteen more years to reach his professional and social peak—1966, when he published *In Cold Blood* and threw his Black and White ball at New York's Plaza Hotel—and then another boozed and bloated eighteen to lose most of his friends and much of his reputation, before dying in 1984, at 59, in a spare bedroom belonging to the second ex-Mrs. Johnny Carson. Gore Vidal's remark (made in private, but widely quoted) that Truman Capote's death was a "good career move" seems almost compassionate now, a look-on-the-bright-side prophecy that didn't pan out. Truman remains stuck in our minds, perhaps forever, in his fat-Elvis phase.

Gerald Clarke's solid 1988 biography, *Capote,* remains the best source for anyone who wants to understand the writer and his work, but George Plimpton's new "oral biography," *Truman Capote*—a chorus of voices speaking their memories, a paragraph or two at a time—will satisfy those who already know TC's story and now wish to see it presented as pure dish: reheated, with a few new anecdotal seasonings.

The book starts with a handful of people recollecting Truman's beginnings in Monroeville, Alabama. Abandoned by his fly-by-night father (Arch Persons) and pretty, promiscuous mother, he was raised mostly by distant female relatives, including the backward, shy Sook, later made famous in the television adaptation of his story "A Christmas Memory." "She had her own little dream world," explains Capote's aunt Marie Rudisill. "And she gave that to Truman. . . . They'd go off in the woods and they'd fly kites. They'd cut these gorgeous pictures out of every magazine in the world and

*Review of *Truman Capote,* by George Plimpton (Doubleday).

paste them on the kites." It was this world that would give rise to his famous early work, delicately gothic stories like "Jug of Silver" and "Miriam."

Preposterously effeminate—speaking in the little voice that, decades later, made talk-show audiences gasp—Capote learned, very quickly, his essential strategy for charming people into submission. A local bully, recalls another relative, "would just be standing, looking at him, and all of a sudden Truman would turn one of his cartwheels. He could do marvelous cartwheels, roll on his hands and land on his feet, and then stop and rotate back and end up standing with his feet right where he had been talking to this bully. And this would just flabbergast the kid, and he would forget all about picking on Truman."

His mother, Lillie Mae—who later restyled herself Nina, just as "Lulamae Barnes" made herself "Holly Golightly"—was not as spectacular a creature as Capote claimed ("She won a beauty contest sponsored by Lux, one of many, many regional winners. Truman expanded this, of course, into her winning the contest for Miss Alabama," explains an archivist), but she did snag a second husband, the businessman Joe Capote, who settled her and Truman in Greenwich, Connecticut, and then on Park Avenue, relocations that began the future author's eventually fatal fascination with the rich.

He started his career as an office boy at *The New Yorker.* "When it turned out to our astonishment that he was a real writer and better than most of the people on the magazine," recalls Brendan Gill, "he made us very uneasy." He made a reputation with short stories in the glossy magazines that used to run fiction (*Harper's Bazaar, Mademoiselle*) and a sensation with Harold Halma's jacket photo for his first novel, *Other Voices, Other Rooms,* a picture that seemed less about precocity than pedophilia. The editor Babs Simpson is certain "he always saw himself for his entire life lying on that sofa. I'm sure he thought he was a beauty till the day he died."

His great luck was to burst upon a literary place and time—New York in the late '40s and early '50s—where, as his friend Phoebe Pierce Vreeland puts it, "he got a wonderful reception because people were fascinated by the artist, but particularly by literature. People didn't talk about money all the time, or movie rights." That they would one day talk of little else is due, in part, to Truman Capote, whose eventual earnings and television celebrity helped turn writers into talkers. But at the beginning he showed more discipline than dissipation. "It didn't matter to me that he was gay and a freak," says his longer-lived contemporary William Styron. "I was very much in awe of his talent."

It is difficult to overestimate the sensation made thirty years ago by *In Cold Blood*, Capote's account of Perry Smith and Dick Hickock's killing of the Clutter family on November 15, 1959, in Holcomb, Kansas. At 14, I plunked down change at the local lending library—run by a white-haired lady named Miss Meek—for the first copy to hit Stewart Manor, New York. My ninth-grade English teacher, seeing me with it, enviously asked how I'd gotten hold of it. Capote appeared on the cover of *Life* and all over television, intriguing initially hostile viewers with the disparity between his lispy persona and this nervy, butch undertaking. The book had taken him six years and was the ultimate cartwheel: He had kicked the bullies right in the balls and left his career contemporaries—the last self-consciously macho generation of American writers—perplexed with envy.

Writers still debate how new the form of *In Cold Blood* really was. Capote called it a "non-fiction novel," and whatever its forerunners, the book was certainly unique to his own body of work, which up to that time had been mostly confections of feeling, like *Breakfast at Tiffany's,* not anatomies of mass murder. The volume does have a personal undercurrent—the author's self-loving attraction to the damaged Perry Smith—but it is more remarkable for its objectivity and *quiet,* the way it regroups authentic details along a narrative arc drawn by life itself.

Time has not validated the criticisms leveled against the book back in 1966, including that of Kenneth Tynan, who argued that Capote didn't fight to save Smith and Hickock from being hanged because *In Cold Blood* depended on their execution for its full impact. (One might as well argue that a war correspondent is obliged to carry stretchers.) But what *does* disturb, and what this new biography enlarges, is the recent, growing awareness that *In Cold Blood* is not as absolutely faithful to the truth as Capote always claimed. We already knew from Clarke's *Capote* that the book's last scene— a graveyard encounter between Nancy Clutter's best friend and the detective who caught her killers—was made up, as a gentle, literary denouement. Now the detective, Alvin Dewey, says Capote's description of his shutting his eyes at the hanging isn't true, either. "I'd seen this thing from the start and I would see it to the finish. After seeing the way that little Clutter girl looked, I could have pulled the lever myself." This may seem like a small thing, but it's not. If novels depend in part on what Coleridge called the reader's "willing suspension of disbelief," *In Cold Blood*'s power derived from the remarkable sense that there was no *need* to suspend disbelief. If that sense collapses, the book—still, I think, one of the most remarkable of its time—goes with it, too.

It made him rich and famous, and it ruined him for anything else. "I think he lost a grip on himself after that," says his friend the novelist John Knowles. Before the book was off the best-seller list, Capote had given his Black and White ball, an enormous New York blowout that had even triple-A-list celebrities begging for invitations. Given mostly to celebrate his own triumph (Katharine Graham was ostensibly the guest of honor), the event is described here, more than once and all too tellingly, as "one of his major works." Diana Trilling makes a fair point that at least Capote's "chic" wasn't the radical-political variety adopted by other '60s sensations, but one has to ask, at this remove, just what was the accomplishment of herding Rose Kennedy, Andy Warhol and Mia Farrow Sinatra onto the same dance floor?

The party was a great showcase for his "swans," those rich, overlunched wives like Babe Paley, Slim Keith and Gloria Guinness. Their friendships with Capote seemed a happy arrangement all around (the husbands liked seeing little Tru perk up their wives), but everyone miscalculated. The swans thought he wouldn't use them as material; Capote thought they wouldn't mind when he did. "I told Truman that people weren't going to be happy with this," remembers Gerald Clarke, "and he said, 'Naaaah, they're too dumb. They won't know who they are.' " *This* was "La Côte Basque, 1965," published in *Esquire* in 1975, a gossipy little short story *à clef*, full of the swans and their husbands and supposedly the harbinger of *Answered Prayers,* a giant and, according to Capote, Proustian novel about the rich and famous that he had (again, supposedly) begun working on even before *In Cold Blood.*

The story's appearance was a disaster. As Norman Mailer shrewdly puts it, Capote had been rash instead of bold. The swans dropped him and went swanning on, leaving Truman a friendless aging duckling who never managed to produce much more of anything. A few additional fragments of *Answered Prayers* were published, and Capote kept promising the rest, but the book is these days chiefly known for its failure to have been written.

Plimpton's new biography contains a number of competing theories about the continuing mystery of just how much work he ever did on it. Princess Lee Radziwill, a defecting swan, "never saw him working," and the film director Frank Perry says the manuscript he saw was "a Missouri bankroll, which is to say, the top three pages had typewriting on them and the rest were blank." No, says someone else, Capote wrote the book but, dissatisfied with it, destroyed the manuscript. No, says another, it was stolen. No, says yet somebody else, it may still be in a cabinet to which the key is lost. (As Holly Golightly would say, Cross my heart and kiss my elbow.)

Are we poorer for being without the whole *Answered Prayers*? Probably not, though one is only now realizing it. Capote did not have the gifts for panorama that the enterprise, as he described it, would require. "The *idea* that he was going to be Proust," says the writer Eleanor Perényi. "I mean, this is again part of the pitifulness of this claim. He never looked at a piece of architecture; he never looked at a painting; he never went to an art gallery. [My mother] dragged him to the Vatican in Rome. He was so bored, he was hysterical."

He managed one more interesting collection of work, *Music for Chameleons* (1980), but its centerpiece, "Handcarved Coffins: A Nonfiction Account of an American Crime," seemed just as broad and implausible as *In Cold Blood*—which it so obviously wanted to follow up—had been painstaking. (The story's first line identifies its location as a "small Western state." There's no such thing, except for Hawaii, and this "nonfiction" tale surely doesn't take place there.) In his last fifteen years, Capote's work appeared less frequently in bookstores than he did on-screen. He showed up in Neil Simon's *Murder by Death,* on *The Sonny and Cher Comedy Hour* and repeatedly on *The Tonight Show,* where he recharged his public feuds.

During the '70s, his longtime liaison with the moody but protective Jack Dunphy gave way to crazier romances with an air-conditioner repairman and an abusive, married banker whose daughter came to live with Capote in his UN Plaza apartment. His drinking and drug-taking reached a point where the art historian John Richardson, an old friend, mistook him for a bag lady on Lexington Avenue.

When he set out for Joanne Carson's California house in August 1984, Capote knew enough to buy a one-way ticket.

———

"Oral biography" came along some years after the nonfiction novel. One of its pioneer texts (edited in part by George Plimpton) was *Edie* (1982), a re-

creation of the blue-blooded, burned-out Warholian superstar Edie Sedg-
wick. That tells you something about the form's natural relation to content,
though it has also been used to reconstruct the life and times and surround-
ing static of weightier subjects, such as Norman Mailer and Marlon Brando.
The genre generally reads like a documentary that's all voice-over, no
images—and winds up being television all the same. The idea of applying it
to the author of "La Côte Basque," a story entirely in the form of lunchtime
gossip, must have been irresistible, though one realizes, from a comment
early in the text by the writer Eugene Walter ("It's a very Southern tradition
to go very deeply into other people's lives, but it's kept within the parlor.
Behind the fan!"), how far from his boyhood customs Capote continued to
travel. His own already well-known incapacity for telling the truth, at least
to his friends, also suits him to the oral-bio treatment. The novelist Alison
Lurie observed the following about this man who claimed to have slept with
Errol Flynn, Albert Camus and André Gide: "Have you noticed that when
the story gets a little bit beyond the credibility—off go the clear glasses and
on go the dark ones?"

These books are only as good as their strongest voices, and the most
entertaining ones here may belong to socialite Leonora Hornblow and
Capote's teenage friend Phoebe Pierce Vreeland: "We were thrown out of
the Pickwick more often than the dust. Dear dear! Golden afternoons in the
Pickwick Theater." One person's devastating remark ("He was probably
one of those people who was good company because you keep expecting
him to be so") can make up for a lot of potted extracts from who-knows-
where-or-when: Elizabeth Bishop has been dead for almost twenty years,
and Plimpton has her talking as if she'd been interviewed last Thursday.

Oral biography's biggest problem, of course, is the lack of any controlling intelligence. People exaggerate and ramble on, often ludicrously ("Had
gynmastics been as popular then as it is today, [Truman] truly could have
been a candidate for possible Olympic consideration"), and even when
Plimpton gives them the hook, his editorial hand is hardly equal to an actual
biographer's interpretations and judgments. Good biographers have it both
ways: They conduct the voices but then turn to the audience to explain the
meaning, or risibility, of what's just been sung. There are stories in this new
book—such as how the Ku Klux Klan disrupted Truman's going-away
party from Monroeville, until his friend Harper Lee's father, the model for
Atticus Finch in *To Kill a Mockingbird,* saved the day—that I don't believe

for a minute. But there's nobody to tell me whether I should trust the anecdote or my own suspicions.

Mailer sums up Capote with as much generosity as anyone now seems able to manage: "The sort of company he kept was part of his destruction. But I don't judge it because he could have died of some inner-crawling disease ten years earlier if he hadn't had that. Maybe he just didn't have long to live. Maybe his life's a triumph, not a failure. Anyone else with that beginning, that size, those handicaps—*true* handicaps—would have gone under." But *Truman Capote* fixes its subject more firmly than ever in the long stretch of his decline and abandonment, reeling between Johnny's couch and Joanne's alimony house. Thirteen years after his death, his best work ought to be coming to the fore, eclipsing the follies of the life that produced it. This is, after all, nature's frequent merciful way with the literary dead. But that is not what's happening in this case. The writer remains terribly present, unable to get out of the way of what he wrote. Capote's tragedy was not early death or even early burnout. It's that, even now, he's outliving himself.

The Novel on Elba

Autumn 1980

ON VALENTINE'S DAY 1965 Immanuel Kant paid a surprise call on Mr. Peter Levi, an exchange student recovering from an infected swan bite in the American Hospital in Paris. News of Kant's message to Peter reached American readers in the spring of 1971: " 'Nature is dead, *mein kind.*' " The carrier of these tidings to the New World was Mary McCarthy, and the vehicle she arrived in was a novel, *Birds of America,* an appealing homemade model whose engine was powered by the spirited inquiries of the *conte philosophique* and whose body was supported by the sturdy facts of realism. Even Peter's hallucination of Kant was entirely plausible: a philosophy minor who carried in his wallet a card saying "The Other is always an End: thy Maxim," he had suffered an ethical shock from the American bombing of North Vietnam on February 7, 1965, and a physical one from penicillin, which had been unwisely administered for the swan bite.

Although this novel was not so very different from others Mary McCarthy had written in the thirty years before it, many critics expressed their perplexity and distaste. Because it reflected at such length on so many of the phenomena that made Kant's pronouncement seem reasonable—bad manners, fast food, mass tourism, irrational politics—it had to be grudgingly pigeonholed. Helen Vendler decided: "if we can have nonfiction novels, why not a new McCarthy genre, the fictional essay? It is not an unworthy form, taken for what it is."

When McCarthy's most recent novel, *Cannibals and Missionaries,* appeared in the fall of 1979, there were again some critics made uneasy by what they perceived as a frail scaffolding of story "overloaded" with ideas— this time about, among other things, terrorism and art. One senses that it was not really the proportion of ideas to story bothering these critics. It was the very idea of ideas, deposited where they should not be. Untidy orphans from politics, philosophy and "nonfiction" in general, they had been plunked onto the doorstep of modern fiction's inner-directed, form-preoccupied house. They were not the novel's responsibility, in the view of these critics, and they were made to feel distinctly unwelcome.

In her new book *Ideas and the Novel*, Mary McCarthy makes clear not only that the so-called fictional essay is nothing "new," but also that "it would have been impossible in former days to speak of 'the novel of ideas.' It would have seemed to be a tautology." This slim, welcome volume recalls and elaborates ideas that first took shape in McCarthy's *On the Contrary* (1961) and *The Writing on the Wall* (1970). Energetically returning to the world of Balzac, Hugo, Stendhal, Tolstoy and Dostoevsky, she celebrates the social and intellectual energy of classical fiction:

> [T]he nineteenth-century novel was so evidently an idea-carrier that the component of overt thought in it must have been taken for granted by the reader as an ingredient as predictable as a leavening agent in bread. He came to expect it in his graver fiction, perhaps to count on it, just as he counted on the geographical and social coordinates that gave him his bearings in the opening chapter. . . .

It was Henry James, says McCarthy, who "etherealized the novel beyond its wildest dreams and perhaps etherized it as well."

This Prufrockian image fixes James as the genre's languid curse. In the gorgeously shaped books of his last period he created a novel

> purged, to the limit of possibility, of the gross traditional elements of suspense, physical action, inventory, description of places and persons, apostrophe, moral teaching. When you think of James in the light of his predecessors, you are suddenly conscious of what is not there: battles, riots, tempests, sunrises, the sewers of Paris, crime, hunger, the plague, the scaffold, the clergy. . . .

After *The Bostonians* and *The Princess Casamassima*, the Master—like his characters—avoided all politics and vulgar day-to-day reality. "What," McCarthy asks, "were Adam Verver's views on the great Free Trade debate, on woman suffrage, on child labor? We do not know. . . . With so much of the stuff of ordinary social intercourse ruled out, the Jamesian people by and large are reduced to a single theme: each other."

As Europe mired itself in the First World War, the novel took its fateful (or fatal) turns into the subconscious and out through the cosmos. Joyce and Woolf published *Portrait of the Artist* and *The Voyage Out,* James died in England, and Hardy continued to shun the novel for poetry. Fiction was getting dressed for *Finnegans Wake,* and criticism would eventually have to face the question of whether or not the "psychological" and technical innovations of modernism were worth the abandonment of so much social and intellectual substance. But for the time being—and it is still more or less that time—the novel of ideas, alive to the manners and ideologies of the way we live now, was sent into exile.

It is, perhaps fittingly, the most famous exile of all—Napoleon—who dominates Mary McCarthy's new book. The Emperor who stole the Continent also invaded the minds of its novelists from France to Russia. Noting Hegel's exclamation that Napoleon was "an idea on horseback," McCarthy looks at him as the father to Stendhal's Julien Sorel ("Stendhal was no revolutionary, but he was very susceptible to being thrilled"), as a source of infuriation for Tolstoy (who "took the trouble to polemicize against Napoleon more than forty years after his death"), and as the perverted inspiration of Dostoevsky's Raskolnikov: " 'Perhaps it was one of these future Napoleons who did for Alyona Ivanovna last week?' " an acquaintance asks him. So powerful and pervasive does McCarthy find Napoleon as Idea in nineteenth-century fiction that his failure to invade England is counted by her as a misfortune for that country's novel: "Victorian fiction, generally, seems to have missed out through insularity, which was a side-benefit of Empire, on the shaking experience of the century: the fact of seeing an Idea on the march and being unable to forget it—radiant vision or atrocious spectacle, depending on your point of view."

At times McCarthy may confuse Napoleon as Idea with Napoleon as *idée fixe*—a very different thing, the aberrant's "complex," clinical and even funny—or as fashion: when she writes of Julien Sorel reading the *Mémorial de Ste. Hélène* we are likely to recall the young men who killed themselves for love after reading *Werther.* And it was probably the English novel, more than any other, that became dominated by an Idea, namely social equality, from the roars of Dickens to the delicacies of Forster. Still, more than anything else, it is her pursuit of Napoleon's long shadow that makes

McCarthy's new book one of the most stimulating about fiction since Forster's *Aspects of the Novel.* There are some flaws in it (putting Fielding's cart before Richardson's horse; a wrongheaded distinction between the novel and film), but its main readings and incidental observations make it just what the classical novel has needed for so long: a champion not beset by the wild punching of John Gardner or the leadenness of C. P. Snow. She makes us wonder whether we aren't on a desert island to which we've brought the wrong books.

In his recent study of Joyce, Woolf and Lawrence (*Beyond Egotism,* Harvard University Press), Robert Kiely defends his modernist subjects against the charge of "indifference to humanity." Far from ignoring the lives of other men and women, he says, they insisted "on searching for general truths by means of concrete characters and situations. . . ." According to Kiely, the "steadiest, most fundamental and significant movement in the works of Joyce, Woolf and Lawrence is outward from the individual and local to the relational and universal." What is missing here, however, is the social. That is the adjective that got leapfrogged in the modernists' rush to the subconscious and the stratospheric. Joyce hovers over the minutiae of Dublin, ingenious and detached like the deists' eighteenth-century God. He plays with the individual parts and bits before him, but never makes the city into the chuffing, consequential machine that is Balzac's Paris. Woolf's London is more an aesthetic bauble than the great cauldron of Right and Wrong that Dickens and George Eliot labored to bring under moral control. D. H. Lawrence's people make love to each other or to the moon, but lose sight of the town beyond the cottage door. (McCarthy admits Lawrence to the company of novelists of ideas, but notes the paradox he presents: "His insistence on blood and instinct as superior to brain was a mental construct incapable of proof except on the mental level.")

Kiely's explorations of the modernists' dealings with nature, maternity, marriage and friendship convince us that the realm of the "relational" rarely admits more than two at a time. The modernists' characters seek to connect themselves to each other or to the stars, but their kingdom is not fundamentally of this world, if one thinks of this world as what it actually is—a social skein of towns and countries and continents, a body politic. The modernists' gift to the novel was their realization that life was not, as Virginia Woolf put it, "a series of gig-lamps"—mere sequence of event and collection of fact—but the novel has suffered from their sense of what Woolf, in her diary, called the "cheapness" of reality.

The heirs of Woolf and her foe Arnold Bennett continue to struggle for possession of poor imaginary "Mrs. Brown." To the former she remains a unique, inviolate soul; to the latter she is a citizen of the realm. There have recently been some assertive signs of a shift back to the real and prescriptive. In novels like *The Ice Age* Margaret Drabble surveys England like a sociologist in a helicopter, a sort of digital George Eliot, and in our own country the free-swinging Gardner picks up Tolstoy's staff and says that good art "claims, on good authority, that some things are healthy for individuals and society and some are not"—he would have no more Pynchonian puzzles and Barthian funhouses. When *The New York Times Book Review* asks novelists if fiction is becoming less experimental and more realistic, Barth himself worries that "The decade of the Moral Majority will doubtless be the decade of Moral Fiction."

McCarthy is not among those so worried—or hopeful. She cites some examples that intrigue or encourage her about a return to ideas, but knows that in their place "images still rule the roost." Not long before his death, C. P. Snow guessed that the realistic novel might appear again in cultures "at different stages of development from ours," but was unlikely to be revived in the West:

> [T]he best conditions [for realistic fiction] appear to be an untidy but energetic social life around one; a public that may be quite small but is ready to respond, appreciate, and believe that such novels are really worth studying and cherishing; and, above all, hope, social and individual, somewhere in the future. Western societies, or at least some of them, possess the first of these conditions, but not the other two.

Snow's realistic novel and McCarthy's novel of ideas are not fully interchangeable, but so often is one the other that the link is indisputable: where there's life, there's thought.

Are we faced with a choice between one sort of novel and another? Barth proposes a synthesis: "My ideal postmodernist author neither merely repudiates nor merely imitates either his twentieth-century modernist parents or his nineteenth-century premodernist grandparents. He has the first half of our century under his belt, but not on his back." And Kiely reminds us that to "pit great writers in deadly warfare against one another can yield insights into their originality, but it is unlikely to exhaust the possibilities of responsiveness to their works." But such a reluctance to fight would have made modernism itself (or any other "ism") impossible. All great artistic changes are partisan, and so is the best criticism. We suffer today from endless structuralism, textualism—and relativism. McCarthy's new book is to be embraced as much for its aggression as its intelligence. She pointedly reminds us how many great novels from *Don Quixote* to *The Red and the Black* comment on "the evil effects of reading." Quixote, Julien Sorel and Emma Bovary were, to a great extent, what they read. Whatever fiction (and criticism) we seek from the future, the idea of reading as a dangerous, infecting thing is something we might once again aspire to. The pen never was mightier than the sword, but it was once less embarrassed than it is now. In *Ideas and the Novel* McCarthy again expounds her unfashionable, career-long belief in knowable truth. In her own novel *A Charmed Life* (1955), one of her characters exasperatedly lectures another:

> " 'How do you know that?' every moron asks the philosopher when he's told that this is an apple and that is a pear. He pretends to doubt, to be curious. But nobody is really curious because nobody cares what the truth is. As soon as we think something, it occurs to us that the opposite or the contrary might just as well be true. And no one cares."

Mary McCarthy still does; but unless criticism (let alone the novel) adds more heat to its current search for questionable light, it may, and probably should, put itself out of business.

Virtual Mary

September 1993 *

IN 1991 I PUBLISHED a novel called *Aurora 7,* and from the start it was my intention to base one of that book's characters, a fifty-year-old novelist named Elizabeth Wheatley, on Mary McCarthy. Mary had been an important person for me—an object of youthful admiration, then a critical subject, and eventually a friend. Her place in my life had been large and complicated, and I didn't know how she would fare as Elizabeth, who disembarks from the *Leonardo da Vinci* on page 35 of *Aurora 7.* The novel is set entirely on May 24, 1962, the day of Scott Carpenter's space flight, and at 9:00 a.m. Elizabeth is wondering how she will spend the rest of the day.

> Perhaps she'll walk all the way home; and maybe, since she'll be walking east on 44th Street, she'll go in the back entrance of the *New Yorker* offices and stop up to see her editor. He'll be pleased when she tells him that at breakfast yesterday she saw a passenger, a rather nice-looking young man, reading *The Committee,* her out-of-print satire about the very literary jury that had once awarded her its prize. . . . What she will spend no part of the day doing is watching this spaceman. Elizabeth's romantic streak, the wide soft spot in her left-wing politics, will permit her to be enthusiastic over, say, an Elizabethan explorer, but as a lover of scratch cakes, natural fibers and manual typewriters she finds herself unable to care about a sterile man in a sterile can being applauded at this moment by every one of her Catholic Rotarian cousins in Wisconsin.

*Remarks at a Bard College conference on Mary McCarthy.

I realized early on in this book that something odd was happening. Not only was Mary, as Elizabeth, turning into a comic character, reduced to her edges and foibles; she was becoming the *only* comic character in the novel. I recalled an answer Mary herself had given in 1961 to an interviewer from the *Paris Review:*

> Something happens in my writing—I don't mean it to—a sort of distortion, a sort of writing on the bias, seeing things with a sort of swerve and swoop. *A Charmed Life,* for instance. You know, at the beginning I make a sort of inventory of all the town characters, just telling who they are. Now I did this with the intention of describing, well, this nice, ordinary, old-fashioned New England town. But it ended up differently. Something is distorted, the description takes on a sort of extravagance—I don't know exactly how it happens. I know I don't mean it to happen.

I didn't mean to do to her what she had done to dozens of characters, not only in *A Charmed Life* but in most of her novels. Yet it turned out that way, and my caricature of Mary McCarthy ended up joining a whole gallery of McCarthy caricatures that have appeared in fiction over the last half century.

Delmore Schwartz refracted what he knew of her into a number of stories, among them an unpublished manuscript called "The Complete Adventuress," whose margin he actually labeled "Mary & Philip (1937)." This small sketch of McCarthy's affair with Philip Rahv puts an emphasis on the ridiculous:

> To their friends who composed a curious circle in which those who were engaged in left-wing politics mixed with those from the theatre and the concert-hall, the infatuation Helena felt and expressed for Stanislaus was such as to make it difficult for one to keep a straight face, for Stanislaus might have remarked merely that the day had been a cold one for early October and Helena then felt compelled to declare that Stanislaus had a consciousness of the external world which disregarded nothing.

In a *Paris Review* story called "Ciao," published in 1961 but set in 1947, McCarthy's third husband, Bowden Broadwater, also gave us a comical glimpse of her as the "dear wife" or "d.w." of the arch, unemployed narrator. While unfailingly good-mannered throughout this short tale, the "d.w." does give some suggestion of being a time bomb. " 'Darling,' she murmurs at the breakfast table, 'may I have the second section now, please?' " After she gets it, in a voice reminiscent of the "morning dew, very fresh," she scolds the husband, gently but unnervingly: " 'But darling,' she said, 'you *can't* have looked very carefully.' She extended the Classified with several items neatly checked for me." When the d.w. straightens up the sitting room, she does so with zealous precision, "three plumps per pillow." Counting the plumps, and being aware of the number's comic value, is exactly in keeping with McCarthy's own methods in fiction; and if the reader of "Ciao," even with all the details about the real-life McCarthy-Broadwater apartment by the Third Avenue El, retains any doubt about the d.w.'s identity, there are her "pretty eyes [that] sparkled like green shampoo shaken well."

For a glimpse (again comic) of McCarthy at her height, two decades and one husband later, one can open James Jones's novel *The Merry Month of May,* set during the Paris *événements* of 1968, and find her as the American writer Magdalen McCaw, married to an OECD official. The narrator worries about a man who decides to bring his mistress instead of his wife to one of Maggie's cocktail parties. "Maybe he thought Maggie and George, Maggie being such a famous American lady writer, were Bohemians—which only shows how little he knew Maggie . . . with her hair skinned back, and her toothy smile, which I have always found innocent and charming, though many others have called it sharklike."

The McCarthy smile—described by Randall Jarrell as "the smile of a suspended, autonomous intelligence . . . [belonging] to nothing, not even itself"—figures with such frequency and prominence in memoirs and fiction that it is almost a separate character. Jarrell's portrait of McCarthy as Gertrude Johnson in *Pictures from an Institution* (he denied the basis to McCarthy but more or less admitted it to Rahv) is the most extended fictional depiction we have of her, as a novelist who comes to a small, progressive liberal-arts college ostensibly to teach, but actually to gather material. Gertrude is tone-deaf; speaks French so badly "that anyone could understand every word of it"; finds the childish behavior of children to be "almost affectation on their part"; and, of course, smiles: "It was like a skull, like a stone-marten scarf . . . torn animals were removed at sunset from that smile."

Above all, as a novelist, Gertrude is preoccupied by facts. In perhaps the book's most famous passage, we are told:

> If one of Gertrude's heroines, running to snatch from the lips of her little daughter a half-emptied bottle of furniture-polish, fell and tore her skirt, Gertrude knew the name of the dressmaker who had made the skirt—and it was the right one for a woman of that class, at that date; she knew the brand of the furniture-polish that the little girl had swallowed; she knew, even, the particular exclamation that such a woman, tearing her skirt at such a moment, would have uttered. . . . But how the child felt as it seized and drank the polish, how the mother felt as she caught the child to her breast—about such things as these, which have neither brand nor date, Gertrude was less knowing; would have said impatiently, "Everybody knows *that*!"

Pictures from an Institution is really no more a novel than McCarthy's own satire *The Oasis,* and if, in Gertrude, Jarrell permits McCarthy more than her usual cameo, the portrait is still less character than caricature. Why, one must finally ask, is the McCarthy fictionalized by all these men almost never permitted more than a few quick comic turns before she's given the hook? In my own novel, Elizabeth Wheatley ends up as a sort of benevolent *dea ex machina,* but there's no soul in the machine. Is it that high seriousness, which McCarthy had, morally and artistically, is inherently comic, and allows for no other sort of fictional treatment? Surely not: think again of Delmore Schwartz, and what Saul Bellow was able to do with him in *Humboldt's Gift.* Were any of the portraits I've quoted motivated by revenge? Certainly not in my case: Mary had never been anything but generous to me. And, even with the others, the results are too likable to have served such a purpose. Simple fascination seems the most likely motive. But why did it always produce comedy?

For one hint of an answer we should go to McCarthy herself, specifically her essay "Characters in Fiction," where she takes exception to the old Forsterian view that comic characters are "flat":

> A comic character, contrary to accepted belief, is likely to be more complicated and enigmatic than a hero or a heroine, fuller of sur-

prises and turnabouts: Mr. Micawber, for instance, can find the most unexpected ways of being himself . . . we really, I believe, admire the comic characters *more* than we do the hero or the heroine, because of their obstinate power to do-it-again, combined with a total lack of self-consciousness or shame.

Even so, in no case can novelists *go inside* comic characters. To Forster's way of thinking that's because they have no interior to reach; by McCarthy's reckoning, it would be more from fear of disrupting what she calls "the principle of eternity or inertia represented by the comic."

McCarthy, the rare non-Communist, nonreligious modern writer who believed that the world contained a knowable truth, did not set any special value upon a second, private life, for her characters or herself. "I grew ashamed to write little observations about [the North Vietnamese] in my notebook," she says in *Hanoi,* "for you ought not to be two people, one downstairs, listening and nodding, and the other scribbling in your room." Her Catholic upbringing had left her with "the idea that it was necessary to be the same person at all times and places." If there *was* such a thing as an inner life, she wanted to see it join the outer one, like one spacecraft coming up to dock with another.

I think that when novelists considered McCarthy as raw material, the task ahead appeared a bit too much like picking up uranium with their bare hands. Writers who knew her were scared of her, less because she herself was so formidable than because she had a way of making you feel weak, ethically and otherwise. Gertrude "had great expectations for humanity," says Jarrell's narrator, and if she "was a sketch for a statue of Honesty putting its foot in its mouth," nonetheless, "After a few minutes with Gertrude you wanted to be good all day every day." I would bet I'm not the only person who used to emerge feeling like that after having had an encounter with Mary.

She had startling gaps in self-awareness, perhaps even more than most people. (Twenty years ago, for instance, she wrote me that when she was writing her essay "The Fact in Fiction," it didn't occur to her that her own books were full of facts.) But more than anyone I have known, she attempted to be honest, sometimes even in the smallest bits of what other people would call social behavior. What I think really made novelists so uncomfortable, once they started to write about her—and made them settle for nervous laughter—was this radical candor, her own lack of respect for that so-called inner life. This was a unique, probably impossible, kind of honesty, and I don't think any novelist, myself included, has ever felt up to portraying it.

On the Fringe

My Fans' Notes

I HAVE LATELY BEGUN to wonder about the extent to which writers would acknowledge what most readers have always been too polite or too timid to admit: namely, that the publication of a book is, as much as anything else, an act of prolonged rudeness. Human discourse is supposed to be a two-way speech, but every book is a monologue, immune to interruption, cut off from the immediate response natural to conversation. Readers may sigh appreciatively, mutter discontent, or even slam the cover shut, but the author hears none of it. His professional colleagues may respond in print, but what of the common reader whose curiosity, intelligence and pocketbook have always sustained authors? How does he make his editorial reply, turn the address into an exchange?

He can write the author a letter.

It ought to be a perfectly natural act. Holden Caulfield spoke some memorable good sense on the subject in *The Catcher in the Rye:* "What really knocks me out is a book that, when you're all done reading it, you wish the author that wrote it was a terrific friend of yours and you could call him up on the phone whenever you felt like it." But most readers who feel the impulse let it subside, probably because they fear being intrusive or predict being rejected.

Certainly there are authors who have been notorious for their annoyance with unsolicited correspondence. Edmund Wilson answered many letters with a printed postcard that began: "Edmund Wilson regrets that it is impossible for him to . . ." Twenty-one possible requests, from appearing on television to supplying "opinions on literary or other subjects," followed, and he would check his refusal of whichever entreaty had been made.

It stands to reason that any extremely popular or controversial author will have trouble answering all the letters he gets. Or that, if he tries to, his career as a publishing writer will come to an ironic end. Margaret Mitchell avoided having to match the success of *Gone with the Wind* by spending most of the rest of her writing life responding to fan mail. There is something sad, of course, in this extended act of avoidance, though it is doubtful her correspondents thought so, however much they may have wished for Tara to rise again.

Most of us who write are neither wildly popular nor particularly controversial. We are surprised at first to get any letters at all, a little bit disbelieving that anyone is actually reading what took such a long and mysterious route from our desks to the bookseller's counter. Far from being indifferent to individual readers, we are eager to make contact with them, to find out just who they are.

About two years ago I published a study of diaries called *A Book of One's Own,* and it was when the letters started coming that I really began to believe there were people reading the book. Some of them seemed as baffled by this new relationship as I was. They might say that they'd never written to an author before, or that they didn't know why they were doing so now, but for some reason they had gone ahead. The act may have been easier than usual with this book, given the kind of person most likely to buy it— someone who was a diarist himself: "I'm not sure why I've written this," confided one woman who told me about the journals she'd kept for more than twenty years. "I guess I just couldn't resist one more opportunity to put my thoughts on paper." A man in Vermont sent me copies from his diaries, entries he'd written on the same days of 1973 and 1974 as some of my own that I'd quoted in the book: "Scary to think how many people must have been scribbling out there," he reflected.

Many people wrote simply to say thank you, to tell me they'd enjoyed the book and that I ought to know it. I realized that in my whole book-filled life I had only once done that myself. The letters I got sometimes seemed apologetic, worried that they might be taking up my time. Their effect was to make me reflect on my own manners: why *hadn't* I written more thank-you notes?

A good letter can help you get over a bad review. *A Book of One's Own* was generously treated by critics, but one day, months after its publication, by which time I thought I'd gotten away without so much as a glove landing on me, a real stinker of a review showed up. Actually it was just a stinker of a sentence within a reasonably positive review, but I began to brood: somebody'd said my baby was ugly. Fortunately, a letter from Mary Taylor of Berkeley Heights, New Jersey, was on its way, assuring me, a few hours after the brooding began, that my book was perfectly splendid. I rubbed on her adjectives like butter over a burn.

For each sheer ego-kiss there was a letter that told me something I hadn't known or thought of. Janet Murray, 81 years old, of Washington, D.C., explained to me that her diary was uninteresting but had come to serve as a protection "against a deteriorating memory"—a purpose I'd not considered in a book that was supposedly organized around diarists' motives. Robert W. Shields of Dayton, Washington, wrote to tell me that he was sure he was the all-time diary-writing champion, with 11 million words (ten times Pepys) to his credit, all put down *"without any inhibitions* whatsoever." (I hope he hasn't seen the recently published distillation of Arthur Crew Inman's 17-million-word diary.)

So inured was I to the idea of writing as monologue that I assumed any question I asked in my book was a rhetorical one. When on pages 103–104 I wondered what had happened to Alan H. Olmstead, the author of a diary coping with retirement (*Threshold,* 1975), I didn't really expect anyone to tell me. But a letter came from Mrs. Olmstead, informing me that Alan Olmstead had written another small volume (*In Praise of Seasons,* 1977) before he died in 1980. He would have enjoyed *A Book of One's Own,* she said, "and been proud and grateful to be included."

Old people wrote more often than anyone else. Presumably they have more time both to write and to read, and perhaps they've also come to see the pointlessness of being shy. That their letters were also the most literately composed may be evidence of cultural decline, or it may have something to do with the lifetime of writing practice they've got from the cozy old habit of diary keeping. I didn't realize my book had a sort of special-interest constituency until their letters came. Elling Aannestad of Rockland, Maine, told me he had gone through the book rather too quickly because it was due back at the library. He is 81 and lives alone except for a cat, and he liked the book because the diarists in it took him out of his solitude. It offered, he said, a "transposition to plurality"—a phrase as nice as any I managed to come up with in 293 pages. Well, who should be thanking whom? Mr. Aannestad and I write each other now and then—conversing, as it were.

Letters from some of Mr. Aannestad's contemporaries sought practical advice: what should be done with their diaries, which had grown to millions of words over thousands of days? "Even if no researcher is turned on by the ego-fueled account of my life," Charles Miller wrote, "the record of half a century (as I saw it) may be worth something to sociologists." Alice M. Irmisch wondered if it would be a "foolish gesture" to leave her sixty years of private writings to Vassar College, where I teach and from which she was graduated. Stanley S. Whitham told me he had no alma mater to which he could bequeath a confessional diary kept for half a century. What should he do? And what should Susan Martinez do with the diaries her grandmother's grandmother wrote in the 1850s? I genuinely didn't know the answers to these questions, and I couldn't help feeling I'd let the askers down.

As Kingsley Amis once said, "If you can't annoy somebody, there's little point in writing." But most of the complaints I received were small and friendly. How could I have left Emerson out of the book, or Henri-Frédéric Amiel, written about Parson Woodforde instead of Parson Kilver? I wrote back to Mr. William Cummings that I had room for only one English country parson and that, under the circumstances, Woodforde looked like my man. A few objections were deeply felt and shyly made. A woman from Massachusetts who had taken one of Ira Progoff's Intensive Journal Workshops (which I'd pronounced preposterous) wrote to tell me that she had found them useful and moving: "I was equally put off by certain wallowings that took place, but that is where some people are. We do not have to accept their limits, but be grateful that the workshops and the journals contribute enormously to the healing of such wounded persons."

Her tone was firm but kindly, her intention not to score a point but to help me. I wrote back, not recanting but expressing perplexity over how her two-page letter contained more clarity, feeling and gracefulness than Mr. Progoff's whole book about his workshops. I couldn't believe these things in her came from or needed him. I didn't want to respond in the spirit of debate, or be proved "right"; I just wanted to register gratitude, and the still-fresh feeling of being taken seriously.

The classiest rejoinder came from Gunther Stuhlmann, editor of the diaries of Anaïs Nin. I'd called him the "keeper of the flame of self-fulfillment," Miss Nin being little more to my taste than Mr. Progoff. Mr. Stuhlmann sent me a copy of *Anaïs: An International Journal* (published by and for the Friends of Anaïs Nin). "With your interest in diaries, I thought you might like to have a copy of our current issue," he wrote. He sent the magazine along with "best wishes for the success of your book." I felt Mr. Stuhlmann had gotten the last word, and so elegantly that I couldn't begrudge him. (Actually, I could: I was glad when a few months later L. J. Wathen, Jr., wrote to thank me for what I said about "that damned bore Anaïs Nin. My God, her father couldn't stand her mother and left the woman—all this futile trying to get Papa back. Bah!")

———————

I keep the letters in a thickening folder in the drawer of my filing cabinet that contains the contract, notes, drafts, publicity and reviews of *A Book of One's Own*. It's just the right place for them, because they're the last step of the whole undertaking. Nabokov said he didn't "think that an artist should bother about his audience. His best audience is the person he sees in his shaving mirror every morning." Perhaps, but once some of these readers are known, one by one in their considerable variety, it is hard not to think about them, gratefully, as one's clientele. I realize that if this were the eighteenth century and I were a Grub Street poet trying to publish by subscription, these letter writers would be my mailing list.

In *A Book of One's Own* I made much of the idea of diaries as pleas to be listened to, to be taken seriously, and in this sense the letters, like the book itself, are all part of a common and somewhat desperate enterprise. All writing is much the same: a series of radio signals shot hopefully, and hopelessly, into the dark—bottled messages awaiting some sort of recognition. Life is, after all, a kind of disaster through which we do what we can to keep up one another's spirits. And whatever these letters may have told me about readers and authors, I would say that they have been important to me more in immediate human terms than any literary ones, that they have been more like than unlike letters I've received all my life, and that they've lifted me in much the same way an old friend's letter might after a few days when the mailbox has yielded nothing but a Con Edison bill and the red light on the phone machine has remained insultingly unflashing. The only difference, over which I feel a certain awe, is that these letters have come from people I didn't know I knew.

A Literary Mugging

February 1997

IN THE SHORT ROW of books I've spent my adult life producing, there's only one I disliked writing—my late-80s' effort about authors who'd plagiarized the books they "wrote." My plans for *Stolen Words: Forays into the Origins and Ravages of Plagiarism* had seemed entertaining enough at the start. I would serve up humorous stories of filching and feuding and fussing among Augustan poets and Grub Street novelists, instructing and delighting the gentle reader from start to finish. But like most books that aren't copied from someone else's, this one didn't turn out as expected. After deciding to venture into some contemporary cases from academe, Hollywood and New York trade publishing, I found—instead of just amusing dustups—plenty of protracted, exhausting struggles that left the plaintiffs shaken and bitter. Their quests for justice were often rendered fruitless by the nature of copyright laws (designed to combat large-scale commercial exploitation, not tweezered rip-offs), and their dilemmas were met with a curious lack of sympathy from other literary people. Plagiarism was, I came to realize, a serious, ugly matter, and when my book came out, I developed a small reputation as a hard-liner on this subject I was by then eager to get away from.

Seven years later, I still get calls from authors, certain their works have been plundered, seeking advice or expert-witness support; and each year the media get briefly excited about a case or two that will prompt a reporter to spin his Rolodex or search his database and give me a call. (It is not fun being asked to go on television to discuss this particular moral failing in Dr. Martin Luther King, Jr.) Most of the cases share the same sleazy features, but there was one I was called about a few years back that seemed to take the cake for perversity. What did I think, the reporter wanted to know, of this guy who was stealing a poet's work and publishing it under a pseudo-nym?

I thought I'd never heard anything like it. The whole point of plagia-rism, for all its dark mental aspects (and they are lulus), is to attach the credit due another to one's own name. Plagiarizing under a pseudonym seemed wildly beside the point, like holding a gun to the bank teller and asking for foreign currency.

Neal Bowers, the victim in this strange case, now tells his story, with con-siderable detail, in a disturbing little book called *Words for the Taking: The Hunt for a Plagiarist.* "Between 1992 and 1994," he states, as calmly as he can, "a person calling himself David Sumner had two of my poems ac-cepted as his own 20 times at 19 different literary magazines. After learning of his activities, I managed to stop 9 of the publications, but my poems still appeared in print 11 different times under someone else's name." Bowers, an Iowa State English professor in his mid-forties, someone who had only "recently vowed to avoid the stress of confrontations with sarcastic waiters and pompous deans," found himself entertaining revenge fantasies as he pursued—and never quite caught—"Sumner," who moved around from Oregon to Japan to Illinois to Germany, or just pretended to. With the over-priced and not-very-helpful aid of a lawyer, and the much cannier efforts of a P.I. named Anne Bunch, Bowers managed to extract a weirdly abject ac-knowledgment of David Jones's (his real name) conduct—" 'This letter is a feeble attempt to apologize to you for embracing and proliferating your ge-nius as my own' "—but not the kind of forthright and systematic amends Bowers wanted him to make with the journals he'd been fooling. He also learned, through Bunch's digging, that Jones, who at one point sent a vaguely chilling letter to Bowers's wife, had served time in prison for child molestation.

Bowers never adequately explains his tormentor's pseudonymous sub-missions, but who could? Admiration mixed up with envy mixed up with a need to get away with something mixed up with a need to get caught? The psychological elements in plagiarism, brilliantly paralleled to those of klep-tomania some years ago by the late scholar Peter Shaw, often make it (except perhaps among students) less a matter of careerism than compulsion. The excuses remain ever implausible. Sumner/Jones told Bowers that he wound up thinking one of the poems was really his after a lot of swapping and cross-critiquing in a writers' workshop—a variant on the "sloppy note-books" excuse so time-honored among literature's double-bookkeepers. (Bowers neatly shoots down another one, the photographic-memory defense: "I have always wondered why the brain's Nikon never gets the name of the real author within its frame.")

It comes as no surprise to me that Bowers met with general indifference from his academic colleagues. As with so many phenomena demanding common sense, on the subject of plagiarism, university professors display an invincible stupidity, a preference for French theory over nasty fact. When confronted with obvious word theft, the same tenured faculty so eager to perish those who don't publish are likely to muse upon the possibility that there is, *vraiment,* no such thing as authorship. Add to this a paralyzing fear of litigation when it comes to disciplining their own.

Bowers, realizing he works in a sphere of society "where 'values' are sometimes defined as 'biases,' " got used to hearing more sympathy expressed toward Sumner/Jones than toward himself. The same people who brought us speech codes and the victim-based curriculum "were often upset when [Bowers] bristled or responded sarcastically" to their saying he should be flattered or that he should just get over it. Journalists, he says, seemed better able to keep their eyes on the ball—something Bowers himself, alas, fails to do in places. The fanciful way in which he sometimes talks about the creative process—"Mind emptied of intent, the poet surprises himself, knows himself to be fortunate to say the things he says, knows the poem is infinitely smarter than he is"—can only encourage the sort of rarefied silliness being thrown at him in the English-department lounge.

Bowers thought that the culture's general inattention to poetry would leave him theft-proof ("Why would anyone steal a poem when the price it commands on the open market varies from a single free contributor's copy to several dollars a line?"), and the titles of some of the literary journals involved in this story—*Half Tones to Jubilee, Mankato Poetry Review, Whiskey Island Magazine*—will reassure even the most skeptical philistine that in this case it really *is* the principle of the thing, not the money, that's at issue.

Bowers has now become identified with a literary subject that never stops vibrating with at least low-level craziness. He has put himself in a position to be contacted by people like the mathematician who sent him "a packet of documents to support his contention that he was robbed of his discovery of several nineteenth-century letters mentioning an ancient pre-cursor to the computer." (I heard from this same man for years.) He knows, too, that in complaining about plagiarism, he runs the risk that "in the long term people might not remember which side of the theft [he] was on."

In being out there with this book, Bowers shows commendable courage, and yet he's a hard person for a reader to like. His language preens with a certain self-cherishing, and he even laughs at the proprietary worries of those would-be poets who send their work to the journal he edited. "[There were submissions] so worn from travel that they broke at their creases," he remarks, "and any carrying a handwritten copyright symbol could be tossed aside." One can't help feeling that, for all the rightness of his position, this whole never-fully-resolved affair bent him out of shape, at least once or twice, into something quite unattractive. When the author and his wife start sending letters to Sumner/Jones's wife and brother, they slide off the moral high ground. And yet even this zealous excess underlines how—in these times when there are fewer and fewer ways to be unlike everyone else—writing, with its fingerprint uniqueness, its irreducibility, may be more precious than ever to those who produce it.

Six Feet Under,
but Above the Fold

November 1997

W HEN BURYING AND WRITING about the dead, the English generally do better than Americans, a people to whom concision, like thrift, does not come naturally. Thus the *Dictionary of National Biography* has set something of a standard these past hundred years, ever since it was first edited by Sir Leslie Stephen, whose posthumous life shows how obituaries aren't necessarily the last word. His own, written in 1904, lacked the information that he would one day be regarded chiefly as Virginia Woolf's father.

I once composed a brief "life" for one of the *DNB* supplements, which are issued every ten years. The "Note for Contributors" was a series of thirteen marching orders, the fulfillment of which seemed an impossibility in the 1,250 words commissioned. Number ten alone decreed it "desirable that the personality of the subject should be conveyed to the reader, with comments upon any particular characteristic in such matters as appearance, manner, recreations, etc." Sound editorial advice, and yet with Brits as the subjects, this is an invitation to spill a cornucopia of eccentricities and tics that may well prevent the accomplishment of the other twelve mandates in the remaining thousand words.

Still, I learned that it can be done. The secret is to avoid eulogy, panegyric, hagiography, pathography and diatribe—all of life-writing's attitude-skewed isotopes—and stick to a selection of the *facts,* which are bound to do their own best work. For example, this past July, when the astrophysicist Gene Shoemaker died, I was surely not the only person to find it interesting that this man, who'd spent much of his career urging a proactive response to the catastrophe a comet or asteroid might one day inflict upon the Earth, should have died in a car crash. Shoemaker's passing was, with all due respect for the dead, a great day for fatalists. Lurking in the event seemed to be some message or truth, not just the cheap irony that had been there for the noting two years earlier, when Orville Redenbacher, whose popcorn popped larger and more frantically than his competitors', was found dead in a whirlpool bathtub.

Mr. Redenbacher's demise is re-created in *The Last Word: The New York Times Book of Obituaries and Farewells,* a new collection that demonstrates how irony, cheap and otherwise, is not the only delight available from this underrated literary genre. One also experiences the more serious lessons and pleasures of history, the ineffable meshings of man and moment. Just listen to the whole world shift its gears in the obit for James J. Shapiro, president of the Simplicity Pattern Company: "Shapiro himself retired in 1976, which turned out to be the peak year for the industry. It has shrunk considerably as women have flooded into the work force." Shapiro's running out of time becomes a reminder of how women ran out of it, too.

The "obits": Even their nickname sounds like a snack, tasty pieces of bite-size prose that some of us consume each morning like Frosted Flakes, when we ought to be eating the big, sober bran muffin that is the A section of *The New York Times.* Perhaps the genre's truest pleasure is Schadenfreude: You, the reader, are alive, while the departed is now twelve column inches of instructive diversion. AIDS took away some of the fun during the past fifteen years, but as that disease's harvest of souls (at least prominent ones) grows less abundant and their ages rise closer to actuarial norms, the obits, as entertainment, have been making a comeback.

The New York Times, like Palm Springs, is really an ideal place to die. Obituaries in the "newspaper of record" have an etched-in-stone, or let's say etched-in-microfilm, quality. In fact, one of their key features is what the *Times* itself had to say about the subject in life: news items, editorial comments and reviews are all quoted, the paper confirming not so much the decedent's passing as the privilege it conferred by noticing him while he was alive. Said decedent might do well to think about shuffling off not too long after he's made his mark. That is the advice of Russell Baker in his foreword to *The Last Word:* "The general rule," writes Baker, "is that an obituary shrinks in proportion to the number of years its subject outlives the deeds that once made him catnip to editors. Fame has a short shelf life in America." Baker also suggests checking out on a slow news day: "Die on a day when war is breaking out or Presidents [are] being assassinated or earthquakes [are] wiping out the city, and you will be lucky to get an obituary at all. Even the most celebrated stars may end up, much abbreviated, far back in the paper." The long New York newspaper strike of 1962–63 famously resulted in the stillbirth of many plays and books, but it gave an odd shot at immortality to the men and women who died during those months when death took a holiday; I'm sure there are readers who think some of them are still alive.

This new collection, a fairly random assortment, activates a reader's categorizing impulse. In it he will find the Inspirational: Hamilton Holmes, who helped integrate the University of Georgia; Angel Wallenda, who stayed on the high wire with an artificial leg; and Barbara McClintock, the solitary geneticist whose scientific peers took decades to accept what she'd already proved. There are also the One-Hit Wonders, like Wrong Way Corrigan (who probably knew exactly what he was doing when he flew to Ireland instead of California) and Johnny Sylvester, briefly "the most famous little boy in America," after Babe Ruth promised to hit a home run for the hospitalized tyke, who ended up living another sixty-four years. Obsessives have their place ("People devoted to a single cause are usually a little crazy," said one friend of Fred Lebow, founder of the New York City Marathon), and the Famous for No Good Reason, such as Jerry Zipkin, society "walker" of the ladies who lunched, also show up on their way out.

The Last Word does perhaps its best work with Hidden Hands, people who built the country we live in without our even knowing who they were—watchmaker gods like James W. Rouse (planned communities), Martin Bucksbaum ("suburban sprawl") and Irwin S. Chanin (city skyscrapers). Some of the most resonant obits here belong to Better Mousetrappers: the inventors of the Rolodex; of Häagen-Dazs ice cream, the Bronx concoction with a meaningless Swedish-sounding name; of the Burma-Shave road signs; the see-through clothes dryer; the see-through cake box. There's no point in mentioning their names; you'll forget them before another paragraph goes by. But each of them is like Christopher Wren, the London architect whose monument, those seeking it in Saint Paul's Cathedral are always reminded, is all around them. (Ironies enter these lives, too. Edward Lowe grew up in a house with no indoor toilet, and his discovery in 1947 of what became Kitty Litter eventually made cats more popular as American house pets than dogs. Who knew?)

A generation or so ago, remarks Marvin Siegel, the book's editor, "the obituary pages would underscore the importance of Pillars of the Community," who were allowed to carry a lot of boring kudos and credentials into the beyond. Today, less privileged characters are more likely to make it in, either for their good works or for having been characters, period.

The obituary desk "is thought to be a kind of Siberia of journalism," says Siegel. The resources of the *Times,* however, have always permitted the salaried presence of someone like Alden Whitman, "who wore a French policeman's cape and a neatly trimmed beard" and, instead of just cobbling together clips (from, of course, the "morgue"), made a practice between the 1950s and 1970s of interviewing his most prominent subjects before their demise. You might say their reputations preceded them. Whitman composed lengthy, updatable obits for his still-walking dead, ready for print at a moment's notice.

The practice continues. Often the paper will lay out the departed in prose by a subject specialist—the science or business or entertainment reporter who covered the deceased in life—but the *Times* continues to employ some full-time undertakers, including Robert McG. Thomas, Jr., whose talents, evident throughout this volume, mark him as Whitman's heir. Thomas displays some formidable tricks of a ghoulish trade, including a mastery of the, yes, deadpan. Obits have to move a lot more quickly than hearses, and he knows how to cut to the chase: "Jerry Siegel, whose teenage yearning for girls gave the world Superman, died in Los Angeles." To succeed in the genre, a writer has got to accentuate the appositive, that key phrase between the first two commas telling you just who the corpse was and what he did. Thomas can hold this syntactical note longer than Placido Domingo: "Benjamin Eisenstadt, the innovative Brooklyn businessman who set Americans to shaking their sugar before sweetening their coffee and then shook up the entire sweetener industry as the developer of Sweet 'n Low, died at New York Hospital–Cornell Medical Center."

After such an opener, good writing is what it is anywhere else, something to be flavored with fine metaphor and, when they're simply too hard to resist, neologisms: Sylvia Weinberger, a chopped-liver entrepreneur, is praised for her "schmaltzmanship." Much to the benefit of both subject and reader, Thomas likes to indulge in parody, especially with the makers of popular culture. A first paragraph summing up the inventor of radio-soap queen Ma Perkins asks, "Can a career woman who sacrificed her leisure to keep a nation of enthralled housewives glued to their radios for the better part of two decades survive a heart-wrenching regimen of producing as many as ninety cliff-hanging episodes a week to live a full, rich, and long life?" And one learns that it was Harold C. Fox who "claimed credit for creating and naming the zoot suit with the reet pleat, the reave sleeve, the ripe stripe, the stuff cuff, and the drape shape that was the stage rage during the boogie-woogie rhyme time of the early 1940s."

"Let no man write my epitaph" is as useless a piece of bravado as one can utter. *Somebody* is going to, and if you've got to go, Robert McG. Thomas provides the best send-off possible.*

The Last Word's arrangement does, however, leave something to be desired. As if dying had caught on only during the last several years, the selection consists entirely of recent pieces (there are none of Whitman's), and the volume has been padded out like one of those upholstered coffins that put the late Jessica Mitford into such a snit. The subtitle calls this a book of "Obituaries and Farewells," and it could have done without the latter. Some of these are from the popular year-end issues of the *Times* Sunday magazine ("The Lives They Lived") and are quite fine, but when added to straight-up obits for the same people—sometimes along with feature articles—they make the number of lives the subject possessed seem more feline than human. Worse than getting the same information a second or third time is how, in these other-than-straight obits, the writer's conscious appraisal cuts down the reader's own room for inference. The narrative propulsion of the daily obit, in whose short newspaper paragraphs sentence-openers like "Then," "Eventually" and "After" keep nudging the subject toward oblivion, is better left unsacrificed to the long view. And there's nothing like the regular obit's bare-bones, obligatory coda of survivors ("his wife, Joanne; their daughter, Laura Carter Larson of Los Angeles . . .") to close the lid and snap the reader back to the land of the living.

Finally, retitling the obits for this anthology strikes me as a mistake. Instead of "Fueling a Legend," Zora Arkus-Duntov should keep waving goodbye the way he did on April 24, 1996: ZORA ARKUS-DUNTOV, 86, WHO MADE CORVETTE A CLASSIC, DIES. The digits of age are an appropriately cold, hard fact; the appositive proves that one is very much what one does; and the final verb, no matter how often you see it, remains a killer.

*Thomas's own untimely death, at age 60, came on January 6, 2000. He got three well-deserved columns from his colleague Michael T. Kaufman.

Indexterity

March 1991

SOME YEARS AGO, when I was looking for lively material to discuss in a book about diaries, I knew, even before I got to the text of her journals, that Betsey Wynne, British naval wife during the Napoleonic wars, would make the cut. A single heading in the diary's index was enough to satisfy me: *dislikes Bombelles family, 119, 157, 164, 165, 170, 174, 175, 177–9, 183, 184, 186, 187, 190, 191, 202, 207, 208, 211, 213, 220, 224, 225, 229, 230, 231, 235, 236, 254, 260, 261, 271.*

Surely this would be a woman with personality.

The etymology of the word "index" takes you back to the Latin for "forefinger." Aside from pointing straight ahead, index fingers can beckon with a come-hither curl, and the pre–Vatican II "Index Librorum Prohibitorum" makes you think of a rigid finger pressed to the lips and signaling silence. It's a tantalizing word. When I finished writing that diaries book I decided to index it myself (do most readers realize that authors must otherwise pay, in docked royalties, to have this done?), and I remember trying to balance considerations of accuracy and appeal. I was delighted to be able to make legitimate headings for "revenge" and "voyeurism," not to mention the exotically pedantic pair of "robbery, grave" and "robbery, highway."

Most indexes deliver on their promises. Almost any column inch of the one for Gerald Clarke's fine biography of Truman Capote ("Kennedy, Rose; Kerouac, Jack; Kerr, Deborah; . . .") gets you set for what's inside. Some indexes, however, tease: how did Brigitte Bardot wander onto page 49 of Gov. Edmund G. (Pat) Brown's book on the death penalty? You turn immediately to page 49 to discover that she once sent a telegram opposing an execution. Oh, well, what were you expecting?

Sometimes an index is so copious that it becomes a readerly pleasure in itself. Surely no index will ever surpass the one in my copy of *The Anatomy of Melancholy. Lovers, Low countries, Lungs, Lust, Lutherans, Lycan-thropia* . . . and that leaves out the subheadings for these six items. Three centuries after Burton, Robert K. Merton devoted much of his delightful book *On the Shoulders of Giants* to tracking the history of a single apho-rism. *The Anatomy of Melancholy* was just one of his hunting grounds, and Merton's latter-day production wound up requiring *two* indexes. One was an "Onomasticon or a Sort of Index," from which follow two sample en-tries:

> *Stekel, Wilhelm: the metamorphosis of a dwarf, 269*
> *Voltaire: splendid vulgarizer of Newton and devoted friend of the Mar-quise du Châtelet, 34–7*

The "Onomasticon" was followed by "Places, Things, and Non-things," the last being defined as "unreified concepts."

The most avid readers of indexes are no doubt writers. In his book *Crooning,* John Gregory Dunne notes: "The first thing I did when I picked up *Spiegel: The Man Behind the Pictures,* Andrew Sinclair's biography of film producer Sam Spiegel, was look in the index, where I found a listing I was hoping not to find: 'Dunne, John Gregory, 131.' " The anecdote on page 131 turned out to be, as Mr. Dunne expected, inaccurate. But more often the authorial ego helps prove Oscar Wilde's axiom that the "one thing in the world worse than being talked about . . . is not being talked about." William F. Buckley, Jr., counted on this when, before sending one of his books to Norman Mailer, he wrote "Hi, Norman" next to the index entry for "Mailer, Norman."

The chief purpose of an index is distillation, and in performing that task it can manage to suggest a life's incongruities with a concision that the most powerful biographical stylist may have trouble matching. The index to *My Turn,* the story of Nancy Reagan's life, is full of juxtapositions that, as they say, Say It All: "Screen Actors Guild" immediately precedes "SDI (Strate-gic Defense Initiative)"; Jimmy Stewart is one line above Potter Stewart; Danny Thomas just before Helen Thomas.

Our indexing expectations are high for biography and history, and higher still for most works of general reference, where an index hardly qual-ifies as "back matter" at all. The index to Bartlett's *Familiar Quotations* is nearly two thirds as long as the book's contents, and *Roget's Thesaurus* comes even closer to textual eclipse: in the version I own, 227 pages of thesaurus come before 201 pages of index. Indeed, the latter often prove so helpful that one doesn't bother going on to the former.

It is novels, oddly enough—those books closest to history and biography in shape and look and spirit—that come to us starkly unappended. There are curiosities like *Pale Fire*, but that is a novel masquerading as something else. "The End" is usually just that, and if you'd like to spend a few more moments reliving the ones you've just spent with some minor character, your eyes and schedule will be out of luck, forced to retrace their whole triple-deckered trek. I can always count on the Cheeryble brothers to give my heart a quick lift, but they're not easy to find when the 7:48 is ready to pull out; and the reason you've sought them in the first place is the same one why you can't possibly bring *Nicholas Nickleby* with you on the train: your lap has been reserved for ungraded papers and an unbalanced checkbook.

There are those who will argue that a full-blown index to a novel would be destructive of its suspense; it would be wrong for a reader to spot "Bennet, Elizabeth, marriage of," before even seeing Mr. Darcy come onto the scene. But this assumes that the first-time reader of *Pride and Prejudice* will lack all self-control (is *that* why the French put the table of contents at the back?), when the last page has always been temptingly there, index or no index.

In any case, it is rereaders I have in mind, especially those of uneven novelists for whom one's feelings are forever mixed. I would be grateful for an index to *The Forsyte Saga* that listed, say, "determinism," in order that I might spare myself Galsworthy's grumblings upon the theme. Irene is perhaps that chronicle's most interesting character, and by the end of the second volume, *In Chancery*, when she has married Young Jolyon, one might enjoy the chance to search an index for any occasions in the first, *The Man of Property*, when their paths may have crossed and one was too dull-witted to imagine the possibilities.

Those who object that such an index would carry the game of make-believe, art's pretense of real-life reflection, a bit too far, might be reminded that the Scribners omnibus edition of *The Forsyte Saga* does come with a family tree, and that after Soames Forsyte finally died in 1926, in a volume beyond the original *Saga*, at least one English paper announced it as news. Now that John Updike's Harry (Rabbit) Angstrom has apparently passed away, on the last page of the fourth eponymous volume about his life (1933–1989), readers and future students of that life might like assistance in tracking the forces at work on it; an index with headings like "Janice, increasing confidence of," would cast important themes into high relief.

In his little monograph *Indexing Books: A Manual of Basic Principles* (1962), Robert Collison, the honorable treasurer of the Society of Indexers, declared that the craft "is only interesting to those people who really like an orderly approach to life." In fact, with today's shrinking production schedules, indexing is often a frantic task. Irving Tullar, a Brooklyn freelancer, talks of twelve-hour days when the crunch is on. Moreover, space can be as bedeviling as time. Laurence Cooper, a manuscript editor with Houghton Mifflin, points out that since books are printed in signatures, the index is the last part of a book to be allocated space during the production process. Indexers are often, in effect, asked to work with what's left over. "They're like reporters," said Mr. Cooper. "They're always fighting for more space. An indexer will say, 'Seven hundred lines? Can't do it.' "

But the craft has its pleasures, too. Mr. Tullar likes "the intellectual challenge" it provides, something akin to "creating a crossword puzzle. I enjoy the books that are well written, and I'm paid to read those books in detail." One thinks of Virginia Woolf gaining unequaled knowledge of "The Waste Land" by setting it in type, letter by letter, for the Hogarth Press.

Ruth Cross—rather a good last name for an indexer—has created more than 250 of them, and the variety of what she's been asked to undertake has made her widely read. She's done biography, memoir, educational psychology, history, psychiatry and literary criticism. "I'll take on almost anything except cookbooks," she says from her home in Maine. "If you've done one of them, you've pretty well done them all."

Irving Tullar makes use of software programs like Cindex—"It would be impossible to meet deadlines without a computer"—but so far Mrs. Cross has stuck to her handwritten citation slips. She can't quite shake the feeling that "in a conceptual index, a computer is not the answer. There are too many shades of meaning, different terms meaning the same thing that a computer won't pick up." Perhaps her fears are unwarranted, but I do know that when she did the index to my book about plagiarism, *Stolen Words,* whose text contained a bare-bones mention of Disraeli's "Calamities of Authors," she needed no one to tell her that instead of adding another page number under the heading "Disraeli, Benjamin," whose light-fingeredness was elsewhere cited, she needed to create a separate heading, "Disraeli, Isaac," for the author and prime minister's father. (Isaac, who spelled his own name D'Israeli, had his apostrophe dropped in posthumous editions of his work that were introduced by his son.)

As for the nonfiction author's own pleasures, there are few keener than seeing the index to his book. The feeling is akin to the kind of popularity one feels when flipping through one's address book, where every name, even those of mere acquaintances, has for a moment an equal voice and presence. It hardly matters how fleeting are the appearances of some indexed items in the text of the book he's written. How learned the author feels just seeing those hundreds of alphabetized subjects and names, and how organized, as if someone had finally gone into his brain and—all for the gentle reader's sake—put those heaps of clutter into a gleaming row of file cabinets.

Minding Your P's and Q's

February 1997

I WONDER WHAT YEATS, who in the 1920s smiled upon Montessori nuns and their students as being "neat in everything / In the best modern way," would have made of my early-1960s public-school classroom. There, a streamlined stainless-steel utility was the rule: under the bold face of the unticking Simplex clock we filled in standardized "California" tests with machine-readable pencil marks and a sense that our labors were leading not just onward and upward but eventually *ad astra*. The clean contours of the Mercury space capsule shining at us through the slide projector were proof.

In defiance of this futurism sat, in a row of alphabet cards above the blackboard, that beautiful ball-gowned version of the numeral two: the cursive capital letter *Q*. One knew, even at eight or nine, that in real life one was about as likely to run into that capital as into, say, the capital of "Chad, fmr. French Equatorial Africa." That *Q* was truly fit for a queen (the stately ancient Victoria, not the slender young Elizabeth II). Its regally useless frills were an extreme case of the curls and pennants flying from the rest of the alphabet—labor-intensive appendages that by sixth grade even strict Mr. Georgi didn't really expect anyone to bother making.

Although I marveled at that *Q,* I grew up with a sense that penmanship was antithetical to the serious business of words, the best of which get set in type. The disjunction was confirmed by my adolescent reading of *Nineteen Eighty-Four,* in which Orwell refers to "the neat handwriting of the illiterate." Years later, doing manuscript research for a doctoral dissertation, I found myself wondering whether my subject, the poet Edmund Blunden,

---

*Review of *Handwriting in America,* by Tamara Plakins Thornton (Yale University Press).

his handwriting calligraphically calm, wasn't a poorer choice than his some-time friend Robert Graves, whose personal correspondence was a storm of black ink. The notion that painstaking penmanship betrays a deficient imagination is fairly common; the discovery, a few presidential campaigns back, that Gary Hart had not only simplified his name (Hartpence) but also modernized the style of his signature made embarrassing political sense.

Handwriting in America, Tamara Plakins Thornton's cultural history of the subject, is filled with interesting and sometimes corrective information about penmanship and its prejudices. In Colonial times, for example, hand-writing, far from being the inevitable accompaniment to instruction in read-ing ("a universal spiritual necessity"), was taught on a need-to-know basis, usually to those young men who would be trafficking in the commercial world. A lingering snobbery against penmanship's mercantile functions re-quired some gentlemen to secure their class identity by adopting a less straightforward script than the one used by the tradesmen they patronized. Even this was a simplification of the "byzantine system of hands" that then prevailed back in England, where according to *An Essay on Education,* written in 1802 by the Reverend William Barrow of London, "a letter was often considered as the more genteel, the less conveniently it could be read."

In the early nineteenth century, a strong connection was made between good penmanship and good character (neatness meant self-discipline), and penmanship itself made the fortune of the writing master Platt Rogers Spencer, who created an ornate feminine hand that kept the fingers busy with all sorts of decorative strokes. With the textbooks he wrote for use in the public schools and a chain of business colleges, Spencer, and a horde of his relatives, dominated the teaching of handwriting well past the Civil War.

At the end of the nineteenth century, another script entrepreneur, named Austin Norman Palmer, came to the opinion that the overly fes-tooned Spencerian hand was lagging behind a restless America. The Palmer method, however billowing and ladylike its results may now appear, was his attempt to butch things up. To Palmer, none of the trick was in the wrist. Thornton explains, "He rejected the use of the fingers to form letters in favor of what he called muscular movement: sweeping motions of the arm from the shoulder powered by a 'driving force' that was both 'positive and assertive.' " The method's rhythms were said to correspond to moder-nity's own, and its advocates claimed for it a "powerful hygienic effect" on immigrant schoolchildren. These were the same proponents who declared writer's cramp to be a form of neurasthenia, and sinistrals to be in need of having their left hand bound up. According to Thornton, aging pupils of the method, which was taught until after the Second World War, recall it with "bittersweet memories of a past when moral certainty still seemed possible."

The history of handwriting analysis—a subject about which Thornton somehow manages to keep a straight face—begins in the Romantic era, when analysts, like that new creature the autograph seeker, hoped to discover genius lurking in the signatures of the famous and the accomplished. (Edgar Allan Poe was not surprised to find William Cullen Bryant displaying "one of the most commonplace clerk's hands which we ever encountered.") The graphologists who appeared later in the nineteenth century concentrated, as phrenologists did, on ordinary folk. Instead of seeking inked evidence of talent, they were on the prowl for "the hidden characters of potentially dangerous strangers" in the ever more urban world. In this same era, another kind of handwriting professional—one who did not claim the ability to analyze a criminal's character, but only to separate forgeries from the real thing—began to take the stand as an expert witness in criminal trials.

The stage was set for a twentieth-century showdown between characterological and physiological notions of handwritten individuality, and Thornton's book is more than absorbing when it concentrates on the former. The potential for self-discovery through graphology ensured that the discipline—which was deemed "intellectually marginal" and therefore practiced largely by women—became wrapped up in the drive toward Dale Carnegie–style betterment. Eager for individuation, the bored and the thwarted began sending letters to graphology columnists in the hope of receiving encouraging analysis. Thornton presents the most popular of these diviners, Louise Rice, as a kind of cursive-conscious Ann Landers, who frequently told her correspondents to wake up and smell the ink. To "Stella," so sure of her own exceptionality, Rice replied, "You bore me more than most persons do."

Thornton, too, brooks little nonsense: *Handwriting in America* is so well organized it sometimes seems to be printed on ruled paper. The author writes with a measured grace, but one wonders whether she would have avoided phrases like "the conceptual space in which the self has been delin-

eated" if she had produced her book by the leisurely means that is her subject instead of, as one suspects, at the computer keyboard. She addresses
the postwar period when progressive education abandoned cursive in favor
of printing and began thinking of "the penmanship pupil as a writer, not a
handwriter—in other words, as an individual expressing ideas," but she
doesn't travel down that slippery slope to a consideration of what has been
lost or gained by our cultural shift toward mouse and screen.

These considerations are perhaps beyond Thornton's subject, but one
does wish she had pondered what lies beyond the extinction phase in the
cultural history of anything American: the comeback. Go onto the Web and
match the words "handwriting" and "recognition": any number of sites will
present themselves, though the "recognition" involved has nothing to do
with character traits—only with the computer's growing ability to interpret
not just keystrokes but handwriting entered on a "digitizing tablet" with an
electronic "pen." Still, even this second act may be short-lived. Computers
have an easier time dealing with print than with cursive, and by the time
they become fully able to "read" the latter, new voice-recognition techniques will probably have rendered the capability obsolete.

The fax and E-mail have brought back letter writing to an encouraging
extent, but the limits of that revival, too, come to mind indirectly from one
of Thornton's rare doubtful assertions—on the subject of autograph col-
lecting. "What appealed to men of wealth . . . was no different from what
drew the lowbrow collectors, namely," she writes, "what one of the former
termed the thrill of 'divining personal character from an examination of
handwriting.' " Physical intimacy—touching exactly what the other person
had touched—was more like it, I should say, just as the photograph on a
signed *carte de visite* gave one the opportunity to imagine proximity, not
just practice physiognomy. *His* hand touched this page: that particular epistolary thrill is gone for the recipient of a fax, and while there is a certain
pleasurable intimacy in the first flash of an E-mail appearing in one's
queue—rather like being tapped on the shoulder at a party—it disappears
when the message itself opens up in the same pixels that everybody else is
sending.

You can't seal E-mail with a kiss, and the latest laptops protect us from
even our own bodily fluids: the Macintosh PowerBooks have eliminated
trackballs in favor of trackpads, so that sweat from one's thumb won't gum
up the works. Handwritten love letters showed a physical motion and inten-

sity that corresponded to what the epistolary couple—one writing, the other reading—were fantasizing about. What Thornton describes in the case of Palmer's method as "endlessly repeated push-pulls" was there on the page, in one way or another, whatever method the handwriter had applied, and it was connected to all those other movements that would make him, once he appeared in the flesh, yours truly.

Bookmobile

April 1998

"H AAA-VA STREET."

"Harvard Street?" we ask.

"No. Haaa-va. H-a-r-v-e."

I am back in Boston, its bowels if not its heart, stuck in the Sumner Tunnel with my book-tour escort of the day, who's just met my plane at Logan and whose car has just died. The local accent, rasping back into my ear as if it were 1975 and I still here in my miserable, grad-schooling twenties, belongs to the tow-truck operator who's materialized without our calling for him: Cameras in the tunnel alerted him to the backup we're creating among the nation's most famously aggressive drivers.

Nice Lynn Cannici is taking this worse than I am. I tell her that an hour from now it will all be an anecdote. In fact, I'm already wondering if I can use it myself, during the dozen interviews that lie ahead in the next two weeks I'll be on the road pushing the paperback of *Dewey Defeats Truman,* my latest novel.

As Truman Capote once observed, "A boy must hustle his book." So while Lynn waits for AAA outside the tunnel, I'm off in a cab to a radio interview at WMJX, where the friendly host has, quite reasonably for a twenty-minute spot, not read much of the book. No problem. It's not as if I can't say things I said scores of times during last year's tour for the hardback and that I'll keep saying over the next two weeks to interviewers from Raleigh's *News & Observer,* Tampa's *Weekly Planet,* the Wisconsin NPR outlet and the *Iowa City Press-Citizen.* "My mother thinks my heroine is a little fast for the 1940s": I've lost count of how many times I've confided this with a wry chuckle. I said it a year ago on the Tom Snyder show, and I'm still saying it, with a better, more spontaneous-sounding spin.

By late afternoon, the car is fixed, and Lynn has brought me over to

203

Cambridge for drop-in signings of stock in the Harvard Square bookstores. Veteran that I am, I keep the same level of grateful amiability whether the clerk's greeting is "Oh, you're him!" or, as it is more frequently, "You're who?" It's a no-win situation for the insecure author. If there are only three copies on the New Fiction table, he thinks, That's all they ordered? If there are eighteen: Oh, God, they aren't moving. But he signs whatever's there and hopes the Autographed Copy sticker applied by the clerk somehow makes it a more attractive purchase.

Once checked into the hotel near the Cambridge Common, I find myself with just enough time to take a twilight stroll through Harvard Yard and into the main university library. How appallingly broke and unhappy I was my first year here, accumulating the comic sorrows that would eventually fill *Arts and Sciences,* my first novel. Climbing the stairs to the library's top floor, I decide to have a retrospective glimpse of the English graduate students' little hideaway, if it's even still there. Yes, it is, across from the open door of a study occupied by—yikes! *he's* still here!—my first-year adviser, a gaunt Elizabethanist named G. Blakemore Evans, now 86 and securely famous as the editor of the magisterial *Riverside Shakespeare.* When I arrived here in 1973, with hair longer than the young Milton's ("the lady of Christ College": it all comes back), Professor Evans looked up from my undergraduate transcript, noting it was from Brown University (whose curriculum had been remade—in time for my entering class—through the efforts of one Ira Magaziner, later the chief designer of the Clinton health plan), and softly asked, "How did you get in here?"

Should I go in and say hello? I try to recall whether he does a walk-on, perhaps uncharitable, in *Arts and Sciences,* but I haven't read the book in ten years and can't remember. It doesn't matter; there's no time for a visit. Lynn has gotten hold of another car, and we're on our way back into Boston for a reading at Waterstone's, beautifully refeathered with books since a fire swamped it a couple of years ago. There's a nice little crowd, including a collector with a whole stack of my oeuvre in plastic see-through covers. I'll sign them after the reading and think, as always, I've got to get some of those.

The real perk of book touring? Seeing the old friends who turn out at almost every stop. I spot a former student in the audience, as well as my dear pal Penny, now sensibly a lawyer but who was an equally miserable grad student with me twenty years ago. And there's Larry Cooper, my eyes and ear for five books and most of a decade, the sharp-eyed copy editor who saved me from a host of howlers with his neat, color-penciled annotations and who didn't hesitate to mark a whole paragraph and let me know it wasn't funny or just wasn't any good. On one page of the manuscript of a book of reporting pieces, he asked why I never mentioned anyone's hair color unless it was red. I had no idea, but together we thinned the Hibernian herd. Larry was always a nonpareil, but these days he's closer to being literally one of a kind—an in-house, on-staff copy editor in a time when even big-ticket books are farmed out to freelancers who share no history with the author and who begin work on the manuscript with no foreknowledge of his quirks (like his almost never writing a straight-ahead sentence if there's a chance to add some semicoloned caboose or parenthesis).

Still, the freelancers do their job as best they can, and I remain grateful to whatever toiler, probably with no medical insurance, saved me from a nice little mess in one of the scenes I'll be reading tonight. My heroine suggests that she and her new boyfriend make love on the couch in his father's garage—the same garage, the anonymous copy editor noted, that I had described a chapter before as "doorless." Did I really want to make them exhibitionists?

———————

The invention of the book tour is generally traced to Miss Jacqueline Susann. Back in the '60s and early '70s, the late-blooming authoress, an unreconstructed broad with a deep voice and an insatiable urge to move wares like *Valley of the Dolls* and *The Love Machine* (each as good as Shakespeare, her husband assured the public), embarked on her bewigged and bejeweled barnstorming of talk shows in cities large and small, making hundreds of what were then called "personal appearances" at the bookstores, selling her stuff.

Over the years, Susann's m.o. trickled down to non-best-selling authors and eventually to the quiet precincts of what publishers call "literary fiction" (a term of economic pessimism, not critical approbation). These tours may involve more radio than television and interviews in the alternative weeklies instead of the big-city dailies, but the highbrows are still taking a page from Jackie's beach book. When a publisher tours an author (the transitive verb a sure sign of established custom) for a paperback, the cities may be smaller (last year I was doing Seattle and San Francisco; this time it's Raleigh and Vero Beach) and the interviews harder for the publicist to scare up, but the drill remains equally exhausting. After the radio stations and the drop-in signings and the evening readings, the game but punchy author, like *Valley of the Dolls'* showbiz legend Helen Lawson, collapses in front of a late room-service dinner and gets ready for the next day's early-morning plane and crazy flight pattern. (Across Florida by way of Atlanta?) In the days before publishers bothered touring me, when I remained at home awaiting word of my new book's stillbirth, I'd get disgusted by fellow lit-térateurs who bitched about their twelve-city ordeals. Why didn't they tour *me*? Three days into my first time out, I realized what my colleagues were talking about. All I did was write a book, I'd think before another Caesar salad in room 723 of the Radisson. Why am I being punished?

Touring authors survive thanks to the escorts, like poor Lynn, who take them through each city. These are typically well-heeled middle-aged women with nice cars who like books and want to work a couple of days a week. They are good company, on the ball but without the shellac that coats the PR lifer. These women are my readers, or at least quite a bit like a big segment of them, and I'm glad we get along. The escorts constitute a small, networked industry-within-the-industry; they hold their own annual gatherings at the American Booksellers Association convention and are rumored to give an award, in absentia, to the biggest pain in the ass they've had to haul around that year. Celebrity memoirists often take the prize: the bigger they are, the not-nicer they are.

The tours turn authors into vaudevillians who ask one another not if they've played the Orpheum in Kansas City, but if they've read at the Regulator in Durham, North Carolina. What's the worst night you've ever had? "Three people in Baltimore," says one well-known friend, who still can't top a novelist buddy who read to two people in Pittsburgh, both relatives. And there are certainly some pretty cozy gatherings awaiting me this time out. But, hey, it's January; El Niño's keeping them home, right? You learn not to take it personally and to spend your psychic energy cheering up the bookshop owner, who's generally gone to a lot of trouble.

Night after night, I read three scenes from the book I'm peddling— "*Dewey Defeats Truman,* a comedy set in the Michigan hometown of the inevitable Republican victor," I can hear myself autodroning at the podium. When the "crowd" is particularly intimate, like the handful tonight at Inkwood Books in Tampa, I forgo the lectern and gather people into a semi-circle for a kind of seminar. It brings back memories of teaching, in particular those days before spring break when the bulk of the Vassar student body would already be in Aruba. But the stalwarts are usually choice. One man here has brought with him a copy of my second book, which he read a dozen years ago and can connect to most of what I've written since. Another fellow waits until the end of the evening to ask how I could let my latest heroine make the absolutely wrong choice between her two suitors. The smaller the group, the longer it goes and the harder you work, and the better you feel at the end.

The owners and small staffs of the "independents," those unchained stores doing battle with every new Barnes & Noble and Borders, not only sell books but read them, too. They'd rather evangelize for favorite titles than talk business, but when asked, they'll tell you they're holding their own—as long as the superstores stay fifteen miles away. You shake your head and sympathize and avoid mentioning the one thing you and most of the writers you know like about the bibliobehemoths: the way they've got room to keep even your oldest, obscurest paperback displayed on their shelves. Still, your heart is with the indies during this bewildering retail revolution that's only begun.

There's also, of course, the Internet. The Seattle headquarters of Amazon.com is now a regular stop on the hardback tour. Members of the staff sit the author down for an interview they'll keep on the Web site, accessible through a dozen links, for years to come. The future of bookselling? One hears talk of publishers' establishing a common Web site, eliminating the middleman entirely, be it Inkwood Books or even Amazon. The future of books? They may survive only in RAM, available for downloading, never going out of print, never *being* in print. The whole business of the book tour, this up-close-and-personal troubadouring, couldn't be more out of sync with the times.

The tour is surely smarter economics than taking out the ads that writers love to see but which, as Maxwell Perkins explained sixty years ago, cannot work because they are "deprived of the great principle of general advertising—repetition." Still, can touring possibly make publishers enough money to justify what it costs to keep the author out on the road? One fellow novel-ist advises me to stop feeling guilty over what they're laying out for the planes and hotels and escorts. "You're working for food," he says, remind-ing me how I'm giving up two weeks when I would ordinarily be writing and earning. I'm still anxious, though: this is the first time anybody's over-paid me for paperback rights, and I'm afraid I'll never earn back the ad-vance.

The question of the advance is always a conundrum. Take whatever you can get, goes one argument—the more money the house has had to shell out, the more incentive it has to push the book and make it a success; and if it doesn't earn out, you still keep the advance money. But I retain a certain puritanism (you shouldn't get paid what you haven't made) and an aware-ness that the last book the publisher and I did together made us both a nice profit; I'm afraid this one will leave me a money loser, box-office poison in the editors' mouths.

A 6:45 a.m. flight to Milwaukee puts me on the ground too early to check into the hotel. Instead, my highly organized escort takes me off to eight drop-in signings she's arranged in advance. By noon I'm wearing my glazed running-for-office look and wet shoes from getting in and out of the car eight times through the slush. So gripped is Milwaukee by Packers fever—even one bookish indie owner wears green-and-yellow earrings—it must be the only city in the United States not talking exclusively about Monica Lewinsky, who has just become the most famous woman in the world. What chance has a novelist got of making a dent in anyone's awareness here?

I make it to my 7:00 show. The audience is attentive, if somehow too po-lite to relax and laugh at the funny parts. My Truman impression—which slew them in Vero—is received in silence. But they're more animated during the Q and A, and afterwards an older man walking with a cane, handsome in the manner of Arthur Miller, comes up to the table to have me sign his copy. Like one of my main characters, Jack Riley, he was a UAW organizer in '48, and like Jack he rode the *Ferdinand Magellan* for several whistle-stops with Harry Truman. In a hoarse voice, he tells me he stayed up the last two nights reading my book and reciting passages out loud to his wife. "You got it all right," he says, thanking me with quiet insistence for an expe-rience that meant a lot to him.

Did I say this was a bad way to make a living?

————

By Friday night, my voice is scratchy from airplane air and hotel heat and talking too much, but I'm looking forward to an evening at Prairie Lights Books in Iowa City, one of the most literate towns in America. My reading will be broadcast live on NPR, and I want to do a good job. ("They ask that you not use the words 'fuck' or 'cunt,' " say my written instructions. "You may use the word 'shit.' ") A nice crowd has come out, a number of them, I'm sure, from the Iowa Writers' Workshop. Its director, my friend Frank Conroy, sits in the last row. Frank discovered teaching when he was about 40, the same age that it was losing me, but I keep my hand in even now, doing short stints at the Bread Loaf Writers' Conference and the Columbia M.F.A. program in New York, where most of my recent crew of second-year students have been writing whole novels for their theses. Twenty years ago, they would have been doing short stories, but the premium on commercial viability and speedy success has convinced them novels have more immediate postgrad marketability.

My hour before the microphone has a pleasant, Garrison Keillor feel, and when I'm done, some young women who've been reading *Dewey* in their book club come up for signatures. Amid so many dispiriting developments, the proliferation of these local groups has been a big boon to literary novelists, and I tell the women to make sure they call my publisher for the official *Dewey Defeats Truman* reading guide, the kind of little pamphlet, now common in the industry, that supports this new demand phenomenon.

I'm happy tonight. An old college friend I've not seen in more than fifteen years heard my voice on the radio and jumped in his car to get here in time for the signing—during which I nodded hello and started chatting before I even recognized him. But if I'm happy, I'm also beyond tired. All the echinacea in the world isn't going to keep me from getting the flu once I get home and the adrenaline subsides. I miss sleeping; and more than anything, I miss working. In my suitcase, I have the outline for chapter four of my new novel, whose characters are far more on my mind than Anne and Jack and Peter, the *Dewey* love triangle I've been vocalizing every night. I have to get back to it. But not tonight and not tomorrow. Tomorrow is Cincinnati, and my escort's picking me up at 6:40 a.m.

Biographical

A Boy of No Importance

"WHY DISTURB THEIR SLEEP? . . . For one likes romantically to feel oneself a deliverer advancing with lights across the waste of years to the rescue of some stranded ghost . . . waiting, appealing, forgotten, in the growing gloom." This, wrote Virginia Woolf, is the impulse that drives a reader to the dust-covered autobiographies of the comparatively obscure. A similar impulse may turn him into the biographer of men and women even more deeply hidden, those whose very existence he may know of only from scattered appearances in the biographies of greater beings, but whose small proofs of existence are tantalizing enough to set the rescuing impulse in motion. The minor figure may first seem appealing as one more key to the personality of a more famous subject, or as evidence of the texture of daily existence in another time; but these odd "lesser lives" may soon begin to exert their own interest and demands. They may cease to function as cultural case histories or clues to another man's life and ask their due as unique subjects.

The downfall of Oscar Wilde offers the biographer an extraordinary interplay of character and action. At the Old Bailey in the spring of 1895, the great and complex wit is brought down, minting epigrams as he goes, by a parade of prostitutes and blackmailers, while much of the society that so recently lionized him jeers. Wilde is the central figure in a courtroom spectacle often farcical and ultimately tragic. But his was not the only disaster reaching its climax in the Old Bailey that spring. There was one witness for the prosecution who was neither prostitute nor blackmailer and whose agony was perhaps as great as the defendant's. This was Edward Shelley, the twenty-one-year-old former sales clerk for Wilde's publishers, Elkin Mathews and John Lane (later the Bodley Head). He was Wilde's own distraught victim, as well as a casualty of his own ambition and hysteria. His

213

story, not surprisingly, has been buried beneath Wilde's more imposing ruins; we have never known more about him than that which contributes to an understanding of the immediate legal reasons for Wilde's destruction. But a search for Shelley's forgotten life ends up telling us something more about Wilde's nature, and bringing us face-to-face with another human story that wants its own reckoning.

––––––––––

The circumstances of Shelley's introduction to Wilde were disputed during the latter's three trials, but the two probably met late in 1891, when Shelley was seventeen, in Lane and Mathews's offices on Vigo Street. Wilde had come to see about plans for the republication of a volume of his poetry. His interest in the sales clerk was quickened, and soon after treating Shelley to some no doubt remarkable conversation, he was taking him to Kettner's restaurant and the Prince of Wales Club, buying and inscribing books for him, sitting him in a box for the first night of *Lady Windermere's Fan,* and escorting him—drunken and protesting, Shelley would claim—to his bedroom in the Albemarle Hotel. At the trials Shelley gave his evidence in great distress, speaking with "considerable pain," according to the reporter from *Reynolds's Newspaper.* During the first criminal trial (which followed Wilde's unsuccessful libel action against the Marquess of Queensberry), he asked that his deposition be read when it became too difficult for him to continue. A reporter described him as "a somewhat distinguished-looking young fellow," who appeared "gaunt." The silk hat he carried with him into the witness-box was a sad vestige of the social ambition apparent in his testimony.

Wilde admitted his own generosities, but denied any impropriety. His counsel sought to discredit Shelley by pointing out that the young man had continued to see Wilde after the Albemarle incident; had asked for money from him (albeit without threats); had dined at the writer's home with Mrs. Wilde; and had carried on occasional correspondence with the playwright until shortly before the trials. It was also brought out, in an effort to cast doubt on Shelley's competence, that he had a mentally ill brother. Most damaging of all was the admission secured from Shelley that he had been arrested for assaulting his father a few months before the trials—and had called Wilde for bail before his father withdrew the complaint.

Despite all this, Shelley must have presented a sad picture of victimization to the jury. They learned of his thwarted plans to study after departing from Lane and Mathews; his painfully sincere literary aspirations; his sense of having committed sin; and his recent determination to " 'accept poverty as part of the Christian religion.' " He confessed to "nervousness," "insomnia," and being "ill mentally"; "people laughed at him and thought him strange." In the first criminal trial, Mr. Justice Charles, the presiding magistrate, noted that the jury's acceptance of Shelley's evidence would become "a question as to whether or not Shelley's mind was disordered. . . . there was evidence of great excitability."* At the final trial, Mr. Justice Wills dropped the charges concerning Shelley for lack of corroboration.

Regardless of this, the young man no doubt haunted the jury's deliberations, as he is likely to haunt any serious student of Wilde's life. With the completion of his testimony at the final trial, Shelley disappears from the front pages and the literary record, but even now one would like to know: Where had he come from? What became of him?

It is difficult to die without a trace. The modern world prides itself on the efficiency with which it keeps track of men from birth to death, and Edward Shelley, though he had reasons to hide an identity that technically had been involved in criminal conduct, cannot completely elude latter-day detection. Shelley was a "stranded ghost," and I was to become, in Woolf's terms, his "deliverer."

In the spring of 1975, after having done some writing on Oscar Wilde, I began to look for Shelley. Inquiries to a great many Wilde critics, editors and biographers yielded for a time nothing except names of other scholars who might be of help. But these responses eventually led to the discovery that there still existed thirty-two letters written by Edward Shelley to his employer John Lane between 1890 and 1895, the period of the boy's acquaintance with Wilde. After lying in a neglected carton for many decades, they had eventually arrived at the John Lane Archive at Westfield College, University of London; Mr. Michael Rhodes, the Lane archivist, transcribed them for me.

Here was Edward Shelley, less *in extremis* than the figure in the newspapers, but recognizable all the same—the ambition, literary pretense and pre-

*"The Wilde Case," *The News of the World,* May 5, 1895, p. 7, col. 3.

carious mental balance all manifested against the goings-on at Mathews and Lane's firm, publishers of the 1890s' most celebrated writers and artists, including Wilde, Aubrey Beardsley, Richard LeGallienne, Alice Meynell and various other contributors to *The Yellow Book*. The partnership of Lane and Mathews was an uneasy one, and Lane, who had to be away from Vigo Street much of the time early in the decade, used Shelley, it is apparent from the letters, to spy on his associate and frequent antagonist. Whether he actually suggested this role for Shelley, or the boy took it upon himself, it was executed with relish. Shelley ingratiates, dramatizes, and aches to please. He reports, for example, Mathews's conduct on June 4, 1891, in a way that is overexcited to be sure, but skillful enough to make his literary ambitions not wholly incredible:

> At half-past twelve o'clock I went up to him, & found him with his coat off, & in his shirt sleeves, *examining your parcels*[.] He was startled at seeing me—(I had come up the stairs very quietly)—& in order to divert my attention he grumbled at me about the dusty state the various parcels were in.

His zeal, though perhaps useful to Lane, seems a bit extreme—even in a seventeen-year-old with his eye naturally enough on the future.

Lane and Mathews's enterprise helped to excite Shelley's literary enthusiasms (on March 10, 1891, he writes of an attempt to glimpse his idol George Meredith at the Garrick Theatre), but the young man didn't neglect the practical aspects of his employment. Throughout the early part of 1891 he attempted to get a raise in salary from Mathews, and counted on the support of Lane in return for the intelligence he had delivered: "Could you give me a notion, (*re* my 'screw') as to what I should say in my letter to M, & when to lay it before him?—I have been here a twelvemonth to day. . . . I intend to ask him to make it a sovereign; I believe I am worth it!!" By the end of June the matter had not been resolved, and Shelley threatened to leave. There follows a gap in the letters until the summer of 1893. By the time they resume, Shelley has left the firm, probably because of dissatisfaction with his salary as well as Mathews's opposition, revealed at the trials, to his involvement with Wilde.

The letters from 1893 to 1895 illustrate Shelley's decline. He asks Lane in July 1893 for a character reference for a clerk's job at the London Library (though he says "my duties will be almost entirely of a literary nature"). He fails to get that position and a month later requests references for employment "in the house of a City firm of tea-brokers." A year later he is asking Lane to take him on in a new publishing venture that the latter has started following the dissolution of his partnership with Mathews: "It is the unanimous wish of my people that I return to the world of books." Lane apparently refused, and Shelley responded in a characteristically overwrought way: "Mr E Shelley would be obliged by your considering the letter of Monday last [an apology for a previous written outburst] null and void."

Shelley's sense of the importance of being earnest leads to near-pathetic lengths of self-advertisement: "I am an early riser"; "I am young and strong, and do not despair of ultimately winning success"; "I am anxious to become an earnest worker." This anxiety seems to have had its psychosomatic counterpart. Absence is explained by "my old enemy—a headache"; he mentions "bad health and nervousness"; apologizes to Lane for one eruption by saying it resulted from "a moment of what I can only call mental aberration." This is the erratic Shelley familiar from the testimony at the trials.

There is almost no reference in the surviving correspondence to his involvement with Wilde, but one may speculate that Lane destroyed letters Shelley wrote between the summers of 1891 and 1893 because they pertained too closely to the playwright. It does, however, seem as if Lane tried to aid Shelley in extricating himself from a dangerous position. In his last appeal for a job in Lane's new publishing enterprise, on August 20, 1894, Shelley writes: "I thank God that I had the courage to live down the terrible blunder of the past at all costs and completely sever my connection with those men, and I only regret that I did not follow your own & Mr. LeGallienne's advise [*sic*] sooner." Shelley's involvement with Wilde had become known to other writers in the playwright's circle, and some of them, too, had come into questionable contact with him. John Gray, the poet of *Silverpoints,* sent Pierre Louÿs Shelley's address with the following advice: "Seulement si tu cherches l'expérience de Shelley il foudra lui expliquer précisement qu'il devra se mettre à vos intérêts et non pas à rigoler." "L'expérience de Shelley" may have been offered to Louÿs for sexual pleasure, or as a case history to that student of homosexuality. In either event, little regard was being paid—except, it seems, by Lane and LeGallienne—to the exploitation of this habitually troubled personality.

By the spring of 1895 he was severely distressed, and the well-reported trials ruined any chances of new employment. Still, he seemed to hope to regain Lane's favor. In his last surviving letter to him, written on April 7, 1895, only pride seems to hold him back from making a direct appeal:

Dear Mr Lane,

You will doubtless have learnt from the newspapers the result of the Wilde case, long before this note reaches you, so that I need not refer to that subject beyond expressing my sense of loathing and regret at being mentioned in connection with Wilde. I am sorry that I had no opportunity of contradicting his cunning lies, especially his statement about your introducing me to him. He withdrew from the Court shortly before I was going into the witness box and is, at this present moment, at Holloway.

With best wishes for your success

I am

Sincerely Yours
Edward Shelley

In the months after his transcription of the letters, Michael Rhodes began his own search for Shelley, and during the summer of 1976 I joined him in London to continue what became a collaborative enterprise. Mr. Rhodes's chief scholarly interest was the history of the Bodley Head, but he too had come to feel the pull of Shelley's story.

We had two starting points available, one gleaned from the printed accounts of the trials and the other from the letters. The first was Shelley's age: if he was twenty-one in the spring of 1895, that meant he would have been born either late in 1873 or early in 1874, and given England's centralized records of births, deaths and marriages since 1837, a birth certificate would not be difficult to find. The second was his address: Shelley wrote his letters to Lane from 3 Hildyard Road in Fulham—although he sometimes listed the neighborhood as the more prosperous, adjoining Earl's Court. Could one learn anything from knocking on the doors of the street on which he had lived eighty years before? It seemed unlikely, but the possibility was there.

Shelley's birth certificate, located at St. Catherine's House, opened up a radial field of investigative alleys, as all such certificates do. It showed that he had been born on January 8, 1874, at 25 Queens Road, Kensington, to Charles John and Sarah Mapple Shelley. A search backwards several years for a marriage certificate revealed that they had been wed on October 30, 1869, at St. Saviour's Church in Chelsea. Mrs. Shelley was the daughter of a watch and clock maker. Charles Shelley, the son of a farrier, listed his own occupation, at the time of Edward's birth in 1874, as "blacksmith."

One is at once struck by the idea of this extremely nervous and "gaunt" young man, Edward Shelley, daring—as came out at the first trial—to assault a father who practiced such a strong man's trade. He must have had, one begins to surmise, a strength and violence not readily visible. Conversely, Charles Shelley, one learns, had weaknesses not usually associated with a vigorous blacksmith: a search, quarter by quarter through the deaths registers after the assault in 1895, showed that Charles died at the age of fifty-eight, on November 4, 1905, in the Kensington Infirmary—from "epilepsy." This raises the possibility that Edward Shelley, so nervous in appearance at the trials, was congenitally defective to a degree, a possibility further strengthened by his brother's having been characterized, at the trials, as "permanently unwell."

Obtaining the story of that brother was the main result of my knocking on doors of the row houses on Hildyard Road. The Shelleys' number 3 is still standing, and its current occupants, Mrs. Emily Reidy and her daughter Patricia, told me to try the house across the street, number 10, in response to my asking if there was anyone who had lived on the block a very long time. Mrs. Harris lived there, they said. She, I found out, had been born in 1896 and resided in the house all her life. She had vague recollections of the Shelley family, but none of Edward. What I wanted, she told me, was someone *older,* and that person would be her sister, Mrs. Grace Carlile, born in 1883 and now living in Tasmania. There she had recently published a slightly fictionalized autobiography.

So I wrote—immediately—to the ninety-three-year-old Mrs. Carlile, and she promptly sent me her book, *Love Holds the Door* (Glenorchy Offset Printers, Tasmania, 1975). It told the story of how, during one Christmas dinner three quarters of a century before, her father had interrupted the carving of the turkey to remark that a hearse had pulled up across the street:

The next morning we heard the sad story. . . . Our neighbours had a secret that none of their children had ever divulged. They had an imbecile eldest son of whose existence no one knew. Since childhood he had lived in an institute, except for brief visits to his home, but we had never seen him on these occasions.

We were both surprised and shocked to hear details of his death.

His mother, having lit a few sticks in the open fire-place, left him alone while she went to get coal from the cellar. When she returned, she found the poor fellow in flames and he died later from shock and burns.

We were amazed to learn that he was twenty-eight years old.

This "poor fellow in flames," Mrs. Carlile wrote me, was Edward Shelley's brother, and a return to St. Catherine's House showed a death certificate for one Percy Charles Shelley, aged twenty-eight, who died at home on December 24, 1899. The cause of death was listed as "Exhaustion, suppuration, following extensive burns received when alone in a room. Accidental."

Mrs. Carlile had other recollections of the Shelley family, and while recovering from a fall, she gallantly typed me her letter containing them. She remembered Edward Shelley "going off to work dressed in a frock coat at the time of his friendship with Oscar Wilde. . . . I often saw [Charles] shoeing horses in the blacksmith's yard in the next street. . . . Charles and Sarah never made friends and in fact were never seen outside, only when Charles came home from work and Sarah did her shopping after dark just before closing time." Mrs. Carlile recalled a number of brothers and sisters of Edward Shelley's, and school records help give evidence of a sizable family, with Edward as the eldest "normal" child.

One can imagine great pressure to achieve conventional success being put on him after the hopelessness of Percy's condition became known. The brother's illness, and perhaps Charles's condition as well, may have forced the Shelleys into the reclusive behavior described by Mrs. Carlile. They may also have prompted Edward's desire to make a distinguished escape from this household—and to accept Wilde's attentions as a means toward that end. Their involvement, when it backfired, must have been a terrible shame for the family to live down, and Shelley's nightly return from the Old Bailey to Hildyard Road in the spring of 1895, just months after he had come to blows with his father, is particularly gruesome to imagine.

Fulham was not an easy neighborhood in which to come of age during the 1880s and '90s. One reason for withdrawal from local schools sometimes cited in the records is "Objection to district." An examination of *The Fulham Chronicle* in the 1890s shows what seems to be an extraordinary number of suicides, murders of children by parents, cases of drunkenness, gangs of boy robbers, fires and deaths by fire. Fulham underwent breakneck urbanization during this period, its population going from 42,900 in 1881 to 91,700 ten years later. Shelley was part of London's ever-burgeoning lower-middle class, with few chances to escape anonymity. However he managed to secure his job with Mathews and Lane, a perception of the difference between Hildyard Road and Vigo Street near Piccadilly must have set his ambitious heart racing.

School records show that he probably did not receive any formal education beyond his thirteenth year; he left the Sherbrooke Road Elementary School in July 1887. Those records also show that the Shelleys made a number of moves during the 1880s, all within a few square blocks' area of Fulham. Their last move, to Hildyard Road, can be explained by the fact that the house there, larger than their previous homes (also still standing), could provide the space needed by the growing family. But an earlier move from 21 Halford Road to 12 Delaford Street sometime in 1886 is more puzzling—the two houses are almost identical in size. Perhaps the reason here is economic: Halford Road would have put Charles Shelley closer to the Lillie Bridge Stables and a more lucrative practice of his trade. Still, one wonders whether unwanted and abrasive contacts with neighbors were ever the cause of a move by the troubled, furtive and, on at least one occasion, violent Shelley household.

The death certificate supplies a biographer with several routes to travel backwards from the subject's demise. So Michael Rhodes undertook the job of finding this essential document for an Edward Shelley born on January 8, 1874—a formidable task, since Shelley could have died any time between May 1895 and the present. It was even possible that he was still alive, a centenarian. Mr. Rhodes began with the deaths register for the second quarter of 1895 and went through 220 ledgers before learning that the particular Edward Shelley we were in search of had died on January 4, 1951, four days short of his seventy-seventh birthday, at "Meadside" (number 13 Westfield Road) in Hertford. Death was due to a coronary thrombosis, and was reported by his wife, "H. Shelley." Mrs. Shelley listed her husband's occupation as "Sergeant, Grenadier Guards (Retired)." One piece of certified paper suddenly added relative longevity, a wife, and military service to the shadowed outline of Edward Shelley.

Mr. Rhodes wrote the Grenadier Guards to inquire if there existed any record that an Edward Shelley had served with them for any period during the decades following 1895. Mr. E. W. Mitchell responded that there was not. But it occurred to Mr. Rhodes that Shelley might have entered the service immediately after the Wilde trials, in which case his notoriety would have necessitated an alias. What name might he have chosen? It could have been any one, but "Mapple," Shelley's mother's maiden name, was the only one to which we knew Shelley had a blood connection. Mr. Rhodes took a chance and wrote again to the Guards, this time asking for the service record of one Edward Mapple; and Mr. Mitchell wrote back that an "Edward Maple" had enlisted in the First or Grenadier Regiment of Foot Guards on July 4, 1895. At the time of his enlistment he was twenty-one years of age, and had given his trade as "Clerk." He was five feet ten and one-half inches tall, 135 pounds, of fair complexion, and had blue eyes and brown hair. He had scars on his head and upper lip. He gave his home address as 3 Hildyard Road, Fulham, and "Charles Maple" as his father's name.

An intolerable situation at home, and the impossibility of finding employment with his new, if minor, infamy, must have prompted his enlistment under the alias just several weeks after the last trial. The physical description aligns with a crude drawing of Shelley that appeared in *The News of the World* on April 7, 1895, and with some of what one knows about Wilde's taste in young men. In fact, in that newspaper sketch Shelley looks like a somewhat less chiseled version of Lord Alfred Douglas. As for the scars on his head and lip, one wonders if they were inflicted by the disapproving father with whom we know he once came to blows.

Whether his military service was undertaken out of sheer necessity or a kind of psychological overcompensation for his homosexuality, it was distinguished, even heroic. Shelley fought in the Boer War and was awarded both the Queen's and King's Service Awards with clasps for participation in action at Belmont, Modder River, Driefontein, Johannesburg and Diamond Hill. The rigor of this combat must have taken a stamina and daring unexpected from the wracked young man who had previously served the crown only as Queen's evidence. On November 27, 1899—a month before the ghastly death of Shelley's brother—Lord Methuen led the Guards to the Riet River, where they

> were at once exposed to heavy Boer rifle-fire from the hidden entrenchments. The Guards were in the worse position: in the confused action which followed they could do nothing but lie on the sand in the blazing heat of the sun, ready to fire if the Boers tried to advance but othewise unable to move. . . . The battle continued all day, and it was not until evening that the Guards could withdraw from their dangerous and uncomfortable position.*

The satisfaction Shelley must have taken from his exceptional service in the five years after the trials was not to last long. In September 1896, he had been promoted to corporal, but on December 15, 1900, just weeks after Wilde's death, his service record shows that he reverted to private. Mr. Mitchell suspects, in his letter to Michael Rhodes, that Shelley "was found out re the assumed name in 1900 and reverted to the rank Pte in order to avoid disciplinary action being taken against him." Whether or not his involvement with Wilde also became known is uncertain, but it was what caused him to assume his mother's name in the first place, and so had caught up with him once again, if only indirectly.

Private Shelley was discharged to the reserves on March 16, 1903. He signed for his medals under his own name and gave 3 Hildyard Road as his address.

The death certificate indicated that there must also be a certificate for Edward John Shelley's marriage to a woman whose first name began with *H*. A search through the registers, forward from 1903, the year of his discharge, showed that Edward Shelley married Henrietta Clegg in Great Amwell, Hertfordshire, on July 7, 1937. Both were sixty-three years old; Mrs. Shelley was the widow of Dr. Richard Clegg of Hertford, and the daughter of

*Edgar Holt, *The Boer War* (London: Putnam, 1958), p. 132.

William Tattersall, a solicitor. A check of the *Hertfordshire Mercury* turned up a report of the wedding and the news that the Shelleys spent their honeymoon in South Wales.

The marriage certificate lists Edward Shelley as a "widower," but a record of his first marriage has not yet been found. There is, however, reason to doubt his truthfulness in giving information about himself. Unless the rank of "Sergeant" recorded on his death certificate is the product of a faulty memory on Mrs. Shelley's part, he deliberately misled her. One assumes that he told the *Hertfordshire Mercury* that his parents were "of Chelmsford": certainly his father had been born there, but Charles Shelley worked all his adult life in London. Edward Shelley also told the marriage registrar in Ware that his blacksmith father had been an "iron merchant," and so one must reasonably doubt the justification for listing "accountant" as his own profession. Perhaps he did spend the years between his military service and marriage to Henrietta Clegg as an accountant in Kensington (given as his residence in 1937). Yet one suspects that "accountant" bears the same sort of relationship to work as a clerk that the term "iron merchant" bears to "blacksmith." Certainly Shelley did not make the sort of living one would expect from such a profession: he died intestate, and his effects were valued at only £312. In the absence of further information, one suspects his life in the early decades of the century to have been fairly much all of a piece; one also guesses that his eventual marriage to Henrietta Clegg was motivated partly by his desire for financial security at the end of a troubled life, and by her hope to escape the loneliness of widowhood.

Mrs. Shelley was a great deal more wealthy than her second husband. She died in 1959, and her will shows an estate worth more than £21,300. As a solicitor's daughter and doctor's widow, she came from circumstances a great deal more comfortable than Edward Shelley's in Fulham. It was her money that enabled him, according to neighbors still living on Westfield Road, to spend a good deal of his last years in two places much enjoyed by Oscar Wilde decades before: the south of France and, ironically enough, Windermere. The Shelleys were away from Hertford much of the time, and have left few memories of themselves on their old street. But in one interview I had with a neighbor, Mrs. Shelley was recalled for her money and property, her eccentricity, her feebleness and difficulty in maneuvering an automobile. (Sometimes Edward Shelley helped her push the car into the driveway, and sometimes he rolled a cigarette while she pushed.) Shelley himself is remembered for being tall and well built in his advancing age, and for having his fatal heart attack while waiting for the tea kettle to boil.

Mostly, however, the Shelleys were out of town. Edward Shelley's obituary in the *Hertfordshire Mercury & County Press* lists his residence as "Bank House, Windermere." Mrs. Shelley died at the Wheatlands Nursing Home there on June 21, 1959. By that time Bank House had been divided into three flats. The bulk of her estate went to a niece and nephew. There seem to have been no children from her first marriage.

––––––––

The embroideries on Edward Shelley's marriage and death certificates are understandable enough. He seems never to have lost the habit of covering his actual tracks and imprinting others where he had never been. One feels, though without certainty, that Henrietta Shelley did not know the story of her husband's involvement with Oscar Wilde. (Certainly the residents of Westfield Road in Hertford did not.) Concealment was probably not too difficult fifty years after the disaster, but Shelley did live to see the rehabilitation of Wilde in the public mind; a number of biographies and studies mentioning his own name; and the publication, in 1948, of H. Montgomery Hyde's *The Trials of Oscar Wilde,* in which he figures prominently.

Before and after his experience with Wilde, Edward Shelley was likely a more troubled than attractive personality. But he was a victim, and it is too easy to say with Lord Darlington in *Lady Windermere's Fan* that "People are either charming or tedious. I take the side of the charming. . . ." For Wilde, Shelley's charms were no doubt primarily physical, although the boy's longings, admiration, and perhaps his suppressed violence—which surfaced in his clash with his father—may have added to his temporary appeal. But he became "tedious." He was not one of the street arabs who would "bray for boots" and eat the fancy dinners they were about to earn with uncomplicated gusto; he was someone who took himself and his two worlds seriously, neurotically so, and Wilde, for all his generous nature and intelligence, did not realize or care that he was helping drive Shelley towards a despair which the recipients of silver cigarette cases (Shelley got books) had little reason or capacity to experience. Shelley's morbidity must have disturbed Wilde, who probably felt well rid of this particular dalliance; but his reaction lacked understanding. He wrote Alfred Douglas in April 1894:

I had a frantic telegram from Edward Shelley, of all people! asking me to see him. When he came he was of course in trouble for money. As he betrayed me grossly I, of course, gave him money and was kind to him. I find that forgiving one's enemies is a most curious morbid pleasure; perhaps I should check it.

The betrayal referred to is probably Shelley's confession to John Lane of the nature of his relationship to "those men," but it was demeaning for Wilde to consider a boy so helpless an "enemy." He was partly responsible for Shelley's longings for distinction; he had helped create a situation he showed he could appreciate in *A Woman of No Importance*. In that play Lord Illingworth and Mrs. Arbuthnot discuss their son, who has recently entered his father's life without knowing of their real relationship:

> LORD ILLINGWORTH: . . . What is our son at present? An underpaid clerk
> in a small Provincial Bank in a third-rate English town. If you imagine
> he is quite happy in such a position, you are mistaken. He is thor-
> oughly discontented.
> MRS. ARBUTHNOT: He was not discontented till he met you. You have
> made him so.

Edward Shelley was never content with life on Hildyard Road. But it is beyond question that Wilde fired his dreams to the point where he was willing to share his mentor's bed in the Albemarle Hotel and return to face his disapproving father at the blacksmith's forge the next morning.

Wilde may simply have been too preoccupied with the sense of his own impending doom, which he famously expressed to Gide, to worry overmuch about another's. But he left himself and Shelley with a quantity of epigrams and speeches that must have rung in his own ears in prison, and in Shelley's on the battlefields of southern Africa. On the night of Wilde's greatest triumph to date, and during the week Edward Shelley was publicly made minion, Mrs. Erlynne spoke to Lady Windermere, who sat left center stage:

> You don't know what it is to fall into the pit, to be despised, mocked,
> abandoned, sneered at—to be an outcast! to find the door shut
> against one, to have to creep in by hideous byways, afraid every mo-

ment lest the mask should be stripped from one's face, and all the while to hear the laughter, the horrible laughter of the world, a thing more tragic than all the tears the world has ever shed. You don't know what it is. One pays for one's sin, and then one pays again, and all one's life one pays.

Shelley's mere survival is remarkable enough.

————

He was buried on January 10, 1951, in the graveyard off North End Road in Hertford, a short walk from the Westfield Road home he shared with his wife. The grave is marked by a stone border somewhat overgrown with weeds. An affable gravedigger, who remembers Henrietta Shelley's first husband, Richard Clegg, as the local school doctor, is willing to lead the visitor from the cemetery's record books—kept in the toolshed—to grave number EC15, Edward Shelley's. The inscription on the foot border is "Blessed are the pure in heart." Presumably, it was selected by Mrs. Shelley. One of course wonders whether she chose it with the miseries her husband had suffered a half century before in mind, wonders again if she knew his early history. Whether she did or not, she had at last, with a beatitude, freed him from epigram.

Held in Check

T HEY HAVE SURVIVED him by thirteen years, in old boxes from the department stores where we used to shop: thousands of canceled checks, a couple of which paid for the merchandise we brought home in those same boxes thirty or so years ago. In 1985, my mother carried the checks with her when she sold the house I grew up in and moved to a smaller place. They look new, much newer than the photographs that accompanied them. The only physical clue to their age comes in handling them; they cover the fingers with a fine blue-green dust—infinitesimal sheddings of bank paper and ballpoint, a spray of volcanic ash from the cultural convulsion that buried this way of life, the American postwar rituals from which people would soon flee, as did the Pompeians from their lunch.

Like the grid of streets in the suburban development on Long Island, where I was born, my father's neatly stacked checks map a whole postwar way of life. To be true dream houses, those little G.I.-financed Cape Cods had to be customized, which meant there were patios to be built and yards to be "landscaped." Every improvement created a bill. On August 29, 1951, my parents paid the Franklin Square Top Soil Company $24, by check, and so there my mother still stands on a late summer day, seven months pregnant with me, watching my father make himself handy with a shovel.

On weekdays, she and the other women would all be home, and fundraisers had no need of direct-mail solicitation when they could just knock on the doors of these young suburban matrons and ask for a check: the Red Cross, the American Cancer Society, the Mental Health Association—one of these, in my mother's curvaceous hand, shows up every inch or so into the stack, and every one is for a single dollar, the sum my mortgaged father would have instructed her to disburse. The Fuller Brush man also came calling ($2.55 on September 5, 1956), and the RCA serviceman, employed

228

in an era when televisions were regularly repaired and even exported, got $12.75 on December 15 of the same year. (You couldn't watch Rosemary Clooney sing on Perry Como's Christmas special if the horizontal hold wasn't holding.) The sums are so small, so tidy, that the few big ones jump out: Joseph P. Doherty, Inc., $1,466, on September 15, 1953? Of course. Our two-tone Nash, with the black body and red roof.

What was never meant to be saved, like what was never meant to be overheard, is usually what contains the truth. The letter and the diary (my father never kept one) are supposed to be the preserved written instruments by which the dead are revealed to posterity, but each of these is a formal communication, and any written communication, from even the least self-conscious soul, is a performance. About ten years ago, in a book I wrote about diaries, I concluded that even the most private diarists are always conscious of an eventual, albeit anonymous audience. Moreover, letters and diaries are written principally about things that have already happened, whereas these checks were not merely a *record* of my father's transactions with the world; they *were* the transactions.

To look at checks—my father's, anyone's—is to see someone on his feet, going about his business at the very moment he went about it. Look at the appointment book of a dead man and see if it doesn't seem curiously more vital than the self-justifying journal he may have kept. The checks were my father's unwitting diary, and I'm their audience.

During the years we lived in the house in East Meadow (1950–1958), Arthur Mallon made his living at the era's most memorably dramatized occupation: traveling salesman, for the Fownes Brothers glove company. It's attested to by the $6 checks to New Jersey hotels and the modest ones to Howard's clothes, just enough to keep him looking smart, "riding on a smile and shoeshine." A gentle, well-liked man (unlike Willy Loman's, his funeral really *was* jammed), he was honest enough to take personal offense at a tax audit. Stuffed in with the checks is an indignant memo he wrote on the back of Treasury Department Form 885B after an appointment with Internal Revenue agent Martin F. Carney in 1954. In his jagged handwriting, he notes:

> During 1st interview in Freeport, Mr. Carney discussed each point of my return, suggesting adjustments both in my favor and in favor of Int. Rev. He adjusted my hotel expenses without suggestion or dis-

cussion and then claimed I owed $65 in taxes. When I objected, he abruptly closed the interview and destroyed notes he had made and complained I had wasted 2 hours of his time. This form claims I owe $194.01. Mr. Carney either does not know his work or is attempting to penalize me for objecting to his adjustments.

Not a bad expository style for a man who left school at fourteen.

Martin F. Carney to the contrary, the checks are redolent of my father's regular habits, his responsible relationship with the world. Pride in that relationship—in having done his mundane duty—is, I suspect, one of the reasons he kept them. I also think they spoke to his own awareness of the passage of time. My father would have been embarrassed to keep a diary; he was just someone who passed his days earning and spending, and the checks were mementos of that. I believe he probably looked at them from time to time, and was aware they were filling up the box, like sand accruing in the bottom of an hourglass.

For all my father's manifest responsibility (he was a "family man" to the point of self-extinction), I confess to a bit of apprehension about going through the checks: Would I suffer some nasty revelation and end up feeling like that other salesman's son, Biff, when he stumbled on the Woman in Boston? No, the only checks I found made out to The Smart Woman shop, for $11.66, and to Ellen's, for $6.56, were written on Christmas Eve and Valentine's Day—last-minute presents for my mother. The Christmas gift would have been a fancy slip, whose routine appearance each December 25 became a family joke; if my father had had a good year, ten-dollar bills would flutter out as my mother unfolded it.

Like many men who served in the Second World War, my father chose an almost passionately unadventurous life in the years that followed. I do not believe he even rode in an airplane until he was forty-six years old, for a one-time-only business trip to Chicago, an event I now remember as a source of some excitement. There it is: February 2, 1960, United Air Lines, $52.75. A month later is the only other record of dealings he had with the land and people of Illinois: a check made out long after he'd returned to New York, to the city of DeKalb, for $1. A speeding ticket, surely; my father could not bear to be a scofflaw even at so great a distance and for so small a sum. By this time he was working in his company's Fifth Avenue showroom, but I can map his earlier road territory from checks he wrote to the traffic-control bureaus of half the towns in New Jersey. Upon first seeing these, I was delighted to imagine him speeding through Millville and Asbury Park, being chased by sirens; but then I considered how these checks, too, were usually for $1. Not speeding, but parking: that was the real story. The poor guy was inside with a customer, schmoozing as fast as he could on the single dime he'd put in the meter. If he made it eleven times out of twelve, he'd come out ahead. Whatever other gambling urges he had were satisfied by the two-cent pinochle hands he played on Saturday nights. "Sweetie! Sweetie!" I can now hear his buddy Hank MacDonald shouting to him and their friend John Molnar, exulting over a good hand, the sound coming upstairs to my bedroom as I lay contentedly under the covers.

Far from being dry, "canceled" instruments, these fiscal madeleines remain sharp with the flavors of memory. February 17, 1957, to Mr. and Mrs. John Moruzzi, $20: a wedding present conveying still the taste of almonds and the feel of satin, things I ate and touched for the first time that night when my mother came home with the reception favor (the almonds) and the swatch of Aunt Rose's bridal-gown fabric. So often these little paper rectangles stubbornly assert the exact circumstances in which they were written. Take pale-green #163, drawn on my father's Long Island Trust account and made out to the First National City Bank of New York. (Banks once had grand, meaningful names instead of today's fused corporate logos.) The check is dated November 22, 1963, and is a loan payment. It was hand-delivered instead of mailed, since there's a bank stamp on the back of it with the same date the check was written. My father probably walked it down to the branch of First National City one floor below the showroom on Fifth Avenue and Thirty-seventh Street, at lunchtime. November 22, 1963, was a Friday, payday, which means the check would have been covered that evening, out of cash from his yellow pay envelope, which he would have brought up to Long Island Trust after we'd met his train and he'd tossed me the *New York World-Telegram* with its 278-point headline.

Occasionally, the checks invite a sort of scholarly detection. The one made out on October 2, 1948, to John Wanamaker, just after my parents had moved to Moorestown, New Jersey, carries a rare memorandum on a line in the lower left-hand corner: "pillows." Were they just getting new things for a new bedroom, or was my mother, pregnant with my sister, beginning to feel that she'd like to prop herself up a bit? Enough faulty memories are corrected, and true ones redated, to make one wonder if psychoanalysts shouldn't ask their patients to go looking among family papers for Oedi-pus's checks. I'm surprised to discover that a Cape Cod vacation, of which I have clear recollections (trampolining on a guesthouse bed, being struck in the eye by a beach umbrella), happened when I was three and a half. I would have put it two years later, but the check made out on April 15, 1955, to the owners of the Wildwood Beach Cottages in Hyannis, tells me I'm not as amnesiac about my earliest years as I sometimes think.

The checks also convince me that as early as 1958, when I was six, I had picked up on my father's financial anxieties and made them my own. That was the year we moved to a bigger house—more house than we could af-ford, as the subsequent twenty inches of stacked checks make plain. What strikes me about the small bundle created by the purchase and the closing is how well I remember the names and sums involved. There's Martha Koch, the German widow from whom we bought the house, whose piano went out one door as our television went in another. There's the realtor, Martin L. Browne; the lawyer, Stanley Fowler; the O'Donnell moving company—their names coming back as familiarly as those of the Yankee infield or the Mercury astronauts. And there is that figure, $127 paid each month to the Greenpoint Savings Bank. I remember it so clearly that I realize I must have been preoccupied by it, afraid that my father might not be able to meet it. That this house was, by the standards of 1950s Long Island, an "old" one (built all of thirty years before) made matters worse. The furnace was al-ways breaking down (checks to the repairman from Dieters-Hagen), and my mother was trying to make do with Mrs. Koch's old washing machine with the wooden wringer (Reliable Washer Service, $4). Nixon would have lost the kitchen debate to Khrushchev if he'd had only us to point to, and I must have sensed that we were in danger of falling behind, of not making it in this big new house with the lovely cool basement. Every night for the next twenty years you could find, by my father's chair in the living room, after he'd gone upstairs to bed, the butt of his El Producto Corona and the columns of figures he'd toted up on the backs of envelopes, the ones that had brought the bills.

A public-policy analyst would note, however, that this was not a family afraid to go to the doctor. It seems clear that the checks written to the gen-eral practitioner were, at $5 and $10 a visit, among the least worried-over in the whole box. No one of the four of us was ever seriously sick, and the frequency with which small sums were paid to our doctors proves it was my parents' habit to nip in the bud any sign of trouble.

I was even born on the installment plan. All those checks written to Dr. Caddy, the pediatrician, after the first of each month throughout '52, show that everything from circumcision to inoculation was done on credit. This friendly arrangement is pleasant enough to notice, but then come, more woefully, the all-purpose credit cards. These were an invention of my father's generation, passed down to mine, in whose wallet they grew into a way of life. My personal fear of plastic (I cannot let a credit-card bill lie unpaid on my desk overnight) clearly has origins in my father's dealings with it. A payment of $14.90 to the Diners Club on March 16, 1956, is the first one I can find, but soon there would be an unending stream to First National City for personal credit—all of this before Visa and MasterCard had even come along. We *were* falling behind, but credit made it barely noticeable, as if we had merely decided to sit facing backward on a forward-moving train. What was really happening is clear from the early 1960s on; the small contributions my father was making to his pension plan were more like the dream of a parachute than a strategy that would actually bring him down safely onto the plains of retirement.

And to see how much he spent on me! I cannot find one check amid thousands for anything that would qualify as a self-indulgence by my father—not so much as a bowling ball. The El Producto cigars (three for fifty cents) and the two-cent pinochle hands were all he allowed himself. But the checks for my upkeep? Start as far back as 1953 for all the ones to the eye doctor (those lenses the size of nickels), and then find ones to the Stewart Manor Little League, and the one on July 6, 1962, to Dick Quigley's Music Shop, for the rented violin I managed (there are no accidents) to break. Eventually you come to the enormous ones, for tuition, to a college that, like the house, was more school than we could afford. Add to those the ones made out to me, term after term, for books and everything else, endorsed with my own rounded signature, which I can see gradually losing its baby fat, becoming ever so slightly like his. My God, I see I was *still* nickel-and-diming him through graduate school, getting him to pay the occasional phone bill or rent notice. On second thought, perhaps a therapist would want to advise his patient to avoid this particular exercise in memory retrieval: it's too guilt-producing. Still, as I think of it now, one of the nicest compliments my shy father ever paid me was in financial language. I was asking him, with some embarrassment, if I could quit my summer job a couple of weeks early to take a youth-fare flight to Paris before returning to college. Reminding me that I didn't take drugs or smash up cars, he reassured me by saying, "You're a bargain."

At the moment, it's hard to see it that way, metaphorically and otherwise. When my father died in 1980, I found the Dime Savings Bank payment book for an education loan with its eighty-four stubs still beveled and bound in; it had kept me safely on an American campus in the last years of Vietnam. My father and I, reserved with each other, substituted a kind of mutual protectiveness for any plainspoken intimacy. I know that this obsolete loan-payment book serves no purpose other than the posthumous one he quite possibly intended: to remind me of how I got started, and of how he ended up in such a mess.

For that's what those last years were. His lungs were bad, and not long before he took early retirement he went into the hospital. There's a spate of checks from that time, written by my mother in handwriting made leaner and faster by necessity. Once he retired, any checks written to Fownes Brothers, for roughly the same amounts as his old pension contributions ($45.27 on November 11, 1975), were to keep his Blue Cross. A first pink check, for Citicorp Credit Services, written that same day, starts a series that appears on the edges of the stack like traces of an infection. These were the days when banks sent credit cards out in the mail, unsolicited, and my father tried to stay afloat by grabbing on to these sandbags, paying off one with the other, BankAmericard with Mastercharge, Chase with Manufacturers Hanover. The last inch of the stack of checks is hard to read in every sense. Checks for refills for the bedroom oxygen tank, written in the shaky hand of a dying man, press ominously toward the very last one, on January 4, 1980, to Visa.

Seven weeks later, he was buried in a veterans' cemetery in Calverton, New York. A gruff military chaplain performed a fast ceremony in the "Committal Service Area" before my father was brought to a grave marked, like the rest of them, by a flat stone, flush with the ground in deference to that symbol of his suburban life, the lawn mower. Grave number 764, section 4, is in a row of other men who died that month. Barr ... Zdunczyk ... Salerno—they're laid, side by side, in nearly the order they died, a procedure one might dismiss as coldly bureaucratic, like the terse rule on the back of the interment record: "Potted plants will be permitted on graves only during the period 10 days before and 10 days after Easter Sunday." But having survived what they did in Europe and the Pacific, the men buried in the rows of section 4 knew that rules and steady habits and orderliness—of lives, of bank checks, even of tombstones—had given them much of what they'd enjoyed in the world.

Sanctified by Blood

Iₙ ᴛʜᴇ ʟᴀᴛᴇ sᴜᴍᴍᴇʀ of 1864, Abraham Lincoln was in the mood to savor any available approbation. He was worried, even expecting, that George B. McClellan, the general he had once mocked for having a case of the "slows," would be elected to succeed him as president of the United States. Just as 100 years later Lyndon Johnson would scan a chattering triptych of television screens in search of good news from the networks, Lincoln must have spent some of the election season poring over newspapers, scissors in hand, looking for whatever comfort he could clip. Two cuttings that he made—or perhaps, knowing they would be favorably received, his secretaries John Hay and John Nicolay handed to him—conveyed support from unlikely quarters.

In Philadelphia, McClellan's hometown, the Reverend Henry Ward Beecher was reported to have told an audience at the Academy of Music that Lincoln might "be a great deal less testy and wilful than Andrew Jackson, but in a long race, I do not know but that [Lincoln] will be equal to him." The newspaper went on to note how the "storm of applause that followed this seemed as if it would never cease. The turn given to the popular enthusiasm, by the mention of Lincoln's name alongside of Jackson's, was wholly unexpected." England, whose early sympathy for the Confederacy was vexing, had often sent bad news; but a second clipping reported that in a letter to Horace Greeley, the British reformer John Bright, who had tried to undo both the corn laws and capital punishment, declared every European "friend of your Union" likely to back Lincoln over his Democratic opponent. The clippings went into a billfold lined with purple silk and divided into compartments for NOTES, U.S. CURRENCY and R.R. TICKETS. There they stayed for the remaining months of the president's life—through Sherman's scourging of Georgia; Lincoln's victory at the polls and conciliatory second inaugural; Lee's surrender at Appomattox. On Tuesday, April 4, 1865, during Lincoln's own visit to the captured capital of Richmond, he added a small trophy to the billfold: a $5 Confederate bank note bearing the portrait of treasury secretary Christopher Memminger.

As Lincoln rode to the theater on the evening of Good Friday, 1865, the billfold rested inside his frock coat with a half-dozen other items, each as compact as the president was rangy. There was a folded linen handkerchief with "A. Lincoln" embroidered in small red letters, and a curved pocketknife he had probably used to repair one of the sets of spectacles he also carried that night—a small gold pair from the aptly named Franklin & Co. firm of Washington opticians. The spectacles' left wire arm had been fixed with string, the way an unfussy person might today apply a Band-Aid. A different pair of lenses folded up at the nose bridge. A thin pencil; some chamois pads with which to clean the eyeglasses; and a substantial watch fob—a pyramid of quartz in a little gold cage, unattached to any timepiece, as if to signify that Lincoln's time was at an end—formed the rest of his pockets' inventory. The frock coat in which the objects rode was protected by a heavy overcoat, a gift from Brooks Brothers for the second inaugural, its silk lining marked by a quilted federal eagle and the inscription "One Country One Destiny."

While the president watched Laura Keene and Harry Hawk grind through Tom Taylor's threadbare comedy *Our American Cousin* (it is doubtful that Lincoln, being farsighted, required either pair of glasses to see the actors), the contents of his pockets, commonplace and useful things (except for the clippings, the pretty watch fob and whimsical bank note), sat there with him, ready to mutate from paraphernalia into relics.

By 10:15 p.m. there was nothing that could stop John Wilkes Booth. The bodyguard at the door of the box had left his post. The assassin, fortified with a gulp of whiskey from Taltavul's tavern downstairs, had only to wait for the funniest line in Act 3, Scene 2 ("you sockdologizing old man-trap"), the one that drew a laugh big enough to drown out the report of his derringer. No appeal to his reason or mercy could any longer be made. And yet, there in the dark, Lincoln had one on his person. Inside the billfold, and generally ignored by historians in their amusement over Lincoln's collection of good press, were a few other newspaper clippings. The additional cuttings spoke to the conversion process; they appealed to rationality and what Lincoln himself had, before the war began, called "the better an-gels of our nature." One of them, printed in the Toledo *Blade,* was a letter written by a Confederate soldier on July 16, 1863, and found in the streets of Brandon, Mississippi, by a captain of the 62nd Ohio Regiment: "It is use-less to discuss the errors of the past," wrote the discouraged Southerner; "possibly there have been none that could have been avoided—certainly we are a defeated and ruined people, shorn of our strength, powerless for a successful solution. . . ."

"Useless": the last word Booth himself would speak, twelve days later, as he lay dying on the porch of Richard Garrett's farmhouse, regarding his own hands. By then he was aware of the futility of the bullet he had fired into Lincoln's brain, and of the great wound his dagger had put into the president's theater guest, Maj. Henry Rathbone, who with his fiancée, Clara Harris, the daughter of a New York senator, had been invited at the last minute to replace General and Mrs. Grant. After Booth severed one of Rathbone's arteries, the major "bled so profusely as to make him very weak," Clara Harris wrote in a letter eleven days later. "My whole clothing, as I sat in the box was saturated literally with blood, & my hands & face— You may imagine what a scene." Like the objects Lincoln carried, Rathbone and Miss Harris arrived at the theater with nothing much for history to re-mark upon. But as they crossed 10th Street to the home of the tailor William Petersen, where throughout the night Lincoln's possessions must have hung from a hook in the back bedroom while doctors attempted to save him, the young couple, drenched with Rathbone's blood, were them-selves turning into relics, doomed to figure in a terrible postscript to the story of the assassination.

It was probably Robert Todd Lincoln, the president's grown son, who took possession of his father's effects, carrying them away from either the Petersen house or the subsequent autopsy at the White House. For more than seventy years they remained in the Lincoln family, until in 1937 Robert's daughter, Mary Lincoln Isham, donated them to the Library of Congress. For nearly four decades after that, the objects rested in the Li-brarian's safe, unseen by the American people as they fought a world war, ventured into space and observed the hundredth anniversary of each Civil War milestone from Fort Sumter to Ford's Theatre. Finally, during the American bicentennial, Daniel J. Boorstin, the historian then heading the Library, arranged for the items to be put on exhibition in the institution's

Great Hall. For the past several years, no longer on display, they have been kept in a cunningly constructed box of beige linen and brown leather. The newspaper clippings are under Mylar in a drawer beneath the box's main display surface, whose sculpted indentations provide a snug holder for each item—including, now, a monogrammed button thought to have come off the president's shirt while doctors removed his garments in search of additional wounds. The smaller box in which the items rested from 1937 to 1976, as well as its silver skeleton key, now sits inside the larger, more recent construction. Another compartment holds a pair of thin white gloves, reminiscent of the ones Lincoln wore to Ford's, for use by any curator who must handle the objects.

Displaying them was probably considered unseemly in the late 1930s, speculates James Gilreath, curator of Americana in the Library's Rare Book division. They were still too close to the living person, having come, after all, not from some distant relative but a grandchild. Today, as the bicentennial of Lincoln's own birth begins to approach, a viewer of the box's contents finds nothing grotesque in the sight, but he does feel an aversion, beyond curatorial rules, to touching the objects. These bits of glass and string and paper are no longer things in themselves.

By saturation or mere proximity, blood is what sanctifies a relic. It is the sulfuric elixir that transmutes what alchemists would call the *prima materia* of the linen handkerchief or the worthless bank note. Blood was the war's literal medium and its rhetorical element—throughout its battles, at its conclusion and for long decades after. The vintage trampled out by the Lord in Julia Ward Howe's "Battle Hymn of the Republic" was the bloody wine press of Isaiah 63:3: "for I will tread them in mine anger, and trample them in my fury; and their blood shall be sprinkled upon my garments, and I will stain all my raiment." The country itself, not just its individual sons, had nearly bled to death by 1865. It was the *nation's* wounds that Lincoln spoke of binding up at his second inaugural, only six weeks before the assassination. And it was the "bloody shirt" that Republican politicians would wave for another generation, any time they wanted to remind voters of the South's antebellum Democratic traditions.

In his *Political Dictionary*, William Safire traces the term to James Baird Weaver, an abolitionist fond of telling "how in the 1850s he acquired the stained and shredded linen of a preacher who had been flogged for inflaming slaves. 'I waved it before the crowds,' said Weaver, 'and bellowed:

"under this bloody shirt we propose to march to victory." ' " Putting the ritual in its long historical context, Safire reminds us that Mark Antony waved Caesar's saturated mantle before a susceptible crowd, and that Abraham Lincoln himself, while serving the prosecution at a murder trial in Illinois, displayed the victim's stained clothing and said: "It is better to wave the bloody shirt than to waive justice."

The blood that drenched the box at Ford's and the gutter of 10th Street belonged entirely to Henry Rathbone, who almost died as Mrs. Lincoln hung on his shredded arm, screaming, while the presidential party made its way through a gathering mob and into the Petersen house. Lincoln, despite his wife's cries ("Oh, my husband's blood! My dear husband's blood!"), had barely bled at all. It was the suffusion of his wound that frustrated the doctors; they kept breaking up the clot to prevent pressure in his skull from building to a fatal level. The temporary success of their efforts could be seen only on the pillows in the back bedroom, where the president rested until his death at 7:22 a.m. on April 15. Incredibly, the bloody pillow he died on remained on display in the house (now a federal museum) until March 1994, sustaining damage from the sun, before the building's curator, S. Marshal Kesler, sent it away for conservation work. While only prudent, indeed overdue, her action was not universally popular, and the pillow remains the first item that many repeat visitors to the house, years after their first trip, ask to see.

Jacqueline Kennedy, a woman with a literary appreciation of ritual, displayed her understanding of blood's mystic and inflammatory powers when, on the afternoon of November 22, 1963, she refused to change out of her stained clothing. "Let them see what they've done," she is reported to have said aboard Air Force One as John F. Kennedy's body was returned from Dallas to Washington. It was this implacable gesture, as much as the killing itself, that turned the bouquet of red roses she had been presented with at Love Field into a terrible foreshadowing object.

Nellie Connolly rejected any such attempt to conjure with the gunfire that her husband, John, had, after all, survived. She expressed surprise at the Warren Commission's apparent indifference to the ballistics potential of the shirt the Texas governor had been wearing:

I had the clothes, but nobody seemed interested. After about seven weeks I took John's shirt . . . it was all smeared with his flesh and blood, and dipped it in cold water several times to try and preserve it. Someone finally came to pick up his clothes. I think the Commission said his shirt was useless as evidence because it had been "laundered." But I never laundered it, I just soaked it in cold water.

The Warren Commission did photograph the shirt, and during his testimony Governor Connally informed its members that he had given it to the state archives of Texas. (The question that elicited this fact was curiously animistic: "What is the permanent home of these clothes at the present time when they are not on Commission business?")

The Lincoln relics had to survive the chaos and violence that created them. The watch fob, now lying peacefully in its customized compartment, looks inevitable and significant, but on the night of the president's killing it would have been just one more nuisance to be frantically stripped away. In 1964, Diana Hamilton Bowron, a young English nurse who had been on duty at Parkland Hospital as Kennedy was brought in, testified to the Warren Commission's Arlen Specter:

> When we were doing a cutdown on the President's left arm, his gold watch was in the way and they broke it—you know, undid it and it was slipping down and I just dropped it off of his hand and put it in my pocket and forgot completely about it until his body was being taken out of the emergency room and then I realized, and ran out to give it to one of the Secret Service men or anybody I could find.

At that moment, it was a piece of property that regulations required returning; thirty years later it would probably seem stately with meaning.

In the jacket he wore over a white shirt with gray stripes (ordered from Cardin's after he'd admired the style on French ambassador Hervé Alphand), President Kennedy was carrying a card that had been handed to him at breakfast that morning by Msgr. Vincent Wolf: "We, the school children, the nuns and priests of Holy Family Church in Fort Worth are happy to offer one thousand Masses for the spiritual and temporal welfare of you and your family, and to show our love and devotion to the President of the United States of America. . . ."

The Mass card, as familiar to Catholics as a rosary or building-fund envelope, was translated by blood into something fateful, cruel in its failure to protect the president's "temporal welfare," which was now, like the thousand days of his administration, one for each of those Masses, at an end. Considering it today, one thinks it should somehow have worked the same miracle performed by the eyeglass case resting in the breast pocket of Theodore Roosevelt on October 14, 1912. That object, along with the folded text of a Bull Moose campaign speech, slowed a bullet fired at the ex-president, saving his life and earning its own magical latter-day presence in Roosevelt's boyhood home, now a museum, on Manhattan's East 20th Street. The thing has a peculiar power, as if the case carried not mere spectacles but second sight, just as Lincoln's four lenses, all of them ready but not in use, make one think of the eyes he would have required in the back of his head to detect Booth's entrance into the box.

The miraculous power of religious relics depends on a willingness to believe in them. In the early Middle Ages, according to historian Patrick J. Geary, the bones of saints provided "the only recourse against the myriad ills, physical, material, and psychic, of a population defenseless before an incomprehensible and terrifying universe." As Geary demonstrates in his book *Furta Sacra,* the monasteries holding the relics counted on them for protection against the same predatory nobles who needed the relics' help against their own foes: "The regional councils at which nobles swore to limit the extension and duration of their violence were usually convened around a particular saint, and it was before the saint that the oath to preserve the peace was extracted."

Our own material world may be more orderly than the ninth century's, but the universe remains "incomprehensible and terrifying." Modern historical relics—the accoutrements of secular figures instead of the body parts of saints—may not be brandished so desperately, but we maintain them as carefully as the Library does Lincoln's possessions because they provide the only human bulwark against time: continuity. They are proof of connections, signs not only of fealty but, more important, of provenance and legitimacy. During the mid-1990s, the White House was damaged by an airplane and automatic-weapon fire. In neither instance was President Clinton endangered, but the incidents appalled people as attacks on the mansion itself, a functioning relic, and all it represents. The plane, for instance, sliced through a magnolia tree planted by Andrew Jackson, a living object seen by thirty-four subsequent pairs of presidential eyes.

The historical relics we prize may run more to items of clothing than corporeal remains, but we have not evolved entirely beyond a wish to traffic in flesh and bone. Recent years have seen a rash of requests for the exhumation of historical figures. Zachary Taylor's skeleton was dug up in 1991 by a group who theorized that he had been the victim of arsenic poisoning and not, as history has always had it, of too much ice milk and cherries (or cucumbers) consumed on the Fourth of July. (No arsenic traces were found, and the American public remains free to honor the memory of Taylor's vice president and successor, Millard Fillmore, who had been mentioned as a possible conspirator.) That same year, the corpse of Huey Long's assassin, the doctor shot by Long's bodyguards immediately after he shot the Kingfish, was exhumed in an effort to show that Dr. Weiss could not have performed the deed after all. Most recently requests have been made to bring up the bodies of John Connally (to retrieve significant bullet particles) and John Wilkes Booth—or whoever was put in his grave after Lincoln's assassin supposedly escaped to the American West.

All these requests—the one for Booth was rejected in 1995—have been made in the name of forensic science, but there is also something grimly ritualistic (perhaps a hope for dark empowerment) in these pleadings to touch the famous dead. For more than three decades after the assassination, Lincoln's body exercised enough of a hold on the national imagination to excite competition among various locales wanting to entomb it more grandly than it had been at Springfield's Oak Ridge Cemetery. In 1876, some counterfeiters, hoping to ransom their ringleader from Joliet State Prison and realize another $200,000 for themselves, broke into the crypt and nearly made off with the body. Before the remains were permanently buried under several feet of cement in 1901, a plumber, according to the authors of *Lincoln: An Illustrated Biography*,

> cut a little window in the lead of the coffin just over Lincoln's face. A pungent odor arose. There was the face, still white from the chalk applied by the undertaker on the funeral trip west back in 1865. . . . Seventeen honored Springfield citizens were asked to peer inside the coffin on this final day, and as each one confirmed the identity of the

coffin's occupant, their thoughts could not have been far different from those of the young doctor Edward Curtis, who had held Lincoln's brain in his hand [during the autopsy] thirty-six years before: "As I looked, I felt more profoundly impressed than ever with the mystery of that unknown something which may be named 'vital spark.'"

To possess Lincoln's corpse would be to own something quasi-holy. The conjunction of the political and sacred has persisted into modern times, most spectacularly in the corpse of Eva Perón, the embalming of which took six months. The body was later stolen, hidden, buried in Italy, returned to Juan Perón in Spain and then brought back from exile, to Argentina, with him. In Buenos Aires's Recoleta cemetery it remains an instrument of wishes. "The sarcophagus cannot been seen," wrote V. S. Naipaul in the 1970s, "but it is known to be there. On the morning I went, white lilies were tied with a white scarf to the black rails, and there was a single faded red rose. . . ." Depending on a country's history, a political corpse is the crime scene, or the better days, to which posterity feels compelled to return.

In modern secular democracies, the relics of history may possess, for many citizens, more potency than religious ones. After viewing the Lincoln objects at the time of the American bicentennial, Stanley Kunitz opened his poem on the subject with a memory of how, during an Italian visit, the effects of real saints had left his imagination cold, whereas Lincoln's button and watch fob now seemed "miraculous."

Here is the American Christ, fit for veneration by even nonbelievers. The centurion at this crucifixion, Major Rathbone, produced three children, the eldest of whom was keenly aware of his ineffable inheritance. Born in 1870 on Lincoln's own birthday, February 12, Henry Riggs Rathbone made Illinois his adopted state and, in 1922, got himself elected its at-large Republican congressman. A well-known lecturer on the sixteenth president, he pressed his connection to the box at Ford's, sponsoring the bill through which the United States acquired a major collection of Lincoln relics in 1926, and rising on the floor of the House to deliver remarks on the 115th anniversary of Lincoln's birth:

As you doubtless know, my parents were the young engaged couple, Major Rathbone and Miss Harris, the daughter of United States Sen-

244

ator Ira Harris, of New York, who drove that fateful night of April 14, 1865, with President and Mrs. Lincoln in the carriage to Ford's Theatre and sat with him in the box, when the bullet of the assassin cut short the life of the President. I am able to say with the utmost assurance of truth and judging from the words uttered by Lincoln in the presence of these persons in his last hour, that his great heart held nothing but kindness and good will toward all his countrymen. . . .

Representative Rathbone did not allude to what did not fit—the unseemly fact that the historical accident which helped make his political career had also destroyed his parents' lives. On Christmas Eve, 1883, while the future congressman slept nearby, his father murdered his mother, in part, it was said, because his mind had been destroyed by years of hearing whispers about how he should have done something more to save the president. Rathbone would spend the rest of his life, until 1911, in an insane asylum, and the whereabouts of Clara Rathbone's bloody dress—not what she wore the day of her own murder, but the gown she had on at Ford's—would remain the subject of inquiry, legend and fiction.

The Lincoln family may also have tried to keep elements that didn't "fit" from being inserted into the legend—or even into the box of relics presented to the Library by Mrs. Isham in 1937. For years, historians have heard rumors that another object Lincoln had in his pockets on the night he was killed—a small pistol he carried to calm his wife's fears for his safety—was deliberately excluded from the gift, lest the firearm somehow detract from the legend of the martyred president.

There is weaponry enough in the Ford's Theatre museum. Booth's derringer is behind glass, along with the knife he plunged into Henry Rathbone. ("AMERICA—LIBERTY AND INDEPENDENCE—THE LAND OF THE FREE AND HOME OF THE BRAVE" is the inscription on the dagger.) Rathbone's white gloves—no doubt, like Lincoln's, balled up in his pockets, and probably the only item of his clothing not to be drenched with his blood—are laid out nearby, somehow more frightening for their pristine condition. A visitor can also see Lincoln's overcoat, a fragment of the wallpaper in the state box, a piece of the theater curtain, and mourning tassels cut from the catafalque that bore the president's coffin. For years after the assassination, the grief-stricken and the curious had to *have* something. The Louis Schade family, who acquired the

Petersen house on 10th Street from its original owner, sold it to the United States government in 1896, after years of trying to escape relic hunters. Today, as the House Where Lincoln Died, it is administered with Ford's Theatre by the National Park Service. The curators had wanted to exhibit the contents of Lincoln's pockets on their own site instead of at the Library. In medieval times, monastic competition for relics gave rise to complicated thefts and "translations"; in our own day, the Library has arranged an unprecedented loan of the items, which are temporarily on display where they last were in 1865.

The Washington tourist who comes to Ford's or the Library may also make a stop at Political Americana, a memorabilia shop that thrives a few blocks from the White House. Buttons, stickpins, fans, pennants, sheet music: American attics are full of them, and what isn't handed down can be purchased. *Hake's Guide to Presidential Campaign Collectibles* lists a Nixon key chain for $15, a McKinley ribbon for $40, and a 1⅛-inch copper Lincoln medal from the 1860 campaign, its reverse depicting the "Rail Splitter of the West," for a surprisingly low $65. But that is the difference between the piece of mere memorabilia and the relic. One is a deliberate artifact, mass-produced and slightly vicarious in feeling; the other is minted by accident, usually catastrophe and blood. One takes the curatorial term "ephemera"; the other belongs to the ages.

Enough About Me

August 1997

As SPRING APPROACHED and I was making the last stops on a book tour, I found myself, one sunny afternoon outside Los Angeles, stuck in the windowless confines of a public-radio station, one more sound-baffled studio with walls like an egg carton. The peculiarly intense interviewer was bent on discerning, among my recent novels, a pattern. Its chief feature, I learned, was the conspicuous absence of my real-life adult self from these books.

Such absence ought to be unsurprising—one might even regard it as a precondition for writing fiction—but the interviewer seemed less to be making an observation than leveling a charge. What was I evading? That was the implicit question—worth asking, I suppose, if all writing were meant to be a projection of the self, with even fiction a chiropractic for the author's psychological kinks. So why had I wandered off to such before-my-birth historical venues as the Civil War and the summer of 1948? And why did my narrative voice hover so far above the action? My books were so removed from my life that the interviewer, while claiming (or feigning) appreciation, pronounced them "very odd."

Well, include me out. After two early novels rooted in personal experience, I said good-bye to myself, at least where fiction is concerned. I now prefer my books to cover parcels of geography and time that I haven't trod with my own two feet. I want to be free of my own small life story. A novelist friend tells me that even in recent ones, I've been more present in my books than I (or that radio interviewer) may think; through the faraway and historical characters, I'm in some ways writing about myself, or at least speaking my mind. True enough, of course. But writing isn't Method acting, and the biggest novels, the ones that made D. H. Lawrence call the genre the "one bright book of life," come out of something other than the writer's needs and assertions. Flaubert's proclamation "I am Madame Bovary" was a eureka of self-extinction, not self-expression.

My doubts about the emergence of memoir as a hot new publishing commodity—it's been variously described as a "trend," an "explosion" and a new "age"—don't just proceed from a belief that too much contemporary fiction is already too autobiographical. My reservations began with a book I published even before my first novel, a study of diaries called *A Book of One's Own*. To write it, I read scads of personal journals and in the process developed a clear preference for those diarists who wrote about something other than themselves. The outer life, let's call it: the weather, the war, the servants, the amusing remark overheard on the street. Anything but the moist quiverings of the writer's moods. To this day, I would rather walk with George Templeton Strong through the "ribs, clavicles, and vertebra" of the dug-up potter's field in nineteenth-century New York than accompany Anaïs Nin on her "step-by-step struggle finally to come . . . into a state of freedom and harmony." In the same way, I would rather experience the more objective truth of a novel—the created world a writer has on a string, at some distance from himself—than the claustrophobic and shaded truth in the memoirs currently trending and exploding.

There's no lack of "step-by-step struggle" in all these books. Kathryn Harrison's *The Kiss* (incest), Frank McCourt's *Angela's Ashes* (poverty), Susanna Kaysen's *Girl, Interrupted* (mental illness) and Mary Karr's *The Liars' Club* (childhood rape and world-class white trashiness) have helped put the genre onto the Op-Ed, front and magazine pages of *The New York Times*. Some of these new books are quite fine (McCourt's in particular), but when a few months ago I sat on an Authors Guild panel, discussing the form with Harrison and McCourt and several other writers, I was the only one firmly to take the retro position that the novel has a capacity that memoir cannot have, that it can be a big truth, whereas the memoir is more likely to be an individual one.

A few weeks later, *The New York Times,* this time in the "Editorial Notebook" written by Brent Staples (himself the author of an interesting memoir called *Parallel Time*), rebutted my objection: "What's obvious is that the devilish little girl in *The Liars' Club* is every little girl. That she bears the author's name makes her no less compelling or universal." If I may surre-but: It's because little Mary Karr is *not* every little girl—but rather because her experiences in god-awful Leechfield, Texas, are so exotic compared with the average book buyer's—that *The Liars' Club* appeals.

To Staples, refracting real-life experience into fiction makes novelists guilty of a fakery that memoirists don't commit: "Memoir writers drop the pretense, which makes the narrative more honest and often more compelling." Actually, it's the memoirists who are doing a lot of faking these days. In certain spectacular instances, such as Lorenzo Carcaterra's *Sleepers,* they seem to be passing off a good deal of invention as fact, counting on the label "nonfiction" to provide buyers with an added emotional jolt ("My God, this really *happened!*"). For a new memoir (*Locked in the Cabinet*) of his term as secretary of labor, Robert Reich claims "no higher truth than my own perceptions"—a good thing, as Jonathan Rauch points out in *Slate,* since those perceptions sometimes don't jibe with anyone else's, let alone available transcripts and videotapes. Other books settle for serving up recollections with a woozy, suspicion-inducing lyricism, or letting their authors be show-offs with their supposed power to conjure details of the past: "In fact," writes Mary Karr, "she hadn't even hauled her Gladstone bag out of the closet yet. The TV was blaring *Dennis the Menace.* I was sitting on the floor with Lecia, cutting fringe on a paper-bag Indian costume, when Mother slammed down the receiver." Susanna Kaysen recalls, from her 1967 hospitalization, a patient named Wade Barker, whose "father had two friends who particularly impressed [him]: Liddy and Hunt." It is absurd to suggest that G. Gordon Liddy and E. Howard Hunt and (presumably) Watergate burglar Bernard Barker were involved with one another before the Nixon administration—demonstrably absurd. But that will not matter to an author self-centered enough to believe that she and her fellow patients "were a provincial audience, New Haven to the real world's New York, where history could try out its next spectacle." She writes, "I can't remember if it was E. Howard Hunt or G. Gordon Liddy who said, during the Watergate hearings, that he'd nightly held his hand in a candle flame till his palm burned to assure himself he could stand up to torture." A trip to the library could have cleared up this matter, and much else.

In his introductory essay to *The New York Times Magazine*'s special issue on the genre (May 12, 1996), James Atlas laid out the memoirists' case in more or less the same way Staples would. "The novelist writes disguised autobiography; the memoirist cuts to the chase." Yes, inexperienced novelists may settle for disguising themselves. But was Defoe shipwrecked? Did Vidal have a sex change? Atlas argues that "the contemporary memoir is like the Nature Theatre of Oklahoma in Kafka's fable 'Amerika,' where everyone can be an artist." Yet Kafka could write a whole novel about America without ever having visited it. What a lot of present-day memoirists are really chasing is their tails, substituting an illusion of truth for the old, vaster truth of illusion. Nineteenth-century fiction, like the world, teemed with characters. After 1900 modernism brought a narrowing of focus, a thinning of the herd: Many novels became like two- or three-character plays or sometimes even one-man shows, in which the "action" was interior, subjective, the famous stream of consciousness. Current memoirs are in many ways the logical extension of this long literary development. Their writers are abandoning a novel that had already lost its outreach and vitality.

Atlas quoted Robert Lowell, the great exponent of modern American confessional poetry: "Why not say what happened?" But there's another line in Lowell, lifted from Milton, that comes to mind when reading many of the new memoirs: "I myself am hell." These current reminiscences suffer from the diseased twentieth-century belief that bad experience is more authentic than good, that misery is truth and happiness deception. In these books, we get the wound without the bow, rawness re-created instead of considered. Their defenders have tried to give them a history and gravitas by associating them with classic autobiographies, but what John Stuart Mill and Saint Augustine and Cardinal Newman and their kind attempted to do was discern the meaning of their lives and pass moral judgment upon them.

Such intrusions of intellect are repelled by many of the new memoirists, who have caught another twentieth-century disease, now at its *fin de siècle* fever pitch: the exaltation of feeling over thought. It is the former, in its messy plural, with which we seek to be "in touch." Detachment and objectification are seen as sterile, suspiciously clinical. The painful memories of *The Kiss* are replicated in a present tense that, perhaps deliberately, suffocates the reader. Metaphor puts in a half day's work at meaning: "My need for him is inexorable. I can't arrest it any more than I could stop myself from falling if, having stepped from a rooftop into the air, I remembered, too late, the fact of gravity."

I would rather end the day having had one clear thought than one strong feeling, which makes me glad that, like any literary development, the memoir explosion has its countertrend, one that's under way in such big, history-minded and cerebral novels as Thomas Pynchon's *Mason & Dixon* and Don DeLillo's forthcoming *Underworld*. Success for books like these, as well as a sudden dip in memoir sales, may muffle the current "explosion." Many of the most successful recent memoirs—including the best written, such as Karr's and McCourt's—have been surprise hits, low-advance bonanzas for their publishers. When, for whatever reasons, a few of the big-ticket confessions now being signed up start bombing at Borders, you can expect to see a rush of think pieces on the New Reticence.

In some ways, the "debate" over memoir has been more depressing than the genre itself. In our Barney-like intellectual climate, my truth is as good as your truth. No one is wrong; others merely have "a different point of view." Even on that Authors Guild panel, we were mostly in a Clintonian rush to find consensus, different ways to agree that novels and memoirs are both just narratives, after all. Two generations ago, a group of New York intellectuals would have been at one another's throats over any such topic, and the most elegant hand on the jugular would have belonged to Mary McCarthy, whose classic *Memories of a Catholic Girlhood* (1957) has now been shanghaied into service as a supportive precedent by the memoir boosters. It may be dangerous to speak for the dead, but I think I knew McCarthy well enough to say that she would be articulately revolted. Her highly analytical, deductive book is almost the opposite of some of the feelfests being offered today. "This record lays a claim to being historical," McCarthy wrote in the introduction to her *Catholic Girlhood;* "that is, much of it can be checked. If there is more fiction in it than I know, I should like to be set right; in some instances, which I shall call attention to later, my memory has already been corrected." When it came to meaning and sense, McCarthy did not admit the slightest relativism: "I believe there is a truth," she once said, "and that it's knowable." Not *your* truth or *my* truth; *a* truth. Certainly not Lillian Hellman's "truth." Forgotten in the current vogue is the credulous reception of Hellman's reminiscences when they appeared in three volumes during the '60s and '70s. When McCarthy uttered her famous imprecation against them—"Every word she writes is a lie, including 'and' and 'the' "—Hellman filed a lawsuit that caused critics to take a closer look at her books and to realize what hilarious, self-serving nonsense (including the whole "Julia" episode) they contained.

Hellman herself stands—lies, actually—exposed as a fraud, but her form of mendacity is more dominant than ever. We are in a chaos of wishfulness and subjectivism, a cultural low point that allows us to deny whatever doesn't fit into our personal or group sense of how things *ought* to be—or have been. "But that's how *I* see it," we reply to one another, secure in a sovereignty that no one challenges with verifiable, inconvenient truth. It's why the memoir has a bigger audience than before. It's why talk-radio switchboards are alight. And it's why O. J. Simpson, albeit with lighter pockets, is playing golf this afternoon.

Life Is Short

September 1999

To THIS DAY, after a lifetime of reading that's worn out my bi-focaled eyes, I still know only one number of the Dewey decimal system by heart: 921, nearly as high as you can go in the three-figure arrangement. It was, if my mind's eye can properly focus on a patch of memory about forty years old, the last section of books on the western wall of the Stewart Manor School library. For a long phase, when our class went to borrow books on Friday mornings, I would head straight to Biography, specifically a series of strictly American subjects, each of them bound in orange cloth and exactly 192 pages long. I would take one home every weekend and read it on a couch in our dark, wood-paneled basement; on Monday morning, I'd put it under the metal clip of my Rollfast bicycle and return it to Mrs. O'Dwyer behind the library desk, now knowing everything there was to know about James Whitcomb Riley or Molly Pitcher or Warren G. Harding, all of whose lives needed exactly those twelve signatures, 192 pages, for the telling. The series seemed to have been edited by God: Everybody's existence amounted to just as much as everybody else's.

I took pride in polishing off a book every weekend—nodding modestly as Mrs. O'Dwyer asked, "Finished already?"—but the series' type was so large that I'm sure each volume could have been printed on fewer than a hundred conventional adult pages. Without realizing it, I had become forever attached to the "brief life," a form that goes back at least as far as the Gospels, whose One Big Life was doled out to me orally, an episode a week, from the pulpit of St. Anne's. Short biographies are now back in vogue with the new Penguin Lives series, and before we survey the imprint's first four productions, it's worth undertaking a survey of the genre's long and attractive tradition.

Not long after Matthew, Luke, Mark and John—biographers all—

Plutarch put together his series of *Parallel Lives*. You can read his treatment of Julius Caesar in under two hours, because the author knows how to hustle even this one of his subjects from cradle to grave: "[Caesar] pursued the enemy for forty miles, as far as the Rhine, and filled the whole of the plain with the bodies of the dead and their spoils." If Plutarch had turned every narrative transition into an agonized Rubicon, he'd never have succeeded in re-creating the classical world's whole history. Instead, he just plunges in and splashes across: "So much for accounts of Caesar's career before his Gallic campaigns. After this he seems, as it were, to have made a new start." Of course, having a subject who recounted his own campaign against Pharnaces II in a total of three words—"*Veni, vidi, vici*"—might spur any biographer toward concision.

Fifteen hundred years later, Giorgio Vasari, quickly chronicling the lives of painters, not emperors, showed that he, too, knew something about writing tight. In reporting how a friar commissioned Andrea del Sarto to paint part of a cloister courtyard, Vasari crams the artist's whole nature into a parenthesis: "Andrea (who was a sweet and good man). . . ." When it comes to critiques of the art, Vasari isn't exactly Robert Hughes. A self-portrait of Andrea is, he lazily declares, "so natural that he seems to be alive," and he weasels out of describing the figure of Abraham in one of Andrea's paintings, "because not enough could ever be said" about it. Plutarch has his lazy formulae, too (an awful lot of trenches are "filled with their dead bodies"), and, not surprisingly, the headlong quality that is the brief life's greatest strength can turn—according to the law of inversion governing every talent—into its most conspicuous weakness. Plutarch is far more absorbing and consistently successful than Vasari, but both retain Olympian confidence about their chosen subject matter. They know they have a good thing going with these little biographies. Vasari tells readers that Andrea's disciple Jacopo Pontormo "will be described in his *Life*," just as, in his life of Caesar, Plutarch cross-references and advertises the rest of his Roman franchise: "All this will be described in detail in my *Life of Pompey*."

By the time history unrolled Britain's bloody but cerebral seventeenth century, brief-life writing had begun to display some disquieting hints of biography's modern expansion and professionalization. Izaak Walton, today more famous as a fisherman (*The Compleat Angler*), also composed a snug single-volume collection of five lives that included one of Sir Henry Wotton, diplomat extraordinaire and provost of Eton College. Though the late

Wotton had been a friend, Walton worries about needing more document sources, frets about digressions and, rather tediously, discovers ancestry, that obligatory preambling of begats that would come to clog the opening pages of so many modern, full-dress biographies. (Emily Dickinson doesn't get born until the second volume of Richard B. Sewall's 1974 life.)

But in Walton's time the short biography was still marching toward its peak of near perfection, which proved to be the mountainous bulk of Dr. Samuel Johnson, onto whose shoulders the genre climbed around 1780. Johnson's *Lives of the Poets* managed to be factual, authoritative and complete, without ever hiding its psychological subjectivity. The interplay between Johnson's personality and his subject's becomes the principal attraction of each poet's life story. Even now one cannot read accounts of Richard Savage's poverty and sleeplessness ("remaining part of the night in the street . . . abandoned to gloomy reflections") without being absorbed all over again by Johnson's own terrible moods and wants. He has, as we might say today, walked the walk.

The brief life never wholly died out; it survives even now, every night between eight and nine on A&E. But for 200 years brevity has been the exception, due in part, oddly enough, to Samuel Johnson, who, a decade after *Lives of the Poets,* himself became the subject of the most famous biography in English, a book destined to remain one of a kind in everything but its considerable length. No other biographer could expect to have James Boswell's access or his ear, and so his *Life of Johnson* ended up setting only a standard of capaciousness for the next century's worth of far less readable lives. The multivolume "life and letters," all scrubbed up for the reader's improvement, took its place as the ugly cousin of the great Victorian tripledecker novel. Most of these nineteenth-century lives now look more like statuary than literature; a "warts and all" approach is eschewed in favor of a marathon chemical peel.

The Life and Correspondence of Thomas Arnold (1844), for example, Arthur Penrhyn Stanley's lengthy tribute to the reforming Rugby schoolmaster (and father of Matthew), survives only as the sort of book that needed shredding by the twentieth century. Lytton Strachey, in 1918, made Dr. Arnold one of his four Eminent Victorians and, in contrast to Stanley, laid waste to the educator's forty-seven years in less than forty pages: Arnold "believed in toleration, too, within limits; that is to say, in the toleration of those with whom he agreed." Decrying conventional biographies' "ill-digested masses of material, their slipshod style, their tone of tedious panegyric, their lamentable lack of selection, of detachment, of design," Strachey, Virginia Woolf's whippet-thin friend, refashioned biography into a sort of elegant graffiti with which to deface a lot of white marble elephants. His subjects, such as Florence Nightingale, almost always emerged, by his own description, more "interesting" and less "agreeable" than before. Miss Nightingale, for instance, was no mere angel of mercy; that lamp she carried into the filthy Crimean War hospital was more like a slave driver's whip:

> Her conception of God was certainly not orthodox. She felt towards Him as she might have felt towards a glorified sanitary engineer; and in some of her speculations she seems hardly to distinguish between the Deity and the Drains. . . . If He is not careful, she will kill Him with overwork.

The sharp, raised nose of Strachey's approach and style could hardly have become the norm, any more than one might have expected a modern parade of Samuel Johnsons to carry the brief life back to the biographical forefront. And so, while the Victorians' reverence might have died out—we now have, at its other, mommie-dearest extreme, what Joyce Carol Oates calls "pathography"—their enormous page count is back in style. Expansion and immersion are the current standards. Contemporary biographers emphasize extended cohabitation with their subjects: Robert A. Caro, for example, lived on and off for three years in the Texas Hill Country when writing about the early LBJ. Comprehensiveness gets equated with comprehension; accumulation substituted for interpretation. At their worst—which, it goes without saying, is biography written by academics—these modern behemoths seem like the twenty-six-volume appendix of the Warren Report. One could read most of Faulkner's important novels in the time it would take to go through Joseph L. Blotner's two-volume life of the author. (Has anyone actually read this book, as opposed to consulting it?) The tendency toward girth has gone unchecked for decades; among the thickest, and most ironic, lives in my bookcase is Michael Holroyd's 1,144-page treatment of—Lytton Strachey.

Modern biographers see their subjects much too steadily and almost never whole. Even Ian Hamilton, a talented writer who has published useful reflections on the life writer's art, submitted to tyrannies of chronology and compilation when he produced his biography of Robert Lowell in 1983. He recounted so many symptoms of nervous breakdown after nervous breakdown that a reader felt as if he'd been locked in the file room of McLean Hospital. It is the full-length biographer's inability to give a reader the whole life, in one or two sittings, that makes the brief life generally superior. Whatever exceptions may exist in practice, the short form is inevitably more memorable and therefore—since learning without retention is useless—more instructive. Modern biography drips toward us line by line and page by page, for days or weeks, like a computer screen being filled in by a 14K modem. By contrast, the brief life is more like a canvas one apprehends suddenly and completely upon entering the gallery. In Isaiah Berlin's famous fauna, the long bio is the fox and the brief life the hedgehog. The latter may impart only one thing, one impression, but done right, it's a big and lasting impression—a sum, not parts. To use a McLuhanesque formula: You'll learn less about Florence Nightingale from Lytton Strachey than from Sir Edward Cook's two-volume biography, but you'll *know* more.

The unpleasant secret of voluminous modern biography, especially when the subject is a literary figure, involves the biographer's forced suppression of his own ego. Time and again, we hear biographers talk of those years spent living with their subjects, of having had their existences devoured by the dead man and his documents: "I came to fear the way in which he would insidiously take over my life," writes Ronald Steel in his essay "Living With Walter Lippmann." The enforced proximity is often presented with humorous resignation, as a sort of internal Oscar-and-Felix standoff. But one suspects real and lingering rage, especially when the book finally comes out and the picture that runs with the review is the subject's, not the author's, and when the biographer notices that even his friends shelve the book alphabetically under "Lippmann," not "Steel."

This problem of hidden animus may be solved by the newest, and most notable, attempt in many years to bring up biography's minor key. The Penguin Lives series, under the editorial direction of James Atlas, has begun issuing brief books, averaging about 150 small pages, at the rate of six per year. Four have already been published, and at least twenty more are in the works. More happily than Holroyd, Atlas too has embraced irony: He says the idea for reviving biographical brevity came to him when his own work on Saul Bellow, which he's been at for at least a decade, went over the 1,000-page manuscript mark. Atlas, who has also written a novel and sustained a literary critic's career outside the university, says his most "immediate model" for this new line is "the Fontana Modern Masters series that was popular when [he] was a student in the early '70s. These were short books, published in paperback, of 120 pages or so, in which an eminent critic or scholar would summarize the work of a significant figure in the culture."

For Penguin Lives, Atlas has raised the level of authorial celebrity with a number of well-known novelists, jazzed up the pantheon of subjects with an occasional sports hero and entertainer and made a generally tip-top series of matchups between the two sets. Before long he will present Edna O'Brien on James Joyce, George Plimpton on Muhammad Ali, and Roy Blount, Jr., on Robert E. Lee. One measure of Atlas's M.O.—and likely success—is that no one will think of mentioning any of his titles without their authors. In fact, the writers are sufficiently well known that a reader will take as much interest in what the books reveal about them as about their subjects—the sort of stimulating two-way street one can still walk between Johnson and Savage. Short-term commitments by authors secure in their own stature would also seem to promise books in which the biographer will keep a firm hand on the subject, instead of being dragged off for an interminable run by whatever Great Dane is at the end of the leash.

Writing on Saint Augustine, Garry Wills, one of Atlas's first quartet, delivers pretty much the sort of exasperating stimulation one expects of him. The choice is perfect: A former Jesuit seminarian, Wills long ago underwent the kind of conversion experience—in his case away from conservatism, not the Manichaean heresy—that Augustine did in the fourth century. Argumentative by temperament (Oh, what a priest the Jesuits lost!), Wills loves rescuing all manner of phenomena from inaccuracy. He insists on calling Augustine's *Confessions* the *Testimony,* in keeping with his overall mission to correct the image of an oversexed, reluctantly penitent saint. The reader probably knows just one quotation from the subject (his request that the Lord make him pure "but not just now"), and Wills is determined to reset the context for these words, even if that means straining against the brief-life format he's signed himself into. He takes more than two pages of a ten-page introduction to prove that Augustine's father did not catch the young man sporting an erection in the public baths at Thagaste; the boy is the latter-day victim of "academic conjecture . . . based on many kinds of ignorance," including poor translation.

The author's stubbornness and eccentricity are entirely to the good—evidence that the series' writers are being allowed to show off the personalities and voices for which, presumably, they were solicited. Like Plutarch, Wills has his subject's writings to pore over—in Augustine's case an autobiographical gold mine of internal dialogues in which, "with a spelunker's hardy nerve," the eventual saint "lowered himself into himself." Wills's own little book, by no means a quick read, ends up being a full, smart accounting, in which the biographer refuses to be a mere archivist or potted plant.

Peter Gay, looking back on Mozart from "the dismal twentieth century," is similarly forthright. He betrays no hesitation about judging his subject's music just because music isn't what academics would wearyingly call his "field." In any case, says Gay, it's "vulgar to read music as a simple translation of its composer's moods or a literal response to private events." So this social and psychological historian enters Mozart's mind with the same Freudian tools he once used to enter Freud's. The root of Mozart's depressions lay in the composer's conflict with his stage-mothering father, says Gay; beyond that, and no biographer has put this more neatly, "A child prodigy is, by its nature, a self-destroying artifact: What seems literally marvelous in a boy will seem merely talented and perfectly natural in a young man." When it's appropriate to shift from the aphoristic to the clinical, Gay shows no reluctance about snapping on, or taking off, the rubber gloves: "Mozart's preoccupation with the anus and anal products never waned. This does not say a great deal about Mozart, except that he yielded more readily than many others to the regressive pull of early fixations. . . . His mother, too, did not hesitate to make jokes about shitting, and so did his father." The panoramic vantage point from which Gay, in *The Enlightenment*, once surveyed that entire era lets him talk easily about the eighteenth century's concert manners ("the habit of listening was at best intermittent") and its artists' gradual shift from patrons' favor to a market economy. (Mozart might not have been "a prudent manager" of money, but Gay spares him the contempt that Vasari can't conceal toward Andrea del Sarto for his tendency to undersell himself. Four times in forty pages, Vasari brings it up, all but calling Andrea a chump.)

Gay seems more mindful of brevity's strictures than Wills. As he moves from musical genre to genre, covering concertos, then string quintets, then symphonies, he sometimes seems to be watching the clock and the page count, and he makes the reader a little nervous. When toward the end he spends a lot of time on the plot of *Don Giovanni,* you want to hurry him along with a whisper, because you have by now a sense of his punctilio, a feeling that he would hate to fail in discharging his obligation.

Still, having too much to work with is preferable to having too little. If the Penguin series has one failure so far, it's Larry McMurtry's *Crazy Horse.* Riding in pursuit of this warrior, man of charity and nonnegotiator, the estimable McMurtry time and again has to acknowledge that he's grasping more at a legend than a life. Faced with a dearth of facts and a surfeit of myths, the author characterizes his own book as "an exercise in assumption, conjecture, and surmise." When it comes to the Sioux fighter, historical novelists have done about as well as historians, says the author of *Lonesome Dove,* who nonetheless often disowns some illustrative tale just before or after he's presented it. (The effect is reminiscent of Butler's *Lives of the Saints,* that brief-life compendium of misty legends. In the couple of pages devoted to the doubting Saint Thomas, the author follows a long, colorful paragraph about the saint's proselytizing in India with the explanation "It is agreed that there is no truth behind the story just outlined.")

If radical compression is the problem facing almost all of Atlas's biographers, McMurtry's difficulty becomes the need to pad. His small book ends up feeling digressive and garrulous: "The Indian and the horse have been together in movies for as long as there have been movies. I now own a tape of a fragmentary silent film called *Old Texas,* made in 1913, in which the great cattleman Charles Goodnight appears briefly at a picnic before the film." Like a well-intentioned cavalry officer attempting to coax his inscrutable subject into the agency and onto the reservation, McMurtry keeps *trying* things. He lengthily compares the army's 1851 Fort Laramie Indian council to "a similar gathering" between the British and the Zulus "in Addis Ababa in 1916" and ten pages later quotes three paragraphs from Peter Matthiessen on tribal warfare in New Guinea. *Crazy Horse* ends up as biography-by-hypothetical-analogy. The overfriendly anachronistic diction ("like a white CEO," "what we would now call a wimp or a wuss") gives off a spray of flop sweat.

Plutarch wrote about Caesar at roughly the same 125-year remove from which McMurtry looks back on Crazy Horse. But the modern interval has proved too fast and vast to overcome. Plutarch could accept that "some heavenly power was at work" in Caesar's assassination—all those portents—and then describe it in the most vivid way imaginable. When it comes to depicting his subject's murder in Fort Robinson, Nebraska, the modern-minded McMurtry is all rational fits and starts: "A variorum death of Crazy Horse would consist of at least a score of versions."

Penguin's decision to publish *Crazy Horse* along with *Marcel Proust* as the first pair of its series was a rangy piece of audacity: one subject thundering on horseback across the plains, the other walled up in his cork-lined Parisian bedroom. The books are further opposite in the way Edmund White's *Proust* remains the new project's standout success. In a press release, White, whose books have run a sort of record gamut from *The Joy of Gay Sex* to highly regarded literary fiction, stressed the author-subject affinities that are the series' biggest draw: "I first read Proust when I was in high school, and even wrote a term paper on him; I read Proust the second time when I was thirty and had hepatitis, then again when I moved to Paris in 1983. He's accompanied me at many of the crucial moments in my life. Like me, he was interested in love, friendship, art, and society."

But the big news about White's little book is that, so far, more than anyone else in the Penguin series, he *gets* the brief-life form, and makes it as elastic as a pair of drawstring pants. He realizes its possibilities and embraces its limitations, setting to work as if he'd never wanted to produce anything but enameled miniatures, and as if his earlier biography of the much less significant Jean Genet didn't run to several hundred pages. When he wants to digress, he just does it ("The Dreyfus Affair is worth a short detour"); and when he's in the mood for an interesting overstatement, he just makes one: Proust's "sophisticated strategies of evasiveness" in fiction come in part from his three years studying law. White pronounces generalizations with a nice, casual sweep that has almost disappeared from biography, locating, for example, some characters from *Swann's Way* "in a period before adolescence was invented, at a time when people passed directly from childhood to adulthood, when a boy would be wearing short pants one day and taking a mistress the next." The modern biographer, who never hears the meter running, has the time—and thereby the obligation—to prove every assertion. He wouldn't make the point White has without statistical buttressing from the retail-clothing and contraceptive industries.

To an extent, all these new brief lives are works of historiography; the famous author of the new, little monograph has to depend on, and acknowledge, the big, classic biographies that have preceded him. White has no trouble getting rid of George D. Painter's "mawkish" and misleading and once definitive *Marcel Proust: A Biography,* which saw Proust as a reluctant "invert" who carried "with him a prisoner crushed beneath the weight of Time and Habit, a buried heterosexual boy who continued to cry unappeased for a little girl lost." To this White all but shouts "Oh, Mary!": "I would suggest that Proust's exclusively homosexual sexual experience might suggest that the only little girl he was crying over was inside him." The author finds a much sounder source in Jean-Yves Tadié's 952-page biography, published in 1996, which does White the favor of being both intellectually sound and badly written. It "lacks narrative sweep and humor value and sometimes looks just like random notes," as if it's been carrying inside it a little book lost—namely, White's—a slim writerly volume dying to get out.

White's admitted "homosexual bias" ends up being not some dreary p.c. cudgel but a sharp lavender-tinted lens: The pastiche-loving Proust, he says, avoided trying to parody writers with a "simple, straightforward style," like Voltaire, the way "drag queens avoid 'doing' unadorned beauties such as Audrey Hepburn and are inspired by highly constructed women such as Mae West or Barbra Streisand." As for the many-volume masterpiece that is *Remembrance of Things Past,* White avoids all the incense and reverence and simply deals with the thing: "If any writer would have benefited from a word processor it would have been Proust, whose entire method consisted of adding details here and there and working on all parts of his book at once, like one of those painters who like to keep a whole canvas 'in motion' rather than patiently perfecting it section by section, one after another." In his breezy movement between the author and the work, White reverses course as needed. When it comes to sex, he uses the novels to get at the life; in most other respects, it's vice versa. In its wit and self-confidence, *Marcel Proust* turns out to be the most Stracheyan volume in Atlas's young series, even if the author is throwing rose petals instead of spitballs.

The Penguin Lives series has so far received almost more press as a business proposition than as a literary venture. (The series is jointly financed by Viking and the investment banker Kenneth Lipper.) But one shouldn't shortchange the intellectual importance of what Atlas is trying here. The project represents, if anything, the opposite of biography lite, as it's sure to be branded. The books' compressive nature calls for a greater attention span in the reader, who must keep up with an argument instead of merely stepping onto a long moving sidewalk. These volumes run counterintuitively to the Information Age, in which the endless availability of data has atrophied our ability to select and synthesize, just as twenty years ago the pocket calculator killed our capacity for simple arithmetic. Facts, in unlimited supply, become enemies of thought—whether they reside in thousand-page biographies or a thousand Web pages forever on call. Evidence of everyone's existence is proliferating in the most ghastly way; but public, eminent lives are becoming electronic Staten Islands, vast digitized landfills of brightly screened recorded info. Against the point-and-click glow of all this raw material, Atlas's brief candles may prove a sight for sore eyes.

Double Dutch

"**R**AWHIDE NOT HURT," radioed Secret Service man Jerry Parr, as the president's limousine sped away from the Washington Hilton on March 30, 1981. In fact, Ronald Reagan had a .22 "Devastator" bullet inside his chest, one inch from his heart and waiting to explode. Parr was lying about Rawhide to mislead any accomplices who might be eavesdropping on the Secret Service bandwidth. Had he not shoved Reagan violently into the car and decided to divert it to George Washington University Hospital, the president would most likely have died.

As it happens, Ronald Reagan had helped to save his own life. About forty years before, when he so winningly played Brass Bancroft, "flying agent of the United States Secret Service," in several Warner Bros. B pictures, he inspired at least one boy in the Saturday-afternoon audience, Jerry Parr, toward his future vocation.

The assassination attempt and its immediate aftermath—Reagan cracking jokes for the doctors through "blood-caked lips"—occasion one of the many superb stretches in Edmund Morris's long-awaited biography, *Dutch: A Memoir of Ronald Reagan* (Random House, $35). The author, a mercurial Anglo out of Africa, impressed both Reagan and serious critics with his 1979 biography *The Rise of Theodore Roosevelt*. A few years later, partly through the brokerage of Senator Mark Hatfield, Morris, a nonacademic historian, came inside the White House as the president's authorized biographer, shadowing Reagan to such an extent that he practically became a member of the second administration. Morris has been at the book ever since, and its appearance at long last feels not just delayed but also, where Reagan is concerned, posthumous: The president's mental death has only added to his lifelong elusiveness. To his severest critics, Reagan was always an idiot. To Morris he is an idiot savant, preposterous and almost certainly great, all at once obtuse and mythic. After the shooting in 1981, he "traded half of his own fresh blood for the staler, cooler contributions of strangers."

From his boyhood in Tampico and Dixon, Illinois (a double rainbow would appear over the first town the day before RR's election as president), Reagan derived what Morris calls "the immense insularity" of his character: "The corn stretched dry and silent, innumerable stalks cut parallel to the horizon. Was there, in fact, a horizon, or had perspective itself gotten bored with the endless retreat, and allowed the sky to cut in? This fertile desert, this universe of sameness, closed off outside experience like a wall." "Dutch" inherited his father's "blarney," though not his alcoholism; from his mother came histrionics and piety. It is, however, Reagan's "preternatural, lifelong calm" and flights from intimacy that most interest Morris. The swimming that made him a local legend as a lifeguard, with scores of rescues to his credit, was really an opportunity for Reagan's simultaneous projection and submergence. Water, the perfect place for "the massive privacy of his personality," both sped and cocooned him.

At Eureka College, "manifestly a loner, Dutch was never alone." He discovered campus politics, which suited his already "urgent desire to tell us what we already knew." He also wrote a good many short stories, which Morris goes through, discovering how in them

> time and again . . . a tall, genial, good-looking boy goes about his business (or lies comfortably doing nothing), untouched by and unconcerned with the agitation of others. He is sexy without being sexual, kind yet calculating, decent, dutiful, gentle—and massively self-centered.

The stories also display "our hero's intense delight in being looked at."

Reagan first went to Hollywood as a sports announcer for Des Moines's radio station WHO, to cover the Chicago Cubs in spring training. On a second trip, he got advice from the young star Joy Hodges ("Don't ever put those glasses on again, as long as you live"), as well as an appointment with casting director Max Arnow, a screen test, a contract and the chance to keep his own name.

> There was a cautious murmur of approval. "*Ronald* Reagan . . . Ronald *Reagan* . . ." Not only were the rhythmic syllables allitera-

tive, they balanced out typographically at six letters to six—ideal for display purposes. "Hey, that's not bad," Arnow said.

When politicians are lucky enough not to have been lawyers, we gener-ally ponder their first careers with serious interest—right now some people are telling themselves that Bill Bradley's time in the NBA makes him uniquely capable of solving America's race problem—but Reagan's movie career was typically the occasion for rolled eyes and scornful laughter. Mor-ris is too smart for that. In it he finds all sorts of clues and confirmations of Reagan's personality and mental habits. When filming, the young star "was completely surrounded by [a] wall of light. . . . He saw no faces and did not miss them. He liked the wall's feeling of privacy." Reagan's presidential for-getfulness of facts and faces was not an early sign of Alzheimer's so much as an illustration of how "*actors remember forward, not backward.* Yesterday's take is in the can; today is already rolling: tomorrow's lines must be got by heart." Most important, Morris makes us see how Hollywood nourished Reagan's black-and-white morality and Technicolor sentiment. Reagan "believed in belief," accepting the bedrock premise of the company town where he worked—namely, that fantasy improves reality. Reagan's 1940 movie *Murder in the Air* has Brass Bancroft "airlifting an enormous, sky-splitting photon machine" against the nation's enemies: "*All right, Hay-den—focus that Inertia Projector on 'em and let 'em have it!*" Who knew, Morris writes, "that the Inertia Projector (that light both lethal and benign, silently purifying the American sky) might one day figure in the strategic defense thinking of Ronald Reagan, Commander in Chief"?

Reagan's bad eyesight kept him at Burbank's "Fort Roach," the U.S. Army Air Forces' First Motion Picture Unit, during World War II. With "800 professional illusionists," he helped turn out propaganda and training films. Army footage showing the liberation of the concentration camps made such an impression on him that he would eventually talk as if he'd been an eyewitness to the events. He made both his sons watch these films when they were old enough to comprehend them, but he would never un-derstand the outrage provoked by his 1985 visit to Bitburg, with its SS graves. He had committed himself to a supposed gesture of reconciliation with the Germans, and no one was going to cut the new movie already run-ning in his head.

In 1946 he was demobilized into a Hollywood version of hard times: His box office and his marriage to Jane Wyman were both taking a dive. Politics—of a liberal, internationally minded sort—filled the gaps in his emotions and time. Morris once and for all buries the myth that it was second wife Nancy who turned Reagan rightward with a strong injection of her stepfather's politics. Reagan's bad experiences with domestic Communists did that. He saw them scuttle the American Veterans Committee, and as an officer of the Hollywood Independent Citizens Committee of the Arts, Sciences and Professions, he heard himself called "Fascist!" and "Capitalist scum!" for speaking in support of James Roosevelt's resolution "in favor of democratic principles" and private enterprise. In 1947, radicals in the Conference of Studio Unions threatened to throw acid in his face, and the future's foremost advocate of defensive weaponry began carrying a gun. Liberals who continue to believe that Communists in Hollywood were few and ineffectual give them insufficient credit for the unconscious work they did in creating America's foremost anti-Communist president.

Television saved his career. Reagan's job as host of television's *General Electric Theater* and traveling spokesman for the company proved "deeply satisfying to his didactic urges" and showcased him to a whole generation of conservative politicians and businessmen, "hard, tanned men who wintered in Scottsdale, talked mostly in digits, and ornamented their dens with Steuben glass eagles." He gave 200 speeches as a Democrat for Nixon in 1960, but Morris judges the election of JFK to have been "good news for Dutch," since "in the end, we voted pretty. For better or worse, film was now a factor in politics." Two years later Reagan finally switched to the Republican Party, and after some boffo performances for Barry Goldwater, accepted the blandishments of California businessmen like Holmes Tuttle, who had a particularly "grand strategy. *He* saw eight years, not four, in Sacramento, followed by four years, maybe eight, in the White House." Tuttle offered Reagan all the money he needed for a twenty-year electoral ride.

Reagan became the ghostly instrument of others' big political wishes; in return they took care of him, polishing and transporting him like a grail. Morris points out that people had always taken care of him in one way or another, even while they failed to detect the underground rumbling of his own ambitions. Reagan "was not by nature appreciative (he merely accepted favors, as he did the mail)." Morris recounts how, in 1988, the aged Holmes Tuttle was "shaking with anger" as he described how long it had taken for Reagan to pay him back with the one thing he ever wanted—"for my wife and I to spend but one night in the Lincoln Bedroom." Did he ever back the wrong guy!

The governor's job suited Reagan perfectly. In Hollywood he had "placed his talents in the hands of other people"; now his aides turned his generalized "feelings" into policy and told him where to show up and what to sign. In the course of eight years, he tamed Berkeley and reformed the welfare system. Morris, who much prefers the mysteries of personality to the arcana of policy, sticks with the latter subject long enough to judge that Governor Reagan "could truthfully boast in later years that 'we reduced the rolls by more than three hundred thousand people, saved the taxpayers two billion dollars, and increased the grants to the truly deserving by an average of forty-three percent.' "

Reagan's time in the political "wilderness"—the exile that Richard Nixon deemed useful for turning defeat into greatness—lasted only four years. In 1976, increasingly remote but still possessed of a "bruising political will," he failed by a handful of delegates to take the GOP nomination from Gerald Ford. Fittingly, the old actor was responsible for the last American political convention with any real drama. Invited to the rostrum by the exhausted victor, Reagan proceeded to give "the acceptance speech he *would* have delivered"—so thrillingly that the delegates went home realizing they'd nominated the wrong man. The ex-governor went back to his radio mike, writing and delivering a few hundred more quick morning political homilies, keeping his prospects alive for one last shot in 1980.

History will record that Jimmy Carter's single contribution to the republic was to fail so completely that he made possible Ronald Reagan's presidency. Morris lashes the little man from Plains with a litany of the malaise he made: "An obsession with allegedly dwindling national resources; a smallness of outlook . . . public lights dimmed, cardigans unbuttoned, hemorrhoids proclaimed, human rights called for, the Panama Canal forfeited; fifty-two Americans taken hostage." After "kissing Brezhnev in 1979 [Carter] had suffered agonies of unrequited brotherly love," most particularly in Afghanistan, which the Soviets invaded just around the time that Reagan, who no longer looked quite so old, was announcing his candidacy.

Morris is sufficiently sympathetic to the Reagan Revolution that his book will incur new displeasure from all the bow-tied professors who write the bulk of American history and already resent the uncredentialed author's literary flair and sales. Morris, for instance, acknowledges the budget deficits but clearly wishes to ascribe the past two decades of prosperity to Reagan's so-simple-it-might-be-profound approach. In the end, though, he can't bring himself to care much—and neither should the reader, since the real drama and achievement of Reagan's presidency took place outside the country, at foreign summits and European missile bases. Reagan's "encyclopedic ignorance"; his "childlike, bipolar" mind; his endless recital of anecdotal "untruisms," most of them to do with domestic policy—they roll right off the president's Teflon biographer, because he understands that the most important thing about Reagan's at-home agenda was its pigheaded resoluteness. If the Gipper was ignorant, he was invincibly so. The Soviets first decided he meant business not when he went after the Sandinistas but when he fired the air-traffic controllers.

"I urge you," he declared on March 8, 1983, "to beware the temptation . . . to ignore the facts of history and the aggressive impulses of an evil empire, to simply call the arms race a giant misunderstanding and thereby remove yourself from the struggle between right and wrong, good and evil." Morris reports how Henry Steele Commager called Reagan's remarks in Orlando "the worst presidential speech in American history." It was actually the bravest, most important executive utterance of the past fifty years, and Morris recognizes that. While the American media roiled the airwaves with liberal shudders, "little attention was paid to Soviet domestic opinion. Not for years would evidence begin to gather that the word *evil* had penetrated the Russian soul as surely as the cadmium poisoning Russian beets." Fifteen days after pronouncing the word, Reagan proposed the Strategic Defense Initiative (SDI), the Inertia Projector that won the Cold War without ever being built.

He rode out the "freeze" movement, skipped Brezhnev's funeral and then Chernenko's, waiting for Gorbachev, the new broom, to sweep his way up the gravel drive in Geneva for the first of their suppressed-rage summits. Morris offers an electrifying eyewitness reminiscence of the encounter: "the surgical sound of a hundred camera shutters slicing the light, and a mysterious roar that gathered overhead as the two leaders drew near. It was, of course, the pass of some military jet, but so intent was I on the business at hand that I subconsciously equated it with blood thundering through Gorbachev's birthmark." The biographer never made it to Reykjavík in 1986

(Don Regan, the chief of staff, bumped him from the plane), but years later Morris flew to Iceland just to walk around the room in which the USSR died.

Mikhail Gorbachev had laid a trap for Reagan. Reykjavík was supposed to be a one-day appetizer for later, full-scale get-togethers in Washington and Moscow, but once the badly "abstracted" president arrived at Höfdi House, the general secretary offered astonishing reductions in nuclear weapons and conventional arms—if the United States would confine SDI research to the "laboratory," which essentially meant abandoning it.

> "It's 'laboratory' or nothing," Gorbachev said at last. He reached for his briefcase. There was a long silence. Reagan slid a note over to Shultz. *Am I wrong?* The Secretary [of State] whispered, "No, you're right."

Reagan made the greatest exit of his career. As his limo pulled out, he barked to his chief of staff, "That son of a bitch tried to shaft me."

The president understood what all the Strobe Talbotts and Walter Mondales and even Margaret Thatcher couldn't grasp: "How the devil can we sit around here," asked Reagan, "and question the validity of the SDI when [the Soviets are] so desperate to get rid of it?" He sent Gorbachev home with no choice but to spend the Soviet Union into its death spiral. Reagan won the Cold War, and as even Zbigniew Brzezinski, Jimmy Carter's long-suffering national security adviser, now admits, he won it at Reykjavík. Gorbachev got the Nobel Prize, and Jimmy Carter will someday no doubt get his, but none of that will change the fact that for the past ten years it's been Reagan's world; we only live in it.

—————

The lady in red is not going to like this book. Morris depicts Nancy as brittle, unsubtle, possessing the blood temperature "of a newt." She dislikes fat people and shares her surgeon stepfather's belief "that all human behavior can be controlled, if necessary by cutting"; she and her predecessor, Jane Wyman, share a tendency "to talk to themselves in the luxury of their mirrored bathrooms." But Nancy, too, is a figure of destiny in Morris's book, the ultimate provider of Reagan's "intense delight in being looked at." The only woman who could "withstand [his] relentless spiel" of political nostrums, she offered "the narcotic of endless attention," a service she practiced during her own theatrical first act: "Even as a stage actress, which Nancy had briefly been on Broadway before coming to MGM, her gift was to vibrate like a membrane to the sonority of other speakers." Ronnie, not the two children she had with him, was her true maternal project. Morris bestows on her a small medal for keeping RR "well fed, well rested, and undistracted by any hint of family problems (of which there are plenty)." During the lowest depths of Iran-contra, Reagan would rush out of the Oval Office "at the stroke of five . . . climbing into his pajamas the moment he had exercised and showered," joining Mommy for a supper on TV trays. His denial was massive—"He can no more comprehend that he has broken the law of the land (a specific embargo against selling arms to Iran) than he can accept a positive biopsy"—and without Nancy, for all we know, his distraction might have progressed to the point where aides invoked the Twenty-Fifth Amendment (there was talk of it), removing him from office for mental disability. Morris offers Nancy the book's most haunting half-dozen lines:

> From the start, I think, she loved Dutch to the exclusion of any other man she had met and anyone else she would ever know. . . . As I write these words, he is drifting beyond all comprehension of who she is and what she has done for him. Cool to her at the start, warm, even adoring, when she suited his larger purpose, he is cold to her at the end.
> Meanwhile, she loves him still.

None of the author's endless thrusts at Nancy—her "weeping fits," her "ditsiness"—kept him from sucking up to her. He had to: Her bony fingers held the keys to the kingdom, the vast, spongy biographical terrain he was trying to conquer. So he flattered her, lunched her, threw a party for her after her breast cancer surgery. We get to see Morris, like Boswell, shamelessly seeking every biographical advantage. He's not only written a book about Reagan; he's also written a book about writing a book. We listen to him fret "for the hundredth time, 'How much does Dutch really know?' " and we watch him squirm over the possible lack of there there: "At times I wondered if he was not simply a polished presence—like those chrome busts that Noguchi sculpted in the Jazz Age, reflecting only outside personalities. Was that James Baker's calculating gaze I glimpsed in the President's right eye? Did his mouth just flash with Ed Meese's pink pout?"

We also hear the subject joking with his biographer. "I'm not going to charge up San Juan Hill for you," says Reagan, who signals that his sessions with Morris are at an end by trotting out a Hollywood story. In later years, when Morris goes into the library or archives, we browse with him; at the end, we watch him read Reagan's White House diary, while in the next room the senescent, retired president reads "Mary Worth." (Morris says that Reagan "retained a useful intelligence throughout two terms as President and for three years thereafter," but one diary entry from 1986 "sounds a quiet, distant gong-stroke. Helicoptering to Los Angeles on August 26, he looked down on the hills and valleys he had roamed for forty years and was disturbed to find that he 'couldn't remember their names.' ")

The author tries a dozen different devices, as if the great, stolid genre of statesman's biography is the Berlin Wall *he* somehow has to tear down. He breaks up the narrative with little memory plays, documentary script, entries from his own diary, an appendix of three poems he has written himself ("1. These Leaves Your Lips. To R.R."). But this is not—would that it were!—the half of it. Morris's biography, one of the most absorbing, and certainly the strangest, I have ever read, is subverted by an ongoing narrative fiasco, the author's decision to construct a fictional persona who can follow Reagan, as if they were both characters in a novel, through every phase of our hero's life. In case the subtitle (*A Memoir of Ronald Reagan*) isn't enough warning that this is no ordinarily definitive tome, reviewers have been sent a memorandum that amounts to a series of instructions on how to read the book.

> The reader will notice . . . that the narrator of the earlier parts of *Dutch* is not quite Edmund Morris. He is, in effect, a literary projection of the author back through time. . . . All good biographical writing strives to re-create for the reader the texture of the times that embraced and helped form its subject. Here Morris does it in a way that is original and vivid, while remaining absolutely true to the historical record.

Well, as Reagan might say, indulgently cocking his head, *not exactly.* The real Edmund Morris, who is, after all, a small part of the historical record, was not born in 1912, did not work as a writer for the WPA, did not fly for the RAF in World War II and was not, as the author imagines in the *coup de foudre* that begins and ends the book, rescued by Dutch the lifeguard on August 2, 1928. The persona—this pickled isotope of Morris—also has a friend, Paul Rae, who sublimates his crush on Dutch into sarcastic letters about the dreamboat's youthful doings, then follows his film career as a West Coast gossip columnist and eventually dies, by implication, from Dutch's neglect, during the first wave of the AIDS epidemic. Further risible narrative aid comes from "Gavin," son of the persona Morris, a student at Berkeley during Reagan's teargassing, National Guard–dispatching gubernatorial rule. Gavin is lost to his father forever when he goes underground with the Weathermen. "And it was you, Dutch, who sent him there."

Eventually, the persona turns into the real-life Morris, writing a biography of Teddy Roosevelt and being authorized to do Reagan's. But how can "I" be both? When Morris tells us that he stood outside the White House, gazing through its railings, on the night Jimmy Carter was dispatching broken helicopters to Iran, how do we know whether to believe him? Are we to suppose that by now he's himself, or that, having swallowed the persona, he's walking around the Reagan White House, doing his authorized eavesdropping, a septuagenarian, just like his old friend Dutch?

One reads on, hoping that this crazy strategy will come to mean something. Did Morris construct the persona because, speaking in its voice, he could be more right-wing than one is normally allowed to be in polite media company? Or perhaps more sentimental? More riffing and writerly? None of these is the answer, and it's doubtful that Morris, after fifteen years and despite that memo to reviewers, could give us one. The persona proves too disposable ever to have been necessary: Dutch might have driven Gavin underground, but the author scarcely mentions him again, thrilling to Reagan's later exploits—his "knightly display of valor" in the face of assassination—with a fluttering, unambivalent heart. The whole rigmarole ends up seeming as silly and cheesy as Herman Wouk's Pug Henry, who was conveniently around for so many of FDR's high spots while *The Winds of War* blew long and hard. One eventually becomes angry over the conceit, which undermines and nearly kills the book; it's a kind of Iran-contra, so *unnecessary* given all the other things that are being done so stylishly and well. Many readers are going to impeach and discard *Dutch* before they get to its most penetrating and delightful stretches.

Morris's observations have, at times, an unbeatable acuity, as when, for instance, he does a physical inventory of pretty, young Jane Wyman, who has a "lovely line from thigh to ass. But her hands are large and cruel." Or when, a half century later, he stands behind her first husband at church back in Tampico, Illinois: "I marveled at the dense lie of his hair, thick and shining as an otter's. Why is it old men and small boys always look so vulnerable from behind? Today, he seemed to belong to both categories." Superbly evocative (a swatch of transcript of a weekly lunch between Reagan and his "distressingly ordinary" vice president, George Bush, reads like Vladimir and Estragon at the country club) and sweetly antic (Morris says it was fortunate for Reagan that the new German chancellor had the same first name as the old one), the biographer brings every man in the two administrations to fast, amusing life. David Stockman, the Office of Management and Budget director who would eventually be taken to the woodshed, "read the federal budget line by line, the way [Lyn] Nofziger read Louis L'Amour"; George Shultz has "a face as blank as a slot machine's."

Patches of the prose are purple and goofy, and completely suitable to the cartoon superhero at the book's center. Once or twice the writing is incomparably tasteless (at Bergen-Belsen, "I thought of my father and Gavin, and Dutch and Anne Frank, and wailed like a Jew"); in other spots it verges on the just plain eerie: The entire production is dedicated to Christine Reagan, the daughter of Reagan and Jane Wyman who was born and who died on June 26, 1947. The book constantly overreaches, puffing out its own dry ice, prowling after every irony, foreshadowing and frisson. And yet, if *Dutch* can be hugely ridiculous, it is also absolutely essential, a work designed perhaps to be as strange as its subject. No one will ever get closer to the mystery of Ronald Reagan than Edmund Morris does in this lyrical passage:

> Out of Tampico's ice there grew, crystal by crystal, the glacier that is Ronald Reagan: an ever-thrusting, ever-deepening mass of chill purpose. Possessed of no inner warmth, with no apparent interest save in its own growth, it directed itself toward whatever declivities lay in its path. Inevitably, as the glacier grew, it collected rocks before it, and used them to flatten obstructions; when the rocks were worn smooth they rode up onto the glacier's back, briefly enjoying high sunny views, then tumbled off to become part of the surrounding

countryside. They lie where they fell, some cracked, some crumbled: Dutch's lateral moraine. And the glacier sped slowly on. . . . *How big he was! How far he came! And how deep the valley he carved!*

Ronald Reagan is alone in forgetting that he was the fortieth president of the United States.

Historical Fictions

Writing Historical Fiction

Autumn 1992

I BECAME A HISTORICAL novelist more or less by accident, and I must admit, upon reflection, to the power of nostalgia in making me into one. When I was writing much of *Aurora 7,* a novel set in and around New York City on a single day in 1962, I was living in New York City in 1988. I thought I was writing a book about childhood and chance and the early days of space exploration, but as I proceeded I realized that what was really pushing me along and making me enjoy this book more than any other book I'd written was that I so obviously preferred the idea of living in 1962 to 1988. Having had the kind of happy childhood that is so damaging to a writer, I couldn't help but like being back in that personal Eden where the crabgrass was high and my mom was good-looking.

I was moved by a civic nostalgia, too. The city in which I lived in 1988 was full of anger and plague and misery, just steps away from chaos; whereas at my writing desk, I had the chance to be back in the city from which I remember my commuting father came home one night, around 1962, angry that he had been given a ticket for jaywalking. By 1988 the quaintness of this seemed something to weep over.* I know, of course, that Mayor Wagner's New York was a city full of groups awaiting their supposed liberation, and that the cop who wrote that ticket for jaywalking was far more likely to be on the take than any cop of today, but you know what I am talking about. I wanted to float, politically incorrect to the point of bliss, through a past where children got their vaccinations, baby-sitters mixed martinis, and the Yankees won the pennant every year.

The attempt to reconstruct the surface texture of that world was a homely pleasure, like quilting, done with items close to hand. Although *Au-*

---

*A dozen years later, the murder rate is way down and jaywalking tickets are back.

rora 7 is set against the background of a very public event—the nearly disastrous space flight of astronaut Scott Carpenter—it was usually what I found in the back pages of newspapers and in advertisements that gave me ideas. I had forgotten, for instance, that the *New York Times* used to publish "Incoming Passenger and Mail Ships," and when I noticed that the *Leonardo da Vinci* docked at 9 a.m. at West 44th Street on the day my novel was to be set, I stumbled toward the scene it would take to put one of my minor characters in motion.

John Updike has written, in an article published in *Picked-Up Pieces* (1975), that in fiction "reality is—chemically, atomically, biologically—a fabric of microscopic accuracies." Only through these tiny, literal accuracies can the historical novelist achieve the larger truth to which he aspires—namely, an overall feeling of authenticity. It is just like Marianne Moore's famous prescription for the ideal poet: He must stock his imaginary garden with real toads.

Is there, though, a point at which the letter begins to kill the spirit? Mary McCarthy once spoke of how, while writing her novel *Birds of America,* she was told by someone that the Sistine Chapel, in which she'd set a chapter taking place around New Year's Day in 1965, might have been closed at that time for a Vatican Council. She was aghast. After making inquiries, she was relieved to learn that the chapel had indeed been open when she had her characters in it; but she insisted that had it turned out otherwise she would have thrown away a whole chapter.

Who, one might argue, besides some terribly pedantic reader bent on ruining the novelist's day with a postcard, would ever have known or cared? While writing the same book, McCarthy called up the Paris weather bureau to check what the skies were doing on the morning of February 8, 1965, a crucial day in the novel, when the hero learns that the United States has begun to bomb North Vietnam. In real life there were showers over Paris, and as a result it is raining on page 330 of my copy of *Birds of America.* But again, one might argue, why bother with such a detail when, at a certain point, since you are writing a novel and not history, reality must give way to lies? After all, there never was this boy named Peter Levi, your protagonist, and he never walked to a kiosk at the Madeleine that morning, as he does in *Birds of America*—so if you put his made-up feet on the real-life sidewalk, why can't you stop the real-life rain over his made-up head?

Every historical novelist will decide these things differently, will calibrate his fidelity to the real past along a different scale. In writing *Aurora 7,* I realized early on that I had to move my main character's entire childhood from Nassau County, where I'd grown up, to Westchester, a place I hardly knew, because Grand Central Terminal was essential to the plot I had in mind. The commuter trains from Nassau County ran then, as they do now, into Penn Station, not Grand Central. So that was that: I could hardly tamper with the underground infrastructure of the city. I did, however, take certain liberties that I'm sure Mary McCarthy would not have. I have President Kennedy making his remark that "life is unfair" a year earlier than he actually made it. But it was useful to have him say it, so I went ahead. More often, I had to wonder if I were not becoming crazily slavish in my homage to Clio: for example, I wrote to Procter & Gamble to make sure that Salvo detergent tablets were on the market in May of 1962 before I allowed my character Mary Noonan to drop them into her automatic washer.

At this remove, I would say that I did not go overboard, because it was often in trying to verify a small detail that I got the idea for a crucial scene. I wrote Kodak, too, to find out what transparency they had up in the old giant Colorama display in Grand Central on May 24, 1962. It turned out to be a shot of the New York City skyline. When I first learned that, I thought it was rather a coals-to-Newcastle banality, but it soon gave me an idea for a way of mentally connecting young Gregory Noonan to his father just before the novel's big moment, and I'm now not sure that any other picture would have worked. Similarly, I overeducated myself about Scott Carpenter's space flight, which was, after all, only the "background" to my story. I had no urgent need to go to the National Archives, but I did. And, if I hadn't gone, I would not have found, in a long-forgotten file, the eerie, never-released press release in which Scott Carpenter, the object of my characters' and the nation's worries, is praised for having died a heroic death. Scott Carpenter is alive and well in Colorado today, but the standby statement that Vice President Lyndon Johnson wanted ready still survives in that folder in Washington. In *Aurora 7* the file provides a creepy touch, one I'm not sure I would have imagined on my own. The point is that I didn't need to. It was there, real. I am not saying that truth is always stranger than fiction, but I would assert that the historical novelist quickly finds that the history in which he must work is not so much a straitjacket as a chariot.

He also finds out, or newly realizes, how quickly the present turns into the past. It is not so much the large official chronicles of history that will tell him this, but the more humble documentation of everyday life. In writing *Aurora 7*, I sought out my elementary-school records from thirty years before and was surprised at the touches of antiquity they contained amidst the predictably modern grids of standardized-test scores. The basic school-record card asked, for example, whether or not the child being registered came from a "broken home"—a phrase that reflects an entirely different worldview from a form that inquires about, as I suspect the forms do now, "single-parent families." The form filled out in 1958 also asked if the child entering school was "unkempt," a word I cannot imagine being used today. And, along with such well-remembered features of the past as named telephone exchanges ("MUrray Hill 3") was a single crystalline flash of an individual personality—my father's—that the school secretary would not have realized she was leaving available for use three decades hence. The form asked that the record keeper take note of "Activities, Hobbies, and Experiences of Parents," and the answer, imparted by my father and still on the form, is "none." That answer verifies my memories of him as incontrovertibly as a fingerprint. He would have said it with a kind of wry mischief, and the secretary would have been charmed, but it would also have indicated both the truth of his privacy-loving nature (what business was it of theirs to know?) and the whole truth of my parents' lives: other than their children and each other, they had no activities, hobbies, and experiences, and they didn't particularly want any.

To a certain degree I am romancing the past, but that is one's privilege with it. One does not have to fear the past, and I think that is one reason why stories about time machines seem more often directed toward the past than the future. We believe in the past because we have all sorts of proof of it. We instinctively disbelieve in the future because we have no guarantee of it, and, if it occurs, we know that it can lead us to only one place—the grave. The future is yawning and vast, and in our imaginations we measure its distance in a different mathematical "base" than the one we use for measuring the past. The years 1962 and 2022 are equidistant from 1992. But which seems closer? Indubitably, 1962.

Why, if the past is so much more familiar and cherishable than the future, is there a smaller audience for historical fiction than for its opposite, science fiction? I would hazard a guess that, with the exception of its young adherents, who feel naive wonder about the future, the readers of science fiction do not love the future at all, certainly not in the way that readers of historical fiction embrace the past. I think rather that science-fiction novels are read and enjoyed as small weapons against the future we all fear. The science-fiction writer has a chance to play God, whereas it is always too late for the historical novelist to do that. The science-fiction writer reassures himself and his readers with a sort of false prophecy; even if it's a terribly dystopian future he is imagining—and it usually is—the act of imagining it implies a certain assertion of control over the world.

Aurora 7 concerns itself in part with space exploration, but even this, I realize, is indicative of my taste for the archaic. I am probably less interested in man's future in space than in his past there, the heroic single-pilot days of Project Mercury. What drove my imagination back to them is the same impulse that made my favorite book—in the list of favorites in my sixth-grade autograph album, another homemade document I consulted—Howard Pyle's *Men of Iron,* a gloriously clunky tale of knighthood, which my eleven-year-old hero returns to the school library in the middle of *Aurora 7.*

I have had it pointed out to me that at Gregory Noonan's age I was interested not only in medieval times but in the American Civil War, too. My fourth-grade teacher got in touch with me a few years ago to ask if I would like to see a piece of juvenilia she had had in her drawer for twenty-five years. It was our school's literary magazine from the spring of 1962, which contained an essay by me, not about Scott Carpenter but about Abraham Lincoln. Though ostensibly history, this essay from my youth manages to display, in a single page, many of the qualities of the most lumbering historical fiction. One climactic paragraph ends: "The Civil War had at last begun!" and is immediately followed by another paragraph beginning: "The Civil War went on and on."

I have no memory of writing this essay, but its rediscovery does strike me as telltale, since for the last couple of years I have been researching a historical novel involving Colonel and Mrs. Henry Reed Rathbone, who on the night of April 14, 1865, when they accompanied President and Mrs. Lincoln to Ford's Theatre, were as yet only an engaged couple: Major Henry Rathbone and Miss Clara Harris, daughter of Senator Ira Harris of New York.

Henry and Clara had been raised more or less as brother and sister, after Henry's widowed mother married Clara's widowed father. Right here the historical novelist runs into a potentially huge pitfall of anachronistic psychology: yes, things were different then, and kin got married as if they were kith, but just how "normal" was it for a young man and woman in that situation to become engaged? Was there, even in unprurient minds, a whiff of incest about the pair? Just before the shooting, Mary Todd Lincoln and the president were holding hands. She asked her husband, in her coquettish way, what Miss Harris would say if she saw her hanging on to him like this. Lincoln's answer, perhaps even his last remark, was: "Why, she'll think nothing about it." One wonders: was that sly, questing mind of his thinking, in its last moments, "After all, she's about to marry a man who's practically her brother"? You can see that I have my research into this little pocket of social-sexual history cut out for me.

At 10:15 that night, Booth stepped into balcony number seven and fired his pistol at Lincoln's head. He then brutally slashed Major Rathbone's left arm, when the major, finally catching on to what was happening, tried to stop him. Rathbone nearly bled to death: any theater relics thought to be covered with Lincoln's blood were in fact drenched with what was pouring from the major's severed artery.

But Rathbone did recover, at Senator Harris's Washington residence, and he did go on to marry Clara, in 1867. Sixteen years later, on Christmas Eve morning in 1883, in a boardinghouse in Germany, Henry Rathbone killed Clara, as their three children slept in another room of the suite. Rathbone then turned a knife on himself and claimed that the violence had been the work of an intruder. Once again he recovered from his wounds, to be committed to a mental asylum in Germany, where he lived until 1911. In fact, he was still alive on the day Ronald Reagan was born.

As I go about reconstructing this story, school records once again prove helpful. Both Henry and his guardian—who was also his future father-in-law—Ira Harris, attended Union College in Schenectady. The school's archives show that Senator Harris was graduated first in the class of 1824, whereas Henry, three decades later, was, to be generous about it, a mediocre student. He was sometimes fined for failing to attend prayers and recitations, and in the summer of 1854 was charged thirteen cents for breaking some glass. My sense of Henry is that he was a bad job from the beginning—not just unhinged by his bloody service with the Twelfth Infantry and the whispers about incompetence that followed his failure to save Lincoln. This broken piece of glass, still present and accounted for in a ledger that has survived for 138 years, has given me the idea for a scene in which he will display, early in the story, a little fit of temper.

Diaries were my first real love as a literary critic, and not surprisingly they are proving useful to me now. There is none by Clara that has survived; but one kept by Henry's cousin, J. Howard Rathbone, now in the Albany Institute of History and Art, has confirmed my suspicion that Clara must have had a lively streak of wit. She was, after all, Mrs. Lincoln's friend, and the clever, high-strung First Lady would have been bored by milksops. Sure enough, I've found that on April 21, 1859, J. Howard Rathbone paid a call on the Harrises in Albany, after which he praised Clara for talking "better than usual, she was less sarcastic."

The National Archives in Washington contain a series of communications—one of them composed on the newly improved typewriter—that passed among the U.S. consulate in Hanover, the U.S. legation in Berlin, and the State Department in Washington at the time of Henry's murder of Clara in Germany. As rich in glimpses of the Rathbones as these documents are, none of them can compare with a letter written by Clara, from her father's house in Washington, on Tuesday, April 25, 1865—eleven days after the assassination and a matter of hours before Booth's capture, which would occur in Virginia at two o'clock the next morning. It is written to a woman named Mary (we don't know any more about her than that). The letter, given to the New-York Historical Society in March 1973 after having been the property of Miss Edith Wetmore of Beekman Place, reads in its entirety as follows:

My dear Mary:

I received your kind note last week, & should have answered it before, but that I have really felt, as though could not settle myself quietly, even to the performance of such a slight duty as that—Henry has been suffering a great deal with his arm, but it is now doing very well,—the knife went from the elbow nearly to the shoulder, inside,—cutting an artery, nerves & veins—He bled so profusely as to make him very weak—My whole clothing, as I sat in the box was saturated literally with blood, & my hands & face—You may imagine what a scene—Poor Mrs. Lincoln all through that dreadful night would look at me in horror &

scream, Oh! My husband's blood,—my dear husband's blood—which it was not, though I did not know it at the time. The President's wound did not bleed externally at all—The brain was instantly suffused.

When I sat down to write I did not intend alluding to these fearful events, at all—but I really cannot fix my mind on anything else— Though I try my best to think of them as little as possible—I cannot sleep, & really feel wretchedly—Only to think that fiend is still at large— There was a report here yesterday that every house in the District of Columbia was to be searched to day—I hoped it was true, as the impression seems to be gaining ground that Booth is hidden in Washington—Is not that a terrible thought!

Mr. Johnson is at present living in Mr. Hooper's house opposite us— A guard are walking the street in front constantly—

It will probably be two or three weeks before Mrs. Lincoln will be able to make arrangements for leaving. She has not left her bed since she returned to the White House that morning—

We expect to be able to leave next week for New York—but on what day, it would be impossible yet to say—I will write you in time however. So that I shall be sure to see you, while there—

Please give my love to all the family, & believe me

Ever truly yours,
Clara H.

There are three details in the letter that arrest me. The first is that small detachment of soldiers tramping outside Mr. Hooper's house, guarding President Johnson: I can now imagine Henry, upstairs, in pain, both maddened and lulled by the sound of their boots. Second is the blood on Clara's face: something literally too ghastly to imagine. Any novelist would think of her dress, of course, but the face? Finally, what interests me most is the information that instead of accompanying her fiancé back to Senator Harris's house at Fifteenth and H Streets, Clara stayed "all through that dreadful night" with Mrs. Lincoln at the Petersen House, across from Ford's Theatre. It is easy to make too much of information such as this, but if a historical novelist scrupulously decides to make too little of everything, then he shouldn't be writing fiction at all.

One of the ironies of the so-called information age we live in is that we are leaving behind less personal written material for the biographer and novelist than we used to.* I would suspect that in November of 1963 after President Kennedy's assassination in Dallas, Mrs. John Connolly was telephoning friends to tell them what she had gone through in Dealey Plaza. One is glad that Clara did not have a phone, but she and Henry were part of the first generation of people to be photographed, and the historical novelist writing about the nineteenth century is always grateful for the glass-plated gold mine left him by Mathew Brady and the new fraternity of portrait photographers. The novelist will want to "read" these photographs for the obvious help they can provide in getting his characters properly dressed and—more perilously—for clues to their psychology. Is Henry's posture neurotically ramrod in that picture? Does Clara's forlorn expression indicate resignation toward a bad mistake she knows she has already made? Or are these just the insignificant products of studio convention and long exposure times?†

When I worked on *Aurora 7,* I was immeasurably helped by the Museum of Broadcasting's acquisition of CBS television's daylong coverage of the Carpenter space flight. I was able to watch hour after hour of old films that had been conveniently transferred to videotape cassettes. Curiously enough, the fuzzy black-and-white images from the still-primitive television of that era make the real-life characters involved in Carpenter's big day look almost as remote as the sepia figures of Civil War photographs. There is a comparable ghostliness about them—a quality that future historical novelists and historians writing about our own day will not have the imaginative

---

*E-mail and the fax have, in the years since this was published, begun a shift, though with respect to E-mail, the archival instinct seems to operate more strongly in the corporate world than the personal one. It will be decades before we know just how much E-mail the ordinary person saves for long periods.

†In 1997, three years after the publication of *Henry and Clara,* I learned that one photograph supposedly of my heroine—identified as such by the National Archives and reproduced in a number of history texts—was, in fact, the picture of another woman entirely. While this new knowledge was disquieting—I had spent a lot of time pondering, and even communing with, that photograph—I soon grew comfortable with the truth. The mistake, or the illusion I'd been under, began to seem appropriate. After all, the Clara I created in words is inevitably different from the actual Clara Harris Rathbone; she's the product not just of research, but of all sorts of surmises and inventions. If I look at Mathew Brady's photo of the actual Clara, taken in the spring of 1865, alongside the one of this misidentified woman, I would have to say it's the latter, the "fake," who's still Clara to me.

opportunity to struggle with. As our century ends, we are thoroughly video-taping it in a high-density, full-color accuracy that will preserve it with an everlasting immediacy. One new fact that the novelist must confront is that from now on history is never again going to look terribly historical.

Getting things to look right is the historical novelist's paramount task. He already faces every other novelist's challenge to keep things moving and to put them into language that has some life, but he has the additional, crucial burden of re-creating a world that functions believably, sentence after sentence, an environment for his characters that is not just a decorated set or a curated museum. Part 1 of my novel about the Rathbones begins on an evening in May of 1845 with the newly widowed Senator Harris writing replies to letters of condolence he has received upon the death of his first wife, Clara's mother. I got a sentence or two into the scene before I had him lighting an Argand lamp: I'd heard of those, and I knew it was reasonable for one to be on his desk in the 1840s. But how exactly did one light them? Would that already have been done by the servant girl? Would she have been Irish? Or maybe, outside Albany at that time, still more plausibly, Dutch? Success, like God, lies in the details, and 1845, I quickly realized, would take a lot longer to reconstruct than 1962. In fact, my publisher might as well know it now: I'm never going to make my deadline.*

Any historical novelist could do well to keep Ford's Theatre in mind as he goes about his business, for the theater as it now exists is really just a persuasive illusion. Converted into government offices in the years after Lincoln's assassination, the structure soon had no more stage, no more orchestra pit, no more balcony. In 1893 a huge portion of this new bureaucratic interior simply collapsed. As if in rebellion against modernity, three floors gave way while the basement was being excavated for the installation of electricity. (If one counts Lincoln, twenty-three people have lost their lives in the building on Tenth Street.) Not until the 1960s was the theater restored to its exact condition of April 14, 1865. As such, it is a kind of parallel universe, and standing in it you can't be sure which items were there on that night and which are copies. In other words, where are the real toads in this imaginary garden? Lincoln's rocker is a replica; the crimson damask

---

*I eventually used the Albany census records for 1850 and 1860 to find out the servants' names and nationalities. (They were Irish.) But see the essay after this one for the much more significant discovery I made from those two sets of data.

sofa, however, is the actual one on which Major Rathbone sat. The flags are reproductions; but the steel engraving of George Washington, which they surround, was in fact hanging there in 1865. Yet, since the whole balcony is a reconstruction, can any of the actual items really be said to be where they were on the night of the assassination? As you think about these things, history turns into metaphysics, a kind of college philosophy problem. Nonetheless, to walk through Ford's Theatre now is to experience an ex-traordinary feeling that you are where it happened and that this is just how it looked. Simply put, it works. Except for the lighted fire-exit signs, the re-storers have done their job without any anachronisms to break the spell for the historically susceptible. In fact, they may have succeeded too well: knowing that performances are once more put on at Ford's, and are on oc-casion even attended by the president of the United States, makes the his-torical novelist wonder if the book he is preparing to set here hasn't vanished, before it is written, in a kind of postmodernist joke.

Why, finally, does one read historical fiction? Victorian theologians fre-quently subscribed to the idea of typology—namely, that almost every inci-dent and person found in the New Testament is prefigured in the Old. Left-leaning literary critics still hope for a similar relationship between the world of historical fiction and the contemporary scene. Sometimes it even exists: William Styron's *Confessions of Nat Turner,* for example, was a con-troversial allegory of the American racial dilemma that existed a century after the novel's action takes place. But for the most part even these political critics will admit that we no longer go to historical fiction for explanation so much as for exoticism. George Lukacs, the preeminent Marxist writer on the genre, lamented in *The Historical Novel* how, a century after Sir Walter Scott, whose historical fiction was prized for its relevance, historical novels were being read because they were so irrelevant, so appealingly strange.

Is this really so terrible? I think the idea of historical fiction as the proto-type of current reality is a bit like a planned Marxist economy—something that looks better on paper than it does while waiting in line. Moreover, I think that readers always liked historical fiction not because they wanted to drag history into the present and make it useful, but because they wanted to put themselves back into history, into the past, to wander around it as if in a dream, to ponder themselves as having been born too late—a much more common feeling than the feeling that one has been born too soon. Avrom Fleishman, author of *The English Historical Novel,* says that historical fic-

tion performs the improving function of making us see ourselves as historical creatures—that is, persons shaped by large forces and currents. I think
that historical fiction more commonly encourages us to see ourselves as historical accidents, to experience what it might have felt like if, my God, it had
been us, not Peanuts John, who innocently agreed to hold John Wilkes
Booth's horse around 9:30 p.m. on that Good Friday evening. The historical novelist will always have to listen to a mass of dismissive wisdom advis-
ing him to abandon his subject. He will be told, by literary theoreticians:
"That was then; this is now." But he should just hold firm, and wait ten sec-
onds before replying, by which time the "now" being discussed will already
have become *his* territory, namely, the past.

The Historical Novelist's
Burden of Truth

February 1998

AT A TIME when important filmmakers and serious novelists are turning to historical subjects with unusual frequency, their audiences find themselves left to ponder and preserve the distinctions between facts and fabrications. Some years ago, in connection with this subject, I noted Marianne Moore's advice that the poet stock his imaginary garden with real toads. After a decade of writing historical fiction, I'm almost inclined to say what Moore famously declared about poetry itself: "I, too, dislike it." The genre is often done badly, and its practitioners have sometimes made grandiose claims for it. In the afterword to my two most recent novels, I've preferred to strike a cautionary note: "Nouns always trump adjectives, and in the phrase 'historical fiction,' it is important to remember which of the two words is which."

I don't believe that the genre, even when done well, rises to a higher truth than perceptively written history. The literal truth, of things judicial as well as historical, is preferable to any subjective one. However differently experienced by its participants, and prejudicially interpreted by their heirs, historical events happened one way and one way only. It's only their meaning that's open to interpretation.

Then why, in considering history, even apply the fictional imagination? Why not rely upon scholarly investigation, which in its rare eloquent manifestations can be quite as powerful and satisfying? Two occasions, I think, best call for the historical novelist: when the facts have been lost to time, and when a time has been lost to the facts.

My novel *Henry and Clara* concerns the engaged couple who accompanied the Lincolns to Ford's Theatre on April 14, 1865. One can find a small

291

collection of published facts about them, often in the footnotes of Civil War histories. And my own best efforts to unearth more—in pension files, alumni records, private diaries and correspondence, contemporary newspapers and diplomatic dispatches—yielded the outlines of a gripping, but by no means wholly connected, story. So I made a pact with myself: insofar as I could discover the facts about Henry Rathbone and Clara Harris, I would pretty much stick to them. In the pages between the facts, I would allow a novel to grow—by imagination, inference and extrapolation. The book that resulted cannot be called history, and yet in places it is more accurate than some of those supposedly nonfiction footnotes about my characters' lives. Clara, for example, is usually said to have been five years younger than Henry. In fact, according to two sets of census records in Albany, she was three years older—hardly an insignificant matter when considering young lovers.

I was well into a draft of the book before I found this out, and the decision to part with what I had already written did not come easily. I could have stuck to the lie about her age that I suspect Clara herself told for many years. I was, after all, writing fiction. But as I considered the matter, I realized how much more interesting—both psychologically and erotically—the truth would be. Having a Victorian heroine fall for the older stepbrother she acquires through her father's remarriage conforms to all sorts of expectations and archetypes. Having her fall for her new *younger* brother, as Clara did, has a bit of a kink to it. This discovery of her real age is the best justification for the rule I've come to write by: don't fight the facts. They'll almost always give you a better story than invention does. It's only after gathering the facts that the historical novelist earns his imaginative elbow room, the right to suggest and invent the rest of his reality.

In a more recent book, *Dewey Defeats Truman,* I again wrote about a real time and place—the Republican candidate's Michigan hometown of Owosso during the months leading up to his "inevitable" 1948 victory—but I tried something quite different from what I did in *Henry and Clara*. However authentically I attempted to reconstruct Owosso, all of the main characters in *Dewey* are inventions. It was as if I'd dropped a neutron bomb (the one that kills people but leaves everything else intact) on the town and then repopulated it with my own imaginings. It's important to remember that the historical novelist's principal obligations are to literature (telling a good story), not to history, but I also wanted to re-create a specific period that history, particularly the televised kind, has rendered rather poorly.

We all know how the "postwar period" gets introduced in documentaries. There's the shot of the atom bomb's mushroom cloud; then the famous Eisenstaedt photo of the sailor kissing the nurse on V-J Day; and then Levittown, TV aerials and baby carriages. But the world did not turn on quite such a dime. In 1948, the bodies of servicemen killed overseas were still being repatriated for home burial; the war continued to lay heavy on many hearts, and towns like Owosso were enjoying a last year without television.

Historical fiction has the leisure to present a more finely sliced and subtly textured time than even good "social history" does. To do the job, a social historian must eventually resort to statistics and comparisons and context; a novelist, in rendering speech and behavior and even the brand names on the breakfast table, can give a more palpable picture of, to paraphrase Trollope, the way we lived then.

Accuracy counts, of course, and the best readers are the ones on alert. I have gotten letters pointing out how, in *Henry and Clara,* no march by Sousa could have sounded at Col. E. E. Ellsworth's funeral in 1861, since John Philip Sousa only turned 7 that year. I'm pleased (and relieved) to respond that the Sousa in question is John Philip's father, Antonio. All the microfilmed newspapers, slang dictionaries and trademark registers in the library won't keep you from making some mistakes, but if you too often fall back on the excuse that, well, it is after all a novel, the accumulated feeling of plausibility is unlikely to hold up.

The other danger is laying it on with a trowel, or what reporters call "emptying your notebook." If you put an antimacassar on what you've already said is a horsehair sofa, the effect will be more pedantic than persuasive. The reader will be fatally aware of the present-day consciousness pulling the strings. *Titanic,* now and forever playing at your local theater, has some hilariously overdone moments: the philistine fiancé can't just sneer at his bride-to-be's newly acquired paintings; he has to chortle that this Picasso chap will never amount to anything.

When *Henry and Clara* came out, I made an appearance at the Abraham Lincoln Book Shop in Chicago. I was the first novelist they'd hosted in some time, pleased to be asked but not surprised at the lack of a turnout.

The serious readers of history who make up the shop's clientele feel toward historical novels roughly what silent-movie enthusiasts felt for the talkies: who needs this loudmouthed stuff? Recently, however, a movement toward "counterfactual" or "what-if" history has been gaining ground among academic historians. Reporting on this trend in *The New York Times,* William H. Honan notes the serious attention being paid to what might have happened, if, for example, the Spanish Armada had emerged victorious. He quotes Niall Ferguson, author of *Virtual History,* on how counterfactualism can "recapture the chaotic nature of experience and see that there are no certain outcomes." I can't help feeling that all this is better left to novelists, for whom the "chaotic nature of experience" is, sentence by sentence, a stock-in-trade. If historians, with their interest in defending a thesis, begin trafficking in the what-if, I'm afraid that what-might-have-been will soon get presented as what-would-have-been.

The historical novelist must grapple with moral considerations, not just aesthetic ones. "Don't you fear the dead?" the Chilean writer Ariel Dorfman once asked me about the dark motives and conduct I ascribed to my character Henry Rathbone. I don't suppose I fear the *long*-dead participants in an event that is by now as much a myth as it was once an occurrence. Immediate families would be, I think, another matter. Thomas E. Dewey's son is justifiably agitated about the portrayal of his honest, crime-busting father as a corrupt prosecutor in the recent movie *Hoodlum.* One cannot libel the dead, but one can refrain from distortions as hurtful as they are preposterous.

Why historical material should be increasingly attractive to both moviemakers (Steven Spielberg) and writers of literary fiction (Russell Banks and Jane Smiley join the ranks of Civil War novelists this season) is the subject of some curiosity. There are those who connect the proliferation of "period" dramas to the way nothing much has been going on in the mid- and late-'90s.* But I think the cause is deeper. The cyber and fiber-optic revolutions have made every person and place on the present-day globe absurdly and instantly accessible to every other person and place. It's not enough that we no longer walk down the street or ride a train with-out talking on the cell phone. We can E-mail and instant-message a thousand people we've never met in Katmandu, and if we're nostalgic for Paris, we can log on to an EarthCam Web site and watch live, real-time images of the traffic. There is less and less need to imagine anybody or any place; we can just access them. We are, as a result and more than we yet realize, becoming sick of one another. The past is the only place to which we can get away, and if I had one prediction for the millennium it would be that all of us, including novelists, shall be spending a lot of time—more than ever before—looking backward.

*This essay was drafted just a few weeks into the Lewinsky scandal and a year before Kosovo. So much for Francis Fukuyama and *The End of History*.

Five Practitioners

The All-True Travels and Adventures of Lidie Newton
    by Jane Smiley

EARLY IN JANE SMILEY'S stubborn new novel, her heroine, Lydia ("Lidie") Harkness Newton, declares: "One thing I've noticed is that when a particular notion enters your head, then its very particularity makes everything tend toward it, and the tending goes faster and faster." It's hard to believe that Smiley herself hasn't constructed this long account of Lidie's "adventures" in order to prove the particular, and much disputed, notion she put forth two years ago in an essay for *Harper's* called "Say It Ain't So, Huck."

In that piece Smiley argued—some would say railed—that *The Adventures of Huckleberry Finn* is not just overrated but deeply destructive. Reading it for the first time since junior high school, she was "stunned . . . by the notion that this is the novel all American literature grows out of, that this is a great novel, that this is even a serious novel." Mark Twain's "moral failure" was perpetuated by critics from "the Propaganda Era, between 1948 and 1955," among them Lionel Trilling and T. S. Eliot, whose collective admiration for the novel served "to underwrite a very simplistic and evasive theory of what racism is and to promulgate it, philosophically, in schools and the media as well as in academic journals." Smiley's suggested curricular alternative was *Uncle Tom's Cabin,* in her view an artistic and moral achievement displaying "the power of brilliant analysis married to great wisdom of feeling." It is Harriet Beecher Stowe's book that she would like to see her own children read.

In *Lidie Newton,* Smiley winds up proving the opposite of what she would like to. Luckily, however, she takes a long time getting around to doing that. The first two thirds of the novel are consistently entertaining, filled with action and ideas, two things sometimes absent from even the author's best work, such as the novellas "Ordinary Love" and "The Age of Grief," in which feelings are diced and worried with a fineness that borders on tour de force. It's rather bracing to have her new heroine out on the Kansas prairie in the 1850s, battling villains and the weather, almost like the Greenlanders of the sprawling saga Smiley published a decade ago.

At twenty years old, Lidie Newton is tall, plain, bookish and argumentative, by her own reckoning "what you might call an odd lot, not very salable and ready to be marked down." Her half sisters in Quincy, Illinois, view her as a problem to be solved, and so one of them furthers the fateful match between Lidie and Thomas Newton, who is on his way to the Kansas Territory ("K.T.") with a dozen Sharps rifles and the support of the Massachusetts Emigrant Aid Company, which hopes to see Kansas enter the Union as a free state.

Smiley may overdo the foreshadowings of peril ("I fully expect that these few conflicts I hear reports of will be as short-lived as they are exaggerated"), yet nothing can take away from Lidie's appeal. Wary but game, she journeys with her new husband to a spot north of the abolitionist settlement of Lawrence, where they bravely resist claim jumpers, horse thieves and Border Ruffians. By insulating their cabin with William Lloyd Garrison's abolitionist newspaper, they are even resisting gag laws imposed by the pro-slavery faction.

The Newtons' fellow Free-Soilers, transplants from back East, are brought to convincing life in Smiley's dialogue and Lidie's first-person voice. The women of K.T., sometimes making cartridges instead of quilts, must rise to a continuous emergency. Mrs. Bush, cool in the face of the pro-slavers' predations, can still be annoyed by a mismatched cup and saucer, while Susannah Jenkins, dismayed over how "coarse and wild" Kansas has made her, will eventually give up and return to Massachusetts. Political events propel the characters through their episodes (Smiley does a fine, harrowing job with the death of a young mother and her baby during the brutal winter) and into a connected, more meaningful narrative. Lidie has so much talking to do over 450 pages that her diction and syntax occasionally lapse into modernity, the way a tired actress will lose an accent, but overall Smiley does a good job antiquing the prose that carries her story.

She establishes the book's atmosphere and period with some creditable research and even a crafty glance forward: "I was always astonished at the speed with which news traveled in K.T. The solitudes of the prairies came later than my time—while I was there, the place was alive with travelers, messengers, and plain old gossips, galloping here and there to keep us all abreast of the latest events."

The novel's greatest strength—one that will haunt its last, unsuccessful hundred pages—lies in the way Smiley makes the Lidie of K.T. less crusading than conflicted. The character's honest doubts, both moral and political, tend to be resolved, or pushed aside, by practical considerations. She may admire the convictions of her husband and her late sister Miriam, who taught Negro schoolchildren in Ohio, but Lidie herself lacks real abolitionist fervor. In pondering her hard prairie life, she confesses to a foremost desire "for the rain to stop and the cabin to be dry and tight." She can see some good in her pro-slavery brother-in-law, but has less trouble with the idea of God punishing the besieging "slavocrats" than do some of the abstract former New Englanders, who are, bewilderingly to Lidie, "a little thrilled" by the threats of violence against them.

Lidie's movement toward commitment and zeal is a fine subject for a novel, but after the sacking of Lawrence and Thomas's violent death, Smiley undoes the character's practicality and ambivalence in such a way that the book never recovers believability. The story lurches into some broad derring-do and then gallops away on a moral high horse, leaving a reader baffled and unsatisfied. Lidie reasons: "I was a good shot and a good horsewoman, a strong girl with no children and no ties that held me to my proper place. Taking care of these Missourians was my business, and I welcomed it." Which is altogether different from making a reader accept the crossdressing, feminist revenge fantasy that follows. "I Go Among the Enemy," Lidie tells us in one chapter title, announcing her entry into slaveholding Missouri. Putting on trousers and an alias, then getting a newspaper job that allows her to pursue Thomas's killers by writing about some proslavery vigilantes, she revels in her peculiar new freedom. "It was eternally surprising to me the way no one questioned my masculinity." To me, too, I must say.

Smiley's real purpose in getting Lidie into Missouri is to rewrite *Huckleberry Finn,* in which, she insisted in that *Harper's* essay, "neither Huck nor Twain takes Jim's desire for freedom at all seriously." If Jim's creator and fictional companion had really cared about him, she argued, they would have sailed the raft across the Mississippi into the free state of Illinois rather than allowing it to drift down river even farther into slave territory. "Twain thinks that Huck's affection is a good enough reward for Jim," she stated. "[A]ll you have to do to be a hero is acknowledge that your poor sidekick is human; you don't actually have to act in the interests of his humanity."

Smiley tries to make her own heroine truly heroic by having Lidie do what Huck, and Twain, failed to. After her Missouri misadventures lead her to the Day's End Plantation, where she is nursed back to health from a miscarriage by a slave named Lorna, Lidie goes along with her new acquaintance's plan for the two of them to escape together: "I ain' gone tell you all de pieces right now," declares Lorna. "When I comes wid you breakfast in the mawnin', I'll tell you a little bit. But you jes' do what I tells you, and we is gone to be fine!"

Complexity now gives way to dutiful caricatures of white degeneracy and black nobility. The "hugely calm" Lorna is further characterized by a hugely predictable "dignity." It can only be Smiley's belief that, in *Uncle Tom's Cabin*, "[o]ne of Stowe's most skillful techniques is her method of weaving a discussion of slavery into the dialogue of her characters," which leads her to create this exchange between Lidie and Lorna:

> "We don' know all dat happen in slavery, an' I always thought we don' want to know. Ifn my days is good enough, an' I hate 'em, den I cain' think about de days of de others, dat is terrible bad, down Louisiana way an' dem other places."
> "You are quite a philosopher, Lorna."
> "Is dat so?"

There may be a crazy bravery in trying to render Lorna's dialect, but everything else about her is the purest p.c. Smiley may sneer that "all" Huck does is acknowledge Jim as human, but that's more than any reader will be able to say about a cardboard slave that exists only to tote Lidie's humanity.

Smiley has marveled at the lack of "personal conflict" Stowe felt in writing *Uncle Tom's Cabin*. "Nothing about slavery was attractive to her either as a New Englander or as a resident of Cincinnati for almost twenty years. Her lack of conflict is apparent in the clarity of both the style and substance of the novel." What an astonishing statement to make about art! What, if not tension and guilt and inner conflict, gave us the great American writing of

Dickinson and Melville and Hawthorne? What, on however less grand a scale, gave Lidie her own most believable moments?

With this new novel, Smiley has put her money where her mouth is. That's admirable, but she has just as certainly, in the book's last section, cut off her nose to spite her face. Her Twain essay ended with a ringing moral aesthetic: "If 'great' literature has any purpose, it is to help us face up to our responsibilities instead of enabling us to avoid them once again by lighting out for the territory." At heart I remain Arnoldian enough to want to agree with her. But it will take a stronger book than *Lidie Newton* to make me break out the old banner, just as, whatever Smiley may say, it's *Huckleberry Finn,* not *Uncle Tom's Cabin,* that's alive enough to get under her skin and, even now, make her want to redeem it.

Naming the Spirits by Lawrence Thornton
and *Voices from Silence* by Douglas Unger

Of all the complaints uttered by characters in fiction, surely none was ever less earned than Stephen Dedalus's cry about history being the "nightmare from which [he was] trying to awake." Even so, like a piece of Polonius's advice, the remark has survived the silliness of its speaker and remained chillingly applicable to those who have experienced slaughter instead of self-absorption. It seems almost to have been made for those who were "disappeared" during Argentina's "dirty war" (1976–83) and still lie in unmarked graves.

The titles of two new novels about the terror's aftermath, *Voices from Silence* by Douglas Unger and *Naming the Spirits* by Lawrence Thornton, hint at an almost literal effort to resuscitate those strangled by history. Each of the books is, like most of history itself, a sequel whose full resonance depends heavily on having read earlier volumes, in this case Mr. Unger's *El Yanqui* (1986) and Mr. Thornton's *Imagining Argentina* (1987). Perhaps the principal distinction between the work of the two authors is that Mr. Unger's novels are the product of fairly extensive firsthand experience of Argentina, while Mr. Thornton writes about a country he has visited only with his imagination.

El Yanqui was a coming-of-age story about an American exchange student called "Diego" by the prosperous Benevento family with whom he spends a year during the period before Juan Perón's 1973 return to power, the trigger for all the calamity that would follow. Fifteen years later, by which time the elected government of President Raúl Alfonsín has begun judicial proceedings against the deposed generals, the adult Diego, now a writer and teacher, returns with his wife to revisit his Argentine family, who have been decimated by the dirty war. Two of the Beneventos' three sons, Alejo and Miguelito, young men Diego considered brothers, were driven underground and killed, and a third has only recently returned from exile in Paris. "Mama" and "Papa" have themselves been repeatedly detained, robbed and forced from their home. Both now do human-rights work, and prepare for Miguelito's case to come before the tribunals, which are conducted grudgingly, with a dearth of publicity and much witness intimidation, in a country that has not fully democratized its way out of repression.

Unger does a fine job reproducing the textures of this era, from its hyperinflation to its still true-believing Perónists. He can render the decline of nightlife in Buenos Aires's port district as vividly as he has Papa Benevento recollect scenes of torture. Much of the country's recent history is given to the reader through Diego's interview with Jorge Gallo, a prosperous acquaintance from his student days who has been impoverished by years of flight, so harrowed by the experience that his chief desire in this tentative new democracy is to be "legal": " 'New driver's license, my own name. New federal identification, my real name. Real estate salesman's card. Library card.' " The changes in Mama Benevento are the most strikingly realized of all. This once-wealthy, convent-educated supporter of the arts, "a tyrant about table manners" in Diego's memory, now gulps her wine and eats her empanadas "as roughly as a dock worker." Her method of survival is hyperkinesis: "She typically had two pots cooking on the stove, items of clothing pulled out with seams to sew and cuffs to raise, clippings to cut out of the newspapers for her expatriate friends."

Unger's Argentina is a place of multiple torments, many of them warring within individuals. Amalita, an unmarried friend of the Beneventos, the boys' devoted "aunt," initially approved of the generals' drive against the urban guerrillas, one of whose bombs killed her cousin. She knew that Miguelito "was in thick with the worst of the militant gangs," but she provided him with the last new clothes and medical help he had before he was killed by the government, whose systematic crimes she insists she was unaware of. Unger gives her a generous, full-throated place in his chorus of ghosts both living and dead.

It is a rare thing these days for any novel to have too much on its mind, but *Voices from Silence* does sometimes suffer from its own urgency and range. Even to a reader of *El Yanqui,* the intensity of the bond between Diego and the Beneventos may still seem more stated than real, and the language of this sequel tends to be more piously rhetorical than what was in the earlier book. Diego stood at the center of that novel, a *picaro* whose every thought and feeling became familiar to the reader. His latter-day version is more narrator than character. Nonetheless, he has done what we never got to see Stephen Dedalus do, which is grow up. His new storytelling responsibilities are heavier than the ones he shouldered years ago, and he keeps the courage of his own well-earned pessimism straight through to the end of his tale. There is no palinode. On the last pages he looks at this rich nation, so instantly ruined it required redemption before it was fully born, and prophesies: "The cycles of power and cruelty would come around again. The recent memories would be erased, the tens of thousands gone, my own two brothers among them."

Lawrence Thornton opens *Naming the Spirits* with a kind of antithesis to Mr. Unger's lament. A group of the dead declare that the perpetrators of the dirty war "overlooked the fact that grief abhors a vacuum. It never occurred to them that even though we were gone we remained alive in the memories of our families." Mr. Thornton is determined to offer as much hope as violence, no matter how much magic that may require. *Imagining Argentina* was the story of Carlos Rueda's telepathic power to envision the location of many of the disappeared and thereby, in some cases, aid their return. *Naming the Spirits* opens with the attempted murder by the police of a teenage girl, whose miraculous survival is witnessed by the spirits of a dozen kidnap victims just massacred nearby. They follow her mute trek to an apartment building in Buenos Aires, the Villa Deamicis, hoping she will come out of her emotional coma to tell their stories and lead others to their grave.

The residents of the Villa Deamicis include an astrologer, a teacher, a womanizing painter, and most important, Dr. Roberto and Mercedes Cristiani, whose daughter Anna Maria is among the disappeared. They attempt to bring the girl out of her trance. In the same dangerously half-realized democracy described by Mr. Unger, Dr. Cristiani works for the Ezekiel Squad, who try to find the dead and gather forensic evidence against their political killers. The girl makes spooky efforts toward her own revitalization, launching origami birds from the Villa Deamicis's balconies. These birds travel miraculously upon the air to some of the key sites in the story, including the mass grave of those who were killed when she was wounded.

Thornton is capable of some lovely effects ("the grief which held her like a setting does a gemstone"), but his magical realism never quite loses the feeling of a knockoff. At its worst, it's like a tango learned at Arthur Murray, something that doesn't look fully comfortable on the American writer. There is a similar generic thinness to the imagery, whose vehicles often seem like emblems from a travel brochure. A disappointment is "as bitter . . . as the taste of day old maté tea"; the girl retraces some steps as naturally "as the River Plate emptying into the thirsty sea."

Historical novelists, from Scott to Vidal, have never been able to travel back to the times they write about, and readers accept that as a simple law of literary physics; and on rare occasions, when only geography is involved, we are sufficiently dazzled to wonder if the writer weren't lucky to have had his imagination kept free of direct experience: *Robinson Crusoe* and *Amerika* may be better books for Defoe's not having been shipwrecked and Kafka's never crossing the Atlantic. But there is usually more to be said for being there. Mr. Thornton's Argentina feels like a tragic myth, whereas Mr. Unger's feels, more appropriately, like history that is still news. (Just this spring Argentines heard new evidence of how drugged political prisoners were thrown into the ocean from the junta's military airplanes.) If Mr. Thornton's country is a sort of whirling Purgatory, Mr. Unger's tantalizes the American reader's imagination as a real place to be found at the end of an eight-hour flight. *Naming the Spirits* remains well worth reading, but *Voices from Silence* seems more in the greatest tradition of the nineteenth-century novel, that powerful scourge of injustice as well as print's most copious form of infotainment, filled with data and sensation and a realism that was magical all by itself.

Ship Fever and Other Stories by Andrea Barrett

THE STORIES in Andrea Barrett's fifth book of fiction all involve the history and revelations of science, with the figure of Linnaeus acting as a kind of muse. The great classifier figures directly in two of the pieces. In "The English Pupil," nearing death, he still makes use of "the thread of Ariadne" that he had strung through nature's species. It now helps his wavering consciousness to keep his daughters straight: "The three oldest looked and acted like their mother: large-boned, coarse-featured, practical. Sophia seemed to belong to another genus entirely." The other Linnaean story, "Rare Bird," tells of an eighteenth-century spinster and widow who forsake the boring company around them to try to disprove Linnaeus's theory that swallows, instead of migrating, hibernate under water—a notion more plausible, if less charming, than a third, competing one that says the birds winter on the moon.

When she leaves historical fiction for contemporary settings, Ms. Barrett hardly abandons taxonomy. She maps her characters' origins, differentiates their inherited and acquired characteristics and, especially, evaluates their attempts (usually failures) at transplantation and hybridization. "The Littoral Zone," one of the best stories in this fine collection, tells of flora meeting fauna: a botanist and zoologist fall in love during a summer of marine-biology research "between high and low watermarks where organisms struggled to adapt to the daily rhythm of immersion and exposure." This is what the two of them are doing as well, moving from collegiality toward a decision to leave their spouses and children for each other. After fifteen years, the completeness of their union will still depend to some extent on whether they can believe Jonathan actually assimilated the bit of Ruby's fingernail that he nibbled and swallowed during their first night together. The scientist in each of them knows that keratin is indigestible; their romantic and moral aspects need to believe otherwise.

"*Soroche*" concerns a working-class Philadelphia woman, Zaga, whose marriage to a wealthy, much older man finally satisfies neither his own children nor her greedy family. From Dr. Sepulveda, the Chilean physician who treats her for altitude sickness while she is pregnant on her honeymoon, she learns the story of Jemmy Button, the Tierra del Fuego native taken to England and returned to his own country in 1835 aboard the *Beagle* with Charles Darwin: " 'captured, exiled, re-educated; then returned, abused by his family, finally re-accepted. Was he happy? Or was he saying that as a way to spite his captors? Darwin never knew.' " Zaga finally judges any connections between herself and Jemmy to be "specious," but they are strong enough for Ms. Barrett to work hard at developing them.

On occasion, a reader will be tempted to say she's worked too hard at establishing such links. One could protest the narrative convenience of Zaga's Chilean honeymoon, or that, in "The Behavior of the Hawkweeds," the possessor of a Mendel letter would meet a young biologist who calls Mendel his hero, but the arbitrariness of Ms. Barrett's inventions is the arbitrariness of the experimenter who deliberately puts one element in contact with another to observe what results. There *is* an artificiality to some of what she does, and a tendency to spell out connections the way one was taught to write "Conclusion" before the last step of a lab report, and yet her scientific bent is sufficiently rare among fiction writers, and her concoctions so cunningly mixed, that dissatisfaction seems out of place. So much fiction now takes place in law courts, those natural arenas for people's passions, that we overlook the ways in which the laboratory offers an even richer stock of metaphor for human contention. An earlier book of Ms. Barrett's, *Lucid Stars,* made use of astronomy in telling the story of a modern marriage.

The title novella of this new collection, "Ship Fever," is based on what seems to be considerable research. It tells the story of Lauchlin Grant, a young Canadian doctor who in 1847 goes to work among the typhus-ridden Irish emigrants at a quarantine station along the St. Lawrence. The emigrants, having exchanged famine for fever, arrive in floating charnel houses that Barrett describes with a rich, horrifying vividness. In the third hold Grant enters, he finds "the rotting food, and the filth sloshing underfoot. The fetid bedding alive with vermin and everywhere the sick. But a last surprise awaited him here. He inched up to a berth in which two people lay mashed side by side. He leaned over to separate them, for comfort, and found that both were dead." Ms. Barrett's customary deliberateness of design becomes less important than a free flow of feeling here; "Ship Fever" has a wholly successful urgency. It also contains the story of Grant's lost love and a quietly moving feminism: some of the isolation techniques with which the doctor tries to save his patients are the same ones practiced, back in Ireland, by the grandmother of Nora Kynd, an emigrant who, because of Grant's care, has lived to tell him about them.

Ms. Barrett's narrative lab is stocked with a handsome variety of equipment. She tells her stories through alternating voices, diaries, letters— whatever seems most promising of result. On a fictional landscape overpopulated with the sensational and affectless, her work stands out for its sheer intelligence, its painstaking attempt to discern and describe the world's arrangement. The overall effect is quietly dazzling, like looking at hand-made paper under a microscope.

Dreamland by Kevin Baker

KEVIN BAKER'S JAM-PACKED NOVEL of New York City "circa 1910" rushes between lower Manhattan and Coney Island like a wild amusement-park ride on a continuous loop. The author shanghais all sorts of real-life Tammany pols, Bowery gangsters, factory girls and carnival attractions to join his own inventions and composites inside a book that teems with violence, humor, information and hustle. *Dreamland* is historical fiction at its most entertaining and, in a number of spots, most high-handed.

The novel's whirligig of plots more or less all proceed from an incident that follows a heavily bet dog-and-rat fight in a basement off Baxter Street. Kid Twist incurs the lasting enmity of his fellow gangster Gyp the Blood when he hits Gyp with a shovel in order to save a newsboy (or so he thinks) from having his back broken across Gyp's knee. Now on the run from "the most dangerous lunatic in New York," Kid soon makes matters much worse by romancing a girl he doesn't know is Gyp's sister, Esther.

The little fellow Kid has saved is actually Trick the Dwarf, a performer at Coney Island's newest and most magical park, Dreamland. Trick sometimes likes to pass for a newsboy, since "With a little make-up, I could not only hide my misshapen body, I could be young again. And what, after all, is the greater deformity—size or age?" In gratitude for his rescue from Gyp, Trick hides Kid Twist at Coney Island's Tin Elephant Hotel, where eventually Esther joins him. Trick himself is in love with the tiny, enchantingly mad Carlotta, whom he contrives to make queen of a built-to-scale Little City, the novel's version of Lilliputia, a community of 300 midgets that actually existed in Dreamland.

Trying to overcome the same tenement life her brother escaped through crime, Gyp's sister Esther first toils in a sweatshop, felling sleeve linings for coats, and later takes a job at the Triangle Shirtwaist factory near Washington Square. With the encouragement of Clara Lemlich—the bravest *kochleffl* (rabble-rouser) of all the young working women, a real-life activist who can be found in histories of the great Triangle fire—Esther is reluctantly transformed from wage-slave to agitator.

Lumbering between the worlds of labor and crime and amusement is the also-real Big Tim Sullivan, the sentimental political boss and investor in vaudeville, nickelodeons and Coney Island. A builder of the crude ethnic bridges that would create the city's modern body politic ("Big Tim's specialty had always been Jews"), Sullivan pushed through labor reforms and the famous law against concealed weapons that bears his name, even as he stole elections and—as Baker has it—stood behind the famous murder of gambler Herman Rosenthal, for which the police lieutenant Charles Becker was eventually executed.

Dreamland is terrific fun, though ultimately something less than the sum of its gaudy episodes. Its gangland and labor narratives tend to move in more predictable increments than the action out at Coney Island; Trick, the only character whose tale gets told in the first person, becomes the most real and affecting one in the novel. The book's best lines belong to him: "Ours was the most credulous of ages, for everything came true." Baker manages to throw everything together for a fiery dual climax—Dreamland and the Triangle factory both burned in 1911—but the 500-page ride to it provides a lot of bumps along with the thrills. The author works his italicized refrains rather hard and occasionally seems to be blocking the movie instead of writing the book. Frequent interruptions to follow Freud and Jung on their roughly contemporaneous American travels add nothing.

Baker is also the author of *Sometimes You See It Coming* (1993), a delightful baseball novel with some of the same vividness and ramshackle construction displayed by *Dreamland.* He has more recently worked as Harry Evans's chief researcher on *The American Century,* an experience that no doubt helped him stuff his own new book with all its song and food and spectacles that run from clip-joint dancing to settlement-house lectures.

In a concluding note on his sources, Baker offers a modest manifesto for historical fiction, saying its essential obligations are to "a good story," "human nature" and "an essential core of truth"—which is to say, the forest of plausibility instead of every factual tree. He confesses to a number of chronological manipulations—allowing, for instance, George McClellan, "son of the famous Civil War flop by the same name," to preside as mayor over the book's action, even though McClellan had left office before all the novel's principal events occurred. Baker hopes that readers "will further amuse themselves sniffing out the real, unnamed, historical personages [he has] stuck into the narrative." Some readers may, but their amusement can only make them conscious of the author and his method; it will hardly keep their disbelief suspended.

All historical fiction requires manipulation and outright lying, but re-arrangement of the public record on the scale conducted by Baker really makes for an allied genre one might call "historical fantasy," a worthy but more perilous endeavor. Readers who don't know the history end up misinformed; those who do know it—if only from other historical fiction—may end up irritated or perplexed.

Baker provides so much pleasure here that one hates to complain, but he might be better off with a clearer set of rules for himself. Naming an amalgam of "great Coney Island entrepreneurs" after his brother-in-law (Matthew Brinckerhoff, acknowledged in the notes) is a charming self-indulgence, on the order of the inconspicuous self-image a cathedral sculptor puts amidst the bigger gargoyles. Naming two Triangle factory foremen "Kristol" and "Podhoretz" is a lousy joke, and a surefire illusion killer for every scene in which the two appear.

Dreamland's publicity inevitably pronounces it "in the tradition of E. L. Doctorow's *Ragtime*," a novel that briefly includes the Becker-Rosenthal affair and a number of other elements in this new one. I would venture to say, even with all the reservations above, that *Dreamland* is the better book. Its history and biography are less potted, and more often than not it truly inhabits its characters and era. There is a coldness to Doctorow's famous and much-more-pulled-together novel, a latter-day superiority that doesn't do emotional or moral justice to the period it's reconstructing. There's nothing arm's-length about Baker. He loves all the "cigars, and oysters, and roasting corn; the shady characters, and the women of bad reputation" he can crowd onto the page. *Ragtime* remains just that, a time, whereas Baker rightly tries to treat the past as a place, whose strange shoreline he's just sighted, like one of the startled immigrants in his bounteous book.

Varlet's Ghost

May 1995

T HE DEVOTEE—which is to say, the reader who has all the books and theories spilled upon a grassy knoll in the back of his mind—will read every page. Will know what the author means when he mentions "the famous morning" in September 1963 when Lee Harvey Oswald did or did not participate in a black-voter-registration effort in Clinton, Louisiana. Will spot mistakes: Officer J. D. Tippit was shot at the corner of Tenth and Patton, not Tenth and Dalton. And will wonder at things left out: no mention of Billy Lovelady, the man with the disquieting resemblance to Oswald, photographed in the Texas School Book Depository's main entrance at the moment of the shots?

The common reader, who cannot number the frames of the Zapruder film and does not immediately recognize 1026 North Beckley as the address of "O. H. Lee's" rooming house, will want to know, caveat emptor, what Norman Mailer is up to in *Oswald's Tale,* his self-admittedly "peculiar" nonfiction treatment of why, and if, Oswald came to kill John F. Kennedy. For a long stretch, the writer's goals seem as difficult to divine as the assassin's. Instead of a preface, we get "Remarks from the Author," beginning on page 197, and the fullest expression of his method about 150 pages after that. Stimulated in part by "an offer from the Belarus KGB to allow a look into their files on Oswald," Mailer has set out to build "a base camp" near the bottom of this mountainous mystery. Although "the materials proved to be less comprehensive than promised, it was still the equivalent of an Oklahoma landgrab for an author to be able to move into a large and hitherto unrecorded part of Oswald's life." To supplement the paper haul, Mailer spent six months in Minsk and Moscow with his old collaborator on *The Executioner's Song,* Lawrence Schiller, interviewing dozens of people who'd had anything to do with Oswald during the years of his defection

(1959–1962) and finding their memories, thanks to years of Soviet oppression, surprisingly fresh: "After the assassination, they had been instructed by the KGB not to speak about Oswald or [his wife] Marina, and indeed they did not. So, their recall was often pristine; it had not been exposed to time so much as sealed against it." In contrast, American memories—including Marina's, after her three decades here—have been corrupted and internally contradicted by their owners' garrulous freedom: thirty years of talking to everyone from Earl Warren to Oliver Stone to *Hard Copy*. So Mailer decided to look, one more time, at all we knew through all we didn't: the largely hidden Russian years would be new lenses, a set of spectacles as magically pickled as Lenin.

No one will fault the author for a lack of enterprise. Mailer and Schiller have gone after Marina's relatives, schoolmates and boyfriends; Oswald's early minders from Intourist; his girlfriends; and his coworkers at the Minsk radio factory where the Soviets decided to put, and watch, him.

What was the steely little nebbish up to? He was so determined to stay that he slashed his wrists when permission wasn't forthcoming; and yet, during his first weeks in Moscow, he never ventured more than a few blocks beyond his hotel, to buy an ice-cream cone at a children's department store. The highest authorities—including Anastas Mikoyan, who four years later would represent the U.S.S.R. at Kennedy's funeral—were in on the decision to let him remain and thereby provide the police "Organs" with a chance to explore some possibilities: "Had some American intelligence service sent Lee Harvey Oswald here to check out their Soviet legal channels? Was he a test case to determine how moles might be implanted for special tasks?"

The KGB followed him with mad thoroughness. July 3, 1960: "Outside he looked around, went to movie theatre Centralny, bought newspaper *Banner of Youth* at paper stand, browsed it through and turned back. At corner of Prospekt Stalina and Komsomolskaya Street he stopped, looked through newspaper again, crushed it and threw it away in trash bin." In July 1961, Lee and Marina's apartment was bugged, and now, thirty years and a world later, Mailer can reproduce careful transcripts of their bureaucratized rows:

WIFE: (*cries*) Why did I get married?
LHO: Well, what am I supposed to do? Is it my fault that you have a lot of work? I mean, you don't ever cook, but other women cook.

It seems clear that Marina married Oswald not because her uncle Ilya Prusakov, an intelligence officer, saw Cold War opportunity in the match (another theory the devotee will know), but because, with his soft drawl and starched shirts, Lee was more intriguing than most of the vodka-belching "Vanyas" on the assembly line. As time went on, Oswald beat her with all the petty viciousness she could have found in a homegrown spouse, but before that, an awareness of the wiretapping was one of a handful of attachments giving the two of them an edgy solidarity.

The Oswalds, with their small circle of friends, were a fairly cheap surveillance operation, and when, in 1962, Lee sought permission to return to the United States, the Organs were inclined to let him go, since all their tedious tracking had produced no evidence he was a spy. It was American organs, the State Department and INS, who couldn't agree on whether to let this "unstable character" come back with his Soviet wife. In the end, the U.S. government loaned him the money to sail home.

The results of Mailer's legwork in Minsk are laid out across his first 300 pages at considerable literary sacrifice—in a flat, almost transcripted, barely third-person style. There is no room for the loud flourishes of his own voice and personality, the outsize ego of his "Aquarian" age, when he could not report the Pentagon demonstration in *The Armies of the Night* without describing his urgent need to use the men's room or, in *Of a Fire on the Moon,* ponder Apollo 11 without musing upon his own marriages and waistline. So brilliantly, too, did he do those things (it will be a sad day if Jimmy Carter gets his Nobel before Mailer does) that now, having read the diligent Russian pages, a reader is ready for a yawping assertion of authorial ego, eager for Mailer, fitted with those Russian lenses, to go to town on Oswald's American years, which bracket the Soviet sojourn.

That American story is familiar enough to make "tale" an appropriate word in Mailer's title. It is, in fact, a twice-a-hundred-times-told tale: Oswald's wildly resentful mother, Marguerite; his time in New York City, at the Bronx Zoo and with the truant officer; his mouthy years in the Marines, learning Russian and spouting a lending-library Marxism. Then—after the Russian years—his return to America with Marina; the grubby jobs he felt were beneath him; the even grubbier apartments; the purchase of the rifle and the bragging backyard photos with it; the attempt to kill the right-wing

General Walker; the summer months of 1963, at the edges of New Orleans's "Bermuda Triangle" of mobsters, anti-Castro Cuban exiles and poetic freaks like the eyebrowless David Ferrie. Finally, the failed attempt to get to Cuba by way of Mexico City; a return to Dallas, where Marina had taken shelter with the kindly Quaker Ruth Paine; one last job, at the Texas School Book Depository, and one last alias, O. H. Lee. In bed at 3 a.m., on November 22, 1963, he'll shove Marina's foot away from his leg. "My, he's in a mean mood," she will think.

Mailer takes hundreds and hundreds of pages to present this, relying on the much-despised twenty-six-volume report of the Warren Commission, "a dead whale decomposing on a beach," for the raw protein of his narrative. The Russian lenses, he hopes, will bring it back to life. He pledges to apply his imagination to this old material, even if he starts out feeling like "a literary usher," escorting all the familiar dramatis personae to their spots on the stage.

The very bad news is that he fails. The Russian lenses, when he even wears them, disappoint like the first pair fitted to the Hubble telescope. The whale, albeit white, remains beached, and onto the huge blubbery slices of Warren Commission transcript that the author serves up (along with great cuts from books by Priscilla Johnson McMillan and Edward J. Epstein), Mailer dabs only smidgens of his own tangy mustard. For chapters at a time, instead of using his own gifts, Mailer displays the KGB's faith in endless accretion. After all the painstaking work of the first third—as Mailer might put it: "Six months in Minsk! By a famous man past 70!"—the author gets sloppier as he goes on, even abandoning Oswald at the most crucial moment in his tale to give us some pointless paragraphs of recollection from Lady Bird Johnson, one car behind Kennedy's in the motorcade.

A reader wants to take a bellows to the sparks and hints of the old, impossible Mailer that are scattered around: the big ideas ("When the frontier was finally closed, imagination inevitably turned into paranoia"), the bravura comparisons (the resemblance of KGB officers to American media barons), the sudden empathies (Ruth Paine and her husband "have been brought up to be so decent to others, so firm and uncompromising about not allowing the greedy little human animal within ever to speak, that one can almost hear the strings snapping"). No one, not even Jean Stafford (*A Mother in History*), has done better with Marguerite, who loves Lee "with a full operatic passion equal to all the unutterable arias of those who are talentless at love. . . ."

But still the whale won't breathe.

Mailer insists that his book "is an exploration into the possibilities of [Oswald's] character rather than a conviction that one holds the solution." He hypothesizes a larger stature for his "protagonist" than the one typically accorded, even as he digs into the young man's "eruptions" of dyslexia; his possibly guilty homosexuality (that Oswald may have killed his fellow marine Martin Schrand is an old speculation, but so far as I know, Mailer is the only writer to suggest the future assassin may have done it after being forced to give Schrand a blow job); and Oswald's wildly dialectical thought process ("To commit his mind to one action sometimes meant no more than that he was constructing a mental platform which would enable him to spring off in the opposite direction"). Maybe there *was* an ideology lurking in Oswald's manifestos (shotguns would be free in his "Atheian system"). Or maybe he was like 95 percent of all the defectors to Russia the KGB encountered—crazy. Or maybe he just desired the attention he could never imagine he would get, incessantly, in these decades after his death, to the point where there now remain no more than 200 undocumented hours of his life between October 1962 and April 1963. And yet, after 600 pages, Mailer must still admit the possibility that the "sad sum" of Oswald was never more than "an over-ambitious yet much henpecked husband, with an unbalanced psyche. . . ."

The author avoids some of the assassination's never-ending debates, such as those over ballistics (thank God) and how Oswald financed his trip to the U.S.S.R. In one place, the investigator in Mailer apologizes for "cross[ing] over wholly into speculation," but why should he apologize, in a book whose approach, he insists elsewhere, "is not legal, technical, or evidentiary, but novelistic"? Early on, Mailer says that he is "studying an *object* (to use the KBG's word for a person under scrutiny)," but *object* is a term of art as well as police work, and Mailer seems never to have made up his mind whether he wanted to approach Kennedy's killing as an artist or as a gumshoe. Even though he confesses to a grander desire than he first admits ("Few who build a base camp have no ambitions to reach the summit"), he keeps tugging himself back.

Why not be the novelist he can still be? Why interrupt a spectacularly imagined paragraph—three minutes after the assassination, Oswald's "[s]tepping out into Dealey Plaza . . . must have been not unlike being hurled through a plate-glass window"—just to dish out the next dozen slices of quotation? Why not, after admitting "the fact that there are no facts—only the mode of our approach to what we call facts," lay full artistic claim to Oswald's mind? Mailer was always a great one for sizing up the talent in the room, and there are those of us who would even now bet on him against Don DeLillo (*Libra*) and D. M. Thomas (*Flying in to Love*), or even James Ellroy, whose *American Tabloid* is a factually risible but triumphantly mythic rendition of Kennedy's killing.

To be sure, Mailer accomplishes much, and it was never unusual of him to achieve in his books something quite aside from what he set out to. He compellingly ponders Oswald's connection with George DeMohrenschildt and the chance that this Dallas adventurer was sent to debrief him for the CIA or even run him as a client. Mailer's pursuit of Jack Ruby during the weekend following the assassination—and of the possibility, however remote, that Ruby did shoot Oswald on impulse, but only *after* he had failed to carry out a Mafia hit—is rather dazzling, enough to make a reader waver, if only for a moment, in his conviction that Gerald Posner earned the chutzpah to title his recent acted-alone book *Case Closed*.

Best of all, if still incidental, is the portrait of Soviet society Mailer creates through his latter-day interviews with the Oswalds' friends and keepers. The boyfriend whose loss drove Marina into the arms of Lee, Anatoly Shpanko, a model citizen, medical student and young officer in Komsomol, insisted to Mailer and Schiller in 1993 that he had no idea the Marina Prusakova he had known went on to marry the man accused of killing Kennedy. The preposterousness of this speaks sad volumes about still-unshakable fears. Dr. Shpanko works today "near the Ukrainian border, and he deals with victims of Chernobyl. . . . For this, or for other causes, he is drinking at ten in the morning. . . ."

Shpanko is now one line in the assassination epic, which Mailer (who sometimes starts sentences with a storyteller's ancient "Yes . . .") can't quite bring himself to release from the world of literal truth into the realm of myth. Even so, he pays "a collegial salute" to a whole shelf of authors whose interpretations of Kennedy's killing are as opposed to one another as those rubber walls in Oswald's dialectical mind, as if he knows these writers are all troubadours singing the same ballad, a tale by now as fluid and familiar as any out of the Bible, one that means what you want it to, one that Mailer *has* let go of enough to cite, a couple of times, his own CIA novel, *Harlot's Ghost,* as if it were part of the historical and not the artistic record. Over time, those two records will further blend, just as John Wilkes Booth now seems little more good or evil than Abraham Lincoln and strikes our eye as one more bright stitch in a tapestry, one more somersault in the historical pageant.

When 1963 is fully released to legend, we will cease to worry about even the last issue tormenting Mailer, the "philosophical crux" of his book: "that the sudden death of a man as large in his possibilities as John Fitzgerald Kennedy is more tolerable if we perceive his killer as tragic rather than absurd." Absurdity, Mailer insists, "corrodes our species," and on the very last page of *Oswald's Tale,* as if to comfort himself, he pronounces the assassin's story to be, indeed, tragic, at least in the common-man sense present in American literature from Dreiser to Arthur Miller. But why should the absurd be so unassimilable, so unbearable? Absurdity is a small secular notion. Who knows what greater, untragic mystery may lie behind it, one explaining why the enormities happening here for no apparent reason may, in a place so distant it's hardly our affair, mean something after all? Here and now we can only marvel at how an angry little man found himself in the right place and time to change the world because a month before, in applying for a warehouse job, he pleased the boss by calling him "sir."

Lens Democracy

*December 1994**

F OR A CENTURY and a half the politician and the camera have been involved in a power struggle, changes in technology shifting the advantage between one side and the other. In the beginning, like anyone else who posed for Mathew Brady or Alexander Gardner, statesmen had to stand still and, even less characteristically, shut up for a moment or two. Early presidential facial expressions run to impatience and bafflement, as their wearers try mightily not to move during the long exposure times: Martin Van Buren leans on a book and John Quincy Adams folds his hands, to steady them, one suspects, in his lap. General Grant stands with his head clamped between the tines of what looks like a giant tuning fork, standard equipment for immobilizing the subject. Lincoln, unsurprisingly, manages to defy convention even as he honors it. Photographed by Gardner in the last months of his life, he adopts the conventional three-quarters profile staring into space, but his lips portray amusement over his son, Tad, who was standing a foot or two away.

After the Civil War, the camera's increasing speed and portability allowed the politician to force it away from portraiture and into witnessing the historical moment. But even in 1862, Gardner was shooting Lincoln and McClellan in a tent at Antietam, the two subjects looking animated and intense, a map or newspaper (it's difficult to tell) discarded at the president's feet, and a Confederate flag folded up on the dry ground. Soon the camera could even travel along with a politician on the mere chance that something might happen. In 1910, William Warnecke succeeded in capturing New

*Review of "American Politicians: Photographs from 1843 to 1993," Museum of Modern Art, October 6, 1994–January 3, 1995, with accompanying text by Susan Kismaric (New York: Harry N. Abrams).

York Mayor William J. Gaynor an instant after he had been shot; the blood pours down from his head and a young man rushes wide-eyed to his aid.

The curators of "American Politicians: Photographs from 1843 to 1993" have tried to keep a balance between general historical significance and important developments in this particular genre of picture-taking. A viewer will find little of Franklin Roosevelt and Ronald Reagan, however much the camera loved each of these titans, and a surprising amount of William McKinley, a dull-looking man whose photographers did an interesting job (in the days before zoom lenses) of capturing the crowds around him.

Probably the best political photographs come out of election campaigns, when the candidates are desperate with self-importance and the voters are jazzed by courtship. Riding through Elwood, Indiana, in August 1940, Wendell Willkie—surrounded by roaring faithful waving their hats and police motorcycles churning up dust—seems so mad with excitement that he can't have noticed how he's just ridden past the undertaker's parlor. Six years later, Congressman Joseph Martin is photographed through the office window of the Massachusetts paper he published, as he listens to election returns over the telephone. So stunned does Martin seem (he's on his way to becoming Speaker of the House), and so in character is everyone else around him, that a viewer wonders just how spontaneous Allan Grant's picture really was. A *Life* photo of John Kennedy from the same year shows the congressional hopeful sitting beneath his own poster, which looks as if it's been designed to tout a film instead of a candidacy—a visual taste of things to come.

When dealing with politicians, art photography is generally no more appealing than state-sponsored painting. Edward Steichen's Theodore Roosevelt, from 1908, is gauzily heroic, and the 1955 Nixon that Philippe Halsman caught for his pointless "jumping" series does have a certain vice-presidential irony to it (as well as the additional merit of giving an aerodynamic lift to Nixon's jowls), but politicians are best captured when they are trying to manipulate people instead of permitting photographers to manipulate them. In 1984, even the still-squeamish *New York Times* could not resist running on its front page a Columbus Day photograph (absent from this exhibit) of Walter Mondale, Mario Cuomo, and Geraldine Ferraro stepping gaily around some horse manure on the parade route; there has rarely been a picture of politicians more joyfully in their element.

The camera may not lie, but that fact has misled many photographers and viewers into believing that every time it opens and closes the shutter it speaks the truth, whereas, like the human mouth, it often says nothing at all. The MOMA show is mercifully short of Avedon, whose coroner's style of portraiture remains utterly unrevealing—totally individuating, yes, but in the way of a DNA smear, and no more evocative of character or essence than that. His Eisenhower, wan and walleyed, is of course meant to surprise us with some sort of meaningfully reversed expectations, but it doesn't, any more than a driver's-license photo exerts any strong claim as truth or art. More thought-provoking, and certainly amusing, is a 1945 *Life* photograph of the general returning to his mother's front porch in Abilene, Kansas. She is the one wearing a big grin, looking more like Ike than Ike does.

When the camera does manage to say something, it often does so by in-direction, or even inversion, like the reliable source whose yes can be counted on to mean no. Jacqueline Kennedy's beautiful face fools the lens into thinking it's being eluded, that her realest part is somewhere else, held in reserve, a glamorous mystery. In fact, Mrs. Kennedy is fully present, fully in control, *projecting* mystery *into* the camera with more art than that mus-tered by most of the thousands of photographers who took her picture. Her talent is almost opposite to that of Ronald Reagan, a man who, in so many photos one remembers, made himself seem fully present to the camera, shaking your hand with his eye, while all the time a part of him, probably the best and most interesting part, was somewhere else. No photographer ever "got" Reagan any more than a biographer will. There's no here there.

Pat Nixon lacked the acting skills of either of these two. Her face, full of intelligence, is more directly present than either Mrs. Kennedy's or Rea-gan's; one sees her straining to cooperate in a situation she cannot bear but knows she must, unable to displace herself mentally to wherever it is she would prefer being. The last thing she appears is plastic, a word with which she was always scorned, but which, in the application of its simple, physical meaning to camera–subject relations, seems made for Jackie and Reagan and painfully inapplicable to her.

The photo opportunity, which came in with Teddy Roosevelt (shown here riding a steam shovel and weighing some skinny boys in a New York hospital), brought politicians to a point of maximum power over the cam-era, allowing them to be a different sort of actor from the kind they had been playing since the Roman forum. The oratorical ham gave way to the silent play of *tableau vivant,* which required little more than the ability, after hours of someone else's advance work, to show up when the flashbulb popped. Even after its cornball apotheosis with Fiorello La Guardia, who drove rivets, cut ribbons, smashed slot machines and pretended to fight fires to shamelessly good effect, the photo op wasn't exhausted. A 1952 Cornell Capa shot of Adlai Stevenson, "Deciding Whether to Run for the Presidency" as he sits beneath a tree on his Illinois farm, can still probably fool some of the people some of the time—though Al Gore, who sits next to Bill Clinton in "Family Help," a 1993 AP photo of the president and vice president "on telephones in the Oval Office . . . to families who were forced to choose between their jobs and time off to care for children or ailing parents," seems to be overacting his way through a tryout for the St. Albans class play. He makes Clinton look positively genuine.

Photo opportunities have, on occasion, undone the lesser lights of political theater. The current exhibition offers two wince-inducing examples, the first of them from September 1947, in which Governor Thomas E. Dewey appears to be performing chiropractic upon a cow. Whatever he's doing in his freshly pressed suit, it's certainly not milking. Forty years later, Michael Dukakis, the closest thing to Dewey the Democrats ever came up with, rides an M1-A-1 battle tank toward a photographer who has just helped to build the George Bush presidential library.

The camera sometimes does succeed in differentiating the mere phony from, to use a term of Truman Capote's, the "real phony," that preferable entity who actually "believes all this crap [he] believes." (In this show, William Jennings Bryan and James Garfield, each of them photographed in a six-button coat and trying to look as Napoleonic as possible, provide a study in contrasts between the former species and the latter.) The current exhibit provides few depictions of politicians in truly unguarded moments, but the most pleasing of these comes from Atlantic City c. 1928, when Al Smith and his plump, giggling wife crowded into a photo booth and made two four-shot strips, unfiltered and fully human.

The Happy Warrior is also shown in an Indian headdress ("Governor Smith Becomes Chief 'Leading Star' "), a venerable subgenre of political photography. The show gives us Jimmy Walker similarly attired, and of course Calvin Coolidge, who looks as sad as one of those William Wegman dogs forced into a negligee for the camera. George Bush, going halfway as usual, accepts a ceremonial pipe from Crow medicine man Floyd Realbird in Billings, Montana, but instead of trying on Realbird's magnificent bonnet, Bush is pointing toward his waiting limo.

In recent years the photographer has regained a certain power over the politician. The lenses are longer and less merciful than ever, and now tricks like "morphing" allow for such uncannily apt editorializing as *Time*'s recent series of a half-dozen photos in which Bill Clinton turns into Jimmy Carter. But current photo ops seem less autonomous than the older ones, more like millimeters of a video you've got on Pause. After all, you've *seen* these images on video; you know what comes just before and after them, and it's frustrating not to be able to scroll forward or backward. Wasn't it, in fact, the waggle, i.e., the movement of Dukakis's helmeted head, like one of those dolls with a spring in the neck, that added to the scene's absurdity? Even so, still photography invites greater contemplativeness, and it's only in Michael E. Samojeden's AP photo that you're likely to spot the person actually driving the tank, who's keeping his head sensibly hidden behind a gun.

Occasionally, a single photograph in this exhibition will call up many moods, such as a group shot from 1977 that gives us Carter, Robert Byrd, and Tip O'Neill, all dewlaps and wattles and perplexity, a ridiculous picture of one-party gridlock—comical until you realize that the emaciated fellow with the wisps of hair at the picture's left is the gallant, dying Hubert Humphrey. But it says something fine about the national character and essentially untragic history of the United States that irreverent and humorous pictures make up as large a part of this show as they do. The camera's true historical focus here is less on the familiar faces than on all the tiny heads looking up at the platforms and waving from the sidewalks, row upon row of them, with blurry bowlers and Gibson Girl hairdos, appearing to be mere extras who made up the crowd scenes, but in fact the people who, however imperfectly, ran the show.

One Small Shelf for Literature

"WITH HOW SAD STEPS, O Moon, thou climb'st the skies! / How silently, and with how wan a face!" Are you looking for your lovers, those Apollonian heroes who pursued you for ten years and were faithful, at intervals, for only three?

Twenty years ago this morning, Neil Armstrong, Edwin E. (Buzz) Aldrin, Jr., and Michael Collins rose off the earth in front of a crowd of a million people. In *From the Earth to the Moon* (1865), Jules Verne had predicted an audience of five million, but he got an eerie assortment of other things right. Florida would be the point of departure; a three-man crew would travel to the moon and splash down in the ocean upon return; and the cannon that launched them would be called the *Columbiad*—the men of Apollo 11 finally went to the moon in a command module named *Columbia*.

Writers have been traveling there for centuries. The real Cyrano de Bergerac (not Edmond Rostand's nineteenth-century creation) had his *Comical History of the States and Empires of the Moon* published posthumously in 1657: "I was no sooner come, but they carryed me to the Palace, where the Grandees received me with more Moderation, than the People had done as I passed the Streets."

By the 1950s science-fiction writers were taking increasingly plausible measure of a place they knew would soon be visited. In the introduction to *Men on the Moon* (1958), a collection of lunar stories, Donald A. Wollheim wrote: "Here then is a science-fiction anthology which may in a little while cease entirely to be 'science-fiction.' " Five years later, when the first Mercury flights were over and the giant Saturn 5 rocket was being developed, Jeff Sutton wrote *Apollo at Go,* a little adventure dancing right on the line

321

between realism and fantasy. His crew took off on July 5, 1969—just eleven days from what would be the real thing.

Apollo at Go contains some enjoyably awful dialogue; one of the descending astronauts tells the one who must stay in the command module: "You have a tough one, Les. We couldn't make it without you." But by the time 1969 actually came around, what would such good-natured clunkiness matter? Now, surely, the great realistic novelists and lyric poets would take over, preserving and giving meaning to the landing, recording and imagining what was happening to those of the species still on the earth and looking up.

It didn't turn out that way. The moon landing now stands as one of the most underwritten of historic events. The reasons that important creative writers might have turned their attention to it seem self-evident, but most of them found reasons to avoid it. To consider the paucity of fiction and poetry on the subject is to feel that Armstrong and Aldrin must have touched down on the moon's dark side and remained invisible to those who had sent them. An essay about literary sightings—uninclusive though it may be—is a survey of exceptions.

———

Harry (Rabbit) Angstrom, John Updike's once-per-decade Everyman, has always, like his creator, had an appreciation of gadgetry. "God, what a lot of ingenious crap there is in the world," he thinks in *Rabbit Redux* (1971) while shopping in a drugstore on Sunday afternoon, July 20, 1969, just before the descent in the *Eagle* to Tranquility Base. Emerging back into the "Sunday-stilled downtown" of Brewer, Pa., he wonders: "Where is everybody? Is there life on Earth?" This is 1969, the age of migration to suburb and mall. Updike uses Apollo 11 as part of the whole Rabbit trilogy's thick historical weave, characterizing the various Angstroms by their reactions to the landing.

Rabbit actually can't work up much enthusiasm for the event's technology, not when his own job as a linotyper at the local paper is being threatened by automation. Also, by the night of the moon walk, his wife, Janice, has left him, and Rabbit's responses to what he sees on television a quarter of a million miles away are tentative, unformed. He is watching at his parents' house but, like the new astronauts, he has been thrust suddenly into a new world:

A man in clumsy silhouette has interposed himself among these abstract shadows and glare. He says something about "steps" that a crackle keeps Rabbit from understanding. Electronic letters travelling sideways spell out MAN IS ON THE MOON. . . . From behind him, Rabbit's mother's hand with difficulty reaches out, touches the back of his skull, stays there, awkwardly tries to massage his scalp, to ease away thoughts of the trouble she knows he is in. "I don't know, Mom," he abruptly admits. "I know it's happened, but I don't feel anything yet."

He's talking not about Armstrong, but Janice.

Novelists, once so confident in telling readers what to feel, didn't seem up to the job with Apollo 11. James A. Michener's narratives have always moved along like big comfortable sedans—dependable, without much vibration—and in *Space* (1982), he does a clever job melding a set of fictional characters and events onto the real ones of the '60s. About 400 pages into the novel, Tranquility Base tells Houston that the *Eagle* has landed. Some of the book's principal characters are watching from the bar of the Longhorn Motel outside Houston. There's a bit of pepper in Mr. Michener's mix of people—Elinor Grant, the right-wing senator's wife, is certain that there's a race of moonlings on the dark side waiting to greet and assist the visitors—but movements and speech in this novel are strictly miniseries: "John Pope started the real celebration by kissing [his wife], who had tears in her eyes, and she turned to kiss Senator Grant, whose fortitude she had so often witnessed. 'We did it,' she cried, 'In our bumbling way we did it.' " *Space* is finally just another place between *Chesapeake* and *Poland*.

Only a few of our best novelists even consented to look up at what was going on. Before discussing moon travel with the scientist Dr. Govinda Lal, Saul Bellow's ruminating Mr. Sammler (*Mr. Sammler's Planet*, 1970) tries to sort his mixed feelings:

This is not the way to get out of spatial-temporal prison. Distance is still finite. Finite is still feeling through the veil, examining the naked inner reality with a gloved hand. However, one could see the advantage of getting away from here, building plastic igloos in the vacuum, dwelling in quiet colonies, necessarily austere, drinking the fossil waters, considering basic questions only.

But Mr. Sammler's planet is earth, and space travel takes up only a small amount of his philosophic time, just as, finally, the moon landing is more a motif than a key to *Rabbit Redux.*

We are told that Tom Gilpin—the millenarian hero of Hortense Calisher's *Mysteries of Motion* (1982), a novel that describes the first space shuttle for civilians—gave himself to the dream of space travel on the night of the Apollo 11 landing, when he was an American college student on a work holiday in a Tuscan village. At a café "a man shouted from the back—*Viv'il machina A-pol-lo!* The old man transfixed in front of the glassy display mouthed it—A-pol-lo. . . . *A-pol-lo* the tables murmured, and crossed themselves. Together, Tom Gilpin and the old man wept." In graduate school, Tom is unable to interest his "intellectual friends" in the idea of new worlds: "Even if he could woo them to a space museum, to join the hoi polloi who were there for the wide-lens movie and any fantasy they could get, their eyes skewed and wandered. It had nothing to do with them. They hadn't yet made the connection."

One thing keeping his fellow graduate students, and most novelists, immune to the lure of spaceships men have actually built and launched is the apparent sexlessness of the enterprise. Before his own flight, Gilpin "feels the removal he always does, from all those still down there in the hot sexual morass." So far spaceships have been clean, well-lighted places whose human occupants have been denied the chance to function in ways other than the all too purely navigational and scientific. Novelists of the here and now have largely assumed the whole business to be devoid of the passions their vocation has taught them to pursue.

But not all of them. Paul Auster's recent, terrifically energetic *Moon Palace* begins in the summer of 1969. The title actually comes from the name of a Chinese restaurant near Columbia University, and it is, in fact, not there but at Quinn's Bar and Grill that the young narrator, Marco (as in Marco Polo), watches the televised descent of Neil Armstrong to the lunar surface. Auster has some of the details wrong (there was no golf cart—that is, lunar rover—on that first mission), and Marco does squirm a bit at seeing a flag planted "in the eye of what had once been the goddess of love and lunacy," but at least both author and narrator are susceptible to the accomplishment's wonder. That summer Marco starts associating the Chinese restaurant's name with all sorts of things: "Perhaps the word *moon* had changed for me after I saw men wandering around its surface. . . . The idea of voyaging into the unknown, for example, and the parallels between Columbus and the astronauts. The discovery of America as a failure to reach China; Chinese food and my empty stomach." Marco is broke and hungry and maybe a little crazy, but he nonetheless feels "a tremendous power surging through [himself], a gnostic joy that penetrated deep into the heart of things. Then, very suddenly, as suddenly as [he] had gained power, [he] lost it." Even so, he and the author who invented him twenty years later have done what few other writers have seemed willing to do: they gave themselves over to the event.

By 1969, the new political incorrectness of the Apollo program left liberal authors feeling guilty or ambivalent toward it. Begun as a progressive Democratic crusade under John F. Kennedy, Apollo would be completed by his 1960 opponent, Richard Nixon. Race riots, Vietnam and the awareness of poverty had come in between. The morning after the landing, *The New York Times* asked a group of prominent artists, thinkers and social activists for their reactions. There was a fair share of joy and awe ("an extraordinary event of incalculable importance," Eugene Ionesco said), but much uneasiness and even outrage. The poet June Jordan asked, "I mean, brothers and sisters, have you ever heard of children—bankrupt, screaming—on the moon?" The odd fact is that, in 1969, a strong interest in extraterrestrial travel usually indicated social conservatism; Hanoi, not Houston, was the typical venue for serious writers of the time.

Norman Mailer covered the moon mission almost in spite of himself. NASA was a place with "no smells . . . hardly the terrain for Aquarius," the name he gives himself in *Of a Fire on the Moon* (1971). The Manned Spacecraft Center was like "one of those miserable brand new college campuses with buildings white as toothpaste . . . a college campus in short to replace the one which burned in the last revolution of the students." Mailer is once again his own picaresque hero, witnessing man's first departure from the planet while preoccupied with such personal earthly problems as his weight and his wives.

"Was the voyage of Apollo 11," Aquarius wonders, "the noblest expression of a technological age, or the best evidence of its utter insanity?" He gives no answer, just consistently fresh speculation. *Of a Fire on the Moon* is a gaudy tumble of humor, philosophy and metaphor: "Physics is the church, and engineering the most devout sinner." On earth the space-suited Neil Armstrong looks like "a newborn cat in its caul," and his first movements on the moon are "not unlike the first staggering steps of a just-born calf." In the midst of thinking big, Mailer the novelist finds all sorts of opportunities to give the reader of his book of New Journalism plenty of old fictive pleasures. For one moment, when the lunar module, still attached to *Columbia,* seems to be tugging on its own toward the moon's surface, the mission even becomes the story of a boy and his pet: "[Michael] Collins was grinding through the anxiety that the lem was behaving most peculiarly, not unlike a dog on a leash who keeps leaning in the direction of a new and fascinating scent."

Potentially so annoying, Mailer's self-absorption in the presence of the epochal ("He too wanted to go up in the bird") proves to be just what's necessary for measuring the event. Aquarius, to his surprise, undergoes "a loss of ego" during his witness, and the Norman Mailer who shines through *Of a Fire on the Moon* has a charm and generosity that he has never conveyed as successfully before or since. His oddball book was the only one worthy of the occasion.

———

Poets acted as if they owned the place. In terms of literary history, this had been pretty much the truth. Milton appraised the moon's "clouded majesty," Blake its "silent delight," Emily Dickinson its "amber hands." Poems by these writers' Apollonian heirs, collected in *Moonstruck: An Anthology of Lunar Poetry* (1974), seem like letters by claimants in a class-action suit. The soft landing by the lunar module is resented as an act of gate-crashing, the astronauts scorned as boorish trespassers.

Babette Deutsch wrote that "for a few, what has happened is the death of a divine Person, is a betrayal." "What Comedy's this Epic!" Allen Ginsberg cried. William Plomer reduced the whole enterprise to six words:

countdown	*takeoff*
moonprints	*rockbox*
splashdown	*claptrap*

In 1930, W. H. Auden had happily noted that the "lunar beauty" he was observing had "no history"; four decades later it did, thanks to "a phallic triumph" at which he blew a bardic raspberry: "Worth *going* to see? I can well believe it. / Worth *seeing?* Mneh!" He decided to pretend that what he couldn't see with his naked eye had never happened: "Unsmudged, thank God, my Moon still queens the Heavens."

Not every poet was aggrieved or contemptuous. May Swenson, for example, settled for quiet speculation about the risks of demythologizing: "Can flesh rub with symbol? . . . Dare we land upon a dream?" But only a few let joy be unconfined. Archibald MacLeish was one: "We have touched you!" he exclaimed in "Voyage to the Moon," a poem that is alert to the landing's narrative opportunities. "Three days and three nights we journeyed, steered by farthest stars."

How many remember, or ever knew, that the astronauts actually did steer by the stars? There were navigational computers aboard, of course, but Michael Collins, more romantically, used a sextant. There was more poetry and personality in the mission than most people, or poets, realized. Who remembers that Neil Armstrong and Buzz Aldrin carried a piece of the wing fabric of the Wright brothers' *Kitty Hawk Flyer* with them, or that Armstrong, on his way home but still more than 100,000 miles away, played "Music out of the Moon," from an old record that he and his wife had liked to listen to in the early days of their marriage? We probably don't recall because we didn't pay attention, having already convinced ourselves that there was nothing emotional or even individual about the explorers. In *Seeing Earth: Literary Responses to Space Exploration,* Ronald Weber writes, "All that writers knew about the new ocean of space came second hand—and second hand from spokesmen hardly notable for their way with words." It's true that space presents particular difficulties when trying to follow the rule to write about what you know. But even after Tom Wolfe's corrective *Right Stuff,* the way in which writers have condescended to astronauts is a kind of imaginative scandal.

Did the journey seem too perfect, too glitch-free, to provide much narrative suspense? In fact, for a while after Armstrong and Aldrin brought the lunar module to the moon's surface, no one, including themselves, knew just where they were. Armstrong saw boulders strewn about the projected landing site, and with less than a minute's worth of fuel left, he had to fly the ship to whatever safe place he could manage to spot through the window. And this antiseptic little lunar module had got where it was because thousands of people on the ground at NASA had endured more than their share of stress and exhaustion. All of this is chronicled, to be sure, in *Apollo,* a new history by Charles Murray and Catherine Bly Cox. But all of it has been left conspicuously unimagined by poets and novelists.

————

Surely science fiction writers should have been ecstatic. Yes and no. Eleven years after publishing his anthology of lunar stories, Donald A. Wollheim reprinted it, along with an appendix by sci-fi writers asked to respond to both the plaque left by the astronauts ("We Came in Peace for All Mankind") and an alternative one proposed by I. F. Stone, which read in part: "Their Destructive Ingenuity Knows No Limits and Their Wanton Pollution No Restraint. Let the Rest of the Universe Beware." Ray Bradbury said Stone was "ancient with Doom, while we stay young with the promise of Space," and plenty of his colleagues offered similar sentiments. But some of the literary space travelers, at least to an extent, had to agree with Stone. The achievement, they felt, expressed arrogance as well as hope. Isaac Asimov wanted to feel the nobility of the mission but acknowledged that "every word [Stone] says has a strong element of truth in it."

Curiously enough, now that lunar fantasy has become lunar history, science-fiction writers seem intent on making up their own past for the space program. In his collection of stories *Memories of the Space Age* (1988), J. G. Ballard imagines Cape Canaveral as a set of rusting ruins and battered heroes. The narrator of Ballard's story "The Man Who Walked on the Moon" remembers reading about an "impoverished American who claimed to have been an astronaut, and told his story to tourists for the price of a drink. . . . His long-jawed face and stoical pilot's eyes seemed vaguely familiar from the magazine photographs." In a 1976 story, "The Eve of the Last Apollo," Carter Scholz places the first moon landing in 1970 and describes the first man to walk on the surface as a self-doubting wreck who is trying to cope (partly through writing poetry) with a sense of futility about what he accomplished: "We took one step out of the cradle; we put our foot out—and drew it back. . . . I think what it is is that we're not *ready* for space, we can't deal with all that emptiness."

He may have been right. Shortly after the voyage of Apollo 11, Arthur C. Clarke wrote an essay reminding us of how the moon originally drew life up out of the ocean and onto land and suggested that it might be doing something similar now—drawing the human species into space. Perhaps the very long run will prove him correct, but much of what he wrote twenty years ago about the moon's manned future—"Well before the end of this century, the first human child will be born there"—was shockingly premature. Most of all, he seems to have overestimated our interest in what was done between 1969 and 1972: "To imagine that we will have discovered all that there is to know about the moon after a few Apollo landings is ludicrous. They will merely whet our appetite."

They haven't. Of course, we may yet go back to the moon, if only to use its light gravity to help us reach Mars. But plans are uncertain, and bets are off. The years of estrangement between man and moon grow longer. I'm more than twice as old as I was that season we first went there, the summer just before I went away to college. A few months ago, I had lunch with an old friend from undergraduate days, and he told me how he has recounted the story of man's trip to the moon to his young and slightly disbelieving son. Twenty years after Apollo 11, moon travel is once more the subject of bedtime tales and childish wonder, though the formula for the prologue has changed, "Many years from Now" becoming "Once upon a time."

The Revolution:
A Minority Report

May 1998*

$$O_{\text{NE}}$$ F<small>RIDAY</small> <small>NIGHT</small> this January I was at Prairie Lights Books in Iowa City, doing a reading that was broadcast live over the regional NPR outlet. When I'd finished, I sat at a table at the back of the store, signing books and chatting with some women who had just done my novel in their local reading group. A man who looked to be about my age stood next to them, smiling, and I tried to draw him into the conversation. He hung back, but didn't stop grinning; not until the scales fell from my eyes.

"I had the radio on," he said. "I got in the car when I realized it was you."

Sixteen years had passed since I'd last seen Tom Lewis, now a professor of comparative literature at the University of Iowa, and the two of us had completely lost track of each other. But we could both still tell you, exactly, the day we met: September 7, 1969, a Sunday, when we arrived as freshmen at Brown.

Tom—like me a literary-minded financial-aid student—had settled in two rooms down from mine on the second floor of Archibald House in the West Quad, and that night we both sat in Arnold Lounge for an orientation meeting. Two upper-class proctors spoke. The first one I recall wearing madras bermuda shorts and dorky black-rimmed glasses (exactly the kind I had on), and he proceeded earnestly to recite the university's restrictions concerning alcohol, drugs and girls in our rooms. The second proctor, an altogether more relaxed presence, followed up with some practical remarks about how we could comfortably accommodate—alcohol, drugs and girls in

**Written for the *Brown Alumni Magazine* as my class ('73) prepared for its twenty-fifth reunion.*

our rooms. I remember, during this latter presentation, watching proctor number one out of the corner of my eye and feeling a sorry solidarity with him: another fish out of the Aquarian Age's water. In case you've forgotten how fast that water was churning, consider that the mere twelve weeks since we'd all graduated from high school had brought the moon landing, Chappaquiddick, the Manson murders, the Stonewall riot and Woodstock.

If that scene in Arnold Lounge were the beginning of an historical novel set during my freshman year, Chapter One would probably end later that first night with me lying awake, too homesick to sleep, hearing this maddening little click, about once every minute. I didn't realize until morning that it was my roommate's digital clock—the kind where the numbers flip like cards on a Rolodex, and the absolute *dernier cri* in mechanical marvels.

In some ways, I might be the ideal narrator of such a novel. I lived as a watchful nonparticipant in the tumult, an even more straitjacketed Nick Carraway, if you moved him from West Egg to the West Quad. Along Brown's particular plotline, the maiden voyage of its New Curriculum, I was a sort of stowaway. The November 25 *Brown Daily Herald* reported that 3.1 percent of freshmen were choosing to take all their courses for grades, instead of the new Satisfactory/No Credit option. I was among the 3.1 percent. And in the year's larger drama, the movement of Vietnam protest from the fall's moratoria to the spring's great strike, I felt similarly offstage, and embattled. On October 14 I argued to my roommate: weren't the professors canceling tomorrow's classes breaking a contractual obligation, forcing me to cooperate in furthering a political position I didn't hold? (I thought Nixon's policy of "Vietnamization" was the most realistic way for us to withdraw from the war.) He countered that I should make a sacrifice for peace by not going to class. "Well, let me tell you how he spent the day 'working for peace,' " I later wrote to a high-school friend. "He slept late—watched television—and then went to his economics class. I asked him what happened to his sacrifice? Well, he just *had* to go to class, he said, because [his girlfriend] is coming up Friday for homecoming and he has to skip class to pick her up and he can't afford to miss it twice."

My high-school friend recently presented me with a whole batch of these letters, and my chief reaction to reading this one after nearly thirty years is: God, how did my roommate stand me? Such a shrill little prig, without a hint of appreciation for the situation's comic aspect. Even now, I can't bear the sound of that voice, let alone the goofy handwriting and bad punctuation. No, for any novel set in '69–'70, I'd have to find another point of view, and certainly another hero.

As I sit here, a few months before my twenty-fifth reunion, my desk covered with these old letters and Xeroxes from the *BDH*, I do see a theme emerging for any novelist inclined to work this material, one that links up to something I remember a professor suggesting in a poetry course I took sophomore year. She said the most forceful literature always arises from inner tension, be it that between the Transcendental and the Calvinist in Emily Dickinson, or the rakish and spiritual in John Donne. In a whole community, not just one poet's head, it would be the cultural contradictions that give a story life. College Hill was full of them that year.

Everywhere on campus one found fusions of the just-born and obsolete, like the modern glass doors stuck into the Romanesque arch of Wilson Hall. The class of '73 was the first to have a racial demographic remotely like the country's, and from week one we did a painfully good job of segregating ourselves ("Blacks, Whites Separated for Talk of Black Experience"). My intense yearlong course on seventeenth- and eighteenth-century French history could not have seemed more sealed off from the "real world," but it ended with slender, severe Professor Church addressing the question of whether conditions for revolution existed in the United States to the extent that they had in 1789 France. (He thought not.) Just as the moratorium and homecoming weekend competed for my roommate's attention, new customs couldn't replace old folkways quite fast enough. One didn't have to take any science or math or anything else one didn't want to, but most professors still called us "Mr." and "Miss." Dr. Roswell Johnson, the sexually hip health-services director, who became infamous for dispensing the Pill to Pembrokers, was also the epitome of WASP tweediness. Which leads me to believe I would probably be better off with a heroine than a hero for this novel, because the last wave of Pembrokers found themselves suspended in an even wider array of transitions than their Brown brethren. The first co-ed dormitory had come into existence, but the headline announcing it read: "Pink Curtains Flutter in Wriston Quad." University Hall might be ringed with demonstrators from time to time, but parietals remained in effect until the end of the academic year.

Present-day consciousness is generally fatal to historical fiction. It would be tempting, in this novel set during '69–'70, to take a mention of the just-graduated and already legendary Ira Magaziner, architect of the New Curriculum, and nudge it forward into his later, gray-haired authorship of the Clinton health plan. Or to conjure up the glamorous future of *fin de siècle* Brown—the high-gloss campus one now sees in *Vanity Fair*—during a scene reflecting its more humble times ("Who rejected you?" a classmate once asked, striking up a laundry-room conversation. "Harvard or Yale?") But one has to let the era-to-era correspondences, and contrasts, come naturally to the reader's mind.

On my last visit to Providence, I walked past the window of my old room in Archibald House and saw the lit square of a computer screen. I wondered if the student sitting in front of it, not far from where my manual typewriter used to rest, was instant-messaging a friend across campus. (Surely no one lines up at the handful of pay phones with which we used to make do.) I found myself remembering the night I played an early computer game with a couple of friends in—would it have been Barus Holley? This pre–Space Invaders competition involved flipping toggle switches on and off as fast as one could: with all the moving parts, it was a lot closer to our fathers' pinball machines than anything that came after.

My first year at Brown is exactly as far from this one as it was, in the other direction, from the Pearl Harbor year of '41–'42. In certain respects, both psychic and technological, '69–'70 may be closer to the earlier time than the later one. The campus I remember walking around at nighttime, three decades ago, was dark to the point of spookiness, or at least romance. It didn't take much imagination to slip back into the Providence of H. P. Lovecraft when you made your way down Benefit Street or even through the Van Wickle gates. Today the university is altogether brighter with ornamental and security lights, and it's hard, when you're there, to lose yourself.

If its sense and meaning remain elusive, the texture of my freshman year—the details through which any book succeeds or fails in re-creating a period—is ready for summons in an instant, so much of it having been printed on my still-adolescent tabula rasa: the orange "bug juice" we drank in the Ratty; the music and clothing shops on a still-unfranchised Thayer Street; the greasy food from the trucks at the corner of Brown and George ("Papa, give me a hamburger grinder, and hold the dirt"—the voice of my friend Jay, I'm sure); the scratchy sounds of the timer lights in the B-level stacks of the Rock, where I fell in love with Keats and worked far harder than was good for me.

A few of the Big Scenes are obvious. The draft lottery, in which most freshmen males had a stake, was broadcast over WBRU, provoking shouts of ecstasy and despair throughout the West Quad as the numbers were drawn. We generally ignored the lunar landings, but the 95 percent solar eclipse on March 7, greeted from the courtyard with loud music and more awe than we were willing to admit, is available for the novelist's symbolic manipulation. Spring Weekend, with James Taylor, whose sweet songs were never off the turntables, could be the interlude, the idyll, two weeks before the convulsion.

———

The student strike, the obvious climax for this novel, caused me a kind of double anguish. I still remember the moment and place I heard about Kent State. I was walking with my friend John Maguire; we'd just finished dinner; it was still light out; a security guard, "Lieutenant" Walsh, told us the news when we crossed Benevolent Street. That night the College bell summoned students to the Green for a vote on whether to suspend academic activities for the rest of the year. When we got there, candles were shining in each of the building's windows—a tribute to the four students who'd been killed, we freshmen thought, until we learned that the candles were there, as they are every spring, to commemorate George Washington's visit to the university. Was—despite Professor Church's conclusion—one revolution lighting another? (Life always does its own best job of making connections; if the historical novelist doesn't fight the facts, he'll have all the allegory—and backdrops—he needs.)

Once again I was in a minority, if not so spectacularly as with the grading option. A total of 1,895 students voted to strike; 884 (more than memory would have guessed) voted no. The real source of my misery lay in the fact that I now no longer believed in the government's policy either, certainly not in this "incursion" into Cambodia. I felt estranged from every side. On the morning of May 5, awakening to the sound of a bullhorn on the street—"BROWN UNIVERSITY ON STRIKE!"—I pulled the pillow over my head. I think this would be the week I hung up on my gentle but still pro-Nixon father from one of those pay phones in the West Quad.

I stayed in my room or at the library, writing a long paper on Romantic poetry that I didn't really need to turn in. Everywhere else, at least for a while, the war protests thrived. A schedule of "Strike Activities" for

Thursday, May 7, 1970, listed twenty-six separate events, four of them at 9:30 a.m.:

- Providence leafletting—need cars and drivers—room 200, Sayles
- Canvassing begins—Sayles
- Guerilla Theatre Meeting—Sayles—participants will go out into community at 10:00 am
- "Big Mother" [coffeehouse]—meeting for home town activities directed toward liberal uncommitted businessmen

As the last item shows, "bringing the war home," a familiar phrase from the era, would soon have to mean, at least for a while, one's actual home. Summer put an end to this academic year as to any other, the dispersal of everyone, as always, so sudden and strange—very much, in fact, like shutting a book.

A character in one of my novels, an old man named Horace Sinclair, divides the world into two kinds of people: those who "when they pass a house, wonder who lives there, and those who, when they pass it, wonder who *used* to live there." The historical novelist will, in part, choose distant subjects as a relief from his own life, but of course he's always present somewhere in the book, and I recognize this passage as coming not from Colonel Sinclair, but myself. For whatever reasons, I get on with the present much better once it's become the past.

A few months ago, when I went back to the John Hay Library, the university archivist brought me that strike schedule, along with hundreds of other stencils run off by the "People's Print Shop" in Sayles Hall. They're now preserved in two brown portfolios tied up with laces—just like the oldest books I'd revered in the B-level stacks. When I untied them, my feelings toward these papers, as dead and not-dead as my eighteen-year-old self, were more tender than anything else. I remember the year that produced them as painful, but as the one that set me on my way, however circuitously, to what I wanted to be doing. The manuscripts of my own novels are now also in the Hay, a sort of advance final resting place, a peaceful eventuality I never considered when I walked the brick sidewalks of Prospect Street that year; lonely, afraid, and constantly excited.

Postscript

On Not Being a Poet

Spring 2000

L AST YEAR A NOVELIST friend of mine mentioned that he'd soon be coming to New York to recite a poem of his choosing at a Town Hall program marking National Poetry Month.

"I'll give you a hundred dollars if you do 'The Highwayman,'" I responded. A joke, of course, and probably unintelligible to anyone much younger than ourselves. Surely today's students don't have to memorize those sonorous lines by Alfred Noyes, which even now the two of us can recall:

> The wind was a torrent of darkness among the gusty trees,
> The moon was a ghostly galleon tossed upon cloudy seas,
> The road was a ribbon of moonlight over the purple moor,
> And the highwayman came riding—
> > Riding—riding—
> The highwayman came riding, up to the old inn-door.

The "ribbon of moonlight"—like Bess, "the landlord's black-eyed daughter"—has stayed with me for forty years now, since grade school, but the success of my joke depended on my friend's knowing, as do I, thanks to all our learning and supposed sophistication, that "The Highwayman" is a *bad* poem, a chestnut, the sort of thing not so much imparted to yesterday's schoolchildren as inflicted upon them.

Like most jokes, mine had an undercurrent of hostility—one directed, I realize, toward poetry itself. Why does it get its own month? Perhaps it needs one, being such a weak-sister genre that almost no one will read it unless force-marched into celebrating it. Even some of the best poets will con-

339

cede that the art is kept alive partly by artificial means. In "The Trouble with Poetry," Charles Simic quickly warms to his own indictment:

> No one in their right mind ever reads poetry. Even among the literary theorists nowadays, it is fashionable to feel superior to all literature and especially poetry. That some people still continue to write it is an oddity that belongs in some "Believe It or Not" column of the daily newspaper. . . . Parents still prefer their children to be taxidermists and tax collectors rather than poets. Who can blame them? Would you want your only daughter to be a poet or a hostess in a sleazy nightclub? That's a tough one.

And yet, for all that, poetry remains the most privileged of literary genres, a gated community at the top of Parnassus, whose lower hills are covered with prose's down-market suburban sprawl. Shelley's "unacknowledged legislators of the world" (a dubious compliment, if you think about it) are typically much more certain of their standing than Simic is. In *How to Read a Poem and Fall in Love with Poetry,* Edward Hirsch declares himself "convinced the kind of experience—the kind of knowledge—one gets from poetry cannot be duplicated elsewhere. The spiritual life wants articulation—it wants embodiment in language." At which point the prose writer may be inclined to raise his hand in the back of the auditorium and identify himself as a fellow practitioner of "language." But it will not do him much good to claim first-class citizenship in the realm of articulation. In an essay titled "Can Poetry Matter?" Dana Gioia identifies the genre as the best and the brightest: "Poetry is the art of using words charged with their utmost meaning." Poetic coinage is nontransferrable. That prose paraphrase can actually make some modern-verse opacities more lucent (Hugh Kenner on portions of Ezra Pound) is a fact the poetry world resists as ardently as the prose world clings to the truism that the movies can only ruin a book.

Gioia's statement is a modernization of Coleridge's famous hierarchical distinction: "prose = words in their best order; poetry = the best words in their best order." Poets have cited his contrasting definitions with smiling self-assurance for nearly two centuries, despite Coleridge's tendency to find other writers' prose so good he wouldn't think of changing a word of it before publishing it as his own, and despite his bifurcation's manifest lack of logic: the prose writer's diction decisions are often *more* exacting than the poet's, given good prose's premium on exactitude, a standard from which poetry is permitted to stray whenever its sound gets in the mood to trump, rather than echo, sense.

When it comes to what each genre might teach the other, poets typically feel they're looking down a one-way street. Joseph Brodsky can barely manage to be polite about the matter:

> What does a writer of prose learn from poetry? The dependence of a word's specific gravity on context, focused thinking, omission of the self-evident, the dangers that lurk within an elevated state of mind. And what does the poet learn from prose? Not much: attention to detail, the use of common parlance and bureaucratese, and, in rare instances, compositional know-how (the best teacher of which is music).

If we hear that someone is "writing a novel" in her spare time, we're likely to think her a casual adventurer, someone taking a long shot on a flashy, rather commonplace dream of literary glory. If we hear that someone is writing poetry when he gets home from the office, we nod appreciatively, our lower lips pushing forward in a how-about-that way, as we acknowledge the monastic seriousness this must entail. It's no wonder Moliere's *bourgeois gentilhomme* had to be told that he was speaking prose. We barely bother to define this mode of writing by anything other than its handicaps and lacks. My *Columbia Encyclopedia* treats it like the plain stepsister patted on her head for the skill with which she does chores:

> meaningful and grammatical written or spoken language that does not utilize the metrical structure, word transposition, or rhyme characteristic of poetry or verse; it is, however, raised above the level of lifeless composition or commonplace conversation by the use of balance, rhythm, repetition, and antithesis.

You can dress it up, but why take it out when you could have a sonnet on your arm?

Alfred Harbage assures readers of *The Complete Pelican Shakespeare* that the Bard moves between poetry and prose according to his own rules, but he won't deny how, in *The Merchant of Venice,* "the most common use for prose was in realistic and common scenes or parts of scenes, just as the most common use of blank verse was in romantic and serious ones." When commentators point out that Hamlet's "What a piece of work is a man!" speech is prose, the observation tends to be made with a slightly awed condescension, like the report of a Special Olympics feat. And it cannot cheer the prose writer to check the statistics and find that, by far, Shakespeare's highest per-play percentage of prose, 86.6 percent, occurs in *The Merry Wives of Windsor.*

In our own time, reviews of novels and biographies pay remarkably little attention to how these books are actually *written,* line by line. Character, plot, and theme gobble up the reviewer's attention, as if all these elements weren't dependent on the DNA in the writer's *écriture.* A perusal of M. H. Abrams's venerable *Glossary of Literary Terms* reveals what an impoverished critical vocabulary we possess for discussions of prose style. Prose is so prosaic it's not even entitled to the term *prosody*—that's poetry's word for its own jewel box of tricks and techniques.

One of the few terms prose can call its own is *periodic sentence,* whose glory is barely suggested by Abrams's definition of it as a sentence "in which the parts, or 'members,' are so composed that the sense remains suspended until the close." Only examples will do this golden staple—the blank verse of prose—real justice. Take this one from *Tristram Shandy:* "Of all the cants which are canted in this canting world, though the cant of hypocrites may be the worst, the cant of criticism is the most tormenting!" Or, from my old *Practical English Handbook,* this one of Thoreau's: "Under a government which imprisons any unjustly, the true place for a just man is also a prison."

The success of a periodic sentence usually depends on what the position of the word "is" is—the later the better. But the form can hide almost any verb under ever more layers, withholding it like the ultimate romantic favor. Norman Mailer, in *Of a Fire on the Moon,* serves up a long, deliberately overwhelming list of the Apollo 11 spacecraft's switches, buttons, and controls, a Homeric catalogue of items in a single ship; but if the author has borrowed this kind of inventory from classical poetry, he follows it, after an em dash, with a fabulous splashdown of the purest periodic prose:

—yes this whole constellation of systems and subsystems of control over power, and control over the beaming out of thought translated into electromagnetic waves, and control even over the disposal of simple human waste sits over, above, around, beneath, yes and even behind the three astronauts in whole congeries of Twentieth Century concepts and forces which have come to focus that this effort may fly to the moon.

"Sits" and "have come" are minimal whiffs of verbal oxygen, all the reader is allowed to inhale as the sentence postpones releasing itself into meaning with the long-withheld "fly." I'm sure schoolchildren still recite some poetry, if not the work of Alfred Noyes. But when was the last time they diagrammed a sentence? The latter activity is a sort of emblem for extinct, parochial-school make-work. But what a grand blackboard trajectory those lines of Mailer would require!

On October 27, 1818, John Keats wrote to Richard Woodhouse about the poet's "chameleon" nature and lack of a stable ego: "A poet is the most unpoetical of anything in existence, because he has no Identity—he is continually in for and filling some other body. . . . I feel assured I should write from the mere yearning and fondness I have for the beautiful, even if my night's labors should be burnt every morning, and no eye ever shine upon them."

I would have to say that poets of my acquaintance have often managed to maintain fixed, solid egos. Brodsky says that the prose writer's "inferiority complex . . . doesn't automatically imply the poet's superiority complex," but I have seen a fair share of poets well aware of their property values at the top of Parnassus, and not at all shy about pointing them out to folks lower down the hill. In summertime, at the Bread Loaf Writers' conference, my literary home away from home, I hear great helpings of generally excellent poetry twice a day for two weeks. It is hard not to notice how comfortably unnatural some poets look behind the lectern. Presentation, for these, is an overdone art, the way it is with restaurant food in northern California. Their declamations and murmurings don't so much paint the lily as outfit it with a Dolby sound system, which between poems shuts down for that silent, please-hold-your-applause moment, when appreciative sighs in the back of the theater will resound like bravas. Last year, in an extreme moment, one young versifier in leather pants came out from behind the lectern to recite his work from memory, with a style of vocal emphasis that can only be compared to the devouring facial expressions of silent film. Between poems, deliberately exhausted from his effort, he gulped water from a plastic bottle, as if it were a medieval jug of mead set out as the troubadour's reward. And when he was through, he left—too wrung out to stay for the much-better-known prose writer who followed him.

Yes, an extreme example, but the absence of the poet's identity seems to me a myth still in need of exploding—even if it means debunking a point from Keats, the first poet I was ever mad for. And yet even here, as I look back on my freshman-year infatuation, I realize that it was those *letters* of his, like the one to Woodhouse—those bouncy, yearning missives about "Soul-making" and the admirable energies of a quarrel in the streets—that held me more than the poems. The truth is I had a crush on Keats himself: we both lacked money and height, but were immensely excited about literature. He, so full of juice and confidence in a way I wasn't, would still somehow have understood me.

But I would have preferred him to send me letters, not verses. In fact, my deepest engagement with poets, then and now, has usually involved their prose. For my doctoral dissertation, I read deeply in the poets of the Great War. Why was I drawn to them? In part, I think, from the way their most startling effects depended on the unexpected use of prose within their poems. Look at the last lines of Siegfried Sassoon's " 'Blighters' ":

> I'd like to see a Tank come down the stalls,
> Lurching to ragtime tunes, or "Home, sweet Home,"—
> And there'd be no more jokes in Music-halls
> To mock the riddled corpses round Bapaume.

The rhyme and meter are there, but all poetic diction and syntactical oddities have been blasted away by a colloquial directness straight out of prose. Even Wilfred Owen, madder for Keats than I ever was, could supplement his poetic mastery of assonance and alliteration ("the stuttering rifles' rapid rattle") with startling outbursts of prose ("Gas! GAS! Quick, boys!"). The war *required* prose (even Brodsky concedes that certain narrative and historical subjects need it), and nothing in the work of my dissertation subject, the poet Edmund Blunden (1896–1974), affected me like the last lines of his prose memoir, *Undertones of War:*

> Could any countryside be more sweetly at rest, more alluring to naiad and hamadryad, more incapable of dreaming a field-gun? Fortunate it was that at the moment I was filled with this simple joy. I might have known the war by this time, but I was still too young to know its depth of ironic cruelty. No conjecture that, in a few weeks, Buire-sur-Ancre would appear much the same as the cataclysmal railway cutting by Hill 60, came from that innocent greenwood. No destined anguish lifted its snaky head to poison a harmless young shepherd in a soldier's coat.

This is lyrical, to be sure—those poetic bird names and the inverted "Fortunate it was"—but the passage also has the direct and *confidential* quality of a letter or diary entry, something every poem sacrifices by putting on its formal raiments.

I never lisped in numbers, and it's hard to say whether my failure to become a poet derived more from temperament or from manifest lack of talent. Even so, there came a moment in my early twenties when I—being serious about literature—not so much aspired to poetry as felt obligated to write it.

The thirty or so poems that resulted still slumber in a little folder in my New York apartment. From an effort (exactly the right word) called "Orbitals," let me quote the minimum number of lines required to make my point:

> I shifted locus a little last night:
> I moved into a blue room with a view.
> The new vantage spies all the clocks and bells
> To the north, instead of the south-southwest.
> The droplet of bright that hailed a delight
> Seems closer, but no longer looks green.

This halting iambic pentameter recounts my move into a house on Well Street, in Providence, Rhode Island, for the last semester of my senior year at Brown. The "blue room with a view"—my attempt at *both* assonance and literary allusion—sat farther down College Hill from the university, and I know that the "droplet of bright" refers to the illuminated top of the old Industrial National Bank building. But "hailed a delight"? What had gone on under that light? Something romantic? Believe me, I'd remember. I cannot now imagine what it was, and the poem exasperates me, because having reread this far, I would like to recall whatever the delight was. My twenty-one-year-old poetic self is so intent on being cryptic, so aware that poetry should be *elusive* as well as allusive, that it won't supply the necessary information. "Orbitals" is a self-conscious attempt at *expression;* what it could now use—what I've tried to achieve in a quarter century of writing prose—is a little *communication* with the reader.

In my post-versifying, and eventually post-academic life, I have never been able to think of myself as an artist. I didn't even know that this was an "issue" for me until a therapist insisted it was. Proud of my ability to earn a living by my pen, I have always preferred to regard myself as a "working writer," a sort of small businessman who took on the most inviting assignments that would still keep his books in the black. In fact, the folder with these college poems has been sitting for years in a box that contains mostly copies of tax returns—what's *that* juxtaposition about? A bourgeois rebuke to the pretentious young poetaster? Or a lingering artistic whimper against the "working writer"?

But the conflict that really bothers me is this one between expression and communication. It is poetry's willful conflation of ends and means—its tendency to put words above meaning—that feels most alien to the prose practitioner. Hopkins's famous prescription to Bridges that "the poetical language of an age shd. be the current language heightened . . . and unlike itself" overfulfills itself most wantonly in "The Windhover," a poem I have always loved to say and to teach, but have never fully been able to accept, with its "rolling level underneath him steady air," as English.

It is my temperament, more than any critical faculty, that makes me regard this sonnet as an extralinguistic instrument of *extasis,* like fasting, or forcing oneself to pirouette at great speed. Love it as I do, I always want to straighten it out, sober it up—and no doubt ruin it—by turning the "achieve" in its eighth line ("the achieve of, the mastery of the thing!") into "achievement."

The idea that poetry should instruct as well as delight did not persist much beyond Dryden. Thought and feeling, said to have been coupled by the Metaphysicals, went their separate ways in the eighteenth century. Thought ruled the Augustan roost, and then, once the Romantics arrived, feeling took over and has reigned ever since. Hazlitt, writing "On Poetry in General," actually made poetry less an art form than a synonym for feeling itself: "All that is worth remembering in life, is the poetry of it. Fear is poetry, hope is poetry, love is poetry, hatred is poetry; contempt, jealousy, remorse, admiration, wonder, pity, despair, or madness, are all poetry." In 1928, Edmund Wilson asked: "Is Verse a Dying Technique?" and bluntly made the argument against its interior preoccupations. By the time of Matthew Arnold, he asserted, "it had finally become almost impossible to handle large subjects successfully in verse."

The modern world, according to Wilson, required the ample, sloppy novel if it was to be engaged fully or indeed at all:

> Even a writer like Dostoevsky rises out of this weltering literature. You cannot say that his insight is less deep, that his vision is less noble or narrower, or that his mastery of his art is less complete than that of the great poets of the past. You can say only that what he achieves he achieves by somewhat different methods.

Anything Dostoevskian might be quite beyond me, but I did find, as I became a writer, that I wanted to reproduce the world's social patterns—small towns, families, institutions—in a series of historical novels. As I became a writer I wanted, above all, at least in fiction, *not* to be writing about myself and my feelings.

Back in the 1970s, Louis Simpson, contributing to an anthology of poets' reflections on "the creative process," explained the origins of his poem "The Hour of Feeling," which begins with the lines:

> A woman speaks:
> "I hear you were in San Francisco.
> What did they tell you about me?"

The woman trembles, and the "sheer intensity" of her feeling leaves the poem's speaker ready to perceive the world with a new clarity and intensity of his own:

Thanks to the emotion with which she spoke
I can see half of Manhattan,
the canyons and the avenues.

There are signs high in the air
above Times Square and the vicinity:
a sign for Schenley's Whiskey,
for Admiral Television,
and a sign saying Milltag, whatever that means.

Only in Simpson's prose explanation, written years later, do we learn that the paranoid woman of the opening lines had come to reclaim a rejected manuscript from the publishing house where he worked: "It was a peculiar piece of writing. She had invented a machine for choosing a mate. It looked like the electric chair. You put your prospective partner in it and the pointer swung to a number." When writing the poem, years after the experience, he "cut out the business about the manuscript. The mating machine seemed ridiculous, and I didn't want to be satiric—I was after bigger game." But what was this bigger game? Simpson says, in the same essay, that he writes poetry to "arrive finally at my true feeling about the experience."

Which is why his prose elaboration interests me more than his poem, even though I get what he's doing there and admire the power of its compressed language. Simpson's poem—like, I think, most modern poetry—remains about him and his feelings, whereas I find myself more curious about the life story of the rejected author and about the city itself—not just images of it, but the way it actually operates, its connective tissues. I would prefer a gradual understanding to a single intense emotion ("The Hour of Feeling"). I don't think I could build something as momentarily powerful as Simpson does from this experience, but I do think I could construct something fuller. I would seek to master the experience rather than to inflame it. My emotion—and, I hope, my readers'—would arise from accumulated engagements with the characters and their world, something I could not achieve by writing a poem or, I suppose, even a short story.

When I now read Keats's contemplation of his nightingale's song—

The voice I hear this passing night was heard
    In ancient days by emperor and clown—

348

I'm inclined to see him as a novelist in the making. *There* is your subject, I want to say: the progression of past to present. When he writes Woodhouse at such a full poetic boil that he must guard against losing "all interest in human affairs," I want to urge him: yes, stay *here,* sublunary and connected.

————

My prose nature betrays itself when I hear music (I have difficulty attending to anything but melody) and when I walk (I set a fast, even pace—pedestrian in more than one sense—with no window-shopping or dilly-dallying). I am writing this sentence in longhand, the blue ink heading toward the right margin of the yellow paper in a way that satisfies both my eye and the flesh on my evenly moving right hand. It's about *getting there,* and hoping the reader wants to come along. One summer at Bread Loaf, Eddie Hirsch jokingly asked why prose writers feel compelled to write all the way across each sheet. "So that the reader will turn the page," replied the perfectly named novelist Francine Prose. In his witty *How to Read a Poem,* Hirsch declares his fondness for Guillaume Apollinaire's *Calligrammes*—those visually imitative poems like "Il Pleut," whose type does a vertical drip down the page. But what about the visual seductions of prose? The proportioned arrangements of chapter division, offset quotation, subheading, footnote? These are things that appeal to me, perhaps inordinately—certainly too much to portend any breakthroughs as a visionary.

The smallness of literary fiction—both its subject matter and its professional world—worries many of those who write it. One often hears these days that the subgenre is "going the way of poetry," destined soon to be published by university presses and read chiefly by other writers of literary fiction. If the serious novel confines itself, as it often does, to the same authorial feelings as poetry, I think this fate of circumscription is likely.

The poetry world is already something of a locked room, partly from the obscurity of so much of its product, and partly—the inevitable flip side—from a surfeit of the "prose virtues" that Robert Pinsky recommends to it. In marked contrast to Brodsky, the current poet laureate cautions poets not to stray too far from clarity and directness, and he draws up a list of current tendencies: "Perception is more to be trusted than reflection, former ideas are obstacles, and the large blank, irreducible phenomena are the truest incarnations of reality." One knows exactly the kind of lazy, portentous verse this leads to. But there is another sort of contemporary verse that resists prose paraphrase only because the effort would be superfluous. Too much of today's poetry, despite enhancement by typographical convention on the page and artificial delivery on the platform, is already essentially prose. Take, from *The Norton Anthology of Modern Poetry*, this portion of Jim Harrison's "Fair/Boy Christian Takes a Break":

> We watch the secret air tube
> blow up the skirts of the farm girls,
> tanned to the knees then strangely white.
> We eat spareribs and pickled eggs,
> the horses tear the ground to pull a load
> of stone. . . .

For all its specificity and evocation, I would characterize this as prose that has been annoyed into verse, to its own detriment. The lines' precise observations are muffled by the reader's being made continually aware, to no particular purpose and by visual form alone, that he is reading a poem. The "prose virtues" are more or less all there is here; but the piece still seems to ask for extra credit because it is, after all, a poem.

I think poetry's best hope may lie in a style proposed by Charles Simic, whose loud denunciation of the genre (partly humorous, to be sure) was quoted near the beginning of this piece. In that same essay, "The Trouble with Poetry," he asks for a style that is "a carnival of styles," a poetry "that has the feel of cable television with more than three hundred channels, facts stranger than fiction, fake miracles and superstitions in supermarket tabloids." Maybe I like his rejection of attempts "to reform poetry, to make it didactic and moral," because that leaves those modes to prose writers like me. But Simic's own poems are a powerful advertisement for his own prescriptions. The *realness* of his surrealism—as opposed to the rote "one-of-the-guys surrealism" that Pinsky scorns as part of today's new poetic diction—has been startling me for years. Perhaps Simic is the perfect poet for a writer like me, because he makes me appreciate what he does without making me feel any desire to emulate it.

Consider "My Quarrel with the Infinite":

> I preferred the fleeting,
> Like a memory of a sip of wine

Of noble vintage
On the tongue with eyes closed . . .

When you tapped me on the shoulder,
O light, unsayable in your splendor.
A lot of good you did to me.
You just made my insomnia last longer.

I sat rapt at the spectacle,
Secretly ruing the fugitive:
All its provisory, short-lived
Kisses and enchantments.

Here with the new day breaking,
And a single scarecrow on the horizon
Directing the traffic
Of crows and their shadows.

Simic starts with an expressed preference for quiet, prosy contentment, but when the light comes, he has to open his eyes to the ominous sights it makes possible. The light itself may be "unsayable," but what it brings are this poet's characteristic visions. It *does* do him "A lot of good."

Looking at this, I think that Brodsky may be right about how "the dangers that lurk within an elevated state of mind" are something prose writers learn only by venturing into poetry. And perhaps what I keep calling my different temperament is really just a failure of nerve. Would I have been a better poet, or a poet at all, if I had been a braver person?

At this point (to take one more term from poetic technique's vast vocabulary), you may ask: Is he about to compose a palinode? Is he going to construct a closing passage that overthrows all he's argued above?

The answer, I'm afraid, is no. I can see myself finding my unmetrical feet in five more tentative lines from "Orbitals," that poem about my move halfway down College Hill in 1973:

The glass and plastic game-board figurines,
The tiny box houses, towers and lights,

Were playfully flung—they landed upright.
Their pegs found new perfect holes in the baize.
I moved down a hill and am higher up.

I now think that hill was really Parnassus. My poetry-writing days had less than three months to go, and I believe I was realizing that the only place I could gain a purchase, with a view, *was* farther down. I needed to be where the air was thicker and the streets more full. I was meant to please, not thrill; to explain, not startle. In any case, down toward town was the direction I traveled; and that has made all the difference.

About the Author

Thomas Mallon's novels include *Two Moons, Dewey Defeats Truman, Henry and Clara,* and *Aurora 7.* He is a frequent contributor to *The New York Times Magazine* and *GQ,* and is the author of books about plagiarism (*Stolen Words*) and diaries (*A Book of One's Own*). He has been the recipient of Rockefeller and Guggenheim fellowships, and in 1998 he received the National Book Critics Circle award for reviewing. He lives in Westport, Connecticut.

The pieces in this book previously appeared, sometimes in slightly different form and under different titles, in a variety of periodicals:

The American Scholar: "Writing Historical Fiction" and "On Not Being a Poet" • *The American Spectator:* "Joan Didion: Trail's End," "*U.S.A.* Today," and "Lens Democracy" • *Biography:* "A Boy of No Importance." • *Brown Alumni Magazine:* "The Revolution: A Minority Report." • *Gentlemen's Quarterly:* "The Fabulous Baker Boy," "Speed the Plot," "Writing Like the Dickens," "Dead Ringer," "Read It and Beep," "And Quiet Flows the Potomac," "The Best Man," "True Crit," "The Bronx, with Thonx," "Book of Revelation," "The Norman Context," "Tom Wolfe Bonfires Atlanta!" "Snow Falling on Readers," "Is God Read?" "A Measure of Self Esteem," "Appointment with O'Hara," "Babbitt Redux," "The Big Uneasy," "Too Good to Be Tru," "A Literary Mugging," "Six Feet Under, but Above the Fold," "Bookmobile," "Enough About Me," "Life Is Short," "Double Dutch," and "Varlet's Ghost" • *Harper's:* "Held in Check" • *Harvard English Studies:* "The Great War and Sassoon's Memory." • *The New Criterion:* "Scrappy Days." • *The New York Times Book Review:* "My Fans' Notes," "Indexterity," "Five Practitioners," and "One Small Shelf for Literature" • *The New Yorker:* "Minding Your P's and Q's." • *Shenandoah:* "The Novel on Elba" • *Washington Post:* "The Historical Novelist's Burden of Truth"